Roberto paused wistfully, then spoke softly in his heavy Italian accent, "When I say long ago that art is my only true love, I knew even then, it is not so—I let my first love slip out of my life. Such a fool am I. When I asked you to marry me, it was a lifetime too late." He pressed her hand to his lips.

"Some things are not meant to be, Roberto."

Beth smiled inwardly, unaccustomed to being this direct with him. Perhaps her heart would always skip a beat at the sheer magnetism of this man. And wouldn't there always be a fire between them—a shared passion for art and the appreciation of each other's talent? His masculine charms had maddened her senses as she put him out of her life time after time through the years. At this moment, she sensed their enduring relationship had comfortably slipped into a newly platonic dimension. But his growing realization of what he'd forfeited appeared increasingly tragic with the passing years, and Beth's heart ached with compassion. She wondered if Roberto would ever allow himself to fall in love with another woman. . . .

Rose-haven

A NOVEL

Lila Peiffer

THOMAS NELSON PUBLISHERS
Nashville • Atlanta • London • Vancouver

Published in Nashville, Tennessee, by Thomas Nelson, Inc., Publishers, and distributed in Canada by Word Communications, Ltd., Richmond, British Columbia, and in the United Kingdom by Word (UK), Ltd., Milton Keynes, England.

Scripture quotations are from THE NEW KING JAMES VERSION. Copyright © 1979, 1980, 1982, Thomas Nelson, Inc., Publishers.

Library of Congress Cataloging-in-Publication Data
Peiffer, Lila.
  Rosehaven / Lila Peiffer.
    p. cm.
  ISBN 0-7852-8227-0
  1. Pastoral counseling centers—California, Northern—Fiction. 2. Middle aged women—California, Northern—Fiction. 3. Family—California, North-ern—Fiction. I. Title.
PS3566.E335R6 1994
813'.54—dc20   93-43512
                                                                          CIP

Printed in the United States of America
2 3 4 5 6 7 - 99 98 97 96 95

In Appreciation

Although *Rosehaven* is only real in my mind, and all the personalities therein are fictional, I am fortunate to have had these special people in their various areas of expertise contribute to the accuracy of the clinical and technical details.

I am grateful: To my husband Rick for his constant support and enthusiasm.

To Eleanor Rosedale for her godly wisdom and encouragement, and Dr. Roy S. Rosedale, Director of International Programs and Faculty at the International School of Theology. To my friend Lynne Logan, Ph.D., a licensed family therapist. To Matthew and Catherine Huffine, who served as missionaries in Irian Jaya, and Joy and Steve King with Mission Aviation Fellowship. To Dr. Jane Bork, Pediatrics/Infectious Disease Unit, Loma Linda University Medical Center. And by no means least, to my "discoverer" Les Stobbe, well known in publishing circles as editor/author/consultant.

A wakened by a chorus of birds chirping across the sloping alpine meadows, Beth smiled at Josh, who reminded her of a sleeping giant, lying beside her. How could she ever have imagined, when they first met over twenty-five years ago, that they'd be here, today, together—honeymooning in Switzerland? Joy washed over her at the wonder of it all. . . .

A cool early morning breeze blew the sweet perfume of clover and tiny blue and yellow wildflowers through the starched white lace curtains, compelling Beth to slip quietly out of bed to the open window.

Filling her lungs with the fragrant air, she shivered, "Oh dear God," not from the chill, but in awe of the scene before her. Parting the curtains, she whispered, "Your creation is magnificent!"

The rugged majesty of the glacier towered almost straight up from the serenity of the valley to the pristine blue sky above the little chalet in Grindelwald. It was a storybook scene. If Heidi and Grandfather appeared up on the high meadow to the right, it would not have surprised Beth.

She tiptoed back to the bed and slipped under the puffy, down-filled duvet to savor the awesome view and snuggle against the warmth of her husband of three days.

Beth savored the luxurious reprieve from the plans, agendas, and names yet without faces that would soon enough consume their lives. They'd spent months focused on the complex details of transforming Rosehaven, the magnificent estate her beloved husband, Charles Townsend, had built for her as a bride. Perhaps the most brilliant achievement in the wealthy architect/entrepreneur's career had been his own home. The 30,000-square-foot mansion and its sixteen acres of grounds, rather than remaining the center of San Francisco's elite benefit balls and garden parties, would soon open as Rosehaven Retreat Center.

Her whole world had changed when Charles died. Josh's did also when his wife Hope, Beth's precious friend since childhood, succumbed after years with cancer. The four of them had been close friends. She felt Charles and Hope were smiling at them from heaven, glad for their happiness and the purposeful new future for Rosehaven.

Psychological counseling and therapy in the '80s had become more than the "in" thing. People now searched in desperation for their "identity," to "get in touch with themselves," and find hope and solutions for dysfunctional families.

But the desire of Beth's heart reached deeper than this. Rosehaven would provide a Christ-centered refuge that offered an opportunity to get in touch with God. And Josh would be beside her—just as he was now.

Beth pushed Rosehaven out of her thoughts. Josh and this moment mattered—nothing else. She gazed adoringly at her sleeping husband. She felt whole again, knit together with him as husband and wife. And it seemed as amazing a mystery of God as the grandeur of the Alps, framed like a painting by the window.

Beth's eyes misted at the incredible beauty. *Lord, it's too wonderful,* she thought, *that You, who created such magnificence, could also be mindful of me. Thank You for the husband You have given me.*

Josh threw a strong arm around her and drew her closer to his lean but massive body, peeking with half an eye. "Mm," he nuzzled sleepily, "please tell me I'm not dreaming. I haven't died and gone to heaven, have I?"

Awake now, propped on his elbow, he searched her violet-blue eyes, curling tendrils of a silver streak in her black hair around his fingers. "Aren't you glad we did this?"

"Glad we're married?" she teased, "or that we're here?"

He smiled, kissing her brow. "I mean, aren't you glad we listened to our family's persuasion and made a honeymoon trip out of my meeting in Geneva? We need this time for just the two of us."

"Mm, yes," she nestled her head against his chest. "We've become accustomed to people constantly surrounding us, and it's going to happen even more so. We've rarely had a private moment since you came home from the mission field in Thailand. And we barely paused before diving into the final stages for Rosehaven."

"Shhh." Josh pressed his lips on hers. "Let's try to remember what two people in love are entitled to do with private moments. . . ."

A hungry passion overcame them. Beth felt electrified as she responded to the current that pulsated between them, trembling with an aliveness once again. The mystery of this physical and spiritual intimacy God gave to man and wife continued to fill her with wonder.

Later, they laid quietly entwined in each other's arms, captive to each other and the splendor beyond the window. Both were reluctant to pierce their tranquil ecstasy by even a whisper.

Long moments passed. Josh gently kissed her lips. "You're staring at me," he smiled.

"I couldn't help thinking . . . we've shared so much of life together; our dreams, joys, and sorrows. We've laughed, cried, encouraged, consoled, and held each other up when no one else could begin to comprehend the depths of our needs. I'm happy I have you so completely now."

Josh cupped her face between his hands, "I can't even begin to put my feelings into words. I want to hold you, forever."

Beth had first loved Josh in a totally different way, since the first day she'd met him as Hope's husband. They'd married in San Francisco while Beth was living in London, studying ballet, just before she'd stunned her parents by announcing her desire to go to Paris to study art. A warm feeling came over her, thinking of her prestigious parents. . . .

Mum, Margaret Sheridan, the famous ballerina of the Royal Ballet, surprisingly and graciously agreed that Beth must follow her heart. Mum knew that every ounce of Beth's being must throb with the desire to dance and nothing else, or she could never be a great ballerina—for her audience would surely know and feel it.

Her father, Sean Sheridan, internationally known for his art and antique galleries in London and San Francisco, desired only that his daughter be happy. Shortly after their family decision, young, innocent, and excited Beth arrived in Paris, at the renowned *École Des Beaux-Arts*.

Beth's thoughts had strayed. . . . She gathered them together again, to Josh. She pictured him as the young missionary pilot, a graduate from San Jose State, beside Hope, who worked with terminally ill children at Stanford's Medical Center. In their first year of marriage, they discovered

Hope had cancer. Surgery followed, and with it the inability to have children.

Everyone loved Josh, a cheerful giant of a man who looked younger than his fifty-three years. Laugh lines radiated around his warm brown eyes, and the only gray in his cinnamon-colored hair was sprinkled through like sugar. But his perpetually jovial smile and kindness of heart were what drew people to him.

They had both been lying quietly, dreaming with open eyes. "What are you thinking?" he asked, brushing her cheek with his lips.

"Just how much I love you, Josh," she breathed, slightly above a whisper. "This moment seems exquisitely fragile. I'm afraid it might explode in my hand like delicate crystal."

The love of her life had been snatched cruelly, suddenly, from her almost two years before by a massive heart attack. Josh had long ago set aside his own natural desires, robbed by the ravages of Hope's cancer.

"Surely life itself is fragile," he agreed. "But look at that rugged mountain. It just stands there, in all its majesty, eternally secure."

"Mm-hmm," she sighed, "it's like an ageless sentinel, appointed to restrict us from plunging too rapidly into the days ahead."

"So do you think that big ole mountain is trying to tell us something?" he smiled.

"I do. I hear a Voice saying, *Be still, and know that I am God.*"

"So do I . . . and in the next breath it's shouting, *put the rest of the world on hold.* Beth, this time belongs to us alone." They snuggled closer and dozed off again. She felt him slip out of bed a little later, but she burrowed deeper, savoring all the reasons why she loved him. . . .

There were many, but the strongest bond between them would endure forever. Hope and Josh had adopted the baby Beth could not keep, raised her as their own, and shared the one secret Beth had kept for nearly twenty-five years. Beth's heart still ached upon countless occasions when it overflowed with motherly pride at Kerry's inner and outer beauty, that she'd never be able to say publicly, *"That's my daughter."*

Kerry and her pastor-husband Bob were told the secret by Hope herself as she lay dying, making Kerry aware she had always had the love of two mothers. And as recently as last Christmas, Beth's precious Mum confirmed what she had only suspected, and asked forgiveness for being proud and unreachable, which had forced Beth to keep her sacrificial secret.

With great delight, Mum claimed her granddaughter and great-grandbaby, Teddy. And six months ago, Kerry's actual father finally learned he had a daughter. Beyond this tight circle, Kerry Sterling Daniels would have to remain Beth's godchild.

For all those years, Josh had lovingly fulfilled the qualities Beth had prayed for in the father of her child. For that alone, she'd loved him.

Beth awoke almost two hours later to the rich aroma of coffee brewing. She followed it and found Josh in the immaculate little kitchen. "What do we have here? Smells heavenly."

"Fresh crusty rolls, butter, our innkeeper's homemade blackberry jam, soft-boiled eggs in these cute little cups, and some suggestions for the day from the lady at the bakery." He had maps, pamphlets, and tram schedules fanned out on the table.

"Mm, Josh—this tastes wonderful! Only in Europe do you find rolls so crusty outside and deliciously soft inside."

"The lady says it's a must: Take the tram and train up to the Jungfrau, the highest of the three peaks—over 13,000 feet. See the track, over to the right and beyond the train station? It winds way up there. The train goes into a tunnel and comes out at one of the famous ski lifts. Then it goes deep into the glacier to what they call 'The Ice Palace,' and you walk through the passages inside the glacier. Are you game?"

"You'll have to hold my hand. Tunnels make me sort of claustro-phobic, but I wouldn't miss it for anything. I wish I had a day to paint, too, but I'll be satisfied to capture it with the video camera."

"I have plenty of film. Then, when we come down for dinner, I've found a restaurant with a balcony and view looking right into the glacier. I've already decided—I'm going to have *weinerschnitzel*," he laughed.

"Again? That's what you had last night in Lucerne! Umm," she smacked her lips, "do you think anything could possibly be as scrumptious as the way the waiter prepared the veal, right at our table, at The Old Swiss Inn?"

"I can tell you one thing, it won't cost that much. But I may have *weinerschnitzel* every night we're in Switzerland."

Early the next morning Mrs. Mueller snapped their picture by the sign on her chalet that read *zimmer frei,* meaning "room available." In her meticulous apron, she insisted on counting out the exact change in francs, refusing anything extra, typical of Swiss precision, and bid them farewell.

Driving back up toward Interlaken, Josh said, "This country is more spectacular than I'd ever imagined, and completely unspoiled. You notice how there's no litter or graffiti anywhere? Interlaken's more touristy than I expected, though. You've probably seen all this before."

"No. I'm afraid I failed to take advantage of traveling around Europe during the two and a half years I studied in Paris. My passion for art consumed all my time." The word passion suddenly sparked a vivid image, a flashback to the night that had changed her life forever. She quickly dismissed it.

"Then you've never been to Geneva, either?"

"Never. And another must is the colorful flower clock by the lake. We'll see what the guidebook calls 'a towering stream of water from the famous fountain, *Jet d'Eau,*' for miles before we arrive. Our hotel reservations are at the Richmonde. My father adored the Swiss family who own it and other prestigious European hotels. He always stayed there."

"Your father was a dear old English gentleman. I'm sure he made friends as well as clients all over Europe." Josh smiled in fond remembrance.

"You'll see the exquisite art and antiques, many of them either procured by our Sheridan Gallery in London or their own family heirlooms. I must warn you," she patted his arm, "you'll think it's frightfully extravagant, but I'd feel remiss if I didn't say hello on behalf of my father. So of course, we couldn't stay anywhere else."

"Extravagance does make me uncomfortable, Beth. I hope you remember, I expect us to live on my administrator's salary, which is far more than what Hope and I received from our missionary support team. But it should be more than adequate, since living as well as working at Rosehaven will cover nearly all of our needs."

"I know, and I respect how you feel. But you must remember, darling, Charles left me with more money than you and I would be inclined to spend in a lifetime."

"That doesn't mean we have to throw it all to the wind, does it?"

Beth blinked, taken back by the only sharp edge she'd ever heard in his voice. Josh was unflappable, even-tempered, always objective. He and Hope had stayed at Rosehaven for long periods during her illness and spent holidays there. No one knew Beth's lifestyle better than Josh, or that she and Charles had given more of their fortune away than they'd ever personally used. Indeed, everyone was stunned by the altruism of her new venture. Was her money suddenly going to present a problem between them?

Her mind struggled for a response that evidenced understanding. *Perhaps it isn't easy for any man to have a wife with independent wealth,* she thought. He'd come into their marriage with only the equity from the humble little yellow and white frame house in San Jose.

After the silence, Josh reached for her hand with an apologetic glance. "I'm sorry. That didn't come out right. The four of us were best friends, and yet more than you can ever know, the generous financial support from Charles and you was often what kept our aviation ministry going."

She managed a smile. "Charles always considered you wise with your resources; he said you enjoyed greater genuine wealth than most people who had money." Beth tried to lighten up. "Josh, your riches are in people and things eternal."

"Well, remind me of that when I order *weinerschnitzel* in the most expensive places," he laughed, "and when you do something I consider extravagant, and I turn blue." He grimaced. "Frugality is not always a virtue. Sometimes it's a downright nuisance, born of necessity, and then becomes a relentless habit."

"Yes, Mr. Josh Sterling, but you have class. I can take you anywhere! You look like a Montgomery Street banker," she giggled. Behind the light talk, the one stumbling block they'd both foreseen in their marriage was money, her abundance and his lack of it. But whatever inner struggles he had in that regard, her statement rang true. He did have class. Josh could and had mixed as comfortably among kings and queens of financial empires as with tribal chiefs. San Francisco's high society admired him, yet so did its lingering hippies when he'd paused on the streets to talk and tell them about Jesus.

In the afternoon, they stopped to stretch in the quaint village of Zweisimmen and ordered apple strudel and espresso in the dining room of a small inn. Delighted with the ambience of the 300-year-old surroundings, they decided to spend the night. In the simple cozy room, with the bath down the hall, the joy of being in each other's arms again caused all other concerns to fade away. . . .

Leaving the village the next morning, Beth spotted a telephone booth. "I've been thinking I'd like to phone home this morning. Would you mind?"

"Should we? Bob and Kerry have Rosehaven under control. Would our calling cause them to think we doubt their capability?"

"I surely wouldn't think they'd feel we're hovering. I want them to be assured we're in touch, that we're available in case something unexpected comes up."

"Well, hon, if it'll make you feel good—we'll call."

"You're more accustomed to international calling from a public phone. Would you ring them up, love?"

Josh assumed a super-dignified stance. "Oh, I say, luv—you're sounding terribly British again, what?" He grinned, the laugh lines radiating around his eyes.

"Well, I say, old chap," she turned it on again, "I suppose I'm a bit anxious for next week, to get home to London and see Mum again. That's quite when my bit of an accent pops up, you know." They both laughed.

Standing at the phone booth, Josh entered the international calling card numbers three times without success. Finally he reached an operator. Receiver to his ear, he waited several minutes for the call to go through. He made absurd faces at Beth, silently mouthing over-exaggerated consonant sounds of the German-speaking operator's *Guten Morgen* (good morning) and rolling his eyes while Beth stood laughing at his antics.

"*Ja—danke schon*," he thanked the operator. "Hi, Becky! How's our number one Girl Friday? . . . Yes it is, beautiful country. Our 'Mother Superior' would like to speak to the 'Most High Reverend'—Pastor Bob, or most likely with Kerry. Okay, thanks." He motioned for Beth to take the phone. "Bob's right there in the office."

Beth's face lit up. "How are my darlings? That's good. Oh, I'm sorry. Yes, this is a dreadful time to be slowed down with summer colds. How's my sweet baby? Oh, no. Teddy's sickly too? Wish I was there to help."

She shifted feet, listening, smiling, frowning, shaking her head with animated responses so Josh could get an inkling of the conversation.

"I thought inspection on the new kitchen adjacent to the ballroom had already passed. There can't possibly be a problem on that vented hood above the ovens. Richard himself, Townsend Enterprises' top architect, specified that particular model! I don't understand. Bob, I'd better let you talk to Josh."

"What's up, Bob?"

"Happy honeymoon!" Bob's jovial voice rang over the receiver. "Beth sounds relaxed and rested; I'm glad. Wish I didn't have to tell you, but we've run into a snag with this one inspector over the new kitchen's hood. Not acceptable, he says, but he refuses to state why or offer any alternatives. He just demands that we change it, so even if we did, there's no way to know if he'd pass that either."

"And did I hear Beth say you've consulted with Richard?"

"He's even come out. What a super guy! Says the hood's totally up to code, there isn't a better one. He's made several phone calls and gone down to Building and Safety, Environmental Health. The inspector won't meet with him or return his phone calls. We're at his mercy and at a complete standstill. It's really holding us up!"

"Can you request a different inspector?"

"Since we're in such a small, rural community, I doubt there is another inspector. There's much wealth here, and it's up to him to pass these things, so I'm wondering if he's not playing a little Napoleon—flexing his limited powers. Maybe the guy's insecure, needs a psychotherapist. Hah! God only knows. But it's possible he could delay us for weeks."

"Bob, I think you've got it. Only God knows. I surely don't have any recommendations. Sounds like you and Richard have done all you can. It's been a piece of cake up until now. Maybe Beth has some clout—she usually does. We'll call you from Geneva for any new developments. Anything else?"

"I think that's more than enough for a couple on their honeymoon. There're several dozen letters waiting on Beth's desk from applicants wanting interviews. I've screened the letters—but that area is her baby. She's the perfect one for the role of admitting, since it's her home she's opening for them, and her whole concept.

"Josh, this entire thing is right. I can't imagine it working as Beth had originally thought, with her just turning it over to professionals, run by the board of directors, and her merely serving as a member of the board. I can see that it needs her heart and your administrative skills, and us working together. I'm excited about what we have going here. I can hardly sleep nights. You'll be surprised at the prestigious names of those waiting to come, and the extent of the hurts they're carrying around. God willing, when we get past this ludicrous inspection obstacle, we can make a difference in their lives."

"I feel that too, Bob. And God's not going to quit on us! I'll pass your enthusiasm on to Beth, word for word. It'll help. This is a beautiful time for us—but I know her well enough to believe that much of her heart is there at Rosehaven, and with you, Kerry, and Teddy. Take care."

As they drove toward Geneva, Beth listened intently to the recap of the conversation, anxious for Josh to fill in what she hadn't pieced together. "There's no clue then, is there, as to how long this stupid inspection thing will take to pass?"

"None whatsoever."

"I'm curious to know who these prestigious famous people are, waiting to come to Rosehaven. I only hope they don't get over-anxious and turn somewhere else. Yet, at least at this point in time, unless it's substance abuse or weight control—there isn't any other facility for people to go to who've discovered money alone won't buy happiness."

At mid-morning, motoring into the fashionable village of Gstaad, a pristine junction of four valleys, they swung around a bend ascending a steep grade. Beth's eyes suddenly filled with tears. "Oh, Josh!" she cried.

"What's wrong?"

"Nothing's wrong, darling. It's gorgeous. The Alps looming above the valley, shimmering pearly white, and that blue sky. . . . It's even more awe-inspiring than in Grindelwald!" Within her head, she could almost hear a thousand-voice choir singing, "How Great Thou Art"! "I'll never forget this moment, Josh, ever." Josh squeezed her hand.

During the drive, Beth read some of Geneva's history aloud from the Michelin guide.

"Interesting," Josh agreed. "But the action going on now behind the Iron Curtain is one of the greatest historical events in the past seventy years. Indeed, 1987 may be the beginning of long-awaited changes in one of the darkest countries in the world. Out of this Geneva meeting of multiple Christian missionary organizations, we'll penetrate with thousands of Bibles into communist countries."

"We've hardly had time to discuss the whole operation, Josh. The call for you to take part in this was sudden. With our wedding and the plans for Rosehaven, I'm not sure I understand what your role will be. Surely you can't *fly* Bibles in?"

"No. It can't be done by air. My part is strictly strategic. They want my experience in getting medical supplies and missionaries into dangerous and politically sensitive locations. You'll never know how many communists, as well as cannibals, we've had to sneak behind. On this operation, the Bibles will be hand-carried—some even sewn into the clothing of those carrying them. Timing is really critical, and these people are hungry, truly starved, for God's Word."

"God's timing is amazing, isn't it? For everything, including this time for us."

Beth shivered, thinking of the magnitude of the commitments they'd made. Their already energetic lives sometimes seemed like a spinning top, but they'd managed to incorporate the Geneva meeting into their schedule, even though Josh had resigned from the mission organization. It was merely one facet of their plans. Rosehaven merited their primary focus. Now, discovering the exasperating detainment by this idiotic inspector, Beth felt even more thrilled for Josh to have this opportunity to lend his experience. The consequences of this historic gathering could result in salvation and hope for millions of lives. The countries behind the Iron Curtain needed the Word of God as never before.

They reached Geneva at five in the afternoon. "Do you have any idea where we're going?" Josh asked Beth, who was studying the map.

"The street is *Jardin Brunswick on the Lake,* according to our reservations. There it is! We can park in front. And as soon as we get settled in our room, we'll call Bob again."

An impeccably uniformed hotel doorman swung open the door of a sleek black limousine in front of them, nodding in recognition as its passenger stepped out. The limo pulled away from the curb, and in an instant, Josh swung into its place. A dark-haired man, elegantly dressed, dashed into the hotel too quickly for Beth to see his face, but she caught her breath and gasped.

"Don't worry, I'm not going to jump the curb!" Josh laughed.

"Oh, I know that! It's the man who got out of the limo. He looks like—well, never mind. That would be too, too preposterous."

The tasteful luxuriance of the Richmonde abounded with massive arrangements of fresh flowers. It bustled with far more activity than Beth anticipated. The stately grandeur of the lobby hummed harmoniously with a stream of continental sophistication. From the impeccably tailored men and women in haute couture designs, she detected dialects as being predominantly French, Italian, and English, and they all flowed in one direction.

Her eyes darted about the lobby for the dark-haired man, up the staircase and down again. *He's been swallowed up by the crowd or the elevator*, she thought.

"Do you suppose it's always like this?" Josh asked.

"It's probably just the five o'clock hour. *Le Gentilhomme*, the bar area, is a famous meeting place."

"Come again, I don't grasp French too quickly."

"It's pronounced *lay john-tee-ohm*," Beth repeated melodiously. "Sounds pretty, doesn't it?" Her eyes still scanned the clusters of people.

Suddenly Beth reeled from the impact of a jolt to her shoulder, throwing her off balance.

A man's arms caught her. *"Scusi, per favore, Signora."*

She turned, startled, as she stared at the same handsome Italian she'd seen entering the hotel, with eyes so deep and beautiful, it could only be. . . .

"Roberto!" she gasped, throwing out welcoming arms.

For the first time since she'd watched him walk away in Paris twenty-six years ago, unaware she was pregnant with his child, this chance encounter was a delightful surprise. The exasperation of his repeatedly appearing at the most awkward possible occasions in her life was a thing of the past. But at last, at least to everyone who mattered, the secret she'd been compelled to keep through the years, even from him, was known. But would she forever feel like putty in the presence of this man? Roberto's ebullient personality enchanted women the world over. Yet men, powerful men, art connoisseurs like Charles, respected the bold Cabriollini style of painting in addition to the vast expertise evidenced by the reputation of the Count's art collections.

"*Signora,* Beth—*Bella Rosa!* You are beautiful as always!"

With more discretion than in the past, those brown eyes swept the length of her trim figure and still shapely ballet dancer's legs to meet her eyes again. Absorbed in kissing her hand, then both cheeks, a look of anguish shot across his face as he noticed Josh. Disappointment engulfed his entire body. Though embarrassed, he quickly recovered his aristocratic bearing.

"Ah, *Signor* Sterling." He embraced Josh's broad shoulders. "It is of course wonderful to see you both!" His eyes searched Beth's left hand. Upon seeing the rings, his exuberance faded. With difficulty he managed to ask, "*Signor, Signora*—what brings you to Geneva?"

Josh rescued the moment, extending his big, warm hand to Roberto in his usual cordial manner. "I'm here for a meeting of Christian missionary organizations. But," Josh made no attempt to camouflage his happiness, "we're combining it with our honeymoon," he beamed.

Roberto's olive complexion paled, seeming almost the shade of the creamy silk shirt he wore beneath the beige Georgio Armani suit. But lifting his shoulders, he extended an amiable hand to Josh. "*Congratulazioni!* You are indeed a fortunate man. When were you married?"

"Last week. From Geneva, we're going to London to visit Beth's mother, then home to Rosehaven," Josh answered.

"Come, let us go to the *Le Gentilhomme* and I will buy champagne. We must talk. You do have time, *per favore?*"

"Certainly," Josh smiled.

Settled in the exquisite lounge, a glass of champagne in his hand, Roberto leaned toward Beth, sipping her Perrier. "How is our daughter? And my grandson, Teddy? I wish to send for them, that they come to see me and stay at Villa Cabriollini for a visit. But of course, her husband too. You must all come, we have a wonderful time together. I will see at last what it is to have a family! They would like Lake Como, *si?*"

"I'm sure. It's very beautiful," Beth smiled, "but it probably will be some time before they'll be able to get away."

Roberto looked disappointed, then brightened. "Ahhh—I have splendid idea! I have one more day of meeting with art museum curators about my collections at the Villa, then I go home to Como. You two must come, *si*? It will be *meraviglioso—scusi—*that is to say, wonderful!" He raised his glass.

"You are gracious as always, Roberto, but we really must get on with our trip and back to Rosehaven," Beth explained.

"Then you are still having benefit balls, many parties, *si*?"

"No, no. Much more important. Rosehaven is to be a place of retreat, where people come and stay for periods of rest and counseling. Josh is the administrator, Bob is resident pastor and spiritual counselor, Kerry will offer Bible studies, and I, well, I'll just be there."

"She's the inspiration, the heartbeat of it all," Josh smiled.

"But of course." Then Roberto looked puzzled again. "*Non capisco*. . . . I still do not understand," Roberto shook his head. "What is retreat? What do people escape from?"

"They're briefly escaping *to* Rosehaven for a month or so, to receive professional help in building a happier life. There's much pain in people's hearts, Roberto."

"*Si*, now I understand. And you are giving up your *magnifico* home. You are happy to do this, I can see, and that is why you hurry to go." His beautiful eyes danced with another possibility. "Ah, but first, you come rest at Lake Como! I will make the arrangements. It is not very far. My private plane will take you there."

She laughed. "Oh Roberto, you are incorrigible. But it's out of the—"

Josh interrupted. "Beth, we can spare another few days," he smiled, reflecting that rare extra sense of perceiving the right thing to do.

Why is Josh doing this? Beth inwardly groaned with impatience, annoyed now at Roberto's fresh intrusion in her life—particularly on her honeymoon. She resented Josh's compliant attitude while she felt an urgency to get back to Rosehaven. Yet she trusted his judgment implicitly. His calm competence was the key to his excellent accomplishments. But would it never end? As much as she'd wanted him to participate in the Geneva meeting, and to visit Mum in London, it had required every bit of persuasion from him, Kerry, and Bob to tear her away from Rosehaven. She likened it to telling a mother her presence wasn't required during the birth of her baby!

"Josh," Roberto turned to him with pleading eyes, "so many things, things of God, I want to ask you through the years. You are the only man I can speak to of such matters. Soon I will be old. Maybe it will be too late to hear. Now is the perfect time. *Grazie.* . . ."

Roberto had his attention fastened on Josh and failed to notice the waiter escorting a stunning woman to their table. Dressed in a form-fitting jet black suit, with warm brown eyes and honey-blonde hair, she flicked the straight and stylishly long locks from her forehead with a jewelled hand.

"Ahh, *scusi,*" Roberto stood, kissing her full lips lightly. "Baroness Franconia Scarlotti, may I present *Signor* and *Signora* Sterling—Josh and Beth, my dear friends from California. We, as they say, ran into each other, in the lobby," he laughed.

"Our pleasure," Josh stood, glancing at his watch. "Roberto, Baroness, would you please excuse us? Suddenly, we're running late for a meeting this evening."

"I will see you to the stairs. *Scusi,*" Roberto dismissed himself to Franconia.

Josh departed for the men's room and to make a phone call. Beth realized any attempt to reverse the decision her husband had made was impossible. It was done. They would go to Lake Como with Roberto, delaying again her return to Rosehaven. She sighed in resignation, wishing she could brush away the unwelcome feelings of resentment.

"It will be wonderful—you will see," Roberto promised.

Beth thought of the many women he had when they were art students, while he waited for two years for her to go out with him. Her mind flashed to sunlit afternoons painting together in the French countryside, the mutual admiration of their work, sidewalk cafes, but never before a date. And how innocent and naive she'd been that night when, filled with the new emotion of love for him, thinking he loved her, she'd finally yielded to his overpowering desire.

Who in the world but a girl who had thought of nothing beyond ballet and art, and knew nothing of the ways of the world but concerts and theater for her first nineteen years, would have fallen for the age-old line to come and see his etchings? Or know nothing of what the consequences might be? She'd overheard the girl-talk at the ballet school, that one couldn't get pregnant the first time. She didn't know what they were talking about—and apparently, neither did they. Because she did. Her adoring parents had lavished her with love and an impeccable education, yet they never prepared her for life. Roberto's cries of remorse, finally realizing she'd never been with a man before, were terrible in remembering.

And yet their child had been to her more precious than life. She could not bear to think that even for a moment she might have considered abortion, depriving Kerry of being born.

Beth's thoughts returned to the present moment.

"Will the Baroness be at the Villa also?" Beth inquired, wondering if Josh had a problem placing the phone call.

"It is planned, but I will tell her—another time." Roberto paused wistfully. "When I say long ago that art is my only true love, I knew even then, it is not so—I let my first love slip out of my life. Such a fool am I. When I asked you to marry me, it was a lifetime too late." He pressed her hand to his lips.

"Some things are not meant to be, Roberto."

Now it was she who caringly clutched his hand, remembering his pleasure when the Baroness appeared. "Are you in love with Franconia?"

She smiled inwardly, unaccustomed to being this direct with him. Perhaps her heart would always skip a beat at the sheer magnetism of this man. And wouldn't there always be a fire between them—a shared passion for art and the appreciation of each other's talent? His masculine charms had maddened her senses as she put him out of her life time after time through the years. At this moment, she sensed their enduring relationship had comfortably slipped into a newly platonic dimension. But Kerry was their real bond, and his growing realization of what he'd forfeited appeared increasingly tragic with the passing years. Beth's heart ached with compassion, and she wondered if Roberto would ever allow himself to fall in love with another woman.

After a long pause, Roberto answered, "True love comes but once, I think. Franconia is a fascinating woman, but . . ." he shrugged his shoulders.

"Now there is something else I know is more *importante* at my age. I must not wait until time takes that from me also. I desire to speak of it to Josh. I will send a car to the hotel for you when his meetings are over. It is arranged," he smiled with a satisfied finality. "I see Josh coming for you. *Addio, cara mia. . . .*"

2

The basket of fruit in their luxurious room would have to suffice as dinner for Josh, for now there was barely time for him to change clothes. An obscure building across the Pont du Blanc in the proximity of St. Peter's Cathedral was selected for the meeting and could be difficult to find. Even in the neutrality of Switzerland, the organization could not risk drawing attention.

"And you're having dinner with this glorious establishment's owners this evening?" Josh confirmed as he quickly kissed Beth goodbye.

"I'm looking forward to it," she smiled. "I wanted to call Kerry as soon as we arrived in Geneva, but it's in the wee hours at home. You're probably going to be late. I'll wait up for you. It'll be morning there, and then I'll call. God be with you, darling."

Her father's dear friends proved as charming and gracious as their famous hotel, lavishing her with a dining experience in their restaurant she would long remember. Returning to her room at eleven and finding Josh not there, she placed a call to Kerry.

"You still sound congested," Beth commented when Kerry answered.

"We all are. But I feel better just hearing your voice. Your lil' grandson is still fussy too, but our Teddy will be okay, and so will we. Don't worry."

"Any more developments with the inspection?"

"Richard's still working on that with Environmental Health. If anyone can make them budge, it's him. I hate to tell you—but we have a new predicament."

"What is it, honey?" Beth frowned. Whatever the problems, it concerned her that they didn't exist when they were there to help, and now that they were out of the country, Bob and Kerry bore the brunt of them.

"We knew we'd have to call you if you hadn't phoned by morning. I'm sure you know Alexander Harding III, the billionaire real estate developer and financier?"

"Of course. He always commanded an audience at Rosehaven's benefit balls. People listened with fascination to his most current ventures. Also, he's been a huge contributor to the arts. His estate, Oakhurst, is in Atherton. He's sort of a neighbor. Good-looking man."

"You may not have thought he looked so good yesterday. He's created nothing short of an emergency situation."

"I don't understand."

"He appeared here yesterday, making demands of Becky, and slammed a huge check on her desk. He insisted on seeing you, Beth, to *admit* his daughter, Shelby Fairchild Harding. She'd made another suicide attempt.

"She's twenty-five and has been under psychiatric care for depression for years. He's leaving in a day or so for a business trip to Japan and doesn't know what to do with Shelby. Rosehaven's publicity impressed him—he'd feel relieved to have her nearby and with you. He threatens to sue if we refuse to accept her.

"Bob explained at great length that we're not medically staffed as yet and don't have all the necessary permits. He responded that we shouldn't 'advertise' if we can't accept people. He vows he'll ruin us before we get started if you don't come home and tend to business."

"Well, perhaps I'll—"

Kerry cut her short. "Don't even consider it. There's nothing you can do at this point. Of course, he can't hurt us legally. But bad press we don't need."

"That poor girl. She could possibly stay there as a friend, except that obviously she needs medical and psychiatric help. We couldn't be responsible for what might happen."

"That's exactly what Bob told him."

"It's for the Shelbys that I wanted to open Rosehaven, Kerry. That poor girl—with a controlling father like Harding, no wonder she's suffering from depression."

"We've no alternative, but the psychological staff and Bob and I feel terribly concerned for her. Bob's calling a Dr. David . . . oh, I'm so upset, his last name escapes me now. A highly regarded, compassionate psychologist. One Shelby hasn't seen yet. The others haven't been able to help."

"I certainly hope and pray he can. Listen to this, Kerry, this is unbelievable. We arrived in Geneva last evening. The first person we literally ran into was Roberto! He persuaded Josh to delay our trip to London for a few days after the missionary conference to go to Lake Como. He said he must speak to Josh, of things of God. I'm delighted for that, and you know how compassionate Josh is. But I nearly fainted. We need to get home, especially with this Harding development, but we're committed now. Roberto's made all the arrangements."

"It's all right, Mother. Roberto's needs are important, too. It's wonderful that he wants to talk to Dad. What we can do for Shelby—and Roberto—is pray."

"You are precious, Kerry. I thank God for you, as always. I'll also pray all of you get to feeling good."

"I love you. . . . Just have a wonderful honeymoon—hear?"

"We are, love. We are. Bye—love you, too."

Tears filled Beth's eyes as she put down the phone, touched by her daughter's wisdom and tenderness. She thought, *Kerry and Shelby are the same age—and what a difference in their two lives.*

She thought about Harding and others, the area's wealthiest, most prestigious citizens who had poured millions of dollars into benefits at Rosehaven—garden parties, medical center auctions, and the legendary Art Guild's Christmas ball. Yet among many of them, Beth discerned the pain their money couldn't hide. Only a few outwardly shared it with her, but she saw it in where they placed their family and material values, in their emptiness, their searching beyond what mere money could buy.

Would the Shelbys and others who were less mortally wounded from all across the country accept the help they offered at Rosehaven? Would they come, not for gala balls, but for rest and renewal, for psychological and spiritual counseling?

During the years of the hippie era, Beth had developed the New Hope Center in the heart of San Francisco. She'd heard the desperate cry for answers to a "meaningful life" that originally sparked that rebellious movement, yet fell desperately short, and hung on and on. Then the yuppies picked up the search. They seemed to think "meaningful" meant something to do with affluence; but they were largely still miserable, requiring more and more toys . . . status symbol automobiles, and jeans, and Rolex watches.

But all stratas of society struggled with shifting values, the compromise of absolutes. Some sought and others fought the awful questioning of the rights of the unborn and a woman's choice about abortion. Beth knew if she never did anything else, the lay and professional counseling at the New Hope Center supplied a need that would not soon be outgrown. But it attracted the moderate- to lower-income groups in the heart of the city.

On the other end of the spectrum, Beth's wealthy peers struggled with corresponding doubts and fears. The vast hours spent in therapy with psychiatrists provided another status symbol, but little relief. They often fell victim to the flattery of humanistic opportunists, rather than qualified professionals, who fed them only what they wanted to hear. This kept them hungry to come back for more . . . while assuring the therapists of endless fees. Present-day idols—the gods of money, sex, power, and controlling others—were as dumb as the graven images of old. These gods could neither hear, speak, nor comfort. They couldn't restore marriages or provide esteem to poor little rich boys and girls who'd grown up like Shelby, with everything their hearts desired—except love.

But Beth, Josh, Kerry, and Bob, with the skilled staff of professional counselors, knew the God who could rescue these lives. The wealthy from all walks of life—new money, old money, the corporate presidents, or college chancellors, those in a position to give true leadership to a wounded world themselves—needed new hope in the worst way.

Other centers specialized in recovery from substance abuse and eating disorders, many exclusively for women. The needs were endless so that Beth's compulsion to fulfill them burned within her. Never had she felt more convinced of Charles's conviction—that to whom much is given, much is expected—or been greater committed to this all-consuming purpose for her life and her wealth.

The telephone rang. Her watch said nearly midnight. The time had slipped away as she'd sat deep in thought and prayer. It was Josh.

"You'd better go to bed, darling. We'll probably be up all night—there's much work to be done. We're taking a short break now. But we knew we didn't come here to play games."

"All right, dear. I'll see you when I see you. Love you, sweetheart."

Josh came in at four in the morning and quietly slipped his huge body into bed. Beth automatically moved into his arms, and both were asleep almost instantly. He arose at eight. Beth had a full breakfast brought up for him while he showered.

Pouring the steaming coffee, she asked, "Did you ever get anything to eat last night?"

"Gallons of coffee and some French pastries. As one of the travel books said, Geneva's as French and international as it is Swiss."

"I hadn't realized that before either. I found it interesting." She'd purposefully opened the breakfast conversation on the light side. Four hours is hardly enough sleep for anyone the day after a long flight, and surely today would be heavy. But that was enough trivia. "What's going on with Operation Bible Smuggling?"

"Last night's meeting centered on determining the most probable location for this particular base of operations. We're coordinating with the other missionary groups to maximize all efforts and avoid duplicity. The communist country's security is tight. It's risky business. But we decided on Vienna. It's already highly concentrated, but it's the gateway to the countries we must reach. We're working with a small, intellectual, highly committed and adventurous cluster of missionaries. They've been in the coffee houses, making friends with the Viennese, appearing very low-key. They don't appear to be suspicious—if there is such a thing. With Vienna thickly infiltrated with KGB, one never knows who's who. But they've established some stable groundwork."

"It will be crucial to pray for their safety."

"Without ceasing. And to pray for top secret security. If it leaks, they're dead. The eastern European pastors will be in the Gulag, and the cover-up will be swift and sure. That's the way the communists work."

Beth shuddered. "But the victory could change the world. We must remember that."

"That's why we're here," Josh smiled, placing his damask napkin appreciatively on the table set with fine china. "Wonderful breakfast, madame. *Merci.* I learned that when I tipped the cab driver!"

They stood facing each other and dreading to say goodbye, even for the day. Beth looked up at him with eyes brimming with love and admiration.

"Are you going to be with your friend today?" he asked.

"Yes. Yvonne has a business appointment this morning, but we'll have lunch and then she'll personally acquaint me with Geneva. I'm going on the tour of the U.N. building this morning. And I don't know when I'll see you—for dinner, maybe?"

"I doubt it. The group has invested months in gathering data on this, but we have only today and tomorrow to put it together. Try and have fun today," he laughed.

"I will. Take care, love." They clung tightly together for a long moment, kissing quickly lest he not leave at all, and Josh was gone.

Beth took her coffee and hotel postcards out on the marble balcony surrounded by the heavy scrolled iron railing. Above the tree-lined boulevard, looking at her location on the map in relation to the fountain, she plotted how far she would walk. She missed her morning exercise routine and was eager to get out and explore. She'd write just one postcard, to her friend Merribelle in San Francisco, who had been stunned, shaken, and just short of angry that Beth would no longer be available to chair her benefits at Rosehaven.

Obviously, Beth would have to do Geneva without Josh. He'd probably see nothing but the route from the hotel to the meeting room. The United Nations building could consume the entire morning, but she had ambivalent attitudes regarding its politics these days. Yvonne mentioned taking her to lunch at some small, very French cafe away from the hotel, and to the shops on the *Rue du Marche*, to the Arsenal with its cannon and the sixteenth century Town Hall where the Geneva Convention was signed. Beth decided to explore Old Town and its small squares with fountains, cobbled streets, art galleries, and antique shops on her own. She also planned to see St. Peter's Cathedral, which started life as a Romanesque Catholic church and became the center of Protestant preaching in Calvin's time.

Genève delighted Beth—French, but unlike Paris; Swiss, but a world apart from Grindelwald; international, but nothing like her beloved London and San Francisco. She fell in love with the uniqueness of *Genevois* in two days.

But all the while she thought and prayed about Josh and the other men, confined to one back room, working almost around the clock. They had answered the call of God to bring His words of hope and truth and light to the oppressed nations. Perhaps those people would never see freedom to worship God and openly read these Bibles in their lifetime, but they could be with Him in eternity.

Josh returned at midnight. "You're exhausted. Let me draw a hot bath for you, darling." She tempted him with the chocolate the night maid had placed on the pillow.

"All I want is sleep, and you beside me. The campaign is well-organized, Beth. With God's help, it will work." Before the next breath, he was asleep.

Josh suddenly sat up in bed, inhaling the unmistakable richness of European coffee blending with the fragrance of summer roses the hotel placed for the enjoyment of its guests. "What time is it?" he asked.

"Eight-thirty. I don't think you moved all night," Beth smiled, looking radiant in a deep lavender satin peignoir.

"Did you say Roberto's driver is picking us up to take us to his plane at eleven?"

"Yes. But you don't have to hurry. I'll check us out and call the bellman when you're ready," Beth answered.

"While you're doing all that, do you think I should call Bob or Kerry?"

"I do, Josh. They need our support, and there's a situation I haven't had an opportunity to tell you about."

In the lobby Josh reported, "Becky filled me in. Says they're being interviewed by the press for another article. Thank goodness the papers haven't heard from Harding—he hasn't made a public ruckus—and Shelby is still in a hospital somewhere."

"Poor dear. Oh, Josh—we've got to hurry. The driver will be waiting."

Roberto's chauffeur, Renzo, drove them in the big black limousine from his private airstrip down the lane of cypress trees to the Villa Cabriollini on the shore of the lake. How well Beth remembered on her honeymoon trip with Charles that he surprised her with an exclusive tour of the famed collection of priceless art by the Count himself. *Surprised* put mildly how she felt that day—*shocked,* rather, to the point of feeling ill. . . .

She'd hated that their marriage had begun with the secret she and Josh and Hope had vowed to keep: that the little girl whom Charles adored and knew as Beth's godchild was her own daughter, and Roberto, who would never have been a strong family man, was the father. When Beth gave Kerry up for adoption, she vowed she would never ask to have her back—she couldn't do that to Josh and Hope. In Charles's heart, pure as it was, he may have coveted Kerry, wishing he could be her adopted father, putting a whole different perspective on something that could never be changed. As it was, they had a treasured and precious relationship.

Then, here in Lake Como, Roberto had denied even the slightest glimmer of recognition that he and Beth had previously met. As mutual admirers of great art, Roberto played this game, heaping one secret upon another. And so, even when Roberto did not know he had a daughter until Charles had passed on and it was Kerry's choice to tell him, Josh knew all these things from the beginning. . . .

"I hope you enjoy Villa Cabriollini, Josh. It's truly fabulous. For me it will be like I'm seeing everything for the first time. My only recollection is just a blur. But I've read of other rare pieces, especially paintings, which have been added since then, and I'm excited." Beth squeezed his hand in anticipation as the chauffeur opened the door.

Josh stretched, catching his breath. "Its beauty is classic. Did you tell me a Prussian prince built it in the eighteenth century?"

"Yes, and it's been in Roberto's family for three generations."

From the driveway, Josh paused to admire the lush emerald lawns, Italian pines, and fir trees. A profusion of rhododendrons lined the terraced path leading down to the lake.

Roberto dashed to greet them. "Ah. You come on most beautiful day. All days are beautiful, but this one—*magnifico*—especially for you."

Rather than using the imposing front entry, he took them through the courtyard to an arched loggia, its graceful curves defined with vines and accented with the family coat of arms. Below, scrolled wrought-iron gates flanked by nineteenth-century statues stood before the steps at the waterside.

Sipping minted iced tea beneath the wisteria-draped arches, Roberto explained, "Tomorrow, we go by boat to enjoy more of the gardens from the lake. Also to enjoy view of the forested hills that rise sharply above. I will show you the Villa di Balbianello, once a Franciscan monastery. A wonderful thing to see.

"For now, we enjoy my favorite hour of the day, before the setting of the sun." He swept his hand across the pink-tinged sky. "We appreciate the colors of the finest *Artista* of all, *si?*"

Beth and Josh exchanged glances as Roberto paused.

"I want to know more about Him—the way I know everything about the great artists of past and present. At last, I want to know about giving God my heart—not just my money. Isn't there more than lighting candles to statues in exquisite cathedrals? Tomorrow, you tell me, Josh. I want to know about God."

As Roberto ushered Josh into the chapel of the Villa Cabriollini, the morning sun cast a kaleidoscope of color through the stained glass window depicting Christ on the cross. The ancient artist portrayed Christ's victory over death, its radiance rebounding almost electrically across the hexagonal walls richly patterned in Cordovan leather.

Two high-backed Bishop's chairs, embellished with tapestried coverings woven with golden threads, and a kneeling rail placed before an elaborately carved altar were the only furnishings.

"You are surprised at my little chapel, I see," Roberto said softly. "The glass is very old, and very beautiful, I think. Part of the early building. I did not know this existed until my father died and I became Count and master of the Villa. I come here sometimes, when I am confused and want to find God.

"What you and Beth, Kerry and Bob have in your lives—I think I want also. I do not understand the man whose figure is on the cross. I am not sure why He died. Some say He died this terrible death out of His love for all mankind. I cannot comprehend that anyone would give his life in such a way.

"But sometimes I go to the beautiful church by the village and I light candles and pray to the Virgin. Still I do not know God—how to talk to Him—how to listen. Will you tell me, *per favore?*"

While the men were together, Beth walked the grounds, praying that Roberto's eyes, ears, heart, and soul would feel God's love speaking through Josh.

She frequently paused, shutting out the beauty around her, to pray that this man with such sadness buried deep in his brown-velvet eyes would find God.

There was a passion for life in Roberto that must come out, a God-shaped vacuum that must be filled, a God-conscious soul that drew unto itself that beauty of creation around him. She'd watched him paint long ago. She remembered her awe of the intensity of color and form on Roberto's canvases. Surely he had a gift from the Master Painter Himself.

But for Roberto, the world had always gotten in the way. The things of this life had been a barrier to discovering the Creator. Yet now, this very moment, he had turned to the perfect man who could show him the way to the true and living God. *Thank You, God, for Josh,* she whispered, *who looks at the heart of a man and not his outside, rich or poor.*

As the morning passed, Beth took her ever-present drawing pad and pastel chalk pencils into the garden. She smiled in satisfaction as she captured the curve of the slate steps, how they nestled in the lush lawns leading to the pink and deep cerise blooms of the rhododendrons. She knew Josh enjoyed the beauty but would be the last man on earth to be influenced by the grandeur of all this, and that it truly was Roberto's heart he wanted to see. That deep compassion for all men is what made Josh God's ambassador—no matter where he was.

It was Josh who told her about the love of Jesus the same day they promised to adopt Kerry. Her thoughts returned to these two extraordinary men, and she prayed Roberto's quest for God was genuine.

Then she heard them talking as they came down the path. She searched for a clue in Roberto's expression but saw none.

"Ah, you still have your way with flowers." He studied her drawing for a quick moment. "*Magnifico!* May I have it, *per favore,* to remember this special time with you and *Signor* Josh?"

"Of course, and I will remember the beauty of these gardens whenever I think of you."

"Come, lunch is ready for us on the upper *terrazzo.*"

"All good things must come to an end," Josh said after the last sip of espresso. "And now we must leave. Roberto, gracious does not begin to describe your hospitality. Thank you. We'll look forward to your next visit to Rosehaven."

"But of course. And I must soon see my daughter, and little Teddy. I want to hear him call me Papa. I do not know when, but we will plan it."

The chauffeur had their luggage loaded in the limousine. Roberto kissed Beth on both cheeks, then embraced Josh with extraordinary gusto. She yearned to know if there was any special significance—some hint of the result of their morning revealed in the embrace.

Roberto's soft brown eyes looked deep into Beth's. He spoke softly, "God is good. He does not let you out of my life—although it is not the way I want. You and Josh are right for each other. Be happy. Serve God together."

As they waved goodbye, Roberto looked older and unbearably sad. Beth's heart went out to him. "*Arrivederci*," she called.

"*Arrivederci, Bella Rosa. Arrivederci,* Josh."

Renzo took them to the Cabriollini airstrip where Roberto's pilot flew them the twenty-three miles to Milan's Maltensa Airport Here they boarded an Alitalia Airlines flight to London. On the plane, Beth laid her head on Josh's shoulder. "I love you, darling, and I'm so glad you accepted Roberto's invitation to Como. And I'm dying to know—what did he say this morning in the chapel?"

"He asked how he could become a Christian, what he must do. I'm afraid Roberto is much like the rich young ruler who asked the same question of Jesus. When I explained Christ had to be not as important, but more important than all his wealth and possessions, he was honest in saying he doubted he could promise that.

"It's not what he wanted to hear. I think he expected to be required to *do* something like a certain number of Hail Marys and more candles and good works and money to the church. He may have said otherwise, but he didn't honestly expect to have to give *himself,* his whole heart."

Beth nodded her affirmation.

"I think being saved by faith and trusting in Jesus instead of *doing* things is a difficult concept for him. Was he able to understand that Christ has already paid the price for our sins on the cross? And that Jesus is waiting to be invited into his life with the same enthusiasm that Roberto expressed when he invited us into his home?

"I made it very clear that when he does that, he will know peace and contentment in his heart now, as well as eternal life. Roberto's an eager listener; he wanted the whole but simple truth. He was totally candid, confessing the reason he lost you—let you slip out of his life—is that loving is too demanding. To give materially is easy. His one fear in life is commitment. He has always used his charm or wealth or both to attain his heart's desires. And now he's being painfully honest about it and can't make a commitment to God either."

"Oh, Josh. We must pray that your sharing with Roberto will help bring about a change of heart. For all his wealth, there's a wrenching sadness within him."

Beth closed her eyes, nestling her head on his shoulder until the plane landed in London.

At Gatwick Airport, Beth's heart searched for her father. Always before, Sean was the one who came to meet her. She would never allow her memory to sustain the white, paper-thin-skinned face as he lay dying of pneumonia, but rather she remembered the jolly, robust, impeccably attired Britisher with bowler hat and black umbrella who had been her father.

Mum waved at them among the other arriving passengers, catching their attention with her lace handkerchief. She looked smaller and shorter than she had the last Christmas she'd spent at Rosehaven.

"Cheerio—there you are, my darlings!" With age, Mum had lost some of her former reserve, but none of the prima ballerina's grace, style, and classic bearing for which she was recognized the world over.

"You both look marvelous. I'm ever so grateful you came to me. I didn't feel quite so chipper so's to come to your wedding, but I'm spry as ever, now. Josh, you are a love, and you know I'm delighted you and my daughter have put your lives together. You deserve one another."

"Oh, Mum, you look wonderful, too." Her silky silver hair was coiled high on her head, held in place with the antique combs Sean had given her years ago. Beth remembered these treasures from an estate collection that he'd withheld from sale in the Sheridan galleries especially for his beloved wife. Beth held Mum close for long moments before they headed for the baggage claim.

When Josh enveloped Mum in a hug while waiting for their luggage, she almost disappeared in his huge embrace. "Where's the car?" he asked.

"No need to fetch it. It's right out the door in the loading zone." She looked pleased with herself for acquiring such a convenient spot.

Beth and Josh exchanged a hint of a smile, hoping the vehicle hadn't been towed away.

At the curb, an attendant, himself aging, smiled, "I'm still an admirer of yours, Mrs. Sheridan. You keep dancing—righto? Have a nice day."

Beth and Josh now beamed openly, laughing at Mum's wonderfully indomitable spirit.

As Josh hoisted their luggage into the trunk, Beth remarked, "Mum, I knew surely the old Bentley wouldn't still be around, but when and where did you acquire this smashing vintage Jaguar?"

"Hop in, love, and I'll tell you."

"Would you like me to drive?" Josh asked.

"Heavens, no, we'd all be killed—unless you are accustomed to driving in London, which I'm not aware of. I still manage, thank you."

Once out of the airport traffic and heading toward her adored home in Hampstead on the Heath, Mum began to tell them about the Jag-u-ar, as the British say it.

"You see, love, the Bentley spent more time in the ga-rage—mechanic's shop to you, Josh—than on the road. I simply couldn't afford it any longer. Sold it for a pretty penny to a collector. I have this friend, an old duchess from Bath, and her husband adored tooling around in this car. But when the duke passed on, she absolutely refused to drive herself any longer. Dear Sean had been more than generous in compensating them for the paintings they'd sell off every time they got hard up, so she simply gave it to me. Jolly good, what?"

"Jolly good, indeed," Josh roared, enjoying every moment of his new mother-in-law's vigor. In all his life, he'd never coveted material things, but if he had, he knew it would be this long, sleek, torpedo-shaped XKE coupe with knock-off wire wheels.

"Josh, love, since this is your first trip to jolly old England, we must introduce you to one of Hampstead's most famous pubs." He later learned they were not far from the North End, at the crossing of Spaniard's Road and Spaniard's End, and knowing that, he would not have been as surprised when she swerved into the countrified parking lot of Spaniard's Inn.

"You see, Josh, popping in at one's favorite pub at the end of the day is one of those British traditions ingrained in our culture. It's where one finds out what's really going on in the world!"

Mum glided confidently ahead with light steps as she directed them to the door of the ancient building, informing them that its finest hour was in 1780. She wasn't even using the cane she'd relied on at Christmas since the weather was warm and balmy and her arthritis wasn't rankled by the chill.

Beth glowed at her mother's happy independence.

"Cheerio, Jack!"

"Cheerio, Maggie," the proprietor responded.

Josh shot a quizzical look at Beth that asked, *Is this the Mum we know?*

Jack approached their table with curiosity, perhaps remembering Beth, but never having seen her with Mum before. It seemed that when Sean delighted in bringing her and Charles here, Margaret thought of nothing but ballet. Obviously, Mum had become a regular.

"What'll it be, m' lovelies?" Jack looked toward the ladies with a broad, friendly smile.

"Just a bit of ale," Mum replied.

"I think you have ginger ale?" Beth questioned.

"Righto, Miss. And you, gov'ner?"

"The same," Josh smiled.

When Jack returned with their drinks, Mum began telling him all about Beth and Josh visiting from California, and how Beth came here with her father years before. Mum knew almost everyone there. An electric crossfire of conviviality swept the room. A genuine warmth pervaded the atmosphere, an evidence of camaraderie. No one remained a stranger, for introductions flew corner to corner if a newcomer appeared. These were the local gentry one could tell their troubles to, knowing someone else cared enough to listen, to give sympathy and understanding, and to share a good bit of English wit and humor at the end of the day.

On their way out they bid everyone goodbye, and while Mum finished chatting with a couple by the door, Beth said to Josh, "What great therapy went on in there! If people were as open with each other as they are in the pub, we wouldn't need as many psychologists."

"Does that mean you think we should open a pub at Rosehaven, then?" Josh laughed.

"Well, why not? Alcohol doesn't have to be the catalyst that makes the 'happy hour' happy. Don't you think residents could just as happily indulge in friendly conversation over beverages other than alcohol? I have to think that's a great way to get people to share their feelings."

"It's worth thinking about, isn't it?" Josh agreed.

The Jag, as opposed to the staid old Bentley, seemed to have restored Mum's youth, even though Beth was crammed into the narrow back seat surely not designed for a third adult passenger. Mum spun down Spaniard's Road to White Pond, explaining to Josh where Kate Greenaway, D. H. Lawrence, H. G. Wells, and other famed old names worth dropping had once lived. Off East Heath Road she turned on Keats Grove and pointed out the arbored path to the poet Keats's cottage, then turned around the corner to her own. "This section remains the prettiest and most romantic bit of it all," she beamed proudly, as she would over a gifted child.

Beth at once felt the joys of her own youth return. She inhaled the remembrance of the fragrant lilacs tumbling over the trellis in the spring on the first day her father had brought them to this wonderful house. With its mullioned windows and English garden, it instantly became their cherished home of fond memories. For a moment, it brought him back to her.

"The roses are splendid this year," Mum gestured as they ambled along the garden path. "Look how healthy they are," she smiled, looking back.

At that, she tripped over a slightly upraised piece of the slate walk. Josh, just a step behind, caught her, but not before her ankle had twisted painfully.

Mum moaned in pain. Josh picked up her light frame and carefully carried her into the drawing room. All the while she told them how she'd meant to tell their neighborhood gardener lad to fix the loose slate. Beth packed the already swelling ankle in ice, elevated her leg, and brought hot tea.

The pain became intense enough for Mum to ring up Dr. Alistair.

"No, I'm not performing at the Royal Ballet Theater very soon," she laughed. "You flatter me, Doctor. I haven't performed on stage for years, but I'll teach ballet until the day I die, God willing. Just order some pain medication, would you, love?"

The Westminster chimes on the parlor clock were striking seven. *What an unfortunate way to begin the few days we have here,* Beth thought.

And already she knew they must stay longer than she'd planned so she'd be there through every moment Mum might need her. Shelby and her plight also weighed heavily on Beth's mind. She'd have to phone Bob and Kerry immediately.

"Bob? How's it going?" Beth asked, mid-afternoon, California time.

"Well, thank you," Bob replied in his normal expedient manner. "How's with you and Josh? Where are you?"

"Oh, this has been a rewardingly wonderful trip! You'll get the details later. And thank you for encouraging us. We're at Mum's in Hampstead. She's incredible—getting younger every day—but she sprained her ankle today, pretty severely I'm afraid, just moments after we arrived at the house. It's not likely we'll be home on schedule. I can't possibly leave until I know she's all right. What's going on? Everything okay?"

The prolonged pause on the line made her uncomfortable. Every manner of complications crossed her mind. "Did we get the inspection passed?"

"Yes. Richard finally solved that."

"How about the Fire Department? Did they approve the kitchen hoods too?"

"Yesterday."

"Wonderful! Then, do we also have the permits?" Beth would have felt ecstatic over the progress except for the restraint she sensed in Bob's voice. Something critical had gone wrong.

"The permits have been issued too, all but the final."

She struggled to draw Bob out, to extract whatever bad news he couldn't bear to reveal. "What about applicants?"

"We've gained several more."

"And Alexander Harding?" She held her breath. . . .

"Dr. Lawford suggested another psychiatrist for Shelby, and he's satisfied for the moment. Still wants her at Rosehaven as soon as we open."

"Well, Bob, I'm delighted. You've survived without me after all, then?" she laughed lightly. "I'm being facetious, of course. I respect your competence implicitly." She'd never had to draw him out before, and there wasn't a glimmer of enthusiasm in his voice.

"Something's troubling you, Bob. Tell me."

"Dr. Lawford asked to be relieved of his position today. I spent the morning with him."

Beth almost dropped the phone. "Dr. Lawford! The whole clinic staff is relying on him! The other doctors and therapists are excellent, but they've never worked with inpatients; they don't have that background. Oh, Bob—that's dreadful. Is it final? Whatever is his reason?"

Beth heard Bob sigh, like relief in having exposed the problem. "Lawford is distraught, and he fully realizes the situation that his departure places us in, especially so near to our scheduled opening. He looked exhausted. He'd not slept, been up all night, and finally came to this conclusion at six this morning."

"Whatever brought him to such a decision in the first place?" Beth couldn't imagine. Lawford was perfect for the position; he had been her strongest encourager and was instrumental in forming the psychotherapy teams.

"For one thing, he's been asked to head the American Council of Psychologists. It's absolutely unheard of for a Christian to have even a voice in this group, and he's convicted that this is a major opportunity to initiate some godly leadership at the top of this organization. It means there is hope of strengthening some major moral issues in this country. That's what he feels God is calling him to do."

Beth's heart sank. "How can we argue with that?" she asked, a wave of discouragement sweeping over her. "Josh made a quick trip to the pharmacy to get Mum some pain medication. I'll have him call you when he returns. I'm keeping Mum's ankle elevated and packed in ice. I think I hear her calling."

"There's more," Bob said in the most serious tone she'd ever heard from him. "Lawford has already spoken to the therapy staff. He wanted them to be aware he won't be taking the position, and asked them to submit their own recommendations to the board for a replacement. He's heartsick because some of them are vacillating. Several accepted mainly because of the opportunity to work with him. Our staff is unraveling."

"What can we do?" Beth's voice broke, nearly in tears.

"Pray. Lawford and I are meeting at six o'clock every morning this week to pray and listen to what the Lord says."

"Of course, and know we're praying with you. . . ." She could barely speak above a whisper over the lump in her throat, and hung up the phone. *God, right when it seemed all our prayers were being answered, when our hopes and dreams and plans were progressing beautifully, why are they now, when we're almost ready to open, falling apart? Lord, surely it's not Your will that we fail. What would You have us do, God?*

She tried to concentrate on the parts of the verse from Philippians 4 that said, whatsoever is honorable, right, pure, excellent, of good repute, etc.—let your mind dwell on these things. She concentrated on smothering the frenzied thoughts racing through her mind, to push out a mental picture of her vision for Rosehaven crumbling before her, and to allow that peace of God that passes all human understanding to guard her mind instead. A repetition of the words she had heard in Grindelwald, the calming words *Be still and know that I am God* swept like a wave over the rubble in her mind. *Why is it so hard for me to remember that?* she scolded herself.

And yet, how could she ever forget? God had blessed her beyond measure. In the times of loss and sorrow that come to everyone, He always comforted her and never failed to work out something better than she'd even hoped for.

"Beth, dear—can you come?" Mum called, the pain straining the usual melody in her voice.

"Oh, sorry, Mum," Beth rushed to the big old chair her father had always sat in, its huge ottoman stacked with pillows. "I had to call Bob. Oh, mercy, the big pillow shifted. I should have stayed right here, and that wouldn't have happened." Now she really felt terrible, seeing Mum's swollen ankle and ashen face.

"Oh," Mum breathed in relief. "That's better, love. Now don't look so worried. This is only a sprained ankle. I've helped many a dancer of mine with a sprain when he or she landed incorrectly. I'll mend. Why don't you make us some tea? You look like you need it more than I do."

Beth bent to kiss Mum's forehead. It felt a little clammy, and she knew the pain was intense. Best Mum think the ankle was her only cause for concern—she surely didn't want her to know a problem, rather a catastrophe, raged at home.

Josh came in with the pain medication the doctor had phoned into the pharmacy at the moment Beth poured the steaming brew into Mum's beautiful Wedgewood cups.

"Wonderful, darling. You're just in time—for tea and to give Mum relief. She's almost in tears, it hurts so bad."

"We really should take you over and let the doctor look at it, like he said, Mum. He's prescribed something pretty strong, but I'm sure he would much rather see you."

"Nonsense. I've *danced* on an ankle almost as bad as this. I don't want to put you both through that dreadful ordeal on your first evening here. I'd planned dinner out. Looks like I botched that, and frankly I've lost my appetite. I don't know what or how I'm going to feed you."

Beth thought of her terrible inadequacy as a cook, and Josh loved good, simple food. Growing up here in Hampstead, there'd always been Tillie to cook for them. It now seemed ages ago that they'd eaten on the plane, and she suddenly realized she felt starved.

"Let's have a breakfast for dinner," Josh suggested. "I can make bacon and eggs and pancakes. How does that sound?"

"Marvelous. I'm famished." She'd never eaten breakfast for dinner in her life. "Glad I married a man of many talents. Sound good to you, Mum?" But mercifully, Margaret now slept soundly. "I think we should let her sleep," Beth said. "She said she wasn't hungry, and I'm sure all that pain did take away her appetite."

Josh obviously enjoyed employing his kitchen skills, while Beth set the table in a little nook with diamond windows overlooking the garden. Kerry had always said her daddy made the best pancakes in the world, and he'd had much practice during the years of Hope's illness. Throughout their simple but cozily delicious meal, Beth stifled her anxiety over the phone call to Bob.

In their room, with Mum still comfortably sleeping in the drawing room, Josh held her a moment, then asked, "Do you think you can get some sleep now? Mum's little accident took its toll on you too. You look awfully tired."

"Not yet. Oh, Josh, we have a terrible situation at home. . . ." She explained it all, as Bob had told it to her. "I told him you'd call him tonight."

"Well, let's see. It's ten-thirty p.m. here, so it's two-thirty in the afternoon on the West Coast. We'll give it a go. What's the new number? I only remember the residential number you've always had—not Rosehaven's new office number."

"Here, dear. I'll dial it." She clicked in the international calling card numbers and returned the phone to Josh.

After hearing a gentle voice answer "Rosehaven Retreat," Josh said, "Hi, Becky—how's our favorite secretary?" Beth watched as he nodded his head, eager for him to reach Bob. "Well, we're eight, or is it nine hours ahead of you, so please have him call us tomorrow morning, London time. We're going to bed now. Beth's exhausted."

She felt an urgency to object before he hung up, but it was too late. "Why didn't you have him call regardless of the time?"

"Bob and Kerry just left for the city to meet with Lawford and the board of directors. It'd be something like three in the morning when he'd return the call. It can wait another few hours," Josh answered calmly.

Beth felt more stressed than she cared to admit to herself, and here was Josh, cool and controlled as ever.

Why hadn't Bob told her they'd be leaving so soon? She'd have asked Josh to call earlier. No. Wrong—they'd both been too tired and hungry, and she'd needed to get Mum settled.

Fending off a gamut of impatient impulses, Beth let go, laying her head against Josh's chest and inviting his arms to encircle her as they stood, not even a breath apart. "I'll tiptoe down and see if Mum's all right—then I'll come to bed." Even in his reassuring arms, sleep did not come easily. She tossed, conjuring yet more problems. At five a.m. she heard faint noises from the drawing room and crept down to investigate. Mum was struggling to position her leg and in the doing, knocked over a glass of water and her pain pills. Her helplessness pierced Beth's heart as she rushed to her aid.

"Oh, Mum, don't strain—I'm here. How's the pain? Let's look at the ankle. I think you did get some sleep, didn't you?"

With a sigh, Mum eased back in the chair. "Yes, love—some. The pain's simply awful. I feel as helpless as a turtle on its back. I need to take a pill, but better have some milk with it, my tummy's feeling empty."

Beth examined the swollen ankle, shaking her head.

"We'd better get you to the doctor this morning. I'll fix you some tea and toast and a coddled egg and get us dressed."

A tear ran down Mum's cheek. The only other time Beth had seen her mother's silver coil of hair so disheveled and the great ballerina's composure shattered was the night pneumonia and the toll of time had taken her beloved husband's life.

At seven a.m. the phone rang twice before Beth could get to it. But Josh had answered it upstairs. She heard Bob's voice. "Good morning, Josh—how's Mum doing? Is this a good time to call?"

"We're going to take her to the doctor's at eight; she's in a lot of pain. There's more swelling. Beth, are you there?"

"Good morning to you, Bob. What happened at the meeting yesterday?" Feeling guilty that her first thought was of Rosehaven rather than her family, she asked, "Are you and Kerry and my Teddy all right?"

"Teddy's learned his first word. It's *no*." He laughed. "So he's normal. We're not much further enlightened after yesterday. Lawford's really upset. He had no idea his pulling out would shake the others up like this. I'm disappointed in them, too. I thought they were motivated by the opportunity to work with patients in a non-clinical atmosphere, rather than just Lawford's brilliance. They're still weighing their options. No one has quit yet. But I don't think we want anyone in our team of psychologists who's lukewarm, do we?"

"Not at all," Josh responded quickly. "Where do you think we go from here, Bob?"

Mum needed help in the bathroom. "I have to go, Bob." Beth's heart felt heavy. She had nothing to contribute to the conversation. No other thoughts. No suggestions. If only she were there in San Francisco to regenerate enthusiasm among these competent professionals who had encouraged her in the beginning. Bob was young; he didn't have the contacts, but he certainly possessed charisma and practical insight to the objectives and concepts, the goals of Rosehaven. The board of directors lacked nothing in these areas either.

Yet all of her reassuring thoughts felt hollow.

Dr. Alistair's office was only fifteen minutes away, on the top of Frognal Lane adjacent to some of the oldest buildings in the district, dating back to the late 1700s. In the 1950s, the good doctor's neighbors had included the ballerina Tamara Karsavina, a close friend of his and Mum's, and perhaps that's how she'd located Alistair. Beth loved the little town, hardly more than a village, with its hilly winding streets steeped in history and tradition. And Dr. Alistair possessed that friendly country doctor demeanor that made everyone's fears vanish at the sight of him.

"Well, Margaret, my dear, what have you done?"

"Oh, Reggie—it was stupid of me. I should have had a slate stone in my garden reset ages ago, and I tripped over the ghastly thing. Do something—it hurts like fury."

After reviewing the x-rays and degree of swelling, Dr. Alistair decided to cast the ankle to mid-calf for about a week's duration. He sent them home, saying he'd then x-ray again and make another evaluation, and advised Margaret in the meantime to take it easy and elevate the ankle as much as possible.

Josh reveled in maneuvering the right-sided steering XKE through the shady, picturesque lanes of Hampstead, Mum beside him with her casted leg stretched out, and Beth again crammed in the narrow ledge of a back seat. The incredible machine was classic red. Josh had never driven such a high-performance automobile, and he delighted in it. He now more fully understood how Mum could feel so revitalized and in control of her life behind its responsive wheel.

Once out of the car, Mum was awkward on crutches, and made her way as far as the garden bench, where she sat to rest. The morning, warm and fragrant with early summer's bouquet, welcomed Beth and Margaret to sit a while as Josh immediately went about resetting the guilty stepping stone.

"Well, isn't this a shame?" Mum sighed. "I'd planned so many things for us to do today and tomorrow, to show Josh. But my dear, I have so much to share with you. At least we'll have a time to talk."

Beth smiled. Time to talk with Mum is what she coveted all her life. But Margaret Sheridan was a private person regarding the things Beth thought mattered most, except ballet.

Her parents' conversations with Josh and Hope, long ago at Rosehaven, had awakened a spiritual awareness within them. But only after Sean's death had Mum shared with Beth and Charles that they had entered into a personal relationship with Christ and assured them He was their Lord and Savior. That beginning of openness was itself an answer to prayer for Beth. It helped fill the void of the great loss of her father to know they'd all be together in eternity.

The years of secrets, at times known only to herself and her beloved roses, secrets Beth had passionately guarded to protect those she loved, especially her mother, were now opened and set free.

Margaret, too, had been set free: free to admit that her ingrown world of ballet had held her captive, blinded to the real world around her. A world in which her precious daughter had to discover the facts of life by herself—the hard way—and suffer the consequences alone. When Sean was living, he'd sheltered and protected his wife from every responsibility and distraction from her career. And yet in many ways, the fame and glamour of Margaret Sheridan lived in the shadow of her husband's outrageously gregarious nature and renowned artistic competence. They had never attempted to compete, only complement one another. But Margaret was more her own person than ever—cherishing the joys of the past, relishing whatever the present and future held with new appreciation.

At this point in time, Beth adored her mother as never before. Age only served to enhance her elegance, yet she had mellowed, grown more believable. Beth could finally approach her, at seventy-five, and they could talk of feelings—about life, and God, and share the depths of their hearts.

Suddenly, the frustrations and delays in returning to Rosehaven lifted, and she realized *these obstacles had also provided a time set apart to cherish.*

How terrible a loss if I hadn't noticed, she thought.

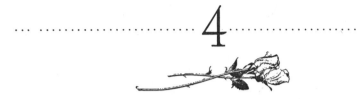

4

Several days passed without their hearing from Bob. Beth applied every bit of fortitude she could rally to suppress her impatience until she could stand it no longer.

"Do you think we should call this morning?" she asked Josh anxiously.

"I think we should let Bob run with it. He's the designated hitter, the one Lawford is placing his greatest confidence in. Let's wait for Bob himself to tell us what is on the minds of our board of directors. That's what they're there for. I'm hungry. I'm going to go down and fix some scrambled eggs. Want some?"

That definitely was not what Beth wanted to hear. Every fiber within her pulsated with urgency to be back at Rosehaven. But Mum still needed them, so she wouldn't leave, no matter what. Furthermore, she didn't have a single solid argument to counter Josh's logic. She must admit, no purpose would be served by calling Bob or any of the board. Clearly, it was not her move.

Perhaps even more frustrating than feeling their hands were tied was that she'd never known herself to be so uptight. Was it her age? She'd certainly survived greater traumas and tragedies. And she'd even coped with the matters of life and death far better than this! Maybe a complete physical would be a good idea when she got home. *Maybe my hormones are going haywire. Maybe I need estrogen,* she thought. All she knew was that not being at Rosehaven right now produced more stress than she felt able to cope with.

Josh felt right at home in Mum's kitchen. She came in on crutches and sat in a chair to chat while he expertly cracked eggs into a bowl. beating them with a wire whisk.

"Did you enjoy your walk this morning?" Mum asked.

"Immensely. My favorite path for walking about the heath begins by entering at West Lodge, through the trellis tunnel. And I'm intrigued with Kenwood. Nothing in my Montana upbringing exposed me to the likes of that neoclassical mansion. I learned construction began in the 1700s, with new wings, then moderate revisions continued until it became a public art gallery in 1928. We can be glad for the bequest by good old Lord Iveagh to English heritage, making it open to the public."

"It's an architectural masterpiece, no doubt about it," Mum agreed.

Beth was getting the plates out of the cupboard.

Josh said, "You know, hon, I think one reason I'm so fascinated with the place is that it helps me appreciate Charles's work and architectural genius all the more. I could be very happy perennially bumming about Europe, going through old buildings," he laughed.

"Let's face it," she agreed, "where *wouldn't* you be happy? You're the most totally adaptable person I've ever known! Can't you manage even a little complaint occasionally—so I'll remember you're a mortal soul after all?"

"I can endure most anything," Josh responded. "Happy is learning to be content where you are, and not like when I thought to be out on the mission field in the jungles of Thailand was the only way to please God. But it was good I went. I now know where my real mission is, one of them at least—at Rosehaven, with you, Beth." He set the steaming platter of breakfast on the table.

Mum's eyes sparkled. "Well, love, if God tells you your mission is to be a cook, you can be mine anytime. Your American-style eggs, bacon, and toast are divine. Thank goodness you don't bother with those dreadful tomatoes at breakfast like we English serve!"

"This is the day your cast comes off, right, Mum?" Josh asked with a last sip of English breakfast tea. "While you ladies are at the doctor's, I'll get the drippy faucets fixed, Mum. Make me a list of any repairs you need."

"Oh, you're a love, Josh. It's impossible to get a good man out to mend anything. You'd be surprised what Mattie can do, though, besides cook and keep house."

"When is Mattie returning from her daughter's in Manchester?" Beth asked.

"Tomorrow, I think. She'll ring me up when she's settled, and I'll see if she can pop in every day, instead of twice a week. I wish that you could stay forever, but I must not be a selfish old woman."

Dr. Alistair cut through the cast, peeled it away, and grinned.

"Well, young lady, don't be concerned if the ankle's a bit shriveled-looking—that's perfectly normal. You'll need to work on some daily therapy, and don't do *Swan Lake* for a while." His eyes danced impishly. "And don't drive that racy machine of yours until I check you again in a week or so. That's your clutch foot. Be a good old girl, and you'll be fit as new."

"Oh, bother, Reggie. Surely you're not going to try to keep me home?"

"Oh yes I am, my dear!"

"Humph—maddening—'don't drive.' Well, then, Josh can drive us to dinner again tonight, and we're going to celebrate my going out of the house without my leg in that awful stiff thing," Mum announced on the way home. "That is, if you can scrunch into the little back seat again, Beth." She did rely heavily on her cane, Beth noticed, helping her out of the low Jaguar.

"Any calls?" Beth asked anxiously, as Josh tugged on a rope, tying up a heavy branch of the cherry tree.

"Not a one," he smiled. "You okay, Mum?"

"Splendid. Except Alistair said, *'don't drive,'* and taking away my wheels is dreadful. The worst."

Through the complaint, Beth caught the twinkle in her eye. Mum would be fine. As for herself, the worst right now revolved around not knowing if there would be a psychotherapy staff to care for the patients at Rosehaven.

Suddenly, a thought flashed through her mind. *There's no problem in calling Kerry. I need to know how she and Teddy are. I don't even have to ask about the other. . . . It would be about eight p.m. there.*

"Kerry, love. I'm missing all of you. How are you—and how is my Teddy?"

"Still pretty sick," she admitted reluctantly. The tiredness in her voice alarmed Beth. "How's Mum? Are you having a good time?"

"Mum got the cast off today. She is making a bit of a fuss because she can't drive yet, but she's mending. Josh loves Hampstead and the people. And he's repairing everything in sight that Mum's needed done for ages. She's bright as a new penny. Incredible, at any age. . . . You sound exhausted. I wish we were there. But I'm glad you have Tillie."

"Tillie's off, and I've been helping Becky with the phone. It's been ringing like crazy. The *Examiner* interviewed Bob just before he learned of Dr. Lawford's decision, and they printed the article immediately. I'm saving it for you, of course. It's excellent. You'll be pleased."

Kerry went on to explain, "The story appeared in the Sunday edition. A whole section on meeting the challenges of changing times—leading off with Rosehaven, and how *your* vision reached beyond the social glitz to the ultimate needs of people in high places under pressures. The article listed 'Charles and Beth Townsend's history of generosity,' your New Hope Center in the city, the philanthropic events held here, the money raised for charities, and on and on. And that now, you and Josh are carrying on—with his daughter and her pastor-husband, and a 'highly accredited professional counseling staff, opening Rosehaven as a place of rest and emotional and spiritual renewal.'

"The exposure is fabulous—all we've ever hoped for. But internally, we must deal with the upheaval regarding the staff. The board of directors is working on drafting a statement that doesn't sound like we're stalling in reply to the calls."

While Kerry updated her on Rosehaven's challenges, Beth sensed terrible dread in Kerry's voice regarding her baby. At this point, Beth's concerns about Rosehaven paled—nothing else mattered, except her grandson.

"Does Teddy have a temperature? How high?"

"Staying at 102.8. I have been giving him Tylenol and tepid baths. He's still vomiting, too. I didn't want to worry you, but Mother, I'm frightened." Kerry began to cry.

Kerry's anguish for her son stirred sorrow in Beth's heart, knowing she would never forget the son she and Charles lost only a few hours after birth. Only a mother knows how another woman aches for her baby. Tears filled her eyes. . . .

"Oh, honey—I wish we were with you. You'll have Tillie back with you tomorrow, though, and—" Beth heard a stifled sob. "Tillie's taken a few days off with the Hartfords' maid. Won't be home for four more days—on the twentieth. She never goes anywhere, so Bob and I thought she should get away before things around here get really hectic. I got sick the day after she left. But we'll be all right. Cookie's here—but she's no match for Tillie. Teddy's crying now. Have to go, Mother. Bob or I will call you soon. Love you."

Beth felt sick. There wasn't a thing she could do, and her daughter and grandson desperately needed her. *Lord, help us all,* she whispered.

Beth shuddered, only now realizing the date—July 16, 1987. At once, July 16, 1965, vividly loomed before her. The tragedy of this day, for twenty-two years, remained indelibly engraved upon the pages of Beth's heart. She'd heard medical terms she never knew existed: autosomal trisomic syndrome, a type of Down's syndrome—and the most severe of mental retardation—claimed their baby's life. Charles had gambled in the hope he did not carry those disastrous genes inherited from his tyrannical father. Tragically, he had lost. And they lost a son.

And mercifully, Thomas Charles Townsend, dear little Tommy—named for Charles's dead retarded brother—had slipped into the arms of Jesus shortly after his brief time in this world. Their double-grief seemed unbearable, and Charles would never take that risk again.

Tommy had died before they knew the joy of his adorable squeals of laughter and the sweet baby love Teddy returned to those around him. Teddy, who by God's grace had survived his difficult premature birth, brought them gladness beyond measure in his first year of life. He'd filled the void and eased the ache that especially came with every July 16th.

God, please heal this precious baby, Beth prayed. *And let Kerry get some rest.*

For a little while, God was the only One with whom Beth could bear this current burden. She couldn't even tell Josh right now, for surely Mum mustn't know, and they were in deep discussion in the garden. Mum would insist on heroics—that she'd be fine, all by herself, with no one to help with the therapy Dr. Alistair prescribed, while unable to drive herself about. All Beth could do was wait for Mattie to come home tomorrow—and pray that she did.

Another whole day went by. No answer from the calls to Mattie. No word from Kerry or Bob. In their quiet, private moments, Josh, her forever-solid rock, assured her God was in control. Their prayer time became Beth's only comfort. She must suppress all forms of anxiety, or Mum would contend that the needs at home were of greater priority than hers. Beth couldn't accept that either. What if, with Mum's weak ankle, she fell and broke a hip, or some other mishap occurred? They kept praying Mattie would come home soon . . . that Teddy's temperature would come down, and he'd be well.

Yet in those moments when Beth succeeded in turning all other considerations aside, she and Mum shared more feelings of past, present, and looking into the future than they had in her whole life. Each day, Beth cherished this intimacy as a gift, as a prize Mum brought out of a previously barred closet, unwrapped with great tenderness, and spread before them to savor.

Beth caught the telephone on its first ring at six a.m., July 17, so as not to awaken Mum.

Bob apologized, "Sorry to call so early. Teddy needs your prayers. It's nine p.m. here. His temp shot up this evening to 104. They've just admitted him to the hospital with a diagnosis of bacterial meningitis. We're frightened, Beth. Kerry's called out the varsity of our prayer warriors, including her faithful Bible study group in San Jose. We knew you'd want to know right away. I've got to get back to Kerry. I'll call immediately if there's a change."

Beth and Josh went to their knees in prayer for the next hour. . . .

The phone rang again, at eight a.m. Mum picked it up in her room, still in bed, at the same time Beth did. To Beth's relief, she heard Mattie's voice and softly set the receiver back in place. Still in her robe, she started downstairs to boil the kettle for Mum's breakfast tea and to serve her in bed.

Passing Mum's door, she heard her tell Mattie goodbye, and poked her head in. "May I come in?"

"Oh, good morning, love. Yes, indeed, come sit on my bed a minute," she patted the down comforter.

Impulsively, Beth climbed in beside her, kissing Mum's cheek. "I came to tuck you in last night and read you a bedtime story—but you'd already fallen asleep."

"A bedtime story?" she beamed. "How lovely! That was Mattie who just rang me up. But the rest of the world can jolly well wait a bit. . . . Why don't you read me a 'wake-up story' instead?"

Beth reached for Mum's Bible on the nightstand and turned to Psalm 23. She needed the words of comfort and began to read—"The Lord is my shepherd; I shall not want. . . ."

"Excuse me, love," Mum interrupted, "but that is true. The Lord is my shepherd, as He is yours—and I shall want for nothing. Mattie is home and she'll come today whenever I ask, and can come and stay with me and do for me as long as I need her. Your heart is troubled with something you're not telling me. And somehow, I must let you go, you *must* go."

Tears of grateful relief swam in Beth's eyes, obscuring the words of Scripture on the page she knew so well.

Mum gently took the Bible from her and continued, "He makes me to lie down in green pastures; He leads me beside the still waters. He restores my soul; He leads me in the paths of righteousness for His name's sake. Yea, though I walk through the valley of the shadow of death, I will fear no evil; for You are with me; Your rod and Your staff, they comfort me. . . ."

Mum stopped reading. "These words gave me comfort when nothing else could, dear, as I cried out to God on lonely nights after your father passed away. Whatever shadows are over you now, whether you wish to tell me, or not—take heart."

Beth slid under Mum's enfolding arm like a chick under wing, laying her head on her breast and cried, releasing the tension, the heartache stored within. Yet hurting tears mingled with tears for the new joy of comfort she found in her mother's embrace—the assurance that she too called upon God to take her through the valley of the shadow of death when her time came.

"The six o'clock call, in case you heard it," Beth dried her eyes, "was Bob. Teddy's in the hospital with bacterial meningitis." She could now relate concerns with the high temperature and symptoms of the past several days and know Mum no longer wanted to be sheltered but to join forces in the power of prayer.

"Hey, got room for one more?" Josh peeked in and balanced his huge frame on the edge of the bed by Beth. His precarious position looked so ridiculous, they all laughed.

Mum sat up, taking charge. "You'd best get on the phone and see to the next possible flight to San Francisco. I'd adore having you stay on, but Bob and Kerry, and my darling little tyke Teddy need you—and now I'll have Mattie. Go on, now—git," she chuckled, flapping her hands, as if to shoo them off.

Beth called the airport. "The only available flight out this afternoon is from Heathrow, leaving at 2:15. Unfortunately, there's a two hour and twenty minute layover in Chicago, so we'd arrive in San Francisco at 9:15 p.m. That's over twelve hours in the air, plus the layover."

"Oh, that's brutal, isn't it? Nothing direct to San Francisco, huh?" Josh groaned.

"British Airways has a 1:15 flight, arriving at 4:05—that's ten hours and fifty minutes in the air . . . but they're booked. Nothing available but standby for two days. That won't work. . . ."

Hurriedly they threw their luggage together. Mum prevailed upon Malcolm Claridge, a neighbor, to drive them to Heathrow for the long, exhausting trip home.

From the San Francisco airport, Max, now more of the family at Rosehaven than the Townsends' faithful chauffeur of over twenty-five years, drove them directly to Stanford Medical Center. The small hospital in nearby Atherton, where Teddy was born, had neither the staff nor facility to handle the dread disease.

A friendly young nurse at the information desk directed them to the pediatric unit on the third floor. It was now nearly eleven p.m. and the halls were quiet.

Bob and Kerry sat dozing, leaning against each other in the adjacent waiting room, as Josh softly gave their name to the nurse at the station. "What's the latest report?" he asked quietly.

Bob sat up with a start, which in turn woke Kerry.

"Mother, Dad." Her eyes bleary, she stood to embrace them. "We're relieved you're here." She began to cry. "Our baby is terribly sick."

Josh wrapped his arms around them both. "What's the latest report?" he repeated.

Bob's handsome young face was gray with exhaustion and Kerry's thick long lashes shadowed hollow eyes. "He's hanging on by a thread of life. The next twenty-four to forty-eight hours are critical," Bob answered. "We've been here all day."

Beth shivered. Those exact words, *a thread of life*, had come from the nurse the night her father died of pneumonia. She refused the negative remembrance, clinging only to the word *life*, clinging to the thought, *Where there's life—there's hope. Strange, how these old clichés pop up in one's mind. Better how God's Word—such as "Yea, though I walk through the valley of the shadow of death, You are with me," gives strength and hope,* she thought.

"Any chance I can just take a peek at our baby?" Beth wanted to know. "I've missed him more than I could ever imagine." The pediatric night nurse compassionately escorted them to the isolation unit. They tiptoed silently around his crib, agonizing over his flushed baby face, his little form heavily sedated against throbbing head pain. Beth gasped, seeing the IV tubes taped to his tiny arms, the monitors tabulating his heart rate and vital signs.

After forming a circle, a holy huddle of prayer for Teddy that he would recover and live, they tiptoed out again.

At midnight, Josh asked, "Is anything open for coffee and a sandwich maybe?"

"Just the dispensing machines around the corner, with a few tables and chairs," Bob said. "Let's see what they have. We need a stretch, at least."

Teddy's condition remained unchanged when they returned to the waiting room. They all dozed, each stretching out on the bench-like sofas to get whatever rest they could through the seemingly endless night.

Beth awoke first, at about seven-thirty, surprised any of them had slept, yet she felt far from rested. Josh sat up, groggy, brushing back his thick brown hair awkwardly with his fingertips.

A silver-haired man with black-brown smiling eyes, wearing an open-collared shirt, khaki-colored cotton slacks, and sandals, paused at the entrance to the waiting room. Seeing the sleeping forms of Bob and Kerry, he moved toward Beth and Josh, extending his hand.

"Hi. I'm Dr. Rosen—David," he whispered. At once, Beth felt comfort in this man's presence—that somehow, beyond all the foreboding evidence, all would be well.

"I'm relieved our little guy seems to be holding his own, although he's far from being out of the woods. Here, let's slip around the corner so we can talk." He guided them down the hall. "I've been praying for Teddy all night. Glad his parents are getting a little rest. It's been rough. Please tell them I was here."

He moved toward the elevator, extending cordial hands to each of them. "I'll look forward to meeting with you. Right now, I must go tend to someone in an acute depressive episode. See you later," he said in a rich mellow voice Beth thought would comfort the most distressed person. With that, he stepped through the elevator doors and they closed behind him.

Beth searched Josh's face as they walked back to the waiting room. "That man has an amazing serenity about him. I can't explain it. I'm also grateful for his prayers, yet I don't understand. How can he be Teddy's pediatrician, whom I thought Kerry said was a Dr. Jarvis, and also have what appears to be a psychiatric patient? It doesn't equate. But undoubtedly we will encounter him again."

"I think so," Josh whispered, studying the deep sleep of Bob and Kerry, which only the younger generation seemed capable of.

"I'm going to the ladies' room to splash some cold water on my face and freshen up a bit. I'll bring some coffee," Beth said wearily.

"Good idea," Josh nodded, now fully awake. At the nurse's window, he asked for any new report on Teddy before Beth returned.

"I'm sorry, sir, the morning shift's just come in and I don't really have anything to tell you. You'll have to wait for a report from Dr. Jarvis."

At eight-thirty Dr. Jarvis approached them with the utmost professional demeanor, a grave expression clouding his gray eyes.

As though intuitively, Bob sat up, at once alert with a look of a hundred questions fixed upon the doctor. "Good morning, Doctor." Kerry sat up too, appearing anxious for a report of her baby.

Josh stepped forward. "Good morning. I'm Mrs. Daniels' father, Josh Sterling, and my wife, Beth."

Jarvis wasted no words.

"Your son has just had another seizure, which occurs in about 30 percent of children with bacterial meningitis within the first several days. It is urgent to initiate antibiotic therapy during early evaluation. A diagnosis can frequently be made from the Gram stain of fluid from the lumbar puncture. His symptoms are classic: nausea, vomiting, and stiff neck. But at least at this time, we're not seeing evidence of stupor, coma, neurologic signs, or paralysis. That is as much as I can tell you at the moment."

Kerry turned white, herself still weak from the flu.

Beth quickly crossed the room to embrace her, fearful she might faint at the doctor's seemingly impersonal evaluation of their baby's condition. Dr. Michael's voice came from a chamber of the past explaining her Tommy's terrible prognosis. Even now, she wondered if the imperative cruelty of truth Dr. Michael delivered didn't bear more compassion than this report of Dr. Jarvis's. Beth's judgment softened. *Surely*, she thought, *making people grasp the situation with such a devastating disease must be one of a doctor's most difficult tasks. Perhaps such professional detachment had become a necessary precaution against lawsuits. But I can't worry about that now.*

Beth heard herself question, as she had with Tommy, "What's the outlook for our baby? What can be done?"

"I believe you realize the first twenty-four to forty-eight hours are the most critical in determining recovery and any permanent neurological consequences. We'll proceed with monitoring heart, respiration, and vitals, and administering IV. Once the culture and sensitivity of the infecting organisms are known, antibiotics will be adjusted accordingly."

Bob settled beside Kerry. Piteously, they clung to each other for comfort. Beth saw a reflection of herself and Charles in their hour of heartache, except Teddy did not have irreversible mental and physical retardation. *Bacterial meningitis is devastating—but even infants do recover,* she thought. *I trust You, God. I know You're watching over Teddy. Thank You.*

Dr. Jarvis's gray eyes softened now, and he managed a half-smile. "Now that I've presented the situation as it appears now, I can tell you that in the majority of case studies similar to your son's, receiving early medical attention makes all the difference in getting those nasty little microbes under control as quickly as possible.

"Now I realize why your names seem familiar. I read the excellent article in the *Examiner* and admire the program all of you are developing at Rosehaven. Wasn't Hope Sterling your mother, Mrs. Daniels?"

"Yes . . . yes, she was."

"I'll never forget the wonderful work she did here with terminally ill children. She possessed the rare gift of imparting dignity and purpose to a dying child."

Kerry, touched by the esteem he had for Hope, could only express "Thank you" in a whisper above the lump in her throat.

Tenderly, Bob brushed the tears from Kerry's thick eyelashes with his fingertips. "I know Teddy's going to be all right, honey."

"Thank God. I know that, too. It's—it's going to be awfully hard, though, being separated from him. Like when he was born and we couldn't take him home from the hospital for several weeks," Kerry sniffled.

"I'll order a bed set up for you in his room this afternoon, Mrs. Daniels. Both child and parents recover much more quickly that way," Dr. Jarvis smiled.

Kerry brightened immediately. "Could you—do you always do that?"

"It's not unusual."

"How long will Teddy be in the hospital, do you think?" she asked.

"With no complications, probably ten to fourteen days. I'll be back this evening. Right now, I prescribe that all of you go home and get some sleep."

"Who is Dr. David Rosen?" Beth asked on their way out of the enormous medical center.

Bob raised his eyebrows and glanced at Kerry. "Why do you ask?" Bob wanted to know.

"He stopped by the waiting room for a minute last night while you two were sleeping," Beth told him. "He's a kind man. Said he'd been praying for Teddy. Then he disappeared, saying he had to go tend what I interpreted to mean in layman's incorrect terms as a nervous breakdown."

"It certainly wasn't his own," Josh interceded. "He seems to be a pretty laid-back guy. But we concluded he must be a psychiatrist or psychologist, not a pediatrician, although he seemed to know all about Teddy."

Kerry and Bob instantly brightened, exchanging big smiles. "You tell them," Kerry squeezed Bob's hand.

"Dr. David Rosen is a psychologist and our answer to prayer," he beamed.

W hat do you mean when you say this doctor is our answer to prayer?" Josh asked. "Has Dr. Rosen contributed to Teddy's treatment or diagnosis in some way?"

"No, but he's sat and prayed with us during some long, anxious hours and been a great comfort." Bob's eyes sparkled above a broad smile. "He's Lawford's replacement. And he's the best there is!"

"Then I wonder why he wasn't considered before?" Beth asked.

"Lawford assumed he wouldn't leave his own out-patient clinic, so he didn't even approach David, but they're close friends. Lawford recommended we refer Shelby to him, and they've conferred several times regarding her. David took her case. It's even possible it was she that he alluded to when he told you he had to take care of someone in an acute stage of depression."

"Oh, dear," Beth frowned. "How terrible. The poor girl."

Bob continued. "David is encouraged by her improvement. She still requires in-patient care, however. Her background suggests she was the abandoned lost child, her spirit and creativity crushed by an authoritarian father who was completely unavailable to her emotionally.

"As you saw, David has a gift of charisma that even exceeds his psychological abilities. You feel at ease the minute he steps into a room, and he's brilliant. A fascinating conversationalist, whatever the subject. We found ourselves pouring our hearts out to him in the first five minutes we met." Bob's face was aglow. Kerry beamed.

"We felt that, too." Beth smiled. "And he's available?"

Bob grinned. "You bet. It happened this way. Lawford confided in David regarding our dilemma. Instantly, David became personally interested, completely surprising Lawford, who then attempted to set up an appointment with us. Learning we practically lived at the hospital to be with Teddy, David came to see if he could help in any way. We talked about everything, including his interest in Rosehaven, and that he had attended numerous benefits held there for Stanford Med Center."

Beth's eyes became misty. "This is wonderful!"

"As we talked, David acknowledged he's dreamed of a concept like Rosehaven for years. He's expressed the need for in-patient alternatives to psychiatric hospitals as well as the need for Christian counseling in a caring, warm, and friendly environment. He also sees the limitations he has with many patients who don't require traditional hospitalization; the minute they leave his office the world swallows them up again. They can't stay focused on the behavioral changes they've recognized are necessary. To his knowledge, there are less than a handful of resident care counseling facilities in the country. He's convinced that two, four, sometimes six weeks, could significantly turn many of his patients' lives around. Some of them would return for shorter periods as they work through issues during recovery. Someone like Shelby might require a longer stay."

"What will David do about his current patients? Surely they're not all candidates for Rosehaven?" Josh asked.

"He has a competent staff of doctors in his clinic to handle the other patients. A Dr. Albertson will step up to replace him and oversee the clinic, but David will retain ownership."

"Did you say his last name is *Rosen*?" Josh raised his eyebrows. Bob nodded affirmatively. "As in *Rose*-haven? That's a coincidence! People might assume he owns the place!" he chuckled, glancing at Beth. "Do you think that's a problem?"

"Not to me. An amazing coincidence, as you said," she smiled.

"It is, isn't it?" Bob agreed. "And yes, if you're wondering, he is Jewish. Rosen is a good Jewish name! He's a completed Jew. Interesting story, how he became a Christian. He was reared orthodox. He and his wife Golda raised their two sons even more strictly because of their fears that they and the Jews in their temple were drifting away from God. His son, Benjamin, at eighteen, couldn't see the point of the hundreds of Jewish laws they were immersed in, especially those involved in keeping the Sabbath. What Ben observed looked like pride. He viewed the old traditions as being puffed up with how religious they were. He asked David, who is a learned Old Testament scholar, to search the Scriptures with him and prove that these laws came from God rather than man. David is a wise father. Instead of insisting they accept tradition without question, David welcomed the challenge. He and Golda made it a family study. Together, they all found Christ. We've met Golda and fallen in love with her, too."

Josh nodded in appreciation. "Has his candidacy been presented to the board?"

Kerry's deep brown eyes danced beneath the long lashes, yet Beth recognized her attempt to restrain any further enthusiasm that might seem influencing.

Bob answered, "They've studied his résumé and personal history. Their approval is unanimous, but your stamp of approval is the final word."

Beth smiled at her daughter, again cherishing the woman she had become. "I think his being Jewish is a definite advantage. I presume that some of our residents will be Jewish. He'll be a tremendous asset in reaching out to them."

"Do you think he and Golda will want to live on the premises—or have you discussed that yet, Bob?" Josh asked.

"They'll keep their home in Palo Alto, at least in the beginning. He said they've discussed selling—it's now too big for the two of them with the boys grown and far away. But they'll be full-time plus on call, and it will be helpful for them to live at Rosehaven eventually."

"Where are their sons?" Beth asked.

Bob looked pleased to answer, "Ben is a Bible translator in the highlands of Irian Jaya—that's in Indonesia. A fascinating story. Ask David about him sometime. Aaron is doing his internship in cardiology—"

"Something else is wonderful," Kerry beamed. "Golda is also a Ph.D. and specializes in family counseling. Their credentials are impressive—and they're both just sweethearts!"

"It's important for you to know they both have Dr. Foster's highest recommendations, since Foster will direct the psychiatric staff and medical team."

"Exactly how do Foster and Rosen work together?" Josh asked. "I must admit, the correlation is still new to me."

"Foster orchestrates the clinical direction, oversees all medical aspects: prescriptions, lab results, consults with the dietician, and orders patients taken out for cat-scans, et cetera, when necessary. He's responsible for daily charting, and coordinates with David on psychological evaluations and with the primary therapist of each patient."

They had been talking as they walked. Josh stopped. A deep frown creased his smooth forehead. "An in-patient retreat center, as you're describing us, almost entails what amounts to a small hospital! Being administrator for so broad a scope of services may be over my head. Beth, I don't want to let you down!"

Bob interjected respectfully, "Josh, we're all overwhelmed by the magnitude of what God has called us to do here. Let me ask you: Did God tell Abraham *exactly* where he was going when He asked him to leave the security of his own country and what he knew, to go into a land that He would show him?"

"Tending sheep I could handle. . . ."

"Josh, be serious. God needed a leader of strong faith. So does Rosehaven."

"Darling," Beth looked up at him. "I can't tell you how many times after I had the trust and all the papers drawn that I'd awaken in the middle of the night in a cold sweat. I'd start thinking of the enormity of what we'd undertaken. And it's still scary—but it's been God's business from the start. When I get cold feet, I look first to Him, then at the quality of our professionals on the board and staff. We're all a team."

Bob smiled. "If each of us felt adequate, I'd be concerned. Josh," he dramatically gestured with his right hand, almost laughing, "I can see you now, *embroiled* in a difficult rescue mission. You engineered the whole strategy—there's jungle on the right of you, guerrilla troops lurking on the left of you, the plane's engine is sputtering, and you're quoting Second Chronicles, 'the battle is not yours but God's!' "

"All right already! Thanks. You made your point. Did you say something about *broiled*? Reminds me of food—I'm hungry!" Josh looked like himself again.

The four of them radiated a circle of huge smiles and suddenly realized people passing through the hospital lobby were staring at them.

Josh wrapped the vast span of his arms around Beth and Kerry, his eyes twinkling. "Let's get out of here and celebrate! I'll spring for Egg McMuffins. It's been a long night!"

It seemed more like days rather than hours since they'd landed in San Francisco. They'd been up for almost thirty hours. Josh thought about food while Beth yearned for sleep. Tired but laughing, she gave him a sideways glance.

"Oh, I forgot," he grinned, "you don't eat fast food. I know a coffee shop we used to go to when Hope worked here."

On the way to the parking lot Josh turned to Bob. "So the board's given complete approval on Rosen—salary and all?"

"David's salary is exactly what we budgeted for Lawford, and Golda's salary equals the two therapists who decided not to join us. She's a bargain."

"I'm totally impressed with the way you handled everything while we were out of the country, Bob. Beth had a hard time of it, being away at such a critical period, but she always felt confident in you."

"What is it they say? It was a *growing experience.* But thanks, I appreciate the encouragement."

While waiting for their food in a corner booth of the coffee shop, Josh gave thanks for all their blessings—for the hope of Teddy's prognosis, the Rosens, and the meal they were about to be served.

"Thanks, Daddy," Kerry kissed Josh's cheek after they'd eaten. "The pancakes weren't as good as yours, but I feel much better now. I know our Teddy's going to be well soon. But I want to get back to the hospital."

"You're going to get some sleep first, honey, and then come back," Bob said, putting his arm around her.

"Well, I do need to get some things to stay over, and I've got plenty of paperwork I can bring to do. It'll pass the time. I'll nap on the way home."

"Me, too," Beth yawned.

Tillie rushed to meet Beth and Josh when she heard the big Cadillac at the end of the long driveway, with Bob and Kerry pulling up behind them.

Josh stepped out, lifting Tillie's slim straight frame off the ground, twirling her around. Beth laughed. Who but Josh would greet this prim, proper, and still very English, gray-haired servant in such a gregarious way? Tillie blushed, smoothing her apron as he put her down, but her faced glowed.

"Tillie!" Beth exclaimed. She threw her arms around her dear friend who had served her faithfully through most of her life. "How are you? We're glad you got away on a little holiday. Was it fun?"

"I'm sorry as I can be I picked a poor time to be gone, Miss Beth, but it was ever so pleasant. Seems like you've been away forever. How's your Mum?"

"Oh, she's priceless, practically invincible. Be assured she'll be diligent about her therapy. She'll want to get back to her ballet students. Mum will be out and about in no time."

"Hi, Tillie," Kerry called. "It's good to be home."

"How are you, Tillie?" Bob asked, already escorting Josh toward the grounds where painters, carpet-layers, telephone linemen, landscapers, and a variety of workmen swarmed. The new cottages, resembling keeper's cottages surrounding a manor house in the Cotswolds, and the immense commercial kitchen on the other side of the mansion were almost finished.

During the next two weeks they worked relentlessly, almost around the clock, exhilarated by how effectively the concepts of the organizational framework unfolded each day. Bob, Beth, and Josh alternately visited Teddy in the hospital while supporting Kerry, who devoted the hours her baby was under sedation to drafting small-group Bible studies. In Teddy's waking hours, Kerry kept him calm and happily entertained with songs as his aching little head and body began to respond to treatment.

Beth worked long hours, yet the days seemed to disappear in a labor of love. The old-world elegance of Charles's study, with its walls of deep Venetian red linen and leather-bound editions in mahogany bookcases, provided an atmosphere of contentment for her office. She'd replaced the rich beige velvet draperies with a floral tapestry, using the same fabric for down pillows on the plump leather sofa. Other than those few feminine touches, she wanted it to remain as he'd designed it. And of course, the hand-blown vases of Murano glass Charles chose himself would always be filled with roses, fresh or silk, just the way he liked them.

She took comfort in the fact that he had often worked at home on the redevelopment projects that had brought a better way of life for hundreds of low-income families. Just sitting in his chair behind his desk energized her and gave her assurance, as though he hovered nearby, guiding and affirming her accomplishments.

Rosehaven was scheduled to officially open for patient residents—the term Beth preferred to use—on August first. In the last few weeks, she had received more than two dozen letters requesting appointments and information for inpatient counseling in this place where someone obviously cared about special needs. The details of providing for residents and the facility at times appeared overwhelming.

One of the main-floor drawing rooms, just off the entry, had become Becky's office and reception area. Josh chose an adjacent former sitting room for his office, requesting that Beth keep the decor simple.

Bob had selected his study with great care, and Beth was amazed and delighted at the thought he invested in it. He chose the ambience of an upstairs sitting room whose burnished walnut-paneled walls exuded an unhurried elegance, calm, and the epitome of confidence. One felt an invitation to settle down in comfort for purposeful conversation, which was the essence of pastoral counseling. This environment might not be significant to less-sophisticated stratums of society, yet Bob innately related it to the tastes of the wealthy and further decided it was well-suited for men's Bible studies. Men usually recognized and appreciated the craftsmanship of the hand-carved fireplace. Charles had commissioned Beth to design the mantel and surround during the time she managed the Sheridan Gallery in San Francisco for her father, before she knew Charles was building the mansion for her.

Kerry preferred a sunny former bedroom to hold the women's Bible studies. She delighted in selecting the sofas and chairs, visualizing how the floral and feminine designs would lift spirits. David chose the office adjacent to Dr. Foster's, some of the large rooms in the main wing had been divided into cozier counseling rooms for Golda and the other doctors, and the dietician's office was incorporated in an addition off the new kitchen.

Beth had arranged for eight regular-sized offices and five smaller offices in the main wing. She'd given Bob and Kerry the former master suite, the rooms where Kerry had fantasized being a princess throughout her childhood. Josh and Charles's friendship went deep, and she would never risk the possibility Josh might feel like an intruder, in another's man's bedroom with another man's wife. The elegant comfort of those friendly rooms overlooking the rose gardens seemed woven into her being. Beth loved the rooms, but she loved Josh even more, which made it easy to forego their luxury. They would reside in a smaller, simpler, more tailored suite, which she enhanced with his favorite colors—deep forest green and rich burgundies.

David and Golda's suite embraced the upper east wing. The servants' areas for the new live-ins were below, while Tillie's, Cookie's, and Max's quarters remained undisturbed, and the rest of the staff would live off the grounds.

Now Beth fully realized the tremendous effort she'd put into the arrangements in the house: ordering the office and other furnishings, and rearranging the existing pieces long cherished.

She closed her eyes and smiled, leaning back in the deep leather desk chair. She reminisced to the first day Charles brought her from San Francisco to view the estate after they'd worked together for months on the plans. He'd consulted with her on the carving patterns he'd retained European craftsmen to do, the two-story rose window she'd designed, and every minute detail. He then laid this magnificent mansion and his proposal of marriage at her feet!

She remembered her awe, not only of his architectural genius in design, but the enormity of the place. And she'd wondered what on earth they'd do with all these rooms. They'd been used more than she'd imagined. Sometimes it seemed like a hotel.

But the main rooms were well-loved for what she'd always called a "sanctuary" from a wearisome world. Through the years her home had been like a precious friend. It possessed the capacity of gathering unto itself exhilarating joy or profound sorrow with equal grace. Only God knew what future souls would find refuge from life's traumas and new paths of direction within its gates.

Surely Charles, by some divine guidance, had always known Rose-haven was destined for a purpose far beyond themselves. . . .

Beth took a deep breath, refreshed by her reverie, and plunged into the final tasks whereby the long-awaited future would become the present. Like fine art, only the finishing strokes remained to complete the complex scene. Soon the characters of the drama they'd been building would take their places, and the action would begin. . . .

6

ello there!" a cheerful voice called out to Beth as she walked the grounds early on a golden September morning. She squinted into the sun, approaching the scrolled iron bench above the corridor of English yew trees.

"Oh, now I can see who it is . . . Shelby! Good morning! How are you?"

"This is the first day in a long, long time that I've wanted to go on living." Shelby paused, waiting for her reaction.

"That's a dramatic statement! You've come a long way, Shelby," Beth smiled.

"I look pretty different from that terribly sick person my father's chauffeur dumped off from the hospital about a month ago, don't I?"

"You do look like a new woman. There's color in your face, and you have a lovely smile, which I've never seen before."

"Even though nothing has changed, no monumental event, and certainly not because my father is paying any attention to me, I feel different inside . . . a peace down deep within I don't think I've ever known before. I don't even feel guilty—and that's really rare."

"Why should you feel guilty?"

"I suppose because I've felt no happiness in being Shelby Fairchild Harding. I'm the only child and sole heir of Alexander Harding III and Gloria Fairchild, and their 'unfathomable fortunes.'" She emphasized a bitter note of sarcasm.

"Who told you that was supposed to make you happy?" Beth asked gently.

"Who else? My father. He's always told me I'm the personification of the ungrateful child. I've never wanted for a single luxury. I guess I've become jaded to material things.

"I'm twenty-five years old, and in my childhood I had every doll, toy, pony, fluff and frill money could buy before I could even think to desire it. The keys to a dazzling new red Porsche were in my sixteenth birthday card. The closets in my suite of rooms bulged with designer labels."

Clearly, Shelby needed to pour her heart out. The review of her progress at the last staff meeting indicated she might still be holding back the deepest hurts.

"Who took the time to go out and buy all those wonderful things for you? How did you feel about that?"

"Father gave the nanny a list and she'd call I. Magnin's or wherever, and have the stuff sent out. I had a continual dream. I saw myself flailing for survival, drowning in a sea of luxurious *things*. I kept beating them off of me, grasping for a lifeline from someone who would pull me out and love me, care about me. By the time I reached eighteen, I'd come to a horrible realization: a loving relationship with a parent would never be included in my inheritance. I came to the conclusion that I'd been born an unlovable person. After that came deeper depression and years in psychotherapy."

"No one is born an unlovable person, Shelby. God loved you before you were born." Beth paused. "What about your mother?"

"Gloria Fairchild was the *crème de la crème* of New York high society before she married my father—heir to another great fortune of old established wealth. My most vivid remembrance of her is looking beautiful in a glittery dress and giving me a quick good-night kiss on the cheek before she went off to a party to drink too much. She died in a private plane crash when I was six.

"I can't push those dark, lonely nights out of my mind, when the nanny routinely tucked me in bed, and I cried into the black shadows. . . . 'Won't somebody please love me?' I've asked myself my whole life—what's wrong with me?"

"Dear Shelby, the need to be loved is the most basic of all human requirements—there's nothing wrong with that. The problem lies with those who withhold love."

Shelby changed the subject. "The warmth of the sun feels heavenly. This is a beautiful spot, overlooking the grounds and gardens and pool. The little tea house is delightful. Does anyone ever use it?"

"Certainly. It's always open—you're welcome to sit and enjoy the fountain and greenery. It's been used a great deal in the past, but we've never planned anything specific there since we've opened Rosehaven for residents."

"Nothing at Fair Oaks was ever used or enjoyed. It's like a well-designed cemetery. Everything feels dead."

"Fair Oaks?" Beth questioned.

"That's my father's estate—not too far from here, where I grew up. Except I almost always got sent away to boarding schools, then college, which I didn't finish because I was too unstable, and then to hospitals. But I never found a place to simply sit and enjoy its beauty, you know? Father sent me on a tour of the continent last year during a 'well period,' and I visited Versailles, outside of Paris. My father had something in common with old Louie the Sun King—they contrived to impress the eyes only with the ornately lavish but sterile. Rosehaven was designed to comfort the soul."

If any soul needed comfort, it's Shelby's, Beth thought, quietly awaiting whatever feelings should come spilling out next.

Both women gazed at their surroundings in comfortable silence, yet Beth felt Shelby studying her trimly classic figure molded into jeans and a violet shirt, her shiny black hair with its silver streak tied back with a matching ribbon.

She also sensed Shelby assessing her own rather scrawny, unkept form, in need of shaping and toning for one yet so young, her hair and complexion dull and neglected.

Shelby broke the silence. "It's wonderful to actually be able to speak to you. I've admired you all my life!"

"Well, thank you, and certainly you can speak to me, dear. That's what I'm here for—and of course, this is still my home. Your comment puzzles me a bit—have we met before you came to Rosehaven?"

"No, no, we haven't. But I know you and the staff study each patient's history—excuse me, 'guest' is the term you prefer, I believe—before accepting us. So I'm sure you know my background. As a fellow philanthropist for the Arts, my father and his various lady-friends have

attended many of the glorious benefits held here when Mr. Townsend was
alive. I've followed the events of Charles and Elizabeth Townsend, everything I could dig out of the newspapers, since I was a teenager. You
changed my concept about people with wealth. You gave me hope.

"I've read the society pages and about your work in establishing the
New Hope Center for counseling in San Francisco. Of course, my father
would have a fit if I went down on Market Street for help. But since we're
practically neighbors, and he has such respect for you and awe for this
place, he was eager that I come."

Beth smiled inwardly. *That's putting it mildly,* she thought, remembering the terror he caused in demanding they accept Shelby before they
were legally able. But this affirmation was precisely what she'd hoped to
hear.

"As I said, I've been in therapy for seven years. I don't know when
I've felt as good as I do today. You are truly a great lady. I've noticed some
of the other 'guests' are perking up, too." Her smile warmed Beth's heart.

"Shelby, you've made my day." Beth squeezed her hand. "Rosehaven
gave Charles and me a world of pleasure in sharing its beauty. I wish you
could have known him, but he'd be blessed to know you're here, being
helped by our excellent staff. This is what he'd want. He felt about his
father much as you do about yours. But take heart. Old TNT was not only
a distant father, he was a tyrant in business, and that hurt Charles very
much."

"I read everything I could find about Charles," Shelby admitted.
"Even some of the features in magazines on the President and CEO of
Townsend Enterprises—his fame and fortune in architecture, his philan-
thropic projects. He was a great man."

"One of a kind," Beth smiled. "It pleases me, knowing he'd also be
delighted I have Josh Sterling for a husband, as well as a fine administrator
for Rosehaven Retreat. We and his deceased wife, Hope, were the dearest
of friends."

"Pardon me, Mrs. Sterling," Shelby said, "I've engaged you in a very
personal conversation. Please forgive me, if that's being out of line."

"On the contrary, Shelby, you're such a sweet, friendly person—delightful to talk with. And I sense a warmth . . . openness, and that's a very
good sign. I usually have a talk with our residents when they first arrive,
to get to know them, but you were very ill when you came and withdrawn

until now. Besides, I have no secrets." Beth caught herself, thinking of her own past heartaches, and added with a smile, "Well, not many, at least."

"Mrs. Sterling—"

"Excuse me, Shelby," Beth interrupted with a smile, "we're on a first-name basis, so please call me Beth." This gorgeous morning, here in the setting she loved, unhurried, with the opportunity to reach out and touch a hurting soul made her heart glad. Looking at this plain and polite young woman, repressed and lacking in self-esteem, she wanted to reach down into her being and draw out her pain, set her free. *That's God's job,* Beth reminded herself. . . .

"Now, what were you going to say?" she continued.

Shelby rephrased. "Beth, then; you said Charles felt similarly about his father. How did he live with that? How does anyone learn to overcome rejection by their parents? I want so much to please, to be accepted, and yet I never measure up. Never seem important enough to be worthy of spending time and conversation together. It's taken me years merely to be able to face these facts. Father isn't the one who's going to change. With three generations of hanging on to all that money and power while excluding feelings—it's just not going to happen!"

"Facing the reality is the first step, Shelby."

"I've come a long way. I know I have. When the doctors diagnosed me as anorexic, Father placed another guilt trip on me. I was starved for affection. He's all I have, but he's indifferent and detached. Charles lived a fabulous life, was successful, loved, and admired. How did he do it? I'm still nothing—but rich."

Beth expected to see tears as she studied the young woman with compassion. Then she realized her pain went deeper. Shelby had cried a river of tears when the hurt was new.

"There's not a simple answer, Shelby. But it does have a happy ending. Yours will, too. You and I will talk as often as you like, and that's what we have a professional staff for. Right now, I'd like to concentrate on why you look and feel much more alive. What brought this about?" she smiled.

"Yes, we must learn to accentuate the positive, right? I feel loved here. I feel a peace inside that doesn't come from me, but it's in me. Does that make sense? I'm not sure who put it there. You, I think, by caring enough about people to open and give over your private estate, all the glamorous events that used to take place here, to help others. I simply can't believe that kind of love."

"You've made my day again, Shelby. Everything comes from somewhere. Let me ask you, where do you think that kind of love comes from?"

"I have no idea. It's a complete mystery to me, foreign to anything I've ever known. I almost don't trust it—but I trust you. I've honestly never felt loved, *worthy* of being loved, before. It's from God, maybe. If there is one."

"Let me assure you, there is a God. But why do you say that?"

"The other day I read a plaque as I walked through the gardens over by the Tea House. What a beautiful little place that is, with its walls of glass and trailing vines, the cool slate floor and the fountain bubbling out of the green dolphin's mouth. Anyway, I sat to rest on a bench and read that sign in the ground."

"And what did it say?"

"*Be still and know that I am God.*" Shelby paused, assimilating its meaning. "That really quieted my anxious thoughts. It made me feel almost loved, like I didn't have to be troubled about anything, because someone stronger than I sat beside me. Could that be?"

Tears danced in Beth's eyes, sparkling like sapphires.

She prized this affirmation of the vision she'd had for Rosehaven, her life, her family. And for all the Shelbys.

"That's exactly right. You have wonderful things to discover about God and His love. We've much more to talk about. I usually walk the grounds early in the morning, turning my thoughts toward Him. I often pause and read from this little Bible I carry before I exercise and start my day. Sometimes Josh is with me." Beth stood up. "I have a board of directors' meeting in an hour, so I'd better scoot back and shower."

Shelby rose also. "Please tell them thanks. Maybe there's hope for me yet!"

Beth extended her arms and drew Shelby into a hug, intending to release the young woman momentarily. Instead, an awareness of something flowing out of her being melted into another's heart. She felt it mingling there. And in turn, a response of cherishing the warmth and tenderness of a motherly hug Shelby had never known reflected back. Beth held her tightly for long moments. Letting go, she whispered, "God bless. . . ."

7

Josh turned quickly as his wife entered the library where the board was about to meet. With admiring eyes he followed her lithe motions. She paused, as though framed by the carved oak doorway, radiant in a deep pink linen suit, a single strand of pearls, her lustrous shoulder-length hair lightly turned under. Josh admired her guileless understated elegance.

He noticed that her presence brought the din of conversation down to a hush as eyes turned in her direction—by no means an uncommon occurrence—and the quick breath she drew before proceeding as though she hadn't noticed. Their eyes met as she threaded her way toward him.

At the same moment, Beth thought about his frequent comment, that almost every day he found a fresh new dimension in their lives together. She tingled, sensing it now. The life experiences of their intimate friendship resembled only a glimmer of the insights as husband and wife. She glowed, knowing she'd stimulated an awakening in him, a great joy in being alive.

"You're absolutely dazzling, but then, what else is new?" he whispered in her ear.

"Just a minor miracle, is all. I had an encouraging conversation with Shelby Harding on my walk this morning. If the rest of you are as gratified as I at how God is bringing precisely the people who need to be here, and touching their lives, we're in for a great meeting today!"

"Did you see Bob and Kerry on the way?" Josh asked, searching the massive doorway. "I believe they'll have some exciting reports, too. Did I apprise you of the agenda? Staff meets with the Board, we have lunch, then Bob and I reconvene with your Board to evaluate progress. I'd like you to attend the meeting too."

"No, I'd prefer the way it is." Beth looked up at him, half-teasing, totally adoring, mustering unusual spunk. "Did you say *my* board? I'm in this with *you*, remember? My original plan specified in the deed of trust for Rosehaven Retreat that I would be a life board member, and otherwise not in a staff position. Then, *you* modified Plan A with the splendid ultimatum requiring me to marry you and work hand in hand or you wouldn't accept the job! What do you say to that, Mr. Administrator?" she laughed.

"I say we've struck a mighty bargain, and we'd better get this show on the road. It's ten o'clock."

Beth overheard two of the other board members, Dr. Malcolm Fielding, one of the hottest Christian authors and psychologists on dysfunctional relationships, chatting with the Reverend Brian Tarkington.

"There's Daniels now with his bright wife, Kerry. I tell you, Tark, I haven't been this excited about my profession since I began my own counseling practice at his age, twenty years ago. Since your church is largely made up of multi-millionaires, you know how tough it is to reach through their pride. Young Daniels is refreshing. His warmth and sincerity will get right to them. But he's an intellect, too. Have you had any direct personal feedback?"

Beth's heart swelled with justifiable pride. Fielding's prestige as a clinical psychologist had importantly enhanced Rosehaven's posture and credibility. Beth admired Brian Tarkington as well, the senior pastor of First Church of San Francisco. Many years ago, Charles had done the architectural design and donated the renovation of the huge old structure. He'd given grace to the tarnished name of Townsend left by his father among its congregation.

"Tark," as his friends called him, was mature in years as well as in preaching the Word of God. He had succeeded the Reverend Goodwin who had been called to a larger church in Washington, D.C., to Beth's great relief. Granted, she rarely drove the twenty-five miles into San Francisco to attend services anymore. But since Charles had much of himself invested there, her heart became glad that the pastor's message was what God, rather than man, would have him preach.

Beth valued Tark's friendship and esteemed his spiritual leadership on the Board. He'd championed the cause of both the New Hope Center and Rosehaven in the pastoral community . . . he'd been invaluable.

At that moment Tark's peripheral glance caught Beth. "Before I answer, I want this young lady to hear, too—" He reached out his arms, "Good morning, Beth. What a splendid occasion!"

"Isn't it? I'm excited!"

"And rightly so. I see God's hand at work. I was about to tell Fielding here how impressed I am with young Daniels's spiritual maturity. The biblical truths he applied in counseling with one member in my congregation who spent two weeks with you brought about nothing short of a miracle. As a pastor, I can't possibly invest that kind of time with one individual. I'd say Daniels, and our entire staff, are truly gifted by God."

Fielding brightened. "And may I add, I was saying to Tark how delighted I am to be associated with Rosehaven, Beth. Your vision and incredible efforts are to be congratulated!"

Beth swallowed the lump in her throat with misty eyes. "I appreciate your support, gentlemen, in all ways. Come, let's find our seats. The meeting is about to begin," she smiled.

In the role of gracious hostess, Beth welcomed the Board and staff to their first official meeting at Rosehaven, her heart pounding with joy as Bob opened in prayer and Josh called them to order.

She hung on every word as she listened to the reports of Dr. Foster's psychiatric staff and medical team, of David's warm professionalism, and of Golda and the other psychotherapists, ending with the dietician. This was not new information to her. This and more comprised the Monday morning team meetings.

Each member of the Board of Directors represented Beth's personal choice, all of whom were highly regarded in their realms of expertise. Now, during this official presentation to the Board, her heart overflowed with gratitude at the accomplishments to date. Within her spirit she wondered, *Charles, do you hear?* and saw his steadfast blue eyes, smiling. Tark had said it, "I see God's hand is at work." *Yes, yes,* she thought, filled with the essence of the most rewarding day she'd ever known.

Following the luncheon, while their men continued the meeting, Kerry took Beth by the hand and led her into the privacy of her own former bedroom suite. "While the others are occupied and Teddy is napping, I want a stolen moment just for us," Kerry hugged her tightly. "Mother, I'm so proud of you!" Her thick dark lashes were moist. "This is when it's

all I can do to restrain from shouting to the whole world—'This remarkably loving, generous, talented, godly woman is my mother!' "

"I know, I know how you feel, darling. That's how it is every time
I look at *you*. It seems unbearable to me at times. Let's be content to share
the glory that belongs to God. I do thank Him for all He's allowed us to
do—and especially that we share it together. I was thinking that today is
the most satisfying day of my life, but it was really the day I gave birth to
you. It remains my crowning achievement. That, too, is a gift from God
. . . that He couldn't allow aborting the life within me."

They relaxed in comfortable armchairs, chatting as two schoolgirls
would on a warm afternoon. Their conversation slid into discussing the
progress of Rosehaven's guests, whose names ranked among the rich and
famous.

"The older I get, the more difficult it is for me not to get really angry
with people," Kerry confessed. "The devastating effects of being totally
consumed with *self*, to degrees I've never imagined, make me furious.
We're surrounded by lives ruined by selfishness!"

"You've been blessedly sheltered, as was I," Beth agreed. "When I
began to realize the hurts and suffering of those who came for help to the
New Hope Center, I could hardly stand it. It's the same here, but with
different names and faces. Are you thinking of a patient in particular right
now?"

"Yes. Trenton Walker. He looks like he's ready to shove his fist
through the wall most of the time while simultaneously looking guilty for
even thinking such a thing. Otherwise, he's really a good-looking guy.
How old do you think he is?"

"Twenty-seven," Beth answered, "an old and bitter twenty-seven.
But considering his mother's image as television's highest paid nightly
news analyst, with her pompous feminist's bias so degrading of traditional
values, Trenton's anger becomes understandable. It's as though he feels
guilty by association when his mother persists at taking nasty shots at
pro-lifers and anti-abortion issues."

"Oh, I know. And Trenton's a Christian. That must tear him apart."

Kerry stood and stretched. "I think I hear Teddy waking up. Better
take a look and get his bottle ready." Opening the refrigerator in the suite's

compact kitchen concealed behind a door, she asked, "Would you like an iced tea?"

"No thanks, hon. I think I'll go see if our men are out of the meeting. Oh, remind me to tell you about my conversation with Shelby this morning."

"Encouraging?" Kerry asked.

"Yes, indeed. It'll make your day."

Kerry hugged her mother. "Lots of good things made our day. Congratulations. Are we having dinner together?"

"If you and Bob don't need some time alone, that would be lovely. I'm all wound up! Maybe David and Golda would like to join us. I'll ask, and then advise Chef."

"I don't know what's cooking for the guests, but if he can, I'd love spaghetti!"

"I'll see what we can do. Better yet, let me go change, then I'll come back to the nursery with Teddy and play Grammy, and you can put all that together."

"It's a go!" Kerry smiled.

Peering into the library through the slightly open door, Kerry caught the scent of the famous Bouchand fragrance. The angry voice of Rochelle Bouchand demanded, "Why did God allow that?"

Bob called out, "Come in, Kerry, and you may close the door, please." Rochelle immediately stood up, obviously annoyed at the invasion of privacy. "I'll make an appointment to discuss this further with you tomorrow. I'm not satisfied with the answers I'm getting." She stormed out.

"What's that all about?" Kerry looked confused.

"I was the last one in the room after the meeting, and she barged in with her usual aggressive manner as I was about to leave. She's in the throes of working out some mixed emotions. Very angry at God, as you can see."

"She's owner, president, and CEO of the Bouchand cosmetics empire, isn't she?"

Bob nodded, absorbed in putting a sheaf of papers together. "She appears to be the epitome of success, quite an achievement for mid-forty. Expensively attractive. I wouldn't want to block her path though—she looks like a barracuda."

"I think that's about right. *Newsweek* recently did an article on her corporate toughness. She's legendary in business but a failure in personal relationships. She devastates everybody she comes in contact with—and it's getting to her."

"Why is she angry at God?"

Bob sank down with a tired sigh into the big leather chair, obviously fatigued from the unexpected encounter.

"She became a Christian at twelve. Persuaded her alcoholic parents to go to church with her, and prayed they'd change. They sure did. They told everyone they were Christians, put on a sanctimonious facade, and continued to drink themselves into senselessness every night. They were in complete denial of their alcoholism. They stopped going to church and were out of it all day on Sundays. The shades were kept pulled down. Rochelle never had friends come to her home—she felt ashamed of her tawdry parents. It was forbidden and instilled in her never to discuss her parents' alcoholism, either in or out of the home. She felt isolated with nowhere to go with her feelings or misery. That's when she became angry with God, asking, 'If He loved me, why did He allow me to grow up in such an unloving home?'" He paused. "Sorry—guess I've repeated some of the history you've heard at Monday team meetings, and of course, there's more."

"Well, darling, that's enough for now. This has been a day to remember. Unless you have something else in mind, Beth suggested we have dinner with them and the Rosens. Chef's going to do spaghetti for us. Okay?"

"Umm—you bet!"

Among Kerry's messages the next morning was one from Rochelle, requesting Kerry to meet with her after her nine o'clock counseling session.

"You are a lovely young woman," Rochelle began the conversation. "For all the claims of my Mascara Magic, one must be *born* with eyelashes like yours. They are to die for!"

"Thank you for the compliment, Rochelle. But what can I do for you?"

A frown clouded her perfectly made-up face. "It's—it's quite out of character for me, but I have a need to apologize to both you and your husband for yesterday. I feel more comfortable with women, so I'll begin with you."

"I commend you for doing the difficult, and my husband has always felt that apologies are good for the soul. What are you apologizing for?"

"My outburst of angry intrusion and rudeness yesterday. I can't stand the person I've become." Rochelle paused, and began to shake.

"What kind of person is that?" Kerry asked gently.

"Well . . . I finally realized I've built a wall around myself that separates me from the world and from sensitivity to other people. I've become a cold, calloused person. I suffer from anxiety attacks, and my doctor told me I was depressed. It's so bizarre. I rank number five among the ten most successful women in business in the U.S., and I'm a failure as a human being. Isn't that a kick?"

"We're here to help you," Kerry said softly, waiting. Rochelle came to make an apology, and it was important for her to accomplish that. Kerry let her talk.

"I can't believe what I did. . . . I had an employee in upper management, Shirlee—the sweetest woman in the world, and loved by everyone. She lost a husband in an auto accident, her father died of a stroke, and her teenage daughter committed suicide—in the last six months. She's brilliant and was valuable to the company's future. My heart truly aches for her now, but when she tried to share her feelings with me about what she was going through and requested some time off—I refused. Can you believe that? She'd been with me ten years, and I can't remember if I ever showed an interest in her as a person. But I paid her well.

"I'll never forget the look of hurt and disbelief in her eyes. Then she quietly walked out of my office, emptied her desk, and left without a word to anyone. Surely she was crushed. No one dared to mention it. She held the reigns of management's morale with her sunny smile—until I'd come on the scene and destroy everyone. I've had two resignations of staff since then. A heartless tyrant, an ogre—that's what I am. . . ." Rochelle's voice cracked, yet her gray eyes were stoic and dull as unpolished steel. "Please forgive me for yesterday."

"I do. And I suspect you also have some forgiving to do. Unforgiveness is a bedfellow of anger. You've been very open with me, as I hope you've been with Jessica, your therapist. I want you to know I'm always available to you also."

Rochelle looked relieved while contemplating her next question. "Aren't you going to insist that I attend your women's Bible study and come to your husband's worship services?"

"Those are available options. Of course we want you to remember—God loves you. But you should come when you're ready," Kerry smiled. Her phone rang. Rochelle rose to leave, and Kerry asked the caller to hold.

"Being at Rosehaven is my first experience in therapy, but it wasn't my therapist, Jessica, who advised me to apologize—you should know that. I just needed to. . . ."

"Thanks," Kerry nodded with a smile.

In Beth's office, Becky informed her that Mrs. Earle had arrived and was waiting in the reception area. "Thank you, I'll be down in a moment," she said, and took another quick scan of the notes she'd taken over the phone.

The sun beaming through the mullioned windows illuminated Allyson Earle's ash-blonde hair in a halo of spun gold. Exquisitely coiffed, she wore a cream-colored linen suit, silk blouse, and gold earrings. The famous teen star that stole movie-goers' hearts in the mid-'60s with her charm and talent stood as Beth entered, a queenly beauty of poise and grace, but she was visibly nervous.

"Welcome." Beth extended her hand. "May I get you some coffee, and show you around the grounds before we go into my study?"

"No, thank you, Mrs. Sterling. I have no doubt that everything is equally as beautiful as what I've already seen. I—I'd like to get on with the interview."

"Of course. Let's go upstairs."

Beth motioned for Mrs. Earle to be seated and threw the French windows open above the rose garden, inviting their perfume to pervade the room. "Will your husband be coming separately, or was he unable to be with you today?"

"Austin considered cancelling a major meeting with his insurance executives, but many had flown in especially eager to meet him, the president and founder, not just the CEO. I assured him I'd go through with this. I can't live with it any longer. . . ."

"I understand. How long ago did your father pass away, Mrs. Earle?"

"A year ago last month. But even in death, the guilt, shame, and dirtiness still haunts me—has haunted me since I was twelve. It consumes me. It affected my acting career. It affected my marriage for too long . . . I must think of my husband. And my sanity."

"I'm certain the devastation of incest is terrible. You said you were worried about your mother and the results if you follow the advice you've been given. I'm sure you'll need more counseling before you decide to go public to expose a man as prominent as your father. What will that do for you?"

"It will expose me, too, and dredge up some painful emotions I haven't dealt with. I hope it will emancipate thousands of other women, perhaps even men, who've been molested or sexually abused. It's shocking how prevalent this is—more than most people can imagine."

"You're taking a courageous step. And what about your mother?"

"My psychiatrist and therapist agree that she can't live in denial much longer. My mother is a dominating socialite. Appearances are more important than honesty or even morality. She refuses to allow disgrace to come to this man who proudly escorted me to my debutante ball, whose millions supported charity drives and was one of the community 'pillars.' She's a proud woman—perhaps she feels she was not enough for him, that he turned to his daughters in the dark of the night."

"Daughters?" Beth asked, surprised.

"Yes. My younger sister Lynette confided in me six months ago, and I felt doubly distressed. It was worse for her after I'd given up my movie career and left for college. I dreaded coming home and didn't when I could avoid it. Mother lived in Fantasyland, insisting that we were a 'close' family, steeped in tradition, and Daddy demanded we be together on holidays as though nothing abnormal went on in our bedrooms."

"You endured that a long time."

"Yes. Until I met my wonderful husband and married. When I was twelve, my father told me the sexual acts were things daughters must do as a special way of 'being close.' I waited in terror every night, not knowing when he'd come into my room. I can hear him still, whispering 'I love you.' When I was fourteen, he threatened to tell Mother, because he knew I was afraid of her, and that she'd blame me. In college, I tried to forget everything. I became overly ambitious, an honor student and drama major.

Appearing on stage helped my self-esteem, and I traveled extensively. I went deeper into denial and thought for a while I'd blocked out my past.

"The early years of our marriage were difficult. I'm surprised we made it, because I soon refused intimacy with my husband. It brought it all back. I finally had to confess to him; he found a therapist, and we've gone as far as we can with the help we have. Is there hope here for us at Rosehaven? Do you believe there's hope for incest victims?"

"We have a God of hope—and especially with Him, all things are possible," Beth assured her with a smile.

"Maybe I can find God again—here. The ironic thing is, my father was a trustee of our church, very involved. His outer image appears impeccable. Our church was imposingly grand architecturally, with a preacher perched so high above the people, I felt he and God were beyond my reach. I didn't think God could hear me, but I desperately wanted to hide the sin from Him. When I stopped going, Father didn't object. Thought I might tell on him, I suppose. I had very few rules in high school, but I was honestly a good kid.

"Mrs. Sterling—I'm searching for wholeness and a new spiritual direction, which may be one and the same. So is Austin."

These were the words Beth had hoped to hear from Allyson. She told her, "When we have a right relationship with God, the rest of our lives are much more likely to come together. That's the desire of my heart for Rosehaven—to introduce hurting people to the healing power of our living God."

"I want that very much. When I telephoned, I asked for an interview and information." She paused, her gorgeous smile illuminating brilliant blue eyes, "but I came prepared to stay, if that can be arranged without a waiting period."

"Let me give you some information to look over," Beth smiled. "Come downstairs with me; here's a diagram of our facility. I believe our Dr. Foster is available this afternoon, and we'll proceed from there."

The mid-September morning, bathed in the amber hues of Indian summer, reminded Beth of a Tintoretto painting. The heavier her schedule, the more she treasured her morning walks and talks with God. She'd pause to read her Bible, then resume her walk to reflect upon what she'd read, asking for God's refreshment of her insight for the day ahead.

A call from the high knoll rose above the melody of the birds. "Good morning! Isn't it glorious?"

"Shelby—good morning!" *Glorious* seemed like a foreign language springing from Shelby's vocabulary, and Beth immediately felt elated. Beth hadn't had a one-on-one conversation with her in weeks but recalled that the reports had shown improvement; Shelby was eating, had greater stability in her emotions, and had become more outgoing. "You're glowing from the inside out," she told her. "You must be feeling as good as you look."

Shelby giggled. "When I look in the mirror, I can't believe it's me. I know David saved my life. He and my therapist, Julie, are helping me understand myself—the things in my life I can change and those I can't. You're all so *caring*. Especially Josh. He's my friend. Kerry is lucky to have a big teddy bear kind of a daddy. I always wished I had one just like him. He's wise, too. My best friend, though, is Allyson. Can you believe a gorgeous creature like her would care about me?"

"Of course I can! God made each of us with our own kind of beauty, but down deep, we're all alike in our basic needs. Sometimes we relate more to the inner person than to what meets the eye. She bleeds when hurt just as you do."

"Allyson and Rochelle and I were having a soda in your charming English Pub a few evenings ago. The pub's neat—what a great place to socialize."

"That's what we thought when we were in England. I'm glad we put it in."

"Anyway, we talked about our inner and outer selves. They both look terrific on the outside. I'm more transparent . . . what you see is what you get!" she laughed. "Rochelle was very tactful, but she volunteered to do my makeup. I found that incredible too. Imagine—the head of a multi-billion-dollar company! I was terrified of any personal conversation when I first saw her in group therapy. . . . She looked so—angry is all I can think of. And I've been trying to shape up in the work-out room. That's all part of the glow in my cheeks. The rest of it comes from. . . . " She stopped.

Beth waited a moment. "From where, Shelby?"

"From that inner peace that's still new to me. I'm often drawn to the Tea House and that plaque that says 'Be still and know that I am God.'

It calms me. But I've never gone in to the Tea House even though you said I could."

"Why not, since you're so intrigued with it?"

"I feel silly saying this, but it's such a quiet, beautiful place. I feel God's presence in there. And I'm not worthy to go in and be with Him." She bent her head and stared at the ground. Beth placed a gentle hand on her shoulder. "God created you to be near to Him. His desire is for you to know and love Him. He sent His Son to—"

"Excuse me, Beth," Shelby stood up, tears in her eyes. "You've lived such a pure life. You just don't know—" She gulped down the lump in her throat and hurried away.

Reach out and touch her, Lord, Beth prayed. *Tell her You love her just as she is. . . .*

As Beth passed through the Pub in the late afternoon, she noticed Shelby and Allyson talking again. Shelby was smiling. *A good sign,* Beth thought.

But the next day, and those that followed, Shelby wasn't smiling anymore. Another stealthy joy-robber had emerged from the dark shadows of her soul and ripped at her heart, exposing a gaping wound she refused to let anyone come near.

Dr. Foster could find no explanation for this new bout of depression. Julie, her primary therapist, grew concerned about her holding back and conferred daily with David after their sessions. Shelby respected and trusted him as he slowly and gently threaded his way into her deeper confidence. The team steadily prayed as they evaluated her progress.

After a diligent week David told the team, "Although she refuses to say the word—I think I know, and hope to God I'm wrong."

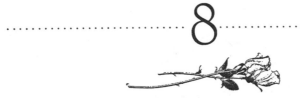

8

Y ou don't understand what Allyson's saying—none of you!"
Shelby burst from her chair, screaming at the therapists and
patients in the group therapy session.

"Allyson's attempting to explain that incest exceeds the humiliation
of a young girl's body being violated. As she grows up, the hideous secret
seduces her mind, and she must put aside her own thoughts and feelings
for lies." Shelby's voice had reached a crescendo.

"You don't understand," she repeated, collapsing into her chair in
sobs, "except me. Oh God, how I understand. I've been there."

David knelt before her, with Golda and Julie giving support on both
sides of her contorted body. "There now, you've said it, Shelby," he
soothed her with his mellow voice. "You're not denying what happened
to you anymore. You've overcome denial and reached the important and
necessary stage of acknowledging the truth. We all care about your and
Allyson's pain." He gave her his handkerchief.

Shelby wiped her tear-blotched cheeks. Her eyes swiftly traveled
around the circle, assessing the compassionate faces fixed on her by fellow
pilgrims in search of wholeness. She looked at Allyson. "You've had the
guts to expose the awful truth I've kept buried since I was twelve. Half my
life! There were times I thought I would go crazy with shame, and that I
dared not divulge the repulsive acts of my father because—because it's too
sick. I was afraid that I'd be judged a pervert too."

Shelby's imprisoned anger exploded in full force. "I see now, I'm
emotionally damned forever if I continue to hide in denial. I realize my
eight years of counseling was a form of religion—and the therapists
believed and taught worship of self. It was all for nothing," she sobbed.

"That can't be all there is to life! How does anyone manage to get outside of themselves?

"I'm wondering how many other women live with the horror of being victims of incest," she demanded of David, expecting no answer to her rhetorical questions. Shelby threw her head back with a resolve they'd never seen before. "All of us must be set free. Allyson, your father is dead." She began to tremble. "Mine is very much alive, but I can't live with the evil hold he's had on me. If you go public with your story, I will!"

A lightning bolt of emotion quivered through Shelby's entire body, followed by uncontrollable shaking. Julie placed a reassuring hand on her shoulder. "I suggest you spend some time thinking that through—proceed with caution before you come to any decision, and carefully evaluate if you can bear the consequences just now." The shaking grew more intense. "Let's take a walk, Shelby. That's enough emotion for one day." Julie steadied her willing follower out of the room.

Concerned eyes of patients and therapists now shifted back to Allyson, visibly unnerved by the testimony of another victim of this cruel exploitation of a daughter by her father. The classic beauty of Allyson's face was distorted in anguish. "Shelby understands. No one can comprehend the painful emotions and betrayal that come with incest."

David stood, his hands thrust into his pockets as he took several paces back and forth. "We psychologists are limited in our ability to heal life's wounded. We can help identify the feelings and take you through the steps to recovery. But it is God who shares your broken heart when you are a victim of another's sin. From the book of the Old Testament prophet, in Isaiah 41:10, God gives us this assurance: 'Fear not, for I am with you; be not dismayed, for I am your God. I will strengthen you, yes, I will help you, I will uphold you with My righteous right hand.'"

David's rich tones and the words he spoke penetrated and dissolved the tenseness in the room. "Remember, God alone knows the extent of your pain. The supernatural power of the One who created you is the infinite source of power that is constantly available. Like electricity—it's always there. But you have to decide to turn it on. God's inviting you to ask for His help."

He paused, scanning the inquisitive faces of his listeners. "I can see that some of you have questions, maybe even doubts whether God really is available," he smiled. "So I'll stay a while to talk with you. I agree with

Julie, however—a little exercise is exactly what this doctor is prescribing. I'm looking for a tennis game a little later, if anyone's interested."

"You're on!" Trenton called out. "After you answer a question for me," he added.

Allyson remained riveted to her chair, while about half of the patients quickly left the room, eager for relief from the strained emotions.

Beth leaned into the room, searching for David. A briefing of Shelby's breakthrough, relayed to her by Jessica, constituted a major event, and she was eager to hear from David firsthand. She heard him fielding lively questions.

"What do you mean by 'God's supernatural power'?"

"How do I plug into it?"

An aggressive male voice layered with skepticism asked, "How can I believe that God will lift my depression when the best shrinks in the country have tried and failed?" Beth smiled, knowing how deftly David would resolve the inflected sarcasm with the Word of the living God.

She slipped silently into the garden to wait for him, her spirit soaring with the victories of the afternoon. "Thank You, God," she whispered, inhaling the spicy fragrance of a favorite rose, Double Delight. "You've done a mighty work in these lives today. Another variety of 'double delight' with Shelby coming out of the darkness of denial and now others searching for the light of Your healing love."

Beth expertly pinched back two small rosebuds below the large one on the stem. It reminded her of the reluctance of people to pinch back or deny themselves even the smallest and most temporary delights in exchange for spiritual growth. From years of nurturing her precious roses, she'd observed a lesson in life—the sooner the undesirable buds were nipped, the less pain and distortion to the bush. She fondled the healthy green leaves of a splendidly tinted red and cream blossom the size of a tea cup. Its stem stood strong and beautiful for having yielded itself to being pruned, fertilized, and pinched back. But it is God who creates the glory of the rose and causes it to grow. *How much more He desires to do for us,* she smiled.

The footsteps she heard on the path were not David's but those of Josh. "There you are," he called out. "I don't suppose you've heard the evening news?" He frowned.

"No. Why? What's happening?"

"It's on every channel. Alexander Harding's been charged with fraud! It concerns the sale of the golf course he negotiated with the Japanese on the Monterey peninsula. The public's been outraged about the prestigious old course and famed club being purchased by foreigners. Now the media reports he surreptitiously closed the deal, is charged with fraud, and is being sued by the Japanese government. Harding's in big trouble!"

Beth froze. "My first thought is to wonder what the effect will be on Shelby, how she'll manage the anger if he's convicted of fraud. How did the Japanese government get involved?"

"Beats me. But I just watched Brenda Walker on TV rip Harding to shreds on her five o'clock news commentary. Trenton and I were in the Pub discussing theology and politics when someone turned on the news— and there was Brenda. I support her point of view, but her demeanor was atrocious. She all but locked the prison door! Trenton literally broke out in a cold sweat and excused himself, mortified by his mother's vicious assessment of Harding. He asked me to tell David their tennis game was off!"

"How awful for Trenton! Harding has power, Josh. He'll bribe his way out."

"Not likely. Harding's sharp attorneys won't halt the wheels of justice this time. The evidence, with or without bias, seems quite convicting."

David came whistling down the path with a smile in his eyes. "Aha, I saw you poke your head in, Beth. Did you hear any of those pithy and profound questions? We've some great spiritual awakenings going on. I'll share some of them at tomorrow's staff meeting. And Shelby's coming out of denial is the breakthrough we've been waiting for. What a day!"

"What I heard delighted me! I felt like a mother hovering in the wings, silently prompting her babies to step out in holy curiosity. But Josh heard a shocker on the news. You tell him, Josh."

Josh repeated the story as David stroked his gray beard. Beth observed the psychologist's mind turning, evaluating the repercussions of Harding's fraud scandal upon Shelby, and Trenton's reaction to his mother's scathing report of it.

"I think we'd better have a staff meeting tonight, and a private session with Shelby and Trenton. I don't suppose anyone knows if Shelby's heard the news yet. I can't predict how she's going to react. What a bombshell!"

"How can we help?" Josh asked.

"Find Shelby, please, and tell her I'd like to talk with her and I'll be in my office. I'd guess Trenton's in his quarters for the night, so I'll contact him. Please inform Julie and also Trenton's primary therapist of the circumstances. Let's have our staff meeting at eight p.m. If any of the patients mention either situation, caution them to be sensitive, and assure them we'll discuss it freely in group therapy."

"Father God," Bob opened the staff meeting in prayer, "I am persuaded by Your Word it is Your desire that none should be consumed by the wicked ways of this world. Be present with us tonight as we commit Shelby and Trenton to Your loving care. Show us Your plan, to enable us to be used in healing the pain of these two wounded soldiers. By the power of Your Holy Spirit, make them victorious over their battles with physical and verbal abuse suffered throughout their young lives. And Father, by the power of Your Spirit, enable us to bring them to a saving knowledge of Christ, and may they seek His peace in their hearts. Amen."

David smiled. "Bob's prayer brings to mind Zechariah 4:6, doesn't it? 'Not by might nor by power, but by My Spirit, says the Lord of hosts.' I'm relieved it's not by our might or power, for we have a complex situation boiling: volatile personalities and interacting circumstances. One could impact another and explode without notice."

"Did you talk with Trenton?" Kerry asked. "It's unfortunate he had to see that newscast. I felt his self-esteem increasing greatly in the past week, and his anger subsiding."

"I'd have to agree, he's been coping much better," David replied, turning to Ryan, Trenton's primary therapist. "How would you evaluate him this evening?"

"His first response was to turn literally purple with rage. But the rage toward his mother was totally justified, properly directed, and he's learning to release it in a healthy form by talking it out. It helped prove to him he can be his own person and isn't responsible for anyone else's behavior. Let's pray he'll allow God to use this incident for good."

"We'll have to encourage him to verbalize *all* of his feelings," David agreed. "I can't believe Brenda's sponsors allowing character assassination under the guise of news coverage. They must think she represents a wide audience of viewers who relish seeing subjects crucified by her sardonic style and interpretation. And I'm glad she's not my mother!"

"Julie, how is Shelby dealing with the charges against her father, and how did she hear about it?" David asked.

"She's livid. Allyson saw the news on television and had the courage to go straight to Shelby to offer her support. She was with Shelby when I talked with her. Shelby immediately released a diatribe of buried anger related to various past projects of Harding's. That's been yet another area of denial. She'd suspected numerous land deals were corrupt. Realize that Harding ingrained a guilt trip on her about every opinion and action that didn't correspond with his objectives, so she condemned and buried her criticism as disloyalty. But already I believe she's releasing some of her guilt feelings. Tonight she reaffirmed her pledge to join Allyson in exposing their fathers publicly," Julie concluded.

"Would you say Allyson acknowledges her own need to forgive her father and get on with her life as more important than being vindictive?" David asked. "And what do you think Shelby's motive is at this time?"

"I'd say that's a correct assessment of Allyson. Her previous therapy focused on dealing with incest as the root of other dysfunctions. She's worked her way past denial, self-degradation, and the rest. Shelby's therapy dealt with depression. She's absorbed all the clinical vernacular—and she's right. The humanistic therapy she's had did become a worship of self. We all know that without God, the power to heal doesn't exist."

Julie paused, then continued. "Forgiveness will come slowly and take time for Shelby. My evaluation is that she's devastated over the scandal on the one hand, and fighting back with the other. She hasn't a glimmer of the degree of emotional trauma involved in publicly exposing her father's incestuous behavior. I advised her and I'm praying she'll weigh that carefully and count the cost."

"Good counsel, Julie. Let's pray Shelby and Allyson will open their hearts and ask God to lead them, particularly and individually with those decisions." Prayer continued until nearly midnight.

A photograph of Alexander Harding III flanked by attorneys and juxtaposed to pictures of irate Japanese officials covered the front pages of the morning papers. The article in the *San Francisco Examiner* consumed page after page of Harding's entrepreneurial career, once called brilliant but now attacked with allegations from all facets of the media. On television, morning talk shows featured the story exclusively throughout the first half of their programs.

Harding had managed to evade personal interviews. He issued only one statement before he and his attorneys departed on his private jet to Japan. "The public may rest assured that this is a matter of cultural miscommunication. The assertion of intent on my part of any fraudulent activity is absurd. Today's meeting in Osaka with Mr. Nakamura will negate this nonsense. I have nothing more to say."

Shelby waved the newspaper article, spewing the accretion of fury long repressed, commanding the attention of every possible listener, charging her father with lies. She was possessed by one thought. Exposure. Now. Today.

"Come, Shelby," David invited her with his warm, compassionate eyes and mellow tone. "Come walk with me. We'll go up to your favorite place on the high knoll, enjoy the sunshine, and you can tell me more about why you're so certain your father is guilty as charged, and exactly how you feel about it."

"I want to go to the Tea House," she said, bargaining in a childish pout.

"Very well. The Tea House is a lovely place."

They talked for hours as Shelby emptied her soul, yet she remained determined to make a statement to the press.

"Wait," David persuaded in conclusion. "I'm not suggesting that this isn't the appropriate action for you or Allyson. But I doubt she'd want to divulge her story on the heels of this scandal that has nothing to do with her. And I believe the timing's wrong for you. The point is, you're not emotionally prepared. You've no idea how the media will wring you out if you add this to the lawsuit by the Japanese."

Her jaw was resolutely set. His plea had floated over her head and fallen on deaf ears. Without another word, Shelby bolted out of the Tea House, running as though she'd burst from the starting block of a mad dash to escape the truth once more.

David ran after her, but she'd disappeared. He went to Shelby's cottage, then Julie's; he searched the halls, but there was still no sight of her. He went next to Josh's office. "Alert Julie and the staff," he said breathlessly. "We must find her. Notify Dr. Foster as well."

Becky knocked and entered without waiting. "A cab just pulled away. I think I saw Shelby in it!"

"Oh, God . . . help her!" David dropped into the chair.

The previous evening's five o'clock news report, castigating Alexander Harding III, paled in contrast to the latest testimony of his daughter's charge of incest. Brenda Walker's on-the-spot interview with Shelby drilled mercilessly for details until Shelby suddenly collapsed in front of the cameras. The live coverage showed paramedics taking her by ambulance to the hospital.

Rosehaven grew quiet with shock at the turn of events. Bob gathered the staff and encouraged patients numbed with disbelief at Shelby's irrational behavior, disregard of counsel, and warning of the consequences, to meet for prayer and comfort.

Beth observed that a new rapport had quickly developed between Trenton and Allyson in empathy with Shelby's newest trauma. He appeared resigned to, or perhaps disgusted with, Brenda's callous disregard for human kindness. Perhaps the compassion he'd received conveyed that he was not held accountable for his mother's acidic tongue.

"Beth," David encountered her somberly moments after the confusion ebbed, "do we have an option other than to go to Shelby?"

Involvement, implications of staff, Rosehaven itself, disruption of the other patients, condemnation by Brenda Walker, newspaper reporters clamoring for interviews—flashed across her mind with dizzying challenges.

"No," she answered simply.

David asked Max to drive him directly to the hospital, accompanied only by Beth.

As Max merged the big Cadillac onto the highway, David looked into Beth's troubled sapphire eyes. "There's just one thing in this world

I'm confident Shelby truly believes. . . ." He paused, touched by what he was about to say.

"What's that?" Beth asked.

"That you alone truly love her."

"I'm glad," she whispered, her eyes brimming with tears, unable to speak above the lump in her throat. Her heart bled for Shelby.

They'd attempted to leave Rosehaven unnoticed but departed in a flurry of anxiety among the patients. Beth recognized the voice of the man in the core of the bewilderment as yesterday's chief skeptic. Howard Klotz, one of the nation's largest retailers, appeared the most perturbed, even offended, at Shelby's defiance of godly counsel.

David apologized for the brisk action. "I felt we had no time to lose in getting to Shelby before she's harassed any further. But I suggest that right now, we telephone our Board of Directors, inform them we're on our way to the hospital, and have Tarkington or whoever we can reach at this hour arrange a conference call. We need to get their sanction if possible before we blunder into this mess."

"I was considering the same thing." Beth found the number in her handbag roster and dialed it on the cellular phone, passing it to David.

"Tark? David Rosen here. You must be the only one still in the office. You've heard the news, I suppose, about. . . ." He paused, "Yes, Harding's bombshell yesterday, Shelby's today. Beth and I are in the car, on the way to the hospital downtown. Let me fill you in. . . ."

David gave him the pertinent details. "Yes, yes. I don't think so either, we can't abandon her. The paramedics brought her in. She's at General. Yes, I was her last doctor before she came to Rosehaven. We've no choice but to get involved. We thought a conference call—what? Can't hear, I'm about to lose you. . . . You'll take full responsibility and call—Tark?" He shrugged his shoulders, "Lost him."

"Apparently you have your answer—let's go for it." A million thoughts crowded Beth's mind. "Who do you know at General that you can call for a report of her condition? We've got to get her out of there without further publicity!"

David calmly dialed the phone, getting the number from information. "Dr. Henry's office, please, Dr. David Rosen calling." Putting his hand over the receiver he winked, "We'll start with the Chief of Staff." He waited only a moment. "Thank you. Paul? David Rosen. I need a favor.

You've a celebrity staying with you, at least she is now: Shelby Harding. Elizabeth Townsend Sterling and I are en route to your hospital. Oh, you heard the crucifixion on TV? Absolutely, Brenda will turn up with hemlock in her tea someday. Right now I need to be apprised of Shelby's condition and how to get her released without further press. Here's the mobile number. We'll be another twenty minutes or more in this traffic. Thanks."

Beth's eyes were closed. "The Man heard your prayers," David smiled. "Try to relax. Paul will meet us at the doctor's entrance."

"You made great time, Max," David praised the driver twenty-three minutes later, spotting the massive San Francisco General Hospital as they pulled off the 101 freeway at Potrero.

Dr. Paul Henry ushered David and Beth through the somber labyrinth of corridors while the media corps clamored outside, haranguing the administrator, ready to kill for a statement from Shelby.

"Disgusting, aren't they?" Dr. Henry muttered, passing a window. An army of shaggy cameramen and Brenda herself tromped the parking lot. Inside, Dr. Henry ordered security to block all interior passageways of the hospital. Attendants and nurses beyond a *Positively No Admittance* area shifted aside as their entourage came through.

Softly, Dr. Henry made his introductions. "Dr. Rosen, Mrs. Sterling—Dr. Greenway. How's the patient?"

"Sleeping. Fortunately, I saw the incident live on TV, moments before she collapsed. Her eyes looked glazed. She O.D.'d on something taken just prior to the interview with Walker. Turned out to be Elavil. Apparently she'd planned to stage her grand finale on camera, before the eyes of millions of sympathetic viewers."

Beth fanned her moist face, struck by the actuality of Shelby's close encounter. Hospitals, crisis, and the taste of death were no strangers. But the desperation of this young woman in whom she'd deeply invested herself became suddenly incomprehensible. Beth recalled Shelby's anguished comment, that her father's greatest concern about her other attempts at suicide accused her of pulling attention-getting tantrums with drugs, stopping just short of a lethal overdose. Did Shelby really want to die? *No! But she didn't know how to live with the pain,* Beth told herself.

David's discerning glance steadied her. "Could Mrs. Sterling have some water, please?" he asked. "Sit down, Beth."

"Thank you, I'm all right now," she weakly assured the nurse. The medical legalese went over Beth's head in a fog. What she did comprehend was that Shelby could not be released until seven a.m. Dr. Henry would endeavor to get the San Francisco P.D. to bar all media from hospital premises for reasons of public safety and noninterference with medical treatment.

"That's all we can do tonight," David commented as security escorted them toward the exit where he'd phoned Max to park.

"David, if you don't mind, let's stay at my penthouse at Townsend Towers tonight. I can't possibly go home to Rosehaven tonight and through this all again tomorrow. You and Max can share the second bedroom."

"I didn't realize you had an apartment in town. Tell me about it," he urged as they kept walking.

Beth glowed, recalling the first day Charles came into the Sheridan Gallery and commissioned her to furnish the Tower's executive suite with specific rare antiques.

"I didn't know the penthouse existed until after we were married. He designed it all. One night after the opera, he had Max drive us to the Tower. We went up the elevator, to the door marked *Private*. He picked me up and carried me over the threshold to our elegant hideaway!"

"A true romantic. If more men developed the art of courting their wives after marriage, we wouldn't need marriage counselors. The question is: Do you have an extra toothbrush?" he grinned.

"But of course, everything you need," she managed a tired smile upon reaching the exit where Max was waiting.

Beth noticed a dark sedan leaving simultaneously from the opposite side of the secured parking area. It seemed to be following them, but she quickly dismissed it as fatigue and an overworked imagination and closed her eyes.

David phoned Golda en route with an update. "Paul's handled this beautifully. Shelby's stabilized after having her stomach pumped. Beth's sleeping—she looks exhausted. Remember the first time we witnessed an attempted suicide? Beth's overwhelmed. . . ." David lowered his voice, giving his wife the clinical details, telling her they'd be staying in town for the night. Beth leaned her head back as he talked.

"You say Josh and Bob are with Trenton? Excellent. We'll be at the Towers in a few minutes, Josh can call her there. She's half-asleep now. Don't imagine she'll be up long. We'll call from the hospital in the morning when Shelby's released and inform Dr. Foster when to expect her at Rosehaven. Good night, dear."

Sensing they were almost downtown, Beth sat up, wondering if that same vehicle had turned left behind them on Market Street onto Montgomery. Max entered the nearly deserted underground parking structure of the professional building, stopped close to the elevator, and opened the car door for them.

"What's the matter?" David asked, as Beth observed a dark green BMW circle the far end of the structure and exit on Bush Street.

"Nothing. Probably my imagination. I'm too exhausted to worry about it." She unlocked the elevator button at the top of the panel for the penthouse.

Inside the apartment, delicate nightlights outlined the perimeters of the room. Beth dramatically flung open the draperies, introducing a multi-layered chorus line of millions of brilliant prisms dancing across the black velvet sky.

David gasped, captivated by the panorama of lights viewed from high above the city. "Magnificent! Almost hypnotic."

"Yes, many a night I've been mesmerized, with my thoughts adrift in the dark."

"If I won't disturb you, Beth, I'd like to sit here and ruminate over my own thoughts a while."

"And if you'll excuse me, I'll see you in the morning, David. Good night, Max."

One day I'll tell her, David meditated in the dark, *that as a psychologist I'm not exempt from being grieved, as God must be, when one comes within a breath of destroying the life He's created.*

The blush of an October after-dawn tinted the heavens in the east above the bay, while a pale handful of scattered stars lingered in the clear morning sky.

"I thought God was the only One who never sleeps," Beth grinned, seeing David in front of the window with a Bible in his lap. "Surely you didn't sit there all night?"

"No. But I slept fast. 'Have you not known? Have you not heard?'" he quoted Isaiah. "'The everlasting God, the Lord, the Creator of the ends of the earth . . . gives power to the weak.' He's given me the strength necessary to help Shelby today, Beth. I couldn't come close without Him."

"And isn't it amazing how many attempt it on their own?" Still absorbed in the unfurling of a new day, she added, "And I thank Him for this glorious morning. It's rare even for October."

David arose with panache, sweeping his arm above the horizon.

Awake! for Morning in the Bowl of Night
Has flung the Stone that puts the Stars to Flight:
And Lo! the Hunter of the East has caught
The Sultan's Turret in a Noose of Light.[1]

"So you also quote Omar Khayyam? Which building out there do you think looks like the Sultan's Turret?" Beth laughed.

"That one," he laughed, waving with an indiscriminate gesture.

"Breakfast is served," Max announced. He poured fresh brewed coffee, juice, and warmed bakery pastries the Tower's housekeeping staff provided for unannounced stays.

"Mm, delicious. Thank you, Max." Beth checked her watch with the final sip of coffee. "It's nearly seven o'clock. Shall we go?"

No evidence of the press lurked about the hospital. Like well-oiled machinery, Dr. Henry's security plan delivered them without interference to Shelby's secluded room. He'd already confirmed by telephone she could be released, had the papers ready, and personally waited to greet them.

He greeted them gently. "She's asking for you. We've had a nice chat this morning—she knows her system won't tolerate another such episode, and that you were here until late last night."

From the bed, Shelby smiled weakly, embarrassed at the turmoil she'd caused them, although unaware of the media chaos. "I'm sorry," she managed with difficulty.

Beth took her hand, kissed it, gently whispering, "It's all right now. Thank God. Let's go home."

Beth's heart ached. Of all past sorrows, all losses, all deaths, this ache for Shelby was unparalleled. Within this fragile creature, life still breathed and hope still reigned through a faithful God. Beth remained determined to protect the body and soul of this one thrust into her care. When Rosehaven was but a vision, Beth's most vivid imagination never painted a scene with so personal a partnership with God.

David rode in the front seat, consulting on the phone with Dr. Foster. Beth, with Shelby dozing in her protective embrace, felt like they'd plucked a precious life from the mire of death and were returning with their prize.

9

This is Brenda Walker, reporting live from San Francisco this evening, in the continuing saga of the sordid affairs surrounding billionaire developer Alexander Harding III and his daughter, heiress Shelby Fairchild Harding. This is day three of the drama here in the Bay area, with yet another interesting development capturing our special feature report. Stay tuned. Also in the news—"

"She's purring like a pussycat this evening, compared to last night," Josh remarked as staff assembled in Bob's comfortable study to critique the five o'clock news.

Brenda returned after the commercial. "Yesterday's aftershock to the first rumble of a gigantic fraud charge against Harding by Japan's power-monger, Ioto Nakamura, came as daughter Shelby sent a 9.9 quake on the scandal scale. Miss Harding claimed she was the victim of her father's incestuous passions since the age of twelve years.

"But a not-so-funny thing happened on her way to our live TV interview twenty-four hours ago. She overdosed on drugs! Moments after making her sensational exposé, she collapsed before our cameras. Paramedics arrived within minutes and raced the clock to get Miss Harding to the hospital. Please note: Reliable sources disclosed Shelby's numerous attempts at suicide and tell us that she's received psychiatric treatment in and out of hospitals for the past eight years.

"Meanwhile, Harding, busily defending 'the international scam of the century,' as claimed in Osaka, Japan, was not available for comment. He had plenty to say today, however, in response to his daughter's piteous cries relayed via his U.S. attorneys across the Pacific.

"Don't be surprised, attorneys hint, if the newest repercussions in this epoch appear in the form of yet another lawsuit—this one by Harding against Shelby's current institution—the prestigious Rosehaven. Grounds? Psychiatric coercion and collusion leading to alienation of affection by his only child!

"The soap operas couldn't compete with the five o'clock news today!" Brenda sneered with an evil wink at her television audience. "But there's more. At the beginning of the Harding report, I used the term 'affair' not lightly or ill-advisedly. I'll be back after the commercial break."

"Oh, dear God, now what?" Beth moaned with closed eyes, supporting her bowed forehead in the palm of her hand. Josh, sitting beside her on the sofa, circled his arm tenderly about her shoulders. The staff froze at the sickening distortion they'd heard as though stunned by poison darts. Numb. Speechless. Waiting for the final death blows from Brenda.

Drilling fixed eyes into the retina of the camera, the commentator scorned, "An abortive attempt to release the young heiress sequestered in tight security last night following life-saving heroics at General Hospital was made by another wealthy heiress and her companion. Who else but the former darling of high society prior to founding Rosehaven Retreat Center, Elizabeth Townsend Sterling? She and Dr. David Rosen, director of the psychotherapy staff at Rosehaven, covertly disappeared together after leaving the hospital. According to an eyewitness report, Mrs. Sterling's chauffeur delivered them to her secret penthouse in the heart of the city for the night.

"What do we say?" Brenda gestured with open hands. "Live and let live?—and disregard the fact that Mrs. Sterling prides her elite counseling facility as being founded on Christian beliefs and behavior? Or shall we coin Shakespeare's 'all's well that ends well' as they whisked Ms. Harding back to Rosehaven early this morning for further 'treatment' of her damaged psyche?" She paused briefly for effect with the comportment of a magistrate, then pressed on.

"The iron gates leading into the Rosehaven estate were locked tightly today, and all attempts to get a statement from Administrator Josh Sterling returned void. And so, I leave the verdict with you. . . ."

Brenda leaned back with a grandiose sigh, as a judge reposes after admonishing a jury to come to resolution. The celebrated sardonic smile curled the right side of her bright red mouth. "And that wraps up The Walker Report for this evening."

Bob snapped off the television. The silence in the room was deafening. Kerry's body began to tremble uncontrollably until her anger exploded. "That's unfair," she shook her fist. "How can she blatantly disregard truth? That woman is evil. Dad! What are we going to do?"

The phone interrupted. Josh slid away from Beth's side to answer it as Bob took his place and held Beth's limp hand.

"Yes, Tark, we heard," Josh nodded his head. "Just turned it off. We're in shock." He stood listening for several minutes while the others stared obliquely at the floor in silence.

Returning to his place, Josh slipped his comforting arm around Beth again and reported, "The Board of Directors held a five o'clock meeting in Tark's office expressly to evaluate the newscast in anticipation of the Harding coverage. They agree Harding probably isn't fool enough to implicate and sue Rosehaven. That doesn't mean he won't, but they think he's bluffing with a counter-offensive. They were appalled at the venomous attack on Rosehaven, Beth, and David. Another example of the popular sport of Christian-bashing by the media."

Josh brushed Beth's forehead tenderly with a kiss, as if to kiss away the hurt written across her face.

He continued. "Their quick consensus is that the media's gone too far. It's tantamount to slander. Tark's call represented a vote of support and confidence by the board. They concur that we have our plates full here and are to leave the media and any legal ramifications to them. I think we'd do well to remind ourselves of their considerable credentials and influence. He assured us that any official statement, if indeed one is made, will be first presented to staff for approval."

Beth blinked back stinging tears. One or two escaped, running down her cheeks. "They're good men," she sighed, relieved of the burden of defending their innocence.

David stepped in front of her, reaching down to take her hands in his. She saw the faith of Abraham shining in his kind, compassionate eyes. " 'Blessed is the man who walks not in the counsel of the ungodly,' " he began quoting Psalm 1, "whose 'delight is in the law of the Lord. . . . He shall be like a tree planted by the rivers of water, that brings forth its fruit in its season, whose leaf also shall not wither; and whatever he does shall prosper.' This too shall pass, Beth," he smiled. "Get some rest now. The

Lord is in control. How blessed are those who take refuge in Him," he added, embracing her.

Josh lifted Beth up from the deep-cushioned sofa. They all stood, automatically joining hands in a circle of prayer. After several minutes, Bob closed, quoting Psalms again. . . .

"The Lord is my light and my salvation; whom shall I fear? The Lord is the strength of my life; of whom shall I be afraid?"

Bob's eyes glistened, shining with admiration for this deeply wounded woman whom he could not audibly honor as his mother-in-law. "Good night, great lady," he said with a hug.

Kerry wrapped Beth in her arms, holding her close, whispering in her ear. "I love you, Mother. Sleep well."

Dr. Foster had ordered complete rest and seclusion for Shelby, with absolutely no radio or television. Mercifully, Shelby was unaware of the furor raging in the media. Physically, she fared better than Dr. Foster expected, but emotionally she'd withdrawn again. She'd see no one but Beth. They sauntered the grounds, basked in the mellow October sun on the high knoll, and in passing the Tea House Shelby looked askance, as though the turmoil in her soul excluded her from its peacefulness. They talked very little. Beth had their dinners sent to Shelby's cottage, where they shared an appreciation of the soothing études of Chopin on tape. When Shelby retired for the night she appeared exhausted, and Beth felt drained of energy.

"Did we get annihilated by the media again today?" Beth asked Josh when she returned to their suite. "In one sense, I'm glad I escaped it." The question was rhetorical, assuming the answer was a foregone conclusion. She longed now to nestle into their massive canopied bed, luxuriate in her husband's lovemaking, and let the world go by.

Josh answered, "Let's say this was a big day in the newsroom. Harding returned from Japan. The papers and TV are saturated with the corrupt corporate deal. He's attempting to divert attention by claiming slander, coercion, and focusing on the lawsuit he vows he's bringing against Rosehaven. We haven't been served yet. Brenda had no need to be any nastier than merely quoting Harding." Josh stopped for breath.

"Allyson requested a meeting with staff today, reiterating that before Shelby dashed off, she was determined to go public with her story. Now she feels as long as there's attention already focused on the incest issue, she and Austin are prepared to go all out and spearhead a support program for incest victims. Consequently, we had a quick board meeting here and determined we really have no authority to prohibit the Earles from making a statement. Allyson's totally rational. Jessica and David believe she's stable and not acting merely on emotion—and of course it's her right to do it. She's written her story, David's critiqued it, and you can bet it will be grabbed up fast. Austin wouldn't proceed, however, without assurance that Allyson will be permitted to return to Rosehaven for counseling in the future. They both realize she'll have new issues to resolve as she goes.

"Shelby's situation increased the Earles' dedication to pioneer emotional healing for other incest victims. The board listened and was deeply impressed. Particularly as a couple, the Earles possess the proper credentials. Allyson's a glamorous, intelligent woman; he's wealthy and influential. They've a cause whose horror stories are continuously coming out of the woodwork. However, it's agreed we'll have to brace ourselves for the possibility of another assault on Rosehaven."

"Mercy! What a day!" Beth gasped.

"That's not the half of it . . . and you can count on the media's pounding for all it's worth. But listen to this," Josh leaned forward excitedly. "Bob arranged a day of prayer tomorrow for the staff, board of directors, and our attorneys. Becky informed and invited the affiliated pastors and lay counselors from the New Hope Center, and they quickly spread the word to numerous other Christian counselors. Rosehaven's fellow residents have risen as Trenton's staunch defenders because the media battle has unified them in a common bond. *Self* is no longer their primary concern!" Josh beamed, "And this is the *coup de gras*—Howard Klotz is the organizer urging the other residents to come to the prayer meeting!"

Beth's weary face lit up. "Oh—this is wonderful! But I won't be able to go to sleep with all this on my mind!"

"Then we'll proceed to Plan B!" Josh smiled brightly, drawing her into his arms with a kiss as he turned out the light.

At nine a.m., Beth looked out with amazement from her study window at the stream of cars entering the parking area.

The scene was not unusual, except this wasn't a garden party or rose show, but a day for prayer. She hurried down to welcome the faithful.

Josh found her among the crowd. "Have you seen anything of the press?" his eyes darted about.

"I've noticed some unfamiliar faces. They're here—you can count on it. They're just not flashing their press passes. Becky looked frantic a minute ago. The phones are going crazy—people calling for statements. I told her to shut them off."

At ten a.m., one hundred and seventy people were seated in the ballroom. Jimmy had enlisted the help of the gardeners, Max, and the staff to set up the room on short notice. Josh welcomed them in prayer as Bob sat at the piano softly playing "Great Is Thy Faithfulness," then with strong chords as they joined in singing.

The power of the Holy Spirit filled the room during the next ninety minutes. It moved upon them as surely as they breathed and glowed upon upturned faces. Burdened shoulders lifted almost in unison, like a field of flowers raising their heads to receive grace and renewal from spring showers.

Bob concluded the meeting with encouragement to go in confidence and faith, that God's will shall prevail, quoting Hebrews 11:1: "Now faith is the substance of things hoped for, the evidence of things not seen."

The hopeful faces of Trenton, Rochelle, Howard, and others prompted Bob to invite those who yearned to know the mystery of God in Christ to enter a personal relationship with Him, to stay and talk or see him at their convenience. As Beth, Josh, and Kerry talked with Brian Tarkington, Beth noticed seven Rosehaven residents eagerly clustered around Bob. "Thank You," she whispered.

Staff convened again in Bob's study for the five o'clock news, including Trenton, who David anticipated would need the total support of the varsity team.

Brenda appeared on screen in a bright yellow and black tailored suit, her lips a brighter red than usual. She created the image of a dragon breathing fire, her fangs bared to sink into the flesh of the day's events. . . .

"A new victim emerged today in the fervor for truth and justice, which seems to be bred among the inmates—excuse me, patients of

Rosenhaven Retreat Center." Trent buried his head in his hands as Brenda went on. "Another name of prominence among the wealthy patriarchs of philanthropy, William J. Cameron, has been charged with incest. Allyson Cameron Earle, movie star of twenty years past and wife of insurance guru, Austin Earle, also claims to have been abused by the sins of her father. Behind the glittering images of her glorious lifestyle are years of pain and shame, she says, for which fame and fortune cannot compensate." Brenda paused for full effect. Trent groaned while she persisted, "Isn't it interesting that these poor little rich girls—Harding and Earle—both happened to seek Christian counsel and sympathy at Rosehaven, and now, with malice aforethought, drag their prestigious fathers' names through public mud? Is this Christian charity? With one father out of the country, and the other in the grave, are these women counseled to seek vengeance in the name of 'freeing' other victims and supporting their cause? I—" She stammered, suddenly appearing distracted and confused, and quickly announced a station break.

Instantly Brenda disappeared from the screen, followed by the commercial and a flustered reporter covering a liquor store robbery in Berkeley.

Bob slapped his hands on his thighs and stood up. "Well, she went too far this time. I've never seen a commentator cut off before. But she'd already shot her poison arrows. Trent, what do you suppose happened?"

White-faced, Trent shuddered, "Oh God, help." He paused, shaking his head. "If you've ever seen all hell break loose, it's when Mother's ego gets trounced upon. I can tell you exactly what happened. Obviously, the news producer gave her the signal. Mother's dragged me into the field and the studio for years as she's clawed her way up; by now she practically makes her own rules and considers herself immune from the news director's questioning on accuracy. And woe unto him who does. Besides, she's been sleeping with the guy for a couple of years.

"Yet the ultra-liberals love her and she's developed her own dynasty. Until now. And you're right, Bob—she went too far! The station had to be getting complaints from the public, the sponsors, or both, or they'd never pull a name reporter just like that!" Trent snapped his fingers for emphasis.

"Brenda Walker is one tough lady. Wrong—she's hardly a *lady*," Trent corrected himself sadly, "but her ego cannot survive such a blow. It's the old story of dishing it out, but not being able to take it.

"I've *hated* her—yes, *hated*," he repeated with a flushed face, "and she claims she's done all this for *me*. For all her faults, I know deep down she's really cared for me—and that's why I've grown up with the guilt. And the anger. And now she's ruined. Her pride will bury her." Trent made no attempt to stop the tears trickling down his face, but he couldn't go on.

"Why do you say she's clawed her way to the top for you, Trent? Aren't you placing blame on yourself for something over which you had no control?" David spoke gently.

"Yes. I know that now. She had an obsession to prove to the world that she'd provided me with all the biggest and best toys—from childhood gadgets to the flashiest sports cars and the finest education. The education I appreciated, at first, and I greedily accepted all the rest while simultaneously shouting that it didn't matter. Her ambitions for me included graduating summa cum laude from Harvard Law School. She even had me set up in the law firm of a famous divorce lawyer, enabling me to provide another symbol of her dazzling success.

"Yes—I graduated, without superior marks, hated law, and couldn't stand the attorney, famous or not. When I sank into depression, unable to function at anything, that meant she'd failed. That's when she rejected me, furious that I no longer reflected her image of success. I'd disgraced her. She kept sending checks, though, with explicit instructions not to engage in any menial employment until she could get me a position with a prestigious firm."

"Where did the roots of Brenda's distorted obsession with success at any price come from?" Ryan asked. "I'm not sure we've explored that in our therapy sessions."

"Her bitterness began, I think, at about sixteen, when her father walked out on her mother and her and a prettier, younger, and more popular sister. Grandmother loved God with all her heart. She told me she got down on her knees and asked Him to be Father and Husband in that family the day her husband left. Grandmother turned the house into a dress shop, and the three of them lived in one cramped room. Mother worked after school, displaying a flair for business and merchandising, appalled that her mother would accept food baskets from the church. The young Brenda was fiercely independent and driven to having respectable clothes for herself, and the shop quickly soared to success.

"She put herself through college, majoring in journalism, graduated cum laude, and landed a writing job in television, determined to succeed at any cost. Part of the price was marrying the highest-paid news commentator, who turned out to be a womanizer. My mother couldn't tolerate second place in anything! I came along. She left my father and poured her life into me, and stopped at nothing to beat him at his own game. She succeeded by knocking him off the ladder of top-ranking commentators. One may truthfully say she gained the world—and lost her soul."

Silence fell upon the group, allowing Trent the prerogative of continuing or not. Several moments passed. He searched the compassionate faces, contemplating his next statement. His eyes filled again. "She's still my mother—and she needs me." He sobbed unashamedly, assured of understanding. "She's all alone."

"What are you going to do?" David asked, his hand upon Trent's shoulder.

"I'm going to her, tonight, if you don't think that's too impulsive. She hasn't a clue I'm a patient at the 'institution' she attacked, and I'm not at all sure how and when to divulge where I've been. But I'll be back. I hope I can call for help. I'm certain I'm going to need it." Trent took a deep breath to finish his story.

"My grandmother remarried—a Christian man who adored her. They taught me to love Jesus. Mother's sister married young and happily, with four children, but Brenda forged through life with a vengeful heart, preoccupied with bitterness. I've never seen that as clearly as this moment. And I pity her." Trent bowed his head, eyes on the floor, and pleaded, "Would you all pray for me before I go, and for my mother . . . even though she's been horrible?"

Throughout the next day, telegrams, phone calls, and messages jammed the lines at Rosehaven. Dr. Tarkington and other board members, as well as Dr. Rosen's clinic in the city, received a deluge of communications. They chronicled overwhelming support for Beth, their image as a family standing firm on just values, and for the staff for providing a refuge of hope, courage, and recovery for victims of a sick society.

The elated staff met in Bob's study in front of the television, as had become the pattern of the past week. The five o'clock news never mentioned Brenda Walker's name.

A scholarly looking gentleman with white hair, Dan Patterson, concisely reported on the public's overwhelming response to the station in support of Rosehaven, Shelby, Allyson, and confirmed statistics relating to the rise of reported cases of incest.

Following the newscast, staff dispersed jubilantly, smiling for the first time that week, eager to circulate among the residents in the Pub and at dinner. Josh passed Becky as she locked her office door.

"You're smiling, but you look exhausted," he noted.

"Wait until you look at the list of calls we've had today. Wish I'd counted the ones who feel they're victims of 'the sick society syndrome' and want to know more about Rosehaven. I'm glad I get to go home, while you live here!"

"You're much appreciated, Becky. Good night."

Phone calls and letters poured in during the days that followed, with requests for interviews and pleas for help, not only related to incest but to a gamut of problems primarily focused on dysfunctional families and their suffering relationships.

Come Sunday morning, Bob stood at the door with Kerry beside him, as the congregation of Rosehaven's residents and those from the surrounding community entered the ballroom for worship services. His audience had grown steadily each week. They came not out of curiosity engendered by the media, but to hear God's Word, undiluted by the world's standards. On this particular Sunday, Bob knew they felt personally grieved by the ugly publicity and distorted information.

"The message today is found in Genesis—the account of Joseph," Bob introduced the text, "whose jealous brothers sold him into slavery. In the household of the pharaoh in Egypt, God caused Joseph to become a man of great power, who rescued those brothers and their families from famine. . . ."

At the conclusion of his sermon he smiled. "Dear friends, we've learned what men meant for evil, God intended for good. So it will be regarding our purpose here at Rosehaven. If it is the true and living God we serve—and not the many false gods of this world—we must believe His promise, 'I will never leave you or forsake you.'

"Now may the God of peace Himself be with you. . . ."

David's usually informal demeanor gave way to unusual intensity as he opened Monday morning's staff meeting. "You all know by now that Harding has been 'detained' on his return trip to Japan if you watched '60 Minutes' on television yesterday. That was the 'interesting' way his attorneys attempted to repudiate his incarceration by the Japanese government. Apparently the connection with the Nakamura deal is that Nakamura is the *Yakusa*, that is, the godfather of the Japanese mafia, the ultimate bad guys, more feared than the Sicilian mafia. Maybe Harding is fortunate the government nailed him instead of Nakamura.

"Anyway, he's not going to be harassing anyone from a Japanese jail, especially when grappling with the newest evidence of swindling American investors. He's also been denied bail, being a 'significant flight risk' in light of his extensive foreign contacts.

"The really good news," David sighed in relief, "is our nasty publicity is superseded by stronger public support than we could ever ask or hope for.

"So now," David's warm brown eyes swept over the group, "our task this week is to help our patients comprehend that God *will* use the trauma of last week's events for His good purposes. This is Romans 5:3–5 in action . . . 'that tribulation produces perseverance; and perseverance, character; and character, hope. Now hope does not disappoint, because the love of God has been poured out in our hearts by the Holy Spirit who was given to us.'"

David beamed. "I observed a transformation of attitudes and a lightheartedness that I attribute to that new hope. It came alive after your sermon, Bob. Last week's tribulations were a dirge through the world's garbage. Yet they presented endless opportunities for God's Word to demonstrate His truth.

"I particularly observed Shelby. Attending the worship service represented a major step for her. I believe the message stirred her soul and that these wounded ones are becoming hungry for a relationship with the living God.

"Now what are your observations, especially correlating to the traumas of last week?"

David's sweeping gesture solicited the opening of staff reports, essential to their common goal of binding up the wounds of the broken lives in their care.

The meeting adjourned at noon with buoyant satisfaction written on every face. As Beth and Josh left the room for lunch, he instinctively enfolded her hand in his. Along the sunny paths bordering the rose gardens he stopped abruptly.

"A wild and crazy impulse to whisk you away to the house in Carmel has suddenly obsessed me," he said with gusto, his eyes sparkling. "It's gorgeous in October. We'll make passionate love, bask on the beach . . . and let you rest now that the commotion's settled down. We could leave this afternoon."

"Mm, you're making me an offer I can't refuse," she beamed. "Sounds heavenly, darling. I'll get David's advice on leaving Shelby right now, but a Monday evening through, say Wednesday should work. I'd love it. Let's check with Becky for messages and hope there aren't any fires to put out."

By four o'clock they'd returned urgent calls, talked with David, Bob, and Kerry, hugged Teddy, arranged their schedules, and tossed a few casual clothes together, eager for their brief holiday.

Moments before they left their suite, the phone rang. "We're out of here," Josh laughed, but picked it up anyway.

With bags in hand, Beth watched his smile fade as he listened. Josh turned to stone, his face white and solemn, mechanically setting the phone back in place.

"What's happened?" She trembled, a myriad of possible tragedies flashing through her mind.

"Wall Street crashed today! Our patients just heard the news and panicked. That was Becky. The phone lines are jammed—it's pandemonium with calls to their corporate offices and stock brokers."

Josh quickly flicked on the television. Every station flashed to grim faces on Wall Street and charts of figures on the decline of the Dow throughout the day. He caught Dan Patterson's special report in mid-sentence.

"—the Dow plummeted a record 508.32 points, exceeding the blackest day of 1929 that began the Great Depression of the '30s. October 19, 1987, will go down in history as Black Monday. Today's crash marks the sharpest decline in the ninety-six year annals of the New York Stock Exchange."

Beth froze in shock as Josh raised his voice above the confusion on the TV screen.

"The commotion I thought I heard in our parking area while we were packing must have been the exodus of diesel Mercedes peeling out. Becky doesn't know exactly how many left, but our patients have gone berserk! Those who haven't already dashed mindlessly off to their offices probably will, and those who remain are going to need some reassurance that this isn't the end of the world!"

He enfolded her in massive arms of consolation.

"We can forget Carmel," he sighed. "Let's go try to pick up the pieces of broken dreams."

10

The unknown faces of brokers from the New York Stock Exchange invaded living rooms across the nation. Frightening descriptions of Black Monday as "a massacre," "a zoo," combined with the complexity of graphs trudging somberly across the screen. They demonstrated the record high of 2722.42 on August 25 to the 200-point drop by October, followed by declines of 95.46 on October 14, and 108.36 on October 16.

The anxious residents of Rosehaven who crowded around the television in the Pub debated the question: Did the expertise of the Wall Street wizards aid or confuse the issues of whether the disaster was real? One Wall Street guru accused big investors, saying they'd practically plunged the entire financial system into ruin. Another said it wasn't an economic problem. The founder of a major electronics firm dismissed Wall Street's influence on his operations: "My concern is that the company's doing well. Stock goes up. Stock goes down. It's all on paper."

Howard Klotz adjusted his horn-rimmed glasses, unnecessarily smoothing the dyed black strands plastered over his balding pate. "I don't know if anyone noticed, but last month's *Forbes* magazine listed me as the wealthiest capitalist in the country. I just called my stock broker. As close as he could calculate, my family's shares in the firm lost $400 million when the market closed today. Hey—it's paper! It was paper when we started—when it's all over, it'll still be paper.

"I called the corporate office. I told them to concentrate on the business of taking care of our customers, and that's all we're concerned about."

Rochelle, groomed to perfection and smartly attired in a precision-tailored saffron-colored pantsuit, raised her eyebrows accusingly and snapped, "That's easy for you to say, but I find this Wall Street crisis a contradiction to the optimistic business forecasts elsewhere across the nation. My export business rose 13 percent during the first eight months of 1987, and you're telling me—" She stopped. "Wait a minute. What's this analyst saying? Something about computer failures being the culprits."

Two expressionless financial journalists bandied about a list of statistics. "Wall Street computers click off as many as sixty transactions per second. The computer sells off a bundle of securities worth millions of dollars with every click. Electronics, not business judgments, are running the market," the man in the gray suit said. The man in the blue suit added, "On this Black Monday, computers pumped out over 500,000 transactions in unprecedented selling, doubling the previous daily peak. This overwhelmed the mechanical printers, and furthermore—"

"Oh, enough of that," Rochelle snarled in disgust. "Oops—what's he saying now?"

The man in the blue suit concluded, "It's ironic that the entire financial system in the United States could be thrown into a complete meltdown—because of failures in mechanical printers worth barely $20,000!"

Howard stood up. "I'm either going to shut this blasted thing off or leave your fine company. They're analyzing the analysts. The reports we've heard account for today's disaster." He clenched his fist emphatically. "The fact remains that neither Washington nor business nor the world community of economics has listened to the warning bells or even begun to take effective steps to deal with the real problems. In the meantime, the rest of us can't do a thing about it!

"You know what I think?" he shouted. "From a poor lad from the streets, to a billionaire—money isn't what matters! It's *here!*" He pounded his chest. "What's in your heart is what matters. Beth knows that. Too few people with wealth do anything of lasting value with it. She's an exception. The bottom line is, I've spent too much of my life making money and too little making a life for my family. The recovery I'm searching for isn't economic, it's recovering broken relationships!" he yelled. "But then, you all know that," he muttered, leaving the Pub.

David jumped up. "Just a minute, Howard. I'll go with you."

The ring of the telephone in the Pub broke the momentary lull of Howard's sudden departure and David's quick pursuit to talk with him. Becky had stayed overtime and switched the call to Beth. "It's Merribelle Matson," she announced.

Beth hesitated in taking the call at this inopportune time while frazzled nerves waited to be comforted. She'd not heard from Merribelle, who claimed to be her dearest friend, since her marriage to Josh. Beth reminded herself that this San Francisco matron, who'd risen from Southern poverty to become the matriarch of the wealthiest social set, remained one of the neediest persons she knew.

"Merribelle—what a surprise to hear from you!"

Beth encountered Merribelle's instant prattle, sans the benefit of salutary beginnings. "Ah jus' know what an absolutely miserable time you-all've been havin', what with the dreadful scandals on TV and all the newspapers to do with Rosehaven, and you and this David fellow. And aren't you positively ruined by this horrible Black Monday?"

"Let's just say we were knocked down, but not out. I think we're back in the race now and have told ourselves that this too shall pass. I appreciate your concern—thank you, Merribelle. And how are you?"

"Ah've had a difficult time Ah want you to know, since you've abandoned your friends in Art League by not havin' the wonderful charity benefits at Rosehaven, an' dedicated your gawgeous home to all those unbalanced folks with their psychological problems. It's simply not the same—" Her voiced cracked. "But Ah'm terrified, if you must know. Ah haven't talked with Henry since this awful Black Monday stuff hit the news. But Ah just know we're ruined! Beth, darlin', whatever shall I do if we've lost it all? Mah marriage is a shambles, just a meaningless facade with Henry's one true love, his mortgage bankin' business. If it's all gone, we've nothin'—absolutely nothin'."

"You sound so calm," Merribelle agonized. "You must have so much money it simply doesn't mattah, or does your new ex-missionary husband have some hidden wealth?"

Beth felt the back of her neck bristle. "The calm you sense has nothing to do with money," she tried to explain before Merribelle cut in—

"Ah suppose you're goin' to tell me again you're so cool 'cause you're trustin' in the Lord!" Anger spouted with every syllable.

"You do get right to the point, Merribelle. Yes. Nothing has changed. That's exactly what I'm telling you." Beth fought to restrain the irritated edge on her comments.

"Tell me this," Merribelle snarled. "If your God is so wonderful, how's come you've had such bad press? It seems to me He isn't payin' much attention to you lately."

"Oh but He is, Merribelle. Trust me. Or rather, trust God. Only the negative news seems to warrant the television spotlight, but you must not have noticed the public letters of support that've been in the papers. God will use it all for good. He's there for you too, if you'll ask Him."

"Well, Henry hasn't informed me of the doom an' gloom yet. Ah'll hope for the best. . . ."

"You're always in my prayers, Merribelle. Good times or bad."

"Well, when Ah become desolate enough to require prayer, Ah'll let you know!" The clank of the receiver resounded in Beth's ear.

Through the years Merribelle had persisted in a propensity for confronting her with crises on the telephone. Beth found it more than difficult to suppress irritation while conveying a genuine caring for this self-bound woman who so desperately needed God, yet vehemently rejected Him.

Terrible Tuesday, commemorating Wall Street's worst ten minutes in history, followed Black Monday. Financial analysts claimed the U.S. split-second information system that tells the big guys on Wall Street when to buy had failed—and could fail again.

The ten days following the crash were a montage of confusion, resolving only that no one had the solutions in their pocket, and that the market mechanisms that came close to setting off an international disaster on Monday, October 19, 1987, would continue to be a ticking time bomb.

Beth and Kerry carved priceless mother-daughter moments out of amber days, sharing the rich jewels of autumn along leaf-scattered paths. Teddy scampered beside them, stooping to examine each vibrantly patterned oak leaf garnishing the earth. They reflected upon the traumas and triumphs of the amazing first few months of Rosehaven, cataloging lessons learned, evaluating their personal growth woman to woman.

Kerry revealed that she felt deep concern and often guilt about the way she expressed anger. Her fury exploded while Beth's simmered in a hot syrup of pain until she could lay it before God.

"My darling," Beth counseled, "you've taught the Bible study of Jesus throwing the money-changers out of the temple in a state of fury many times. There's no cause for guilt for justified indignation. The problem in our society today is the mindless acceptance of corruption and blatant immorality. Gray is too popular, black and white are out of vogue."

The crisp air that gilded the grape arbor also inspired them to design heartening celebrations for residents who would not be going home for the Thanksgiving and Christmas holidays.

"Let's invite our church family who regularly worship with us, and the neighbors and their household staffs like we did last year," Kerry's huge dark eyes sparkled at the thought. "Or will we have enough room?" she wondered.

"I've no idea how many locals to expect, or how many residents are going to find the holidays too painful to be with family or friends. But numbers shouldn't inhibit us. We'll set up tables outside if necessary, like the pilgrims' first Thanksgiving. If it's as warm as last year it'll be fine."

"I hope Cookie will let me make cut-out cookies. I miss having my own kitchen, sometimes. Must admit, most of the time, it's nice not having to prepare meals."

"I never learned how," Beth laughed. "Kerry, on a more serious note, Bob's spending more time than ever counseling on spiritual matters. His sermon on Joseph and forgiveness opened eyes, ears, and hearts. It was an answer to prayer. Unlike going somewhere to work, we're all on call part or all the time, even though we don't schedule it that way. Hopefully it won't always be like that. But you two need more alone time. So do Josh and I. Why don't you plan candlelight dinners for two in your room?"

"Mother, you're a such a romantic! But I think you're promoting another grandchild!"

"You noticed!" Beth's sapphire blue eyes twinkled mischievously. "I happen to think it's a splendid idea. . . ."

"Shelby's all excited about Thanksgiving," Josh remarked to Beth. "That's two weeks away, and it's all she can talk about. She asked to run with me this morning, and we had a great discussion afterwards. Her progress since she came out of denial thrills me. I never have to ask myself if Rosehaven is making a difference when I look at Shelby these days."

"Oh, I know! It's all the reward I need too. She looked pitifully glum when someone mentioned the holidays recently, though. I guess she thought everyone would leave, like at boarding school. She has nowhere to go. I assured her we'd have a bountiful Thanksgiving, and she cried, Josh. She's never been thankful before, or had anyone to be thankful with."

"I'll join her in giving thanks to God for you. I don't tell you often enough, dear . . . I love you," Josh drew her close.

"No, you certainly don't! Not since last night. Remember?" she teased.

"Of course I remember. Kiss me. . . ."

"Beth," Shelby shouted, her hair flying as she ran toward her the next day after her counseling session. "Look at the gorgeous leaves I gathered this morning. Remnants of our late fall's color. If I press them, don't you think they'll be beautiful for Thanksgiving?"

The wealthy heiress's childlike simplicity touched Beth's heart, and she wondered if Shelby had ever experienced a meaningful Thanksgiving. Beth examined the leaves, certainly not as richly colored as a few weeks ago, turning them with reverence in the garden basket. "Absolutely perfect," she smiled.

"I'm rather artistic. Could I make floral arrangements for the tables? It'll be so much fun!"

"What a grand idea. Thank you, Shelby. No one else has even thought of offering to do that. Give Becky a list of materials and we'll get them for you."

An outpouring of testimonies of God's abundant grace persisted for hours, intermingled with singing and praise after the Thanksgiving feast. "Oh Josh, the sharing flowed as freely as an open faucet, and I loved the encouragement of applause they gave one another." Beth sighed as they relaxed before the fireplace in their suite. "I felt a wonderful sense of community, within and outside of Rosehaven. And Shelby looked radiant. Did you notice her hair and makeup? Rochelle did it for her, and Howard's accolades for the table centerpieces showed honest appreciation for Shelby's talents. Weren't the baskets gorgeous? Every one of our patients told me they'd never experienced a real Thanksgiving before. There must be a clue there somewhere.

"Some confessed they'd reluctantly followed the tradition of stuffing themselves with more food than they wanted, and toasted relatives they didn't even like with too much vintage wine in order to fill the emptiness in their souls. Rochelle actually hugged me, saying she'd never be the same."

"Neither will the budget," Josh scowled. "You realize, of course, Thanksgiving proved to be an extremely lavish affair. My job as administrator is to keep expenses in line. Only part of the invoices are on my desk, and I'm sure there'll be more. Besides, the cost of this one day could feed the same amount of people for weeks in Thailand."

Beth bolted upright. "Josh, darling! What are you saying? I can assure you, the board isn't going to criticize your financial accountability. Rosehaven's operating budget set up in the trust is your baby, but I'm familiar enough with the system to know part of it is outreach and part is Rosehaven's operational expenses. Whatever receipts are on your desk are probably all of them. Please remember, our neighbors who came with their families and household staff also prepared food, and we served 150 people! The participation is what made it extra special!"

"It seemed terribly extravagant," he brooded.

"I—" Beth bit her tongue with tears in her eyes at this senseless conflict over finances, giving her rebuttal second thoughts, sensitive to his feelings stemming from a well-managed and frugal background. The only cross words they'd ever had related to money. She had an excess, he'd lived comfortably within limited means. She swallowed the lump in her throat, remembering the scriptural warning—"Do not let the sun go down on your anger." Clouds over Josh's sunny nature were unbearable to her.

"Josh, dear, first of all, you must remember we're not in Thailand—our mission is directed to spiritually and emotionally starved people who have the ominous good fortune to be wealthy. Many don't know how to be thankful, to God or anyone else. But praise shone on the faces of everyone here today—residents, neighbors, children, staff workers. Tell me what you thought was extravagant."

"It . . . it's a large sum of money."

"We served a large group of people. The floral supplies for the centerpieces looked professional, but Shelby made them and I paid for them. The compliments she received, the lift in her self-esteem yielded therapy no amount of money could duplicate. I'll be delighted to write the trust a check for the whole amount. I'm a wealthy woman, but I've never been flamboyant. It gives me great personal pleasure to do what we did today." Beth's voice quivered as she felt the volume rising.

Josh said nothing. They stared into the fire for a millennium of fifteen minutes.

"My Montana farm boy and missionary conservatism influence my judgment at the most inappropriate occasions," Josh said sadly. "I get hung up on the cross-cultural differences, that Asians and other Third World people are grateful for having little, and Americans aren't content with abundance.

"But your elation is well justified, and I totally agree—everyone was richly blessed. Forgive me for spoiling it for you."

Beth slipped her hand into his in the firelight as Josh philosophized, "I've never drawn lines between rich and poor; they're all God's creatures. But I must admit, the very wealthy are a greater challenge to me than supplying the Word of God, food, and basic necessities to simple people."

"Darling Josh, remember you told me those 'simple people' from Asian and Third World countries have every manner of hang-ups with the spirit world, superstitions, and witchcraft. Their culture is every bit, if not more complicated than the dysfunctions of Western society and our own spiritual confusion.

"Basic needs were what we met today," she stressed. "The ambience provided familiarity with what they're accustomed to. *Basic* is beyond the desire to satisfy our stomachs and have a roof over our heads. It's acceptance, sharing, loving one another. *Basic* is the need you're meeting for Shelby right now. You're modeling the father image she's never known, and without it, how would she ever come to the basic need of trusting a loving God? Or trusting a man enough to one day be a wife? You're a master at those kinds of basics . . . and that's one more reason for my loving you."

"Please be patient with me. And I'm grateful that your loving heart provided a memory-making day for everyone . . . even me. I love you, sweetheart."

On December 15, Mum arrived on the British Airways flight from London at San Francisco airport.

"Cheerio, darlings," she waved gleefully with one hand amidst the bustle of arriving passengers, leaning heavily on her cane with the other.

Josh made his way to relieve her of her carry-on bag. "You look younger every time we see you, Mum!" She temporarily disappeared in his embrace, and emerging she laughed, "I made such a hash of your last visit to Hampstead, I'm relying on my cane to assure I don't bungle this trip. I've so looked forward to it. Beth, love," she held out her arms.

Despite the slight limp, obviously a lingering affliction from last summer's sprained ankle and the arthritis of the dancer's advancing years, Margaret Sheridan retained the regal bearing of the world's most-loved prima ballerina.

"Oh Mum, you're an inspiration. You never change, only improve with age."

"Oh, tish, tish," she fluttered her hand, smiling. "And you look splendid, love. A few more silver strands, but immensely becoming with those amazing blue eyes. Are we going straight away to Rosehaven? How's my dear little Teddy? I'm perishing to see everyone, of course, but especially Teddy."

Mum stepped into the hexagon-shaped entry with unabashed anticipation, pausing to appreciate the Victorian spindled arches and Waterford chandelier she'd always admired. She inhaled the pungent scent of fresh cedar garlands and juniper berries festooned with enameled della Robbia fruits and entwined with rich ruby velvet.

"Splendid, the touch of an artist! I do believe dear Charles designed Rosehaven especially for you to embellish with your endless creativity at Christmas, Beth. It's marvelously welcoming. I'm relieved to see it's not been 'institutionalized' now that it's a retreat center or whatever term is proper."

"Perish the thought," Josh quipped. "Our patients, whom we refer to as 'residents,' find the warmth of its elegance contributes to their sense of well-being."

"Mum-Mum," Teddy squealed, flying into his great-grandmother's knees before she could manage to lift him up. "Wuv you!"

"Careful, Teddy," Bob dashed to retrieve his son. "We don't tackle Mum-Mum. Okay?"

Kerry embraced her grandmother. "He's been kissing your picture and chattering 'Mum-Mum . . . coming soon' for days."

"Teddy, precious, I 'wuv' you too!" Margaret seated herself in the giltwood entry chair and Teddy instantly clamored onto her lap, lavished for a full minute with her undivided attention before climbing down to examine the cloisonne head of her cane.

Appearing with her customary English reserve, Tillie announced, "It's four o'clock and tea is served in the parlor," then flew with smiles and joyful tears to embrace her former employer and dear friend of nearly forty years.

After tea Beth asked, "Mum, would you like to get settled into your room and have a little nap? The trip is always exhausting."

"Heavens no, thank you, love. Max may take my bags up, but our stimulating conversation and the sheer bliss of being here wound me up! Rosehaven has aged with grace; it is lovelier than ever. Show me what you've done to the place, and where your residents live. I insist on seeing it all."

Rochelle and Howard, with anger resolved and depression healed, regenerated physically, emotionally, and spiritually, had returned to test their new relational skills in the real world immediately after Thanksgiving. Trent and Allyson reported minor setbacks as well as major and lesser victories in getting on with their lives. Shelby befriended Kimberly, another incest victim, and Marion, who was encumbered by depression following the drug overdose death of her twenty-one-year-old daughter.

Gradually Shelby's past became less significant than her future as she gained new confidence in herself and her abilities, new insights of God's love. But often she struggled with the sadness of identifying herself as a homeless person. Rosehaven represented the only real *home*, with the only real *family* she'd ever known. Upon her first introduction to Mum, she adopted an instant grandmother.

"Look at those two, Kerry," Beth giggled, observing Shelby and Mum engrossed in conversation in the Pub. "Mum is delighted we recreated the ancient ambience of her Spaniard's Inn in Hampstead. She adores relating the history of the original!"

But that wasn't at all what Mum and Shelby discussed.

Shelby devoured the fascinating tales of the glamour and the glitches of performances of the Royal Ballet in some of the theaters she'd seen in Europe.

"At this stage in life," Mum's eyes twinkled, "I do believe I'm happier than any of the others whose entire existence has revolved around their ballet careers. One tends to become dangerously out of balance with taking self too seriously in such a highly disciplined art. The end result is a distorted view of one's own importance. I became real frighteningly late in life—but I was blessed with a husband who put up with me, and a daughter who forgave me."

Shelby remarked in awe, "You seem to have had it all. What would you do differently, if you had it to live over?"

"I'd have learned to laugh sooner and eat more ice cream!" Mum quickly replied.

11

I took a telephone message, Miss Beth, while you were tucking Teddy in bed," Tillie informed her. "You've had a full day, this Sunday before Christmas; I thought you'd prize that time with the little tyke. Here's the number, with the message to call as soon as possible."

"I appreciate how protective you always are, Tillie. Who called? I don't see a name."

"I have only the room number at the Mark Hopkins Hotel. The operator placed the call."

Beth dialed the number.

"The Executive Suite, please."

"Buona sera, Bella Rosa mia?"

"Roberto?" Beth gasped in astonishment, simultaneously rationalizing that Roberto was quite capable of being anywhere in the world at anytime.

"But of course! I call to wish you and yours happy holidays."

For the millionth time, her heart involuntarily skipped a beat at the voice of her first love, now an enduring friend.

"How were you so certain it was I calling?" she asked, amused at his immutable aristocratic boldness.

"Semplice. You are only one I ring up. . . ." His voice now sounded searching, wistful, twinged with loneliness.

"How dear of you. Happy holidays to you also. I presume you are in San Francisco on business? For how long? I do hope you'll arrange your schedule to allow us to reciprocate your hospitality, to stay with us and spend time with Kerry and your adorable grandson—all of us."

"Ah, *si.* You are gracious as always. *Grazie.* I would but of course love to come and be with my family."

Beth heard Roberto's acute longing for familial intimacy, his genteel aspiration to be included in what is the loneliest or loveliest season of the year. She sensed that this aspiration alone brought him to San Francisco.

"Could you possibly come tomorrow and stay through Christmas? Or as long as your agenda permits. . . ."

"Ah, *si*. I will come. Tomorrow is *magnifico*, if that is convenient with you."

"Perfect! My mother arrived a few days ago. She'll be delighted to hear of your visit. I'll send Max for you. What time?"

"*Grazie*. That is not necessary. I have much to do tomorrow, and cannot say the hour. I have engaged a driver. He will bring me. Sometime in late afternoon, *per favore. Addio, Bella Rosa.*"

"*Addio*, Roberto. We'll look forward to your visit."

A black limousine arrived at five p.m. Max alerted Beth and Josh the moment he opened the electronic gates. They'd been waiting, expecting him earlier. Roberto burst out the limousine door the instant the wheels stopped, not even waiting for the driver to open it, as they dashed to greet him with Teddy. The limousine looked fuller than Santa's sleigh, laden with packages with the unmistakable Christmas wrap from Saks Fifth Avenue.

"Papa!" Teddy ran to his grandfather, ready to fly into his arms.

"Papa?" Tears sprang into Roberto's eyes as he scooped up the child, surprising no one more than himself. "He called me *Papa*! It's *impossibile* for this baby to remember me, and yet he called me Papa!" His deep brown eyes tenderly questioned Beth's.

"Teddy has pictures of all the family in his room," Beth explained, "and we pray over them every night, so you are not a stranger."

Roberto pressed Teddy against the shoulder of his navy blue cashmere blazer, clutching him tightly before the child squiggled out of his arms and back to his familiar grandparents.

"And what is all this?" Beth asked in amazement as Max filed past them with a procession of gifts the driver instructed him to unload.

"This," Roberto smiled broadly with a sweeping gesture, "is Christmas for *my family*! Presents. Did I not tell you I had much to do today?" he beamed.

Margaret appeared to greet Roberto. "Ah, Signora Sheridan," Roberto bowed graciously, kissing her hand extended in welcome. "It is my pleasure to see you again. You are forever a queen, on stage and off."

The words had barely escaped Roberto's lips when Kerry and Bob returned from a shopping excursion in Palo Alto. Max, Tillie, and others had gathered around them by now, prohibiting Roberto and Kerry from exchanging father-daughter greetings, yet Roberto devoured the sight of his beautiful daughter, with the deepest of dark brown eyes so like his own, and warmly embraced her, then Bob.

Only a few residents, with nowhere to go that did not arouse the pain of broken relationships, remained at Rosehaven for the week of Christmas. The staff would be leaving the afternoon of December 23rd, but David and Golda had decided to stay on. Both of their sons were unable to come home for the holidays, and Rosehaven now seemed their home more than their own empty residence in Palo Alto.

These became days of bonding into a large, closely knit family, who sometimes engaged in decorating the ballroom with fresh greens for the candlelight Christmas Eve community services, sometimes sang Christmas carols with Bob at the piano, and sometimes just gathered around the glowing fireplace to talk and reminisce.

The foremost therapy taking place was in the kitchen, which Cookie graciously supervised for Christmas baking.

Beth popped in to observe the activity. "I remember when no one but Tillie or a bona fide caterer dared to set foot in your kitchen, Cookie. For sure, Chef would never permit such homey goings-on in *his* kitchen! You're wonderful!"

"Well, ma'am, we've all done a heap of attitude adjustment, haven't we? I'm learning to 'go with the flow,'" she laughed.

"I'm delighted you even thought of such a thing. And our two men over there, both corporate presidents, are practically up to their elbows in cookie dough and seem to be having a ball! How did all this come about?"

"This one," Cookie answered, pointing to Shelby, "she asked me so sweetly, said she saw some magazine articles with dazzling holiday foods, and learned for the first time that folks actually baked homemade cookies and goodies at Christmas. I couldn't resist. I said, 'Sure, honey, and if the others want to help, that's okay, too. I'll show you how.'"

"You're a sweetheart. Above and beyond the call . . . thank you," Beth smiled.

David wandered in, tracing the origin of the delectable aromas wafting through the halls.

"I found myself irresistibly tempted to follow my nose to the source of this divine fragrance and decided to volunteer to be your sampler," his eyes twinkled.

Shelby handed him a star-shaped cookie, lightly sparkled with red sugar. "Try this," she beamed. "And over here we have snow balls, Spritz, English toffee bars, fudge, chocolate chip, Santa's Whiskers, and I'm about to take peanut butter cookies out of the oven, especially for Josh. They'll get chocolate drops on the top. We baked tons . . . we'll serve them after the Christmas Eve service."

Becky interrupted. "Excuse me, Shelby, the postman has certified mail you need to sign for . . . right here on this line."

Shelby quickly jotted her name with floured hands, shoving the mail in her pocket. "Thanks, Becky," she said, turning back to David.

She glowed on, "I've never had so much fun! I've always dreaded Christmas. It's supposed to be about God the Father, loving the world so much He gave His only begotten Son so we could have eternal life, and our loving one another as Christ loves us. I've read that, but it didn't line up with anything in my life. I couldn't relate. Bob's sermon, the love I feel at Rosehaven, and baking cookies are making this my first *real* Christmas. David, I feel like I've awakened from the dead into a life that's finally worth living!"

David smiled at her with soft brown eyes as warm as melted chocolate. "That's what God is all about."

Mum delighted in sharing Teddy with Roberto. "He's the brightest little fellow," she chuckled, "surely advanced for his age."

"*Si.* He is adorable. I have never been around a small child in my life. Tell me, *per favore*, do you think he suspects I am, how you say, a 'klutz' with children?" he laughed, awkwardly chasing and throwing a ball that Teddy missed with regularity. "I do not huff and puff this much playing tennis!"

"Just let yourself go!" Mum giggled. "Winning with your grandson merely requires loving attention. And when you become weary, you turn him over to someone else."

David came wandering through the terrace, retrieving Teddy's errant ball, and tossed it back.

"Cheerio, David!" Mum waved. "I say, have you had the pleasure of meeting Count Cabriollini?"

"Only a passing introduction. We've not had an opportunity to get acquainted, which I'm looking forward to. Is the little fella wearing you out yet?"

"*Buon giorno*, Dr. Rosen. Ah, *si*. He is a busy one."

"Come, Teddy," Mum held out her hand, "let's you and I locate your dear mother. I believe it's nap time. Tell them goodbye now."

"Bye, Day, bye, Papa." Teddy flopped his hand at them.

"Papa?" David replied. "Teddy, this is Ro-ber-to."

The baby shook his head. "Papa," he insisted.

"Never mind," Mum covered the awkward moment. "He's tired."

Suddenly, Roberto felt robbed of his joy. He smiled proudly, but in his heart he yearned to say aloud, "But of course, this is my grandson." Instead, he told himself, *You threw that privilege away, remember?*

"Let's sit here in the sun, while it's still warm." David gestured toward the cushioned wrought-iron chairs on the terrace. "I'd enjoy knowing more about your fabulous villa on Lake Como."

"Of course, and you must tell me about your work here, and your family. I love to hear about families. You have children?"

The doctor and the Count engaged in conversation until long shadows patterned the terrace and the December chill crept over them. Still they talked.

"I must learn more about your son, Ben, his remarkable work as a Bible translator, and that remote place, Irian Jaya. This is where again? I think I've never been in that part of the world."

"It's one of the islands of Indonesia, actually western New Guinea, north of Australia. It became part of Indonesia in 1963. Tropical jungle, hot and humid, agricultural, some mining. Ben is 16,000 feet up in the mountains, translating God's Word into the difficult language of an extremely primitive tribe."

"He is very dedicated man of God to do this," Roberto reflected pensively. "I cannot imagine one doing such a selfless thing in the jungles. He is an adventurer. A good man, like Josh."

"Ben loves God with all his heart. He's said of risk and danger that he plans to die with his boots on. I'd be justifiably proud to have Ben equated with Josh, whom I've heard say the same thing. They both took seriously what is known as the Great Commission—when Jesus told His followers to make disciples of *all nations*, baptizing and teaching in the name of the Father and the Son and the Holy Spirit."

Roberto touched himself with the sign of the cross.

David continued, "One last note of interest especially to you, and then we must go in. These people's tools remain primitive beyond imagining, yet the translators have discovered their stone axes are of significant relevance to their language as well as culture. Some of the stone axes are exquisite works of art, highly prized for their refined craftsmanship, with the appearance of polished jade. Quite a treasure for an art collector, I would say."

"I am fascinated. I will go to this Irian Jaya place one day, see your fine son Ben, and have him find one of the beautiful stone axes for me."

"I may do that myself, one day. Let's go in, it's cold out here." David smiled, rubbing the chill off his arms.

"Take me seriously, David. I will do it," Roberto promised.

Seeking a quiet moment after midnight and the Christmas Eve candlelight service, Roberto took Kerry's hand, his whole being immersed in great emotion as two sets of identical deep brown eyes met.

"My daughter," he whispered, "something happened in my heart this night. I wish to talk of it to you, *per favore*. It is late, *si*, but I must," he pleaded.

Kerry embraced this elegant man she'd come to love and could not deny his request, no matter the hour. True, they'd had precious little time for deep conversation since he'd arrived, which she hoped to compensate for on or after Christmas Day. Intellectually, she considered Roberto highly acceptable as her biological father, and a charming, generous, kind friend. Josh was her *daddy*.

"Let's go into the library, where the fire's still burning," she said.

Roberto led her to the comfort of the tapestry down-cushioned sofa, seated himself beside her, and began. "Christmas Eve is beautiful. Always I go to the little village church in Como, and the candles and music, they touch my heart, and I pray to the Virgin Mother. Josh, the man who loved you like a *real* father, who raised you, has told me when I asked him of the Son of God. I could not accept Jesus as personal Savior before, because I am too filled up with myself. There was no room in my heart, like there was no room at the inn in Bethlehem. Tonight, I meet the Christchild for first time, as God's gift for eternal life—and I believe. I wish with all my heart to accept this *magnifico* gift, to ask Him into my life."

Roberto's eyes shone brightly in the firelight. "Christmas helps me to see how I break God's heart. It would be sad for me if my family turns away from the gifts I bring for tomorrow. Does it not break God's heart when I do not accept His gift of eternal life for which His Son died? I wish no longer to break God's heart, but for Him to fill up mine."

Tears splashed down their cheeks. Roberto pressed her hand. "My daughter, who knows and loves God, how do I do this? How do I become Christian, like you and this blessed family?"

"Roberto, you've told God everything He wants to know . . . that you believe Jesus is the Son of God who takes away our sins, and in Him we have eternal life. And are you asking Him to come into your heart and live within you?"

"Oh, *si*, that is what I want for my life!"

"And that is all God wants of you. Welcome, Father, into the family of God."

"That is all? I am now a Christian? I am baby, an infant Christian. Will I grow to be like you? Could I become as fine a man as Josh?" he beamed.

"God wants you to be yourself, the finest man you can be!" Kerry leaned forward as they held each other close, sharing tears of joy.

"I am happy man." He stood, lifting Kerry to her feet. "One more thing. I am so very glad that when I come, Teddy runs to me and calls me Papa. I did not do the right thing when you were a baby; I do not deserve the kindness and love you give to me . . . but between us, when no one else is around, would you, could you . . . also call me Papa?"

The tears started down their faces again, Kerry's thick lashes heavy with their weight. "Papa, I will call you Papa not only when we're just family who knows the secret. I will call you Papa anytime, because you have no child to call your own, and I look so much like you, others will only think it's for fun. Josh legally adopted me, but now I will adopt you into my heart. You are my Papa, forever!"

Before they gathered around the tree on Christmas morning, first to sing Happy Birthday and celebrate Jesus' birthday, then to celebrate their love for one another with gifts, Roberto could not contain his joy.

"I am now Christian! You are my only family and I am in the family of God. Merry Christmas! Merry Christmas!" He ran to Teddy, picked him up, and twirled him around. "Papa is Christian!"

Teddy clapped his hands, "More, more," he giggled. Roberto twirled him around again and again, then put him down and then went around the room hugging everyone, stopping at Beth.

"This is the happiest Christmas of my life, *Bella Rosa. Grazie.*"

"This is a wonderful celebration for all of us, Roberto. Merry Christmas indeed. . . ." Her voice quivered with emotion.

Roberto waited politely for the appropriate time to give his gifts. For Teddy, a white bear, so cuddly and big that when he picked it up, the bear's arms hugged him, and another—a bear rug with its rump padded so it was a pillow to lay his head on. Roberto also brought Teddy a small carousel horse that rocked, and boxes of exquisite clothes. Everyone received lavish gifts, except the Rosens.

"*Scusi,*" Roberto explained, "I did not know there were other *family*-type people here," he flashed a smile. "But may I send a gift, a check to your son, Ben, to help with his work in Irian Jaya?"

Golda smiled graciously. "That's generous of you, Roberto, and there are always needs in the mission field. The gesture is lovely, but totally unnecessary."

"It is more than gesture, but my pleasure to do it; tell me the address, *per favore.* I will go there too, one day.

"Merry Christmas, everyone," Roberto bowed formally as they thanked him, "but I have received a gift, the most excellent of all, which you have accepted long ago. I am now Christian!" He smiled from his heart, stretching his arms wide, as if to share it with the world.

Beth's heart silently sang as Josh embraced Roberto.

Oh God, You know whom You have called to be Your own, but You continually amaze me—truly You are working in wondrous ways, beyond my hopes and dreams. Thank You.

The joyful celebration of the morning gathered momentum through the afternoon, through the bountiful Christmas dinner, winding down into the peacefulness of Christmas night and a scene of perfect contentment.

"I didn't need that last piece of pecan pie along with Tillie's fabulous plum pudding," Josh groaned on the floor before the fire, rubbing his stomach while Teddy tumbled with his bears.

"Oh Dad, pretty soon you'll be in the refrigerator searching for a slice of turkey. It's Christmas—you can handle it," Kerry chided him. "Eat, eat, and be merry, for tomorrow we run it off!"

"I overdid the desserts too, Josh," Shelby sighed. "I've said it before, but this really is the most wonderful Christmas of my whole life. Thank you for including me as family. The other residents had somewhere to go today, at least with friends. Your love is extraordinary." She jumped up. "I just remembered. I didn't open the certified mail that came when I was up to my eyeballs in cookies." She ran to her cottage, returning promptly with the letter in hand.

"Certified mail is like a telegram," Shelby said, opening the envelope. "One always expects the worst. Let's see what it says."

Beth studied her expressions, a spectrum of curious to somber, from amazement to shock, as Shelby frowned, attempting to comprehend the content of the document.

Josh got up off the floor and sat beside her in a fatherly manner. "Trouble? What is it, Shelby?"

"It's from my father's attorneys. I'm wading through the legal mumbo-jumbo explaining my position as beneficiary in the trust. It names his assets in property and the liabilities in mortgages, liens, and back taxes against them, a staggering sum of stock losses, and an even longer list of personal notes past due. He hasn't paid taxes in five years for Fair Oaks, the estate where I grew up. This letter explains that in those circumstances, the state takes over the property, and in addition to that, the bank has called the loan!" Shelby turned white, then added stoically, "and there he sits, in a Japanese jail. . . ."

The firelight flickered, dancing about the hushed room in a kalei-doscope of colors reflecting the Christmas lights. The jubilation of the day suddenly became quelled by fear of Shelby's reaction to Harding's latest disaster. No one dared speak.

The same question burned on every shocked face. Would she explode in hysterics, fly off in rage, bury herself in depression, even attempt to take her life again?

Josh took Shelby's hand, massaging the smallness of it between his own huge ones without a word.

They all sat, waiting. Beth, Josh, Bob, Kerry, David, Golda, and even more ill at ease as to what words of comfort might be uttered, Mum and Roberto.

Even Teddy sat immobilized by the tension of the frightening circumstances that froze them in limbo, clutching his bear.

12

Shelby's glance traveled across the dismal faces. A faint smile gradually broadened into peels of laughter as she threw the sheaf of papers into the air, watching them flutter to the floor.

Sighs of relief mingled with expressions of utter astonishment.

"Relax, everybody," Shelby kept smiling. "I may be penniless, but I'm free! You're all looking at me like I've flipped out, totally lost it. 'Poor girl,' you're thinking, 'the shock was more than she could bear.' The truth is, now I'm free to find out who I am. I don't have to interface with the power of my father's wealth. I'm freed of feeling guilty about my ingratitude for the material things he's provided. And I will not carry my father's shame." She stood over David, affectionately rocking his shoulders with both hands. "I promise you, dear David—*I will not!*"

The tenseness of a moment ago broke loose into an air of celebration for those who had supported Shelby through her darkest hours, but Mum and Roberto struggled to comprehend this strange behavior.

Mum turned to Beth in bewilderment. "I say, love, did I miss something? If I heard correctly, I believe this dear young woman's inheritance of her father's fortune has gone down the drain. Afraid I'm a bit boggled by the gaiety of this seemingly disastrous turn of events!"

Beth smiled in empathy. "Yes, Mum darling, you heard correctly. It's a long and complicated story. I'll fill you in later."

"*No comprende*," Roberto held up open palms. "Where will you live, what will you do if you have no money?"

Roberto's concern warmed Beth's heart, and the group launched immediately into the challenge of his practical question.

"You have a home here for as long as you like, Shelby," Beth assured her.

"Congratulations, Shelby," David's tone validated her resolve. "You've taken a positive view of a new beginning, which in this particular situation is incredibly courageous. You're a survivor. Have you any thought as to what you'd like to do with your life?"

"Oh, yes," she smiled. "I'm fantasizing about completing my degree in psychology. Instead of succumbing to the temptation of self-pity, I look at other people's desperation and realize I'm not the only one to whom life seemed unfair. And Bob, I've thought a lot about your sermon on Joseph and how it's possible for God to use my adversities for good. Who is in a better position to understand broken hearts, depression, and being violated than I? I'll have to find some way to make a livelihood. Presently I have no skills. I believe I could be an effective psychologist. David, do you think I could?

"I'm grateful to all of you at Rosehaven for the support you've given me. You've also given me hope, and I want to give back. And I'm serious about joining Allyson and Austin's crusade to assist in forming incest support groups."

Mum gasped under her breath, "Incest, oh dear girl, how dreadful."

"To answer your question, Shelby, I believe you could be a fine psychologist," David assured her. "Once you're committed to a goal, anything is possible."

Roberto's brown eyes lit up. "I will pay for your education—whatever you need, I will do it. It will be my honor to do it!" he beamed. "You should have the finest education. What is it you Americans say? *Go for it!* " He thrust an upward fist, and they all laughed in agreement.

Mum stood up, positioning her cane for support. "This has been an absolutely marvelous Christmas, darlings, and Shelby, while I can't quite fathom your exuberance, I do gather you've made some remarkable attitude adjustments and I'm happy for you. Now, if you'll excuse me, I'm quite done in. I intend to retire to my bed before some other curiosity occurs. Good night, love," she turned to Beth who drew near for a hug.

Beth chuckled as she lay in Josh's arms that night. "I'm with Mum. This Christmas overflowed with miracles almost beyond my comprehension, and all within twenty-four hours. What a great God we have, who caused Roberto to come to Christ on Christmas Eve. But you, Josh, are my greatest blessing of all."

"There's another blessing I haven't told you yet," he kissed her forehead. "As Roberto thanked me for our hospitality, he asked if it was possible for him to stay on a few days to learn from Bob and me about the Christian life, and how to apply the Bible as the living Word of God. This is no light decision on his part. He's entirely serious, and so on fire, I wonder if he'll sleep tonight," Josh laughed drowsily.

Beth pressed her lips on his. "Shhh . . . you whetted his appetite with meaty food for thought when we were in Lake Como, and now he's hungry to taste it. God's timing is incredible. But enough. It's *us* time. . . ."

"Grazie, grazie," Roberto embraced them all on January 2, as Max loaded the last of his luggage into the Cadillac.

"This has been the most fabulous time of my life! The New Year's party, it was *magnifico*. I celebrated a new year, my new life. The old Roberto has gone away, the new Roberto now sees beyond himself. I once heard someone say that one tied up in himself is small package, and did not understand. I had to become older, much older, to do so, and now I am indeed happy!"

He flung his arms around each one: Bob, Kerry, Teddy, Mum, Shelby, David, Golda, Josh, and finally Beth. "*Bella Rosa*, I at last know why you are so beautiful all of your life, and now more than when we were young. God placed a sunbeam inside you to warm others' hearts."

He turned to David. "I will look forward to a photo of the stone axe, and send other checks for the work of Ben and the translators. You will see, some day I will go to that strange country. And Shelby, I shall pray for you, every day, and you go to college again, and follow your dream. You can do it!"

Roberto bent down, holding out his arms to Teddy, and twirled him around for the last time. "*Addio, bambino.* Let me hear you call me 'Papa' one more time."

"Bye, Papa." Teddy kissed his cheek with a loud, wet smack.

"Goodbye, Papa," Kerry embraced him with tears swimming in her eyes as deep and brown as his.

"*Arrivederci*," Roberto waved from the open car window.

"*Arrivederci*," the throng on the driveway waved back.

Beth caught David and Golda's exchange of glances and realized that they'd apparently connected the link between Kerry and Roberto. And surely the intimacy of her relationship with Kerry must be highly transparent to the psychologists.

In an instant, it struck Beth that the secret of Kerry's parentage that she'd painfully endured had outlived its purpose in this tightly bound group. Those whom she'd protected with the secret either now knew or had passed on, and those who didn't would derive no benefit. But David, Golda, and Shelby merited sharing in the mystery, and were trustworthy in keeping it from being wantonly abused. She would explore the disclosure carefully with Josh, Kerry, Bob, and ultimately—Roberto. The decision surely rested with them as well as her.

Within the next few days, the mandate took the form of complete agreement. Roberto became ecstatic, yet promised discretion. And for Beth, Josh, Kerry, and Bob, the very thought of openness within the confines of even these three—David, Golda, Shelby—felt like a fresh breeze blowing in the January air.

The evening of January 10, 1988, Roberto telephoned, requesting a conference call wherein all of them could share.

"With your kind permission, I wish to proclaim Sunday evenings my time to talk with *family*, whoever is available," Roberto said with his usual aristocratic courtesy, "and we talk of things to do with God, and that which *matters, si*? And David, do you have a picture of the stone axe? And how is your Ben? You have close family, like I now desire and had not enough sense to pursue in my youth. But now, I have all of you I do not deserve, like God's love I do not deserve, and I love you . . . each one."

After Roberto's call, Kerry remarked, "He's always been thoughtful and generous, yet he truly is a new man." It became a meaningful bond that they all prayed for Roberto following their Sunday evening telephone chats.

After a few weeks in this pattern, Shelby appeared troubled. She confided in them after such a call, "I join with all of you in prayer, and yet I don't know if I'm considered a Christian—I just go with the flow. I've never made the commitment that Roberto obviously has, but you love me and include me anyway. I've always been commanded, unconditionally, to conform in a certain way, with horrific repercussions if I didn't. Frankly, I don't know how to deal with the latitude you've given me. I don't want to be an outsider, yet I've no right to be an insider. What do I do?"

Bob responded instantly. "Shelby, it's your choice. There's a verse in the Bible, in the book of Revelation, where Jesus says 'I stand at the door and knock. If anyone hears My voice and opens the door, I will come in to him and dine with him, and he with Me.' Jesus is always there waiting to have that special relationship with you; Jesus waited for Roberto to hear Him, and He'll wait until you're ready to invite Him into your life too. He never forces His way, and neither will we. You know we're always available and delighted to talk to you about Jesus. It's your choice."

Shelby nodded pensively and simply said, "Thanks."

Toward Easter, Roberto's Sunday night phone calls centered around the subject of the resurrection and new life, especially the newness of life in Christ as he was perceiving it in his daily walk.

After such a call, with everyone gathered about the speaker-phone talking with Roberto, Bob said, "Kerry and I are also thrilled about a new life . . . we're having a baby in late November!"

Amidst shouts of joy and Roberto's *congratulazioni,* Beth and Kerry exchanged glimpses in acknowledgment of past conversations. "Those candlelight dinners?" Beth whispered. Kerry affirmed it with a wink and a smile.

Later, a buzz of questions filled the room about the due date, names, how Kerry was feeling, and comments that Teddy would be the perfect age for the new baby.

"I feel wonderful! No sicky mornings or any of that!"

"Isn't my wife beautiful?" Bob beamed, kissing her tenderly.

Beth held her daughter close as they said good-night. "We'll have yet another blessing to count this Thanksgiving. I'm excited about our coming grandchild. I'm hoping for a girl, too. Angela, right?"

"Angela Elizabeth. There was never a doubt about a girl's name," Kerry glowed.

In their rooms, Beth and Josh talked some more about the new baby and all the changes in their lives. "Darling, it's more than thinking about being a grandmother, but physically I'm really feeling old. I need a lift. While we're in between traumas let's slip away to Carmel, like we'd planned B.C., that is, before the market crash and Christmas."

"Frankly, my Wonder Woman, we've all been hoping you'd realize the marathon you've endured this past year or so. You begin your day earlier and end later than the rest of us. So I promise you, *nothing* will prevent us from escaping to Carmel this time."

The guard at the gate into Monterey's Seventeen Mile Drive welcomed them. "Nice to see you again, Mrs. Sterling. Have a nice stay. Everything is ready for you, as usual."

The first glimpse of the mansion on the cliff stabbed at Beth's heart. She'd invariably thought of it as the "castle." It housed Charles's cherished memories of boyhood holidays with his beloved mother before she disappeared, yet also made him wonder where she was in the mire of a life made unbearable by his father. The castle was the one truly gracious legacy he'd left to Charles, along with the perpetual membership at Cypress Point. Charles considered the prestigious club a golfer's dream come true.

She and Charles had also escaped here in weariness to be rejuvenated. And here Charles happily spent his last day on earth, which ended in a massive coronary on the golf course.

It exacted a certain courage each infrequent time she returned, an amount of bracing herself for the memories of mixed joys and sorrows. But she now had Josh, dear Josh, who knew every secret of her heart, and filled each suffering with his godly goodness, steadfast love, and his lighthearted humor.

After their second day of resting, the powerful beauty of the shimmering silver sea and the constancy of the surf lapping, slapping, crashing on the rocks below lulled away Beth's anxiety and exhaustion.

As she brushed her hair, scrutinizing the widening silver streaks at her temples, Josh brought her fresh coffee while bacon sizzled in the kitchen.

"I've been thinking I must be going through menopause, that my anxiety's due to runaway hormones or something," she sighed.

"I'd say your anxiety is an accumulation of the extreme demands you put upon yourself. You keep on giving, and never count the cost. But you probably ought to have a checkup," Josh said thoughtfully.

"Mum got through menopause in a breeze. That's what I'm planning on too. But I'm due for a complete overhaul. Look at this salt and pepper hair. It's stunning on some women—but not me!"

"You look lovely to me," Josh smiled at her in the mirror.

"This is the day I come out of my cocoon," Beth announced with resolve over the breakfast Josh had prepared. "Let's go for a run on the beach. It'll be too chilly for a swim, but we might lie out and even get a little color on these pale bodies!"

Mid-afternoon, as the breeze became cool, Beth sat up in the sand. "I'd like to take a quick shower and drive into Carmel. Want to come?"

"I think I'll stay. I should call Becky and go over some reports I left with her. But that'll be good for you."

Beth returned at five-thirty. "Wow!" Josh let out a whistle. "You looked fine to me before, but you're suddenly ten years younger! What did you do?"

"No more gray . . . you like?" She did a model's turn, exhibiting her shining silky mane restored to its natural deep, rich black.

"I do indeed. You managed to go to the beauty shop and shopping too? Isn't that a new sweater and pants? That's a great shade of blue, but not as beautiful as your eyes."

"Thanks, darling, but only the hairdo's new," she laughed. This was high praise from Josh, who always thought she looked gorgeous yet seldom made complimentary comments.

"I made reservations at my favorite little Italian restaurant in Carmel to celebrate my revival. And for you, my love—wouldn't you like to play Cypress Point tomorrow? I'll ride along in the golf cart with you."

"I would indeed!"

Josh finished the game by dropping a one-putt on the eighteenth green. "Having the advantages of the country club set is pretty nice," he laughed. "What an absolutely magnificent course—and I'm surprised I even broke a hundred. The last time I played was with Charles!"

Josh put the putter in his bag and turned the golf cart toward to the clubhouse. "Let's go into the pro shop and see if I can get a starting time for tomorrow." He stopped the cart, allowing Beth to step out as he made the turn to the bag area.

Without warning, another golf cart slammed into the rear of Josh's cart, snapping him backward in a sharp whiplash.

The driver of the other cart staggered toward them, obviously drunk. "Uh, sorry about that," the drunk muttered with bleary eyes. "Uh, here's my card. Let me know if there's a problem," and he stumbled off to the bar area of the clubhouse as the golf pro rushed to the scene.

Excruciating back and neck pain immediately overwhelmed Josh. "I suggest you take him to the emergency hospital in Carmel," the pro urged Beth.

"I'll just go home and put ice on it," Josh moaned.

"No, darling, I want you to be x-rayed," she insisted.

At the hospital, she stroked his head and prayed over him as he lay in pain waiting for the x-ray results.

The emergency doctor recommended, "Mr. Sterling should be under observation for twenty-four hours. While there's evidence of severe injury, the x-ray does not indicate skeletal impairment or articular damage. Exercise, traction, and physical therapy are prescribed. We'll put him in a cervical collar. I'd suggest a minimum of a week's therapy here before attempting to resume any normal activities."

During the hours of Josh's therapy treatments to relieve the debilitating pain, Beth's old friend Annie again proved to be a comforter. They reminisced over the days of Beth's reclusive stay at the Bluebird Cottages that Annie managed in Carmel. At that time, Beth was alone, unmarried, and pregnant with Kerry, and Annie was an unmarried woman raising her son, Ali. Mostly they talked about Annie's discovery of Jesus Christ as Savior.

"I surely would never have met Jesus except through you," Annie confessed to Beth. "He's made the difference between the loneliness and bitterness of a single mom and a full life. No other man has come into my life to be the husband Ben never intended to be, but I've not been alone."

"Annie, Jesus' love is often seen in those He brings into our lives, and I've always thanked Him for you. Please pray Josh's pain is quickly healed. We go home tomorrow."

He returned to Rosehaven wearing a neck collar and still in fierce pain. "My prayer," Josh winced as he explained his injury at the staff meeting, "is that Harry Wolff gets help for alcoholism before he actually kills someone. There are more lethal weapons than golf carts when driving under the influence. The guy was decent enough to drop into the hospital, but he was drunk even then."

When Shelby learned of the injustice toward her mentor, she shouted, "I'd be mad as blazes at some bozo ruining my vacation and causing so much pain. And you're still thinking of everyone else. I can't believe you're not suing him." Beth noticed Shelby was the first to leap to Josh's aid whenever pain prevented him from bending or reaching normally.

As Beth immediately turned to the correspondence and notes on her desk, she told Kerry, "We're not surprised, but you and Bob are to be commended that everything ran like clockwork while we were gone. I've thought of the four of us as the catalysts to our excellent professional staff . . . but we aren't as indispensable as we thought," she smiled.

"Don't entertain the idea that you weren't missed," Kerry warned. "Allyson returned while you were away. She's developing an excellent support program which David heartily encouraged, but emotionally she's still fragile. Of course that's to be expected. Shelby's making great progress and she and Allyson have a superb working relationship for their project. But—" Kerry's eyes filled with emotion as she faltered.

Beth stopped scanning the papers before her. "But what, darling?"

"Oh Mother, Bob and I had a terrible row," she choked over the words. "It's my anger again, and I feel like a screeching fat shrew."

Beth left her desk and sat beside Kerry on the leather sofa, placing Kerry's head on her shoulder. "I thought you were feeling so well with this pregnancy, and you don't even show yet, so *fat* is totally negative thinking. But go ahead and cry it out, love, then begin at the beginning."

"I flew into a jealous rage the other night. I'm ashamed of myself, but I couldn't help it."

"Who or what do you think you're jealous of?" Beth asked.

"Shelby! Bob spends several hours in spiritual counseling with her every day, but as if that isn't enough, she has become more demanding of his evening hours. He sees more of her than me, and he becomes defensive, saying that's his job. I agree. But I've reminded him that patients often think they've fallen in love with their pastors and psychologists, and I think he's courting disaster."

"What's been his response to that?"

"He says my jealousy is unbecoming of a woman of my faith and that I'm self-centered and should be more concerned about saving Shelby's soul. That's when I blew it! I'm as interested in Shelby's salvation as anyone, but I think my husband's zeal for her spiritual well-being over-shadows his good judgment. We've had some very ugly scenes, and now we can't even discuss it. Fine examples of a Christian marriage we are," Kerry scowled, irritated at her flare of anger again.

"So you're at a standoff? What are you going to do about it?" Beth asked gently.

Kerry kept silent and shook her head, indicating she had no solution.

"Why don't you suggest to Bob that you both need David's counseling?"

Kerry took a deep breath, sitting upright. "I'm all right, now that I've gotten my frustration out of my system."

"Kerry, you know better than that. I'm glad you're relieved for the moment, but nothing's resolved."

"Yes," she acquiesced. "You're right, Mother. Thank you. I do believe David can help, because if we simply gloss this over, it will rear its ugly head again, with Shelby or someone else.

"You can go back to work, Mother. Teddy's ready to get up from his nap and I'll go play with him before it's time to do the afternoon Bible study. Love you. Thanks for listening."

Three days later, Bob sought Beth in her study. "I wanted you to know that after we met with David, Kerry shared with me that she'd talked with you. You gave good counsel, and I appreciate that. The advice we received from you and David is exactly what I would have told someone else. Pastors aren't above being blind, and David felt the same concerns as Kerry. He validated her feelings of anger while showing her how to express them constructively without feeling guilty."

"I'm glad, Bob," Beth sighed. "She continually struggles with that. Those two words, *I'm sorry*, work wonders, though, don't they?"

"You bet," he smiled. "And we both agreed to focus on giving our marriage a higher priority than our work. I bought this little plaque on 'Rules for a Happy Marriage' and hung it in my office. One of them says,

'Neglect the whole world rather than each other,' which is advice I'm going to take as well as give out."

"I need to remember that, too. You and I seem to have a greater propensity than Josh and Kerry to let work come first, so keep your eye on me, will you, please?"

"My pleasure—you look terrific, Beth. Certainly not like a grand-mother," Bob beamed proudly. "Your hair is gorgeous."

"How's a grandmother supposed to look?" she laughed.

"Old enough to be one. And you don't. You look like a bride, which you still are until next week. Isn't May 20th your first anniversary?" Bob asked.

"Yes, and what a fast, full year it's been."

"Happy anniversary, darling," Josh drew her closer in bed, and then gasped as a hot arrow of pain shot up his neck.

"Umm, happy first anniversary to you, and I'm sorry you're hurting this morning," Beth kissed his warm lips.

"Now is when I'd like to kill that stupid Harry Wolff. I can't even consummate our anniversary properly," Josh groaned.

"This isn't how I pictured celebrating our first anniversary either. We'll concentrate on our blessings anyway," Beth kissed him again. "I must admit, sweetheart, in my vision for sharing a life together at Rose-haven, I underestimated the extent of this ambitious undertaking. Tell me, is it worth it?"

"How many noble dreams do you suppose would actually material-ize if the entire cost in human endurance were known before the first step? In a mere nine months, abandoned hopes have been salvaged, broken lives were made whole beyond our ability to measure, and we've only begun. We're a dynamite team, Beth, with an inspired group of players on our side, as long as we recognize that God gets the credit."

"I agree," and she kissed him again.

"You'd better stop that," he warned playfully. "You're driving me out of my mind." Josh shifted his enormous body out of bed.

Over breakfast in their suite, Josh smiled in adoration at Beth. "It is exciting that since our honeymoon only a year ago and the Geneva meeting, thousands of Bibles are reaching beyond the Iron Curtain. It's what we'd prayed for. *U.S. News & World Report* stated that under the

Reagan administration, the U.S.S.R.'s *glasnost* policy by Gorbachev seems to be ushering in a new era of proposed economic and social reforms. But only time will tell."

Beth mused, "Talking about world events isn't how I thought we'd spend our anniversary, but it's been an eventful year outside our private world of Rosehaven. A year of oil tankers in the Persian Gulf, Iranian and Iraqi missiles and warplanes in conflict, U.S. military retaliation against Iranian targets. . . . Who knows where the strife will lead?"

"God does."

"True," Beth agreed. "*Only* God knows. It's a world gone berserk. But anniversary dialogue should be either nostalgic or peacefully prophetic," she rebuked their seriousness.

"Peace in the world is impossible," Josh noted. "I'd rather think about Jesus' promise: 'Peace I leave with you, My peace I give to you; not as the world gives do I give to you. Let not your heart be troubled, neither let it be afraid.'"

"Thank you, darling, for that reminder. I love you with all my heart," Beth kissed him. "It's true, the peace and joy within us are totally independent of the struggles of life around us. It comes *only* from within."

"We'll find joy at the party Kerry thinks she's surprising us with tonight," he laughed, "and then maybe. . . ."

"Maybe what?" Beth looked hopeful.

"Maybe I'll be rehabilitated by then," Josh winked.

Under Josh's tutelage during the summer, Shelby polished her confidence and study skills as her transcripts proved to be sufficient for returning to college as a junior. She surprised no one more than herself by being accepted at Stanford University for the fall semester and came home to Rosehaven for the Thanksgiving holidays exuberant with her adaptation to academia.

"I'm averaging a 3.2 GPA, and expect to do even better," Shelby was telling Kerry when a sudden pain made Kerry wince.

"What was that?" Shelby asked.

"My lower back's been aching this morning. I've had one or two of those pains. Maybe our baby's coming today. . . ."

At two o'clock on Thanksgiving Day, November 24, 1988, all of Rosehaven celebrated the uncomplicated and joyful arrival of Angela Elizabeth Daniels.

Beth rang up Mum with news of the baby. "Oh splendid, love!" she commented from her cozy cottage in Hampstead. "I shall exercise great restraint by not appearing until December 15th to meet my great-granddaughter, permitting you time to settle in. Surely she's quite adorable."

Roberto immediately sent masses of pink roses and telephoned Kerry in the hospital. "Your granddaughter is beautiful, Papa," she told him.

"But of course," he said. She easily visualized the smile on his handsome face. "When I come December 23, I will bring surprise. Tell Beth, *per favore*, to be prepared for the surprise."

"Oh, Papa, the surprise would be if you weren't laden with a carload of gifts."

"This is different. You will see. Congratulate your husband for me, kiss your *bambinos. Ti amo*—I love you."

13

The welcoming entourage assembled to greet Roberto for his holiday visit after Max phoned en route from the airport, informing Beth they were a few minutes away.

Roberto leaped from the car to open the other rear door, extending his hand to assist a slim woman with black hair and sapphire blue eyes who alighted with the grace of a dancer.

"Ladies and gentlemen," Roberto beamed, "I am pleased to present . . . Maria!" He slipped his arm around the waist of the stylish woman in a lavender suit as impeccably tailored as his own. "On January l, Maria will become my wife!"

Josh was first to recover his faculties as a mute gasp of astonishment froze in mid-air. He stepped forward with a broad smile, extending his huge hand to Maria.

"Welcome to Rosehaven," he beamed, concurrently embracing Roberto while Max proceeded to unload their luggage and a bounty of gifts.

Teddy bolted toward Roberto with open arms. "Papa!" he shrieked, and instantly the welcoming process ignited in full, with introductions to Maria and jubilant exchanges of Merry Christmas salutations.

Roberto's gaze searched past Kerry, Bob, and the others toward Beth. She caught her breath as his deep brown eyes met hers, and immediately regretted her immutable reaction.

"May I present Maria Sophia Carducci . . . Signora Elizabeth Sterling. My hope is that you two become fine friends."

"I'm pleased to welcome you to our home, Maria," Beth smiled, at once amazed at their physical similarities. "And I should like for us to be friends," she said sincerely, intrigued with whether they shared other characteristics.

"We could go in instead of standing out here," Josh laughed into the crisp air.

"Yes, indeed," Mum agreed. "It's nearly tea time. . . ."

Fewer patients had stayed on at Rosehaven through the Christmas holidays than the previous year. Bob's community worship services reached an all-time high in attendance with a group of the surrounding neighbors eagerly volunteering to host the cookie party Shelby initiated the year before.

Beth delighted in the luxury of family privacy and relaxation. Angela and Teddy captured the center of attention, as did Roberto and Maria with sharing plans for their future. Roberto smiled constantly, the epitome of a happy man.

Later in the evening, sipping eggnog before the crackling fire, Mum said, "I say, you two make a smashing couple. You're stunning together, and perfectly suited. How did you meet?"

"You tell them, *per favore*," Roberto beamed proudly at his fiancée.

Maria, not in the least shy among her gracious hosts, spoke impeccable English, with barely a hint of an accent.

"At a dinner party at the Embassy in Rome, and—"

"*Scusi*," Roberto interjected with a brilliant smile. "It was like this . . . I see this be-ooti-ful woman standing in the moonlight on the terrace. We engage in conversation, and she is also intelligent and kind of heart. An eclipse of the moon happened, and I think God is saying to me, 'This is the woman I have for you' and I say to myself . . . *I think so, too!*'" he laughed.

"I've never seen you look quite so happy, Roberto," Beth smiled. "I'm overjoyed, for both of you. Maria, you are from Rome? It's one of my favorite cities."

"Yes, I am. My father was a high-ranking merchant before reaching a high position in government in Rome. When I was fourteen my parents were mysteriously assassinated in their bed, with never a clue as to the motive or identity of their murderer. I was an only child. My father's brother was also in government. He and his wife were unable to take me into their home, being fearful for my safety under the bizarre circumstances. They entered me into a convent.

"The sisters at the convent were exceedingly kind, and in time the terrible nightmares ceased. I proved proficient in my studies, developed both artistic and administrative skills, and felt content that I would spend my life there in obedient service to God for His protective care.

"A few years ago, I began to struggle with doubt about whether my seclusion in the nunnery truly pleased God. I wondered, was I merely hiding from life? For over a year I prayed for an answer, until it burned in my heart and affected my work, and the Reverend Mother felt God had spoken.

"I left the convent. My aunt and uncle introduced me to friends in Rome, and that's where I met Roberto, at a dinner party at the Embassy. I'm convinced God has chosen Roberto for me. Oddly enough, I didn't truly know Him until I met Roberto," Maria sighed. "I'd obediently served God, but Roberto introduced me to Jesus Christ as my personal Lord and Savior. Now that I've become a Christian, we will serve God together."

"You have made some sort of plans then?" Josh asked, stoking the fire.

"I am excited," Roberto glowed. "We have investigated forming a world orphanage organization, perhaps a Christian home for the aged. God will tell us. We will do something for Christ that will matter in eternity!" Roberto spread out his hands, as though encompassing the whole world.

"We are eager to return to Como and get on with our lives," Roberto said on December 26. "Christmas at Rosehaven has been *magnifico*. *Grazie*. Think of us and pray a blessing on January 1. We will be married in the little chapel in Villa Cabriollini. It will be a very small, very precious wedding." Roberto smiled as he kissed the women and embraced the men in farewells.

Kerry telephoned the Villa Cabriollini on the evening of January 1, Italian time, excited to offer congratulations.

The houseman answered, "*Buona sera*," converting immediately to English upon hearing Kerry's voice and her request to speak with Roberto and Maria.

"Sorry," he said politely, "the Count and ah—*Signora*, are not available at this time. I will be most happy to inform him that you called."

Disappointed yet imagining the happy couple were romantically secluded or perhaps already away on their honeymoon, she left a message that she'd call at another time.

Kerry smiled as she envisioned the wedding scene: a bower of flowers in the historic chapel, the bride's bouquet, which Roberto would have meticulously chosen, the perfection of detail he'd have specified for the small yet exquisite ceremony. Imagining Maria in bridal white lace came easily as she supplanted Beth's image next to Roberto, who'd likely worn a black Italian silk suit, completing her mental picture. *May they be wonderfully happy,* she prayed.

Roberto telephoned on a Sunday evening in late January.

Kerry answered the phone, hoping it was him. "Papa, I'm delighted to hear from you! Beth and Josh are in the city at a concert with David and Golda. We weren't sure you'd continue to call on Sundays."

"But of course, you are my daughter, my family."

"Tell me about your wedding, your honeymoon—you must both be very happy. May I speak to Maria and congratulate her too?"

An uneasy silence followed. "Ah, Maria is not available. We are both, ah—doing well. Tell me about my grandchildren."

Kerry obediently complied, disturbed at his evasiveness, endeavoring to ease the tension she perceived. She purposely rambled about the gifts he had given the children for Christmas, and finally ran out of conversation. *What is the problem?* she wondered. *Was there some area of disappointment in his marriage to Maria?*

With no further mention of her, he said, "Pray for me, my daughter. I have been a Christian one year. Pray for God to give me something *importante* to do with my life. My passion for art, my villa, my wealth, they no longer are my world. They cannot please God the same as they please men, as I cannot." His tone was downcast.

Kerry blinked back tears. *What about Maria, what about the plans they'd made together?* But instead she responded to his question. "That's what God wants to hear, Papa—that He is more important than the things of this world. That's what pleases Him, more than accomplishments. He knows your heart. Ask for the power of the Holy Spirit to work within you and show you what to do. There's a verse in Micah, that's Old

Testament, that says all God requires of you is to 'do justly, to love mercy, and to walk humbly with your God.' "

"*Grazie,*" he sighed. "I am better now, you are good teacher. Wish a Happy New Year to the family for me, *per favore.* Hug your Grandmama, and ask David and Golda to send my regards to Ben in Irian Jaya. Perhaps I will still go there, see the stone axes and people who are new Christians, like me, but do not make life so complicated. As Beth says—God only knows, and who but He knows what this year will bring?"

The new year of 1989 tumbled along not unlike most years, with the pages of the calendar flipping through the days, blending one season into another. Rosehaven's flow of patients consistently mirrored the compromises of shifting social values. These compromises ultimately diluted previously held absolutes in standards and behavior, plunging their victims into progressive emotional misery. They arrived with every outward manifestation of prosperity, yet impoverished in their spirits, wearing intricately patterned masks that hid their consistent inconsistencies.

At mid-year, David made a summation to staff on effective concepts to help people cope with the most common anxieties of life in these times. "It's a jungle out there! Every year, I'm observing deeper depression, extensive abuse, and growing malcontent in the midst of the worldly definition of success. The one element that distinguishes our counseling from the myriad of other psychotherapists who have tried and failed to help our patients is the hope we have in Christ."

On October 17, following an extraordinarily intense day of counseling depressed patients, David told the staff, "The glaring lies that most Americans embrace—'no such thing as absolute truth,' 'people of different religions all worship the same God,' 'God helps those who help themselves without Him'—must be revealed as such at Rosehaven. Our task is to explode the myths; to disentangle half-truths of consequences of behavior and the me-isms of pop-psychology. To send whole, functioning people back into the world, we must never relax in presenting that the truth of the living God is for yesterday, today, and forever. . . .

"Whew—what a day," David concluded as the staff filed out. "My throat's parched from talking. Let's go into the Pub for a soda and cheer for the Giants. What magnificently sunny October weather for the World Series."

David flicked on the television. The waving crowd of spectators who came to Candlestick Park to root for their home teams, the Oakland A's and San Francisco Giants in the third game of the World Series, suddenly gave way to fear.

"The entire stadium is reeling!" the reporter shouted. "We're having an earth—"

Power lines, including those at Candlestick Park, were severed, cutting him off midsentence.

ABC switched to emergency generators, and both ABC and ESPN were on the air from the stadium within minutes. The camera in the booth picked up a shot in the monitor of a collapsed section of the Bay Bridge from a camera aboard the Goodyear blimp.

"We've just had a major quake," he finished. "We're okay here in Candlestick, but the rest of the area is not. We've just experienced fifteen seconds of terror, and I'm amazed this maligned old concrete bowl is still standing," the veteran sportscaster sighed in relief. "Some of the players' families are coming onto the field for safety . . . and this is unbelievable— over 62,000 people, some perched 100 feet above the ground—are acting as if nothing extraordinary has happened!" he said excitedly. "At this moment there's no evidence of injuries—but wait! I've been handed several notes; an angina victim has had an attack, but others are shouting 'Play ball!' The game will obviously be postponed for tonight, and we'll look to baseball commissioner Fay Vincent for a statement regarding its continuance tomorrow. He's commending the crowd for the orderly fashion in which they're leaving the stadium."

"Thank God those 62,000 people weren't crushed in a collapsed ball park," David observed. "And that the Series game kept thousands off the freeways, both at the Stick or in their homes to watch it."

"And isn't it miraculous that we didn't feel the slightest tremor?" Beth said as Josh flipped to various stations for coverage of the catastrophe by innovative news teams of correspondents, producers, and directors.

"Our latest report," one commentator said, "that the major 6.9 quake that struck the Bay area at 5:04 p.m. during rush-hour traffic and stopped the third game of the World Series has killed at least six people by flying bricks. The Marina District, built on a landfill, appears to be hardest hit in San Francisco, where homes and apartments lay in rubble, and an entire city block is on fire. An untold number of motorists were entombed in the twisted mass of steel and concrete when the upper deck of the buckled Nimitz freeway fell. Motorists are also stranded by a collapsed section of the Bay Bridge."

They watched in horror at the devastation wrought in that fifteen-second period.

The newscaster continued, "The old Ferry Building at the foot of Market Street appears largely unharmed, and San Francisco's skyscrapers downtown also seem virtually unaffected. Power is out in most of the city, and further shock waves are jolting Californians with reports that telephone systems are down in some areas. Many residents are—"

The telephone rang. "Thank God!" Merribelle's shrill voice erupted in Beth's ear. "Ah was petrified Ah couldn't reach you! Some people are totally isolated with the phones out. Are you all in a shambles down there? And the news is so sketchy, isn't it? Have you heard if your Townsend Tower is still standing? It's in the same block as Henry's bank, you know, and Ah certainly wish the reporters would be more specific! The buildings could be layin' in heaps for all they're tellin' us. Have you heard?"

Without pausing, Merribelle spouted, "Ah'm terrified that what we didn't lose in the market crash is devastated in this disaster. Ah swear, it's one catastrophe after another, so unfair, isn't it? Ah'm simply terrified of goin' downtown to look—couldn't bear to find a heap of rubble. But we're cautioned not to go downtown anyway, it's like a blackout with the power not workin', and what with streets buckled, and fires breakin' out. You didn't tell me—are you in shambles down there or not?"

There was no quarter for humor in the rampant devastation Beth saw on the screen, nor with Merribelle's legitimate concern for their possible losses. Yet Merribelle fired questions with machine-gun rapidity impossible to respond to, and Beth suppressed a smile at her friend's pathetic yet comical panic.

"Whatevah are we goin' to do, deah?" she wailed again.

"Until the freeways, overpasses, and fires are under control, there isn't any way to see for ourselves, but the media hasn't reported major damage on Montgomery Street, Merribelle, and they did say the skyscrapers appear safe. Try not to worry. It won't accomplish anything."

Beth sympathetically continued attempting to console her. It was entirely possible that the Townsend Towers, representing Charles's millions of dollars of personal investment and the base for Townsend Enterprises, of which she was the controlling stockholder, could also be in jeopardy.

Beth asked, "Is your area of Pacific Heights safe? Do you have any damage?" She was quite familiar with the exclusive neighborhood a half mile up the hill from the Marina District.

"Oh, mah home's not damaged, but expensive paintings flew off the walls, and mah priceless Meissen porcelain dishes crashed out of the cabinets. Ah'm simply sick about it. The house is in one piece, thank God."

"Thank God, indeed—that's exactly what we need to do, Merribelle. The news is covering heavy damage in Los Gatos and Santa Cruz, which was the epicenter. We can thank God again that we weren't in it."

"Beth, you *still* haven't told me. Is your gawgeous Rosehaven just ruined? They're saying the greatest damage is south of San Francisco."

"We didn't feel the slightest tremor. We didn't know there was an earthquake until we turned on the television to watch the World Series. Dating back to when the house was built, I remember Charles saying it's close to the San Andreas fault, but it's also built on rock."

"Well, honey, pray our downtown property's still standin'. Ah'd simply perish, can't fathom how we'd get by if we've lost it. Ah'd die! Ah'm not prepared to be a pauper at this stage of mah life. Hope the Tower's safe too, of course."

"Thank you, Merribelle. It was thoughtful of you to call in the midst of catastrophe, and be assured I'll pray God's best for you, and that our properties are unscathed."

"Ah wish Ah had your faith and cool, deah."

"Faith is available for the asking by believing in the One you ask. And with it, trust in God's help and peace of mind come in times of trouble," Beth felt compelled to remind her again, after the endless instances through the years when Merribelle had desperately sought God's mercy yet denied His grace.

As Beth hung up, Josh asked, "Who was that? I'm surprised the phone's working . . . Oh wait . . . seismologists are reporting on Santa Cruz. Six lives were lost, with tremendous damage. The business area's demolished, homes are destroyed, huge cracks have opened the ground. It's catastrophic! Now, what about the phone call?"

"It was Merribelle. Don't ask me how, but she thought I may have heard if Townsend Towers was damaged. Henry's bank is within a block, and there are fires nearby. She's near hysteria worrying if it's been destroyed. She's still paranoid over their financial losses in the market crash last October. I know her well enough to realize she's even more upset than she sounds."

"How ludicrous for her to think you'd know something she doesn't. Beth, that's not really why she called," Josh said with convincing finality.

"It isn't? Why did she call then?"

"All I heard you say was that Rosehaven is built on rock. Poor Merribelle is terribly insecure, she lives totally on the shifting sand of material wealth. When it's shaken, she identifies you as the stable one to calm her down. You are her rock. She needs you."

"Mmm—you're an excellent analyst. She needs God, Josh. We must persist in asking Him to be patient with her, but I always wonder how many times He will endure rejection."

"He sees within the human heart, which we cannot. Only God knows."

"Yes, I've heard that before," Beth smiled with an upward curve of her mouth.

"I think you invented it," he winked.

During the next four days, they kept close watch on the television for continuing news of the aftermath, calling as many friends as they could reach to ascertain their well-being.

"San Franciscans are a resilient lot," the commentator opened that Saturday morning. "Although the week's aftershocks ranged from 3.0 to 4.67, our camera caught these stalwarts out running, and others in their gardens only a mile from the height of the disaster, and people helping people.

"Family and friends, indeed all in the Bay area, grieve the loss of life," he continued, "yet mercifully the victims were by the score rather than hundreds, and not 26,000 dead as in a quake of the same magnitude in last year's Bosnia disaster. Experts credit California's strict building codes.

There might have been thousands killed in San Francisco if not for the steps taken by civil engineers' preparation in past years.

"As in many calamities, people come closer together. We've received stories of miraculous timing or luck, as you choose, of despair and courage and heroism in those who endangered their own lives on Highway I-880 to rescue others trapped in their cars. Although some of the damage will take time to remedy, San Francisco is a city of survivors."

"I wonder how well Merribelle is surviving," Beth mentioned to Josh over coffee in their suite.

"You should call," he said, reading the morning paper's account of the massive clean-up in Santa Cruz and Los Gatos.

At ten a.m., Merribelle sounded half-asleep.

"How are you?" Beth asked.

"Well, of course, Ah'm a wreck. These dreadful aftershocks have me undone, Ah can't get any decent sleep. Henry's more concerned about havin' the buildin' inspected, which had no damage to speak of, than he is about me. Ah feel so alone. When will it evah stop, Ah'd like to know!"

"But you're safe—there's no damage since I last spoke with you?" Beth asked with concern.

"Ah live a well-ordered life, and Ah'm simply not prepared to be all shook up. Ah loved mah fine china. God is up there, rattlin' His cage, punishin' us all. I see mah neighbors out, goin' about life as usual, like they're unconcerned as can be. What am Ah to do, Beth?"

"Join them! Get down on your knees and be thankful you're not dead and that your house and precious possessions are still intact. It's a beautiful day out there."

A click and a dial tone indicated Merribelle had no intention of listening to encouragement to proceed with life.

Beth heaved a deep sigh of exasperation.

"What now?" Josh looked up.

"Unlike the city of San Francisco, Merribelle has consistently refused to prepare for the slightest displacements in her life. Can you believe she's grieving the loss of her Meissen china while shaking her fist at God?"

"No way," he shook his head. "Like the commentator said, it takes years of developing building codes to prevent disaster. It's no different when one is without a spiritual foundation. It's too late to begin when your world starts to shake."

Three weeks later, shock waves of a different nature reverberated around the globe. Masses gathered before their television sets and devoured the newspapers to venerate history in the making.

The epitaph, *Charlie Is Dead*, blazed triumphantly in red paint on that dread checkpoint of the dividing wall between East and West Berlin. Checkpoint Charlie, where Russian soldiers had struck terror in the hearts of people crossing from one Germany to the other, had fallen to the sledgehammer of those pounding it to pieces for souvenirs.

Hundreds of thousands of East Berliners romped through the broken barrier between the two Germanys that communist rulers held captive for more than forty years.

At Rosehaven, patient Ilse Von Kleinschmidt wept. She identified with the emotional crowd of East Berliners rejoicing with relatives from whom they'd been long separated. "My mother illegally escaped to take me to the U.S. from East Germany in 1949. My father died there. I've inherited her fears, guilt, insecurities, and the constant worries she took to her grave. I'm afraid I've passed worrying on to my children as well. I never knew my mother to have a day without worrying. It became a pattern because of past suffering. My grandparents died in the gas chambers at Auschwitz. Mother always felt guilty for leaving her two sisters in the West, and a brother and two other sisters in East Germany. But at last they can be united as Germany is finally united," she sobbed. "I wish my mother could have lived to see this."

Along the glittering Kurfuerstendamm Boulevard, East Berliners received the 100-mark "welcome money" West Germany had traditionally given East Germans on their first time into the West. The Rosehaven audience vicariously lived the excitement of those who drank in the heady new feeling of freedom.

On November 11, watching the giddy celebration of West Berliners greeting long-oppressed East Berliners with champagne, cheers, hugs, free food from the restaurants, and free theater tickets, Ilse searched David's kind face.

"At this great historic moment, I too feel set free. Is it too abstract, David, to suppose I can celebrate freedom from worrying over the past and be united with a whole self again? The 'End of the Wall' has no direct bearing on my life, yet it strikes me as symbolic. This revolutionary people's movement has brought into motion a process of sweeping change, a new start from a lifetime under a government they loathed. I've loathed and never looked squarely at the oppression over me, or realized I continued to worry in mother's place. Until now. I feel change within me, like another kind of wall is down. Does that make any sense?"

"I'm sure there are millions of people working through mixed emotions right now, Ilse. Changes that break down walls and bring inner peace and unity make excellent sense. The crumbling of communism is not only symbolic of, but gives testimony to, a failed system. I'm delighted that you can apply these world events on a personal level and recognize a failed system that you are willing to change. That's a double celebration!"

A commentator on the evening news reported, "Washington, like the rest of the world, is scrambling—attempting to keep pace with the changes unfolding in Eastern Europe almost moment by moment. Secretary of State James A. Baker III is astonished at notes from his aides informing him of major changes in Eastern Europe. Only a week ago no one imagined, let alone predicted, the Berlin Wall would be down today.

"American officials are guessing that President Mikhail Gorbachev of the Soviet Union will attempt to use the December 2 meeting with President Bush to address the fate of Germany and to press for a dissolution of NATO and the Warsaw pact. Administrative officials declare they have no intention of such negotiations. But in the same breath they're interested in how far Gorbachev is prepared to let events in East Germany develop and the implications this will have for the East-West security balance in Europe.

"Meanwhile, in Montreal, Solidarity leader Lech Walesa said Europe is witnessing 'a new generation' of leadership, and. . . ."

The group in the Pub began discussions among themselves. "I don't think we're capable of assimilating any more change for today, thank you," David spoke directly to the commentator, and turned off the television.

"Have a good evening," he waved around the room, considering it a healthy sign of interaction that he left virtually unnoticed.

Later, at the dinner that Beth, Josh, Bob, Kerry, David, and Golda enjoyed together once a week, David shared Ilse's revelation of her own newfound freedom.

"How is it that during Ilse's therapy we never drew out that her worry was related to her mother's fears growing up in Nazi Germany? It brought to my mind the seventeenth-century poetry of John Donne, and how germane it is to now . . . 'No man is an island, entire of itself; every man is a piece of the Continent, a part of the main; if a clod be washed away by the sea, Europe is the less, as well as if a promontory were, as well as if a manor of the friends or of thine own were; any man's death diminishes me, because I am involved in Mankind; and therefore never send to know for whom the bell tolls; it tolls for thee.' "

"How relevant, maybe more today than then," Josh agreed. "I haven't read Donne since college. While the media depersonalizes in many ways, it does make it impossible to escape that we are all 'involved in mankind.' "

Beth reached for her husband's hand. "When we first heard about the Wall coming down," she smiled at Josh, "we thought about the meeting in Geneva on our honeymoon, and how we laid our hands on the map of communist countries, praying not only for the Bibles to reach the people and that the Word of God would set them free, but also that the Iron Curtain would be torn down. This is an answer to that prayer."

"The world becomes smaller every day," Golda added. "The East-West security balance in Europe, with Washington scrambling to keep pace, is in some ways symbolic of the big picture of us—trying to cope with our individual security balance."

"I agree," Kerry said. "I feel insecure in this society in which our children must grow up. I felt anxious when I took them to the mall shopping today. I felt that if I turned my back for a second, they could be snatched or kidnapped. And our judicial system might protect the offender rather than the offended. The political upheaval in Eastern Europe is bringing pressure upon the Soviet Union for change, but the pressure for change in this country is going in the wrong direction."

"True," Golda agreed. "That's evident with Marta. You all know her case. She revealed much in her therapy session today. My heart aches as I take her through the stages of grief over her fourteen-year-old son killed by a drunk driver who pleaded guilty. She just learned that due to a discrepancy the attorney found in the police report, the court date was cancelled and the offender was released, likely to kill again. She's in the midst of so much anger . . . a long way from forgiveness. She and her husband own a major restaurant chain, and he's now living with another woman. Now he insists on his rights to come home but is not giving up the mistress. He's obsessed with the idols of money, sex, and power. The final blow is that Marta just learned her sixteen-year-old daughter had an abortion." Golda looked down, exhausted.

"Forgive me for bringing clinical talk to the dinner table," she said, "but I pray with each word of counsel for God's wisdom, knowledge, and divine insight that He will use us to bring hope and healing to ones such as Marta."

Bob, who sat beside her, touched Golda's shoulder. "Throughout the Scriptures we are girded with the hope we have in Christ. In 1 Peter 1 it says, according to His great mercy we are born to 'a living hope . . . to an inheritance incorruptible and undefiled and that does not fade away.' A few verses on, it says, 'gird up the loins of your mind . . . rest your hope fully upon the grace that is to be brought to you at the revelation of Jesus Christ.' I like the verse in 1 Timothy 4—'For to this end we both labor and suffer reproach, because we trust in the living God, who is the Savior of all men, especially of those who believe.' Also, in Hebrews 6 the Word says, 'This hope we have as an anchor of the soul, both sure and steadfast. . . .'"

Bob went on, "Contrast that with a survey I read as we go into the '90s. It said that only 13 percent of Americans believe in all Ten Commandments. I guess the rest go through them like a smorgasbord, picking and choosing, overlooking adultery and justifying it by not being murderers. One in five loses his or her virginity before age thirteen. One in six was physically abused as a child, and one in seven was sexually abused."[2]

Bob's determination shone. "The hope we have to share is not of the world's systems, not in governments that come into political power and then crash to defeat, not in piecing together broken dreams on empty promises.

"The hope we have to offer Marta and the others is based on faith in God's promises that say He is sufficient to meet all our needs; we can do *all* things through Him who strengthens us; He will never leave us or forsake us!"

14

T hanksgiving will arrive at the perfect time," Beth happily volunteered as she ran beside Josh in the crisp morning air. She'd elected to forego exercising at the ballet barre, to seize these stolen moments with her husband before the day's heavy schedule engulfed them. She smiled up at him with sparkling eyes, watching her breath float before her.

Josh slowed his stride to a brisk walk, looking puzzled at her comment. "Yes . . . it's quite customary to observe Thanksgiving in late November—but I suspect something pithy and profound is hidden in that statement, hmm?"

"I'm still ruminating on what Bob said the other day, about 'the hope that is our privilege to instill in others. . . .' Massive changes are taking place in political systems abroad, which you and I are especially aware of through your involvement with world missions. Some changes are nothing short of miraculous. Others are unbelievably horrifying. But none is more appalling to me than the breakdown of the family and the traditional value system in our country; the people are getting trampled in the shuffle."

"So what does that have to do with Thanksgiving?" Josh looked puzzled again.

"Remember last year," Beth continued, "after the turmoil of the Harding scandal? Shelby's attempt at suicide, the bad press, and the panic of Black Monday?"

She paused only to catch her breath, but Josh immediately jumped in. "It seems I recall those traumatic incidents," he mocked with a smile.

"You're incorrigible," she scoffed. "What I'm trying to say is that when Thanksgiving came, everyone—that is we, the staff, and the residents—turned our focus on thanking God. We took our minds off of circumstances and concentrated on who He is. The *circumstances* may not have changed, but attitudes toward them did. It brought out the best in everyone. It brought out hope in God, more than anything we'd ever done. Remember the open sharing and the exchanges of encouragement? We need to repeat that stimulus *now*. And that's why Thanksgiving is coming at the perfect time this year," she finished.

Josh slowed down. "Okay. Gotcha! And I promise not to pull a budget number on you. I've realized many times that I was stuck in a 'penny wise and pound foolish' episode. But I think we should take 'hope in God' more seriously than we have . . . live like we truly believe it. Our concept at Rosehaven is effective because we're praying, but not enough. Patients who are striving to fill the voids in their lives with the same old idols and excesses we've talked about before—money, sex, and power—are destitute for the reality of a Savior. At Rosehaven, we want to reinforce Christ as the solid rock in a world whose foundation shifts without giving notice.

"So . . . with those goals in mind, my dear, I must agree, Thanksgiving *will* arrive at the perfect time this year."

"Good! I'm glad to hear you finally agree. My casual comment got 'pithier' and 'pithier' . . . heavy duty while trying to keep up with your long strides. And Thanksgiving will be even more special because of Angela's first birthday. Kerry's having fun planning her party."

"Teddy loves being big brother," Josh chuckled. "He meticulously laid out all the plates, poppers, and party stuff to show me yesterday, explaining the sequence of events."

Josh took Beth's hand, gradually slowing their pace before coming to rest beneath a spreading oak. She leaned back against the massive trunk, inhaling deeply as he pinned her body against it, planting his strong hands on either side above her head. He tilted her chin upwards to meet his lips. Nothing else existed in that moment.

Josh gazed deeply into her eyes. "Beth, you're beautiful in a refreshingly uncomplicated way. But inside, you operate on a highly complex network of transmitters that hold me in awe of your ability to connect hurts and needs, and dispatch love. And thanks for running with me this morning . . . everything is better with you beside me."

By early December, Bob professed that the Thanksgiving season had indeed evolved into a bona fide "revival," hoped for yet rare in these times. The staff attained an inspired new high of commitment, which in turn sparked the patients toward a stimulating search for intimacy with God.

"I don't dare risk the word 'revival' among either the patients or the community. They're far too sophisticated," Bob laughed. "They could conceivably conjure up antiquated images of tent meetings and Bible-thumping, and some of the televangelists expounding what appears to be trumped up miracles. But in reality, that's what we have . . . a genuine Romans 12:2 experience, recognizing that conformity with the world's system is what leads to problems—and here I see a transformation by the renewing of minds, and a sincere effort to 'prove what is that good and acceptable and perfect will of God.' That's exciting!"

The new high of inspiration carried the family through the Christmas and New Year's holidays, and eased the pain of Mum's absence, as she was confined in London with a mild case of pneumonia.

"I'm simply not well enough to travel, love. I dreaded to ring you up with such dismal news. Don't even think of coming to London. It's wet and cold, and I'm less than marvelous company. Mattie takes excellent care of me. Let's save our visits for when I'm myself. I'm sending new photos instead for you to show to my Teddy and Angela, so they won't forget their great-grandmummy."

"Dear Mum," Beth sighed when she rang off. She missed her mother's delightful, positive spirit. Their intimacy still felt remarkably new, and their time together never seemed enough.

Roberto's Sunday evening calls poignantly revealed his reaching for a deeper relationship with Christ, yet with an incongruent sadness, searching, and unfulfillment. He felt pressed to 'do something meaningful in the sight of God,' knowing not what it would be. Kerry earnestly comforted, counseled, and assured him his passage to eternity with Christ was already paid for on the cross, reserved for him with the unconditional love of the Father, and that peace in his heart was possible in this life. Roberto's former beliefs died hard. Grace remained difficult for him to comprehend and accept. He felt certain there must be more required on his part.

"I regret I cannot come to be with you and your family this Christmas, my daughter," Roberto explained sadly via the telephone.

"Papa, we'll all miss you," Kerry said wistfully, tempted to pursue the whys of his decision not to join them but quickly realizing Roberto and Maria had their own lives, their own traditions to establish. He talked for another thirty minutes, requesting a full account of the children's newest words and phrases, and of her and Bob's roles at Rosehaven.

Kerry concluded with, "Give our love to Maria, and may your first Christmas together be filled with joy."

David and Golda were also far away, spending the holidays in Baltimore with Aaron, an intern at Johns Hopkins Hospital. Shelby's return to Rosehaven seemed as normal as any student coming home for a break, and she was warmly welcomed as family.

At the Christmas Eve service, Shelby seemed to further distance herself from God as a heavenly Father. She appeared incapable of accepting any gift from God, much less that of His only Son. Kerry mentioned to Beth, "Shelby looks exhausted, completely drained. Reaching out to these groups of suffering women while carrying a full class schedule is a heavy load. I hope she can handle it without breaking."

Beth agreed. "She's attempting to fill others' needs for survival while she is empty herself. She shared with me that anticipating the Christmas break and quiet moments here at Rosehaven is what's held her together."

Kerry nodded, "And I think she's drawing closer than ever to Josh, vicariously relating him to the type of father she longed for and never knew."

Marta and Ilse stayed on for the holidays, clinging to the security of each other's company, seeking detachment from extracurricular activities or the family's invitation to participate. Most patients eagerly returned home to reunite with families, while others found that impossible to cope with and equally unthinkable to deny themselves a luxury outing even if alone. Four of the lonely male patients flew together to ski in Aspen for two days and referred to the trip as "Christmas."

Angela's first steps, her sweet baby laughter, Teddy's bright observations and expanding vocabulary kept their family delightfully entertained, totally absorbed, and desiring nothing more than the joy of being together.

Beth sifted through her nostalgic thoughts . . . *the lavish Christmas Balls of Rosehaven's celebrated past, the great and grand gatherings of patients, community, immediate and extended family, seem far removed from the quiet peace of this holiday season.*

The festivities felt incomplete without Mum and Roberto, yet she shifted her reflections to the positive . . .

Thank You, God, that You lifted us out of the fast-paced daily demands we willingly yield to, and saw the need for this rare and precious time of privacy with my husband and family. And thank You, too, for bringing Shelby home for rest and encouragement.

Becky interrupted a Monday morning staff meeting. "There's an urgent person-to-person call, actually a request for a conference call for David, Golda, and Josh from Irian Jaya," she announced. "I'll put it through in Josh's office —it's closest."

The three hurried to gather around the speaker phone.

"Josh Sterling here, with David and Golda Rosen."

"I have a message from Ben Rosen. I am Hank Whitaker calling from our missionary headquarters in Wamena. The voice you are about to hear is a message which I received and taped from Ben's two-way high frequency radio to relay to you, as it is impossible to make calls to the States from Langda."

"Thanks, Hank. I understand. Go ahead, please," Josh replied.

"Hi Mom, Dad, Josh," they heard Ben saying. "We desperately need help up here! There's an epidemic of typhoid and cholera raging among the villages. It's out of control. We've exhausted medical and other needed supplies, and to complicate matters, the area is ravaged by unusually severe storms of the March rainy season. Crops have been washed out, the people are hungry. They've suffered some injuries, too. Open ditches are teeming with bacteria. The loss of human lives will be catastrophic unless help arrives soon. Don't worry about me—I may sound tired, but I'm not sick.

"The missionary team and translators are calling every possible resource for planes to meet the emergency. Our own planes are mechanically down, and the few that are available can't possibly meet the demand of the whole island. Josh, I don't know how familiar you are with the terrain in Irian Jaya, but the altitude of our particular missionary station is the highest at 6,000 feet, in dense jungle. Between this mountain range and the coast are hundreds of miles of impenetrable swamp. That's why the people living in the interior mountains were cut off from the rest of the world for centuries, until the age of aircraft brought the missionaries and then us translators."

As they listened, David put a comforting arm around Golda while they observed the wheels in Josh's mind churning to render a solution.

Ben explained, "Josh, I don't know what missionary aviation organization you were with, but could you possibly arrange for the use of a plane and pilot experienced in maneuvering high altitudes? There are dangerous updrafts and downdrafts in these dense forests. The dirt airstrip is short, set in a narrow valley of rugged terrain. A Cessna 206 is the largest plane we can get in here, but that's what it'll take to fly in the supplies we need. I wouldn't ask if there was any other way to go." The connection began to sound fuzzy.

"Hank will put you in contact with our organization in the States who will give you details of the flight route and necessary supplies. Don't worry, Mom and Dad, just keep praying. I love you."

Beth had entered Josh's office in time to hear the desperation of the need and the danger of the mission. Her color went ashen. *Dear God,* she prayed silently, *send someone else—please, not Josh.*

Hank came back on the phone.

"I'll see what I can do," Josh promised. "Tell me how to contact you, Hank, and give me the particulars and I'll get back to you as soon as I have some information."

As Josh wrote down the data, Beth admired his immediate command of the crisis, the glint of the old war horse yearning to be where the action is. And she knew, if it were humanly possible, he would go.

Within thirty-six hours Josh contacted the resources of his twenty-five years as a missionary pilot and set a plan in motion. "We've located a Cessna 206 for the difficult trip that's going to take four days," he explained to Ben's anxious parents and his own apprehensive family.

Beth groaned inwardly. Josh had found the available plane. The available pilot was himself.

"The plane is equipped with special ferry tanks to carry enough fuel to make the eighteen-hour nonstop flight to Honolulu. I'll refuel there, take the mandatory rest period, and continue the next leg, which is Majuro in the Marshall islands. It takes almost as long. The third leg for refueling is to Ponape in the Caroline Islands. Then at Wamena, I'll pick up an old buddy I used to fly with, Roy Allgood, and he'll fly us into Langda, which I'm not currently certified to do. Besides, one could fly right over it and never find the airstrip without having been there. We'll have to go through customs and all the red tape. The Indonesian government people are a particularly proud lot, most of them Melanesian from other islands who have come to 'rule' the Irianese tribal people and fiercely cling to their authority. To the best of my knowledge, we've been granted approval to fly into the country and bring medical supplies. I want you to know that's a major miracle, so pray they don't renege—and keep on praying about that one!" He laughed. But Beth realized the seriousness of his concern that on a whim, the whole venture could be foiled at the end.

"Anyway, after Roy joins me at the mission headquarters at Wamena, and with less fuel, we can reload with about 1000 pounds of cargo—standard supplies like rice, boiling pots, and other needed items. The monsoons have washed out the sweet potato and other crops that comprise the native diet along with wild pig, so they'll have to teach them to cook the rice."

"What medical supplies are you taking from here?" David asked. "Do you have all you need?"

"The biggest problem with cholera and typhoid is dehydration—so lots of intravenous fluids, syringes, some sulfa-based antibiotics. We'll have water-purifying tablets. We'll take standard first-aid stuff of course, and try to do immunizations for those not yet afflicted, but there are many strains of both diseases, so let's hope it helps. I think we're ready to go."

Beth insisted that she alone drive him to the airfield, where the plane sat finally loaded and ready for Josh to take off on the long and tedious mission of mercy. She made a valiant attempt at lightheartedness, struggling to send him off with a smile.

"You were preparing a plane to take off for some faraway place the first time I met you, remember?" she smiled, heading toward the freeway.

"I remember meeting my wife's best friend, who asked me how she could have a personal relationship with Jesus Christ. We've had a beautiful and growing relationship with Him and each other ever since, haven't we?"

"You gave me hope, courage, faith, and changed my life forever," she said just above a whisper.

"Christ did that. I merely had the privilege of introducing you—and He did the rest," Josh grinned broadly.

"I'm not sure I'd ever have found God without you, Josh."

"Oh yes, you would—you were looking for Him, and He chose you before the foundation of the world. You remember Scripture."

"All I can think of now is that you come safely back to me. I can't imagine flying eighteen hours, nonstop, alone. Please don't take any chances, Josh, I—"

"I won't be *all* alone. Besides God as my copilot, there's a fantastic new device—the G.P.S.—Global Positioning System, which gives me longitude and latitude and coordinates everything I need to know from an orbiting satellite system above the earth." He placed a finger across her lips, which she kissed. "Shh, no more worrying. You're frowning."

They held each other in a long embrace moments before he boarded the plane. "Clear across the Pacific, the picture of you I'll carry in my heart is wearing a smile of that same hope, courage, and faith. Right?"

"Right," Beth bravely complied with his request, smiling back at him. She pretended to hold a camera and snap a picture. "And I have your smile to carry in my heart."

Driving away from the airstrip she prayed, *Watch over him. Keep him safe, Lord.*

Beth arrived back at Rosehaven in time for the casual worship service open to the community on Wednesday evenings. This particular night was devoted not only to worship, but to prayers for Josh's safety, for Ben and the missionaries, and the suffering people of Irian Jaya.

Virtually no one had ever heard of this primitive province, though most had a vague notion of Indonesia as a whole. Now they passionately insisted on knowing how they could help and where to send money for relief.

Bob illustrated the location of San Francisco on a big green chalkboard, charting Josh's flight pattern along with the time schedule across the Pacific, down to the East Indies. Spanning the map, Bob wrote, *A Journey in Prayer.* Everyone—the staff, the patients, the community—became deeply involved in praying especially for their beloved Josh and for David and Golda's son.

David remarked to the family during the singing, "This is the healthiest sign of people bonded together helping people and getting outside of themselves that I've ever seen among the residents at Rosehaven. More so than the time of the media crisis and its attack on Rosehaven, Shelby, and Allyson. Take heart, Beth—this is a positive thing happening here."

Shelby had come home for spring break from college, unaware with the pressures of mid-terms that Josh had already left, and slipped into the service that was underway.

Her participation in Sunday and Wednesday services, Bible studies, and spiritual counseling had been haphazard. Since these events were purely optional as a patient, she'd usually chosen to refrain, doubting God could really love her, or that Christ would die to save a person as unworthy as she. But she'd come tonight. The congregation was singing songs of gratitude and praise to God. Worship flowed from their hearts, with hands lifted up to the heavenly Father.

Father. The word suddenly invoked new meaning. Shelby could finally disassociate it with the earthly father who had pillaged her body and soul and nearly destroyed her life. The word had a broader dimension made possible by Josh, who manifested an earthly portrayal of the heavenly Father—loving, caring, never leaving or forsaking her. Being there—except for now.

She needed Josh *now.* New uncertainties threatened her sense of security. And he had flown off on a perilous mission fraught with innumerable catastrophic possibilities to an insignificant, obscure, inconsequential, uncivilized section of earth.

David was showing slides that Ben had sent of the country when he first arrived at the mission station. Shelby shuddered at the primitive, black, naked bodies. The women wore only grass skirts and the men wore strangely ornamented gourds over a portion of their private parts, with pig tusk ornaments through their noses and ears. She felt further jarred by David's profundity in saying "Our cultures are worlds apart, yet God loves them just as much as He does you and me."

Shelby realized Josh had answered to distress exactly as an impartial God would do . . . because Josh truly was God's man. He needed her prayers. But why would God pay attention to her? She'd shaken her fist at Him, or at best, pretended He didn't matter or exist. . . .

Bowing her head and uncertain if she was praying or listening, Shelby heard Bob's voice quoting Hebrews 11:6—that " 'Without faith it is impossible to please Him, for he who comes to God must believe that He is, and that He is a rewarder of those who diligently seek Him.'

"The power of the Holy Spirit is in this room tonight," Bob proclaimed, "inviting those to come forward who want Christ in their lives. Or you may raise your hand so I can talk with you later."

Shelby trembled. She yearned to go forward or raise her hand that refused to move. The impulse of this earnest desire throbbed within her, yet she held back. God couldn't possibly love *her*. She slipped out the back door as two others went forward to accept Bob's invitation.

Beth took Kerry's hand in hers, joyful tears streaming down their cheeks for those who came to receive Christ, to enter into the family of God, and to join their prayers for Josh and Ben. David and Golda closed the evening in prayer while the congregation sang "I Have Decided to Follow Jesus."

Ten days later, Ben managed to get another radio message through to headquarters in Wamena from Langda. Hank telephoned at 2 A.M.

"Dr. Rosen, I apologize for calling at this hour but it's the only time I've had to call. I have word from Ben that Josh arrived safely, but the next day a major earthquake occurred up in the mountains. Langda is completely cut off, and they're still experiencing aftershocks. The missionary station is in worse shape than ever, and the need for supplies is even more desperate. The tribal people are helping to clear the landing strip of debris and fallen rock, but the plane has been damaged beyond repair. Without a mechanic and replacement parts, they can't fly out."

David felt numb as Hank explained, "Ben, Josh, and Roy escaped injury, but many are seriously hurt. Pleas are going out for doctors and emergency assistance from every missionary organization, the Red Cross, and even privately financed resources. As yet, there's been no response because Langda is so geographically inaccessible."

The line began to crackle. "Can you still be reached through the information Josh has?" David asked quickly . . . then the line went dead. "God, let this be only a temporary interference. We must be able to communicate somehow," he prayed aloud.

David and Golda got out of bed and down on their knees. "God, would You bring the right names to mind, to tell us where to turn? Josh provided help to rescue Ben and the people in the villages, and now they're all trapped in a hostile jungle with no way out."

At the Wednesday night Bible study, Bob applied the faith chapter of Hebrews 11 to trusting God in everything, using the examples of Abraham and the saints of old.

"I don't understand God," Shelby angrily told the new believers standing around after the service that night. "If God really cares about people, how can He let good men like Josh and Ben be in this terrible situation? It makes no sense to me. I'm not sure we can trust Him at all."

Beth overheard and silently found herself demanding answers to the same questions. Alone in their big bed, she whispered, *God, I'm afraid for my husband. Help me to trust You as much as I've always thought I did.*

"What is the matter, *Bella Rosa?*" Roberto asked when Beth answered the phone on Sunday evening. "I can tell, in your voice, you are troubled."

Beth turned on the speaker phone where the family was gathered after dinner, realizing it was Roberto's customary weekly call. She concisely apprised him of Josh and Ben's critical situation, the urgency for medical aid, and above all, their rescue from the treacherous terrain.

"Do not worry. Tell me what they need. I'll ask God what to do. I know many people. Someone will help," Roberto assured them.

"We'll transfer your call to David and Golda. He has the information at his fingertips," Bob answered, smiling after he'd hung up. "Such confidence. What simple faith. Undauntable. And I have no doubt he possesses considerable resources. Roberto's not just blowing smoke."

Within twenty-four hours, Roberto called back, again for everyone to hear on the speaker phone.

"This is what I have done. You have met my personal pilot, Emilio. He will fly a Lear jet with supplies and a doctor from the airport in

Milan—remember how close it is to Como? From there it is a long, complicated flight, passing over the Middle East. Hopefully he'll have no problem flying above those troubled countries, then over India, Malaysia, and Borneo, to a major airport in the Celebes, and proceed to Wamena. Emilio and the jet will stay there, then a missionary pilot Hank has contacted will fly a Cessna to Langda with the doctor and supplies. I have discussed these details extensively with this Hank person. A good man. We must pray he has convinced the Indonesian government to allow the plane to come in. But we cannot wait for them to make up their minds. The flight must begin now. The plane leaves tonight at midnight, and I will be on it!"

15

Josh settled against the base of a tree. Under the morning stars, he sat surrounded by the lofty mountains as though in a bowl of night illumined with the dawn. The first syncopated sounds of the jungle awakening to the new day began to reverberate with increasing cacophony, bent on setting his mind in motion. He resolutely ignored this invasion of privacy. His Bible and journal lay across his lap while he savored a few quiet moments with God, hoping to gather and record his thoughts and emotions of the past tumultuous days.

He'd witnessed terror, death, disease, and heartbreak while praising God for sending him into the field again. He wrote in his journal:

> *I'm not so sure that the greatest purpose for being here isn't the missionary families themselves. They're not as subject to disease because of hygiene and their use of water purifiers. But they're as subject to exhaustion, depression, discouragement, loneliness, and spiritual dryness as any of the rest of us.*
>
> *One couple in particular, Dan and Rachel Westergard, were on the brink of emotional breakdowns. They weren't due for a furlough for another ten months and wondered how they could hold on. They'd struggled with problems at home in the U.S.— elderly parents, a daughter going through a brutal divorce, a home they'd rented out and were about to lose. Dan felt spiritually ineffective. Rachel thought she was losing her faith and her mind, and their marriage was unbearably strained.*

Josh paused, thinking it looked like rain, and resumed his writing.

Another couple also, Mark and Rosalie, were affected by the Westergards' depression, constantly anxious about their children getting sick and dying, and felt oppressed by demonic forces.

We prayed against all those things. The physical needs of the people have demanded our efforts night and day. Roy's worked almost nonstop. Our original task was to deliver life-saving supplies, yet another aspect of life-giving has come upon the mission station with each day we've been delayed here.

It seems God has held us captive for a reason . . . and He has multiplied the time we devote to prayer and counseling. The couples have rediscovered the joy of their salvation, are recommitted, uplifted, and encouraged about their missions. What a great God we have—and He allowed me to have a part in it!

Josh's thoughts turned to his brief time in Thailand and his opportunity to serve as a missionary, rather than a missionary pilot. He recalled the joy on the faces of the hundreds of Asians who received Christ, but mostly he remembered the missionaries themselves, and that when his time there came to an end, he knew God's purpose in sending him had been in the role of an encourager.

That seemed also his greatest gift at Rosehaven. He felt confident in his administrative skills, yet his personal rewards were in edifying others. He'd not had the luxury of time to yearn for family and home. For a painful instant he contemplated the perils of his rescue and how and when he'd see his beloved Beth again . . . and quickly turned his attention back to the journal.

I've spent little time with Ben. He greeted us at the mission station the day we arrived. I briefly shared news from his parents, but after the initial earthquake, he's been primarily ministering to the people in the villages. He hopes one day to meet Roberto and personally convey his appreciation for his generosity in supporting the missionaries.

The full light of day suddenly captured his attention, and, realizing he had work to do, he closed his journal.

When the sun was high, Josh peered into the heavens. He respected the manifest skills of the pilot making several passes to assess the narrow, short, crude airstrip before landing the single engine Cessna. He'd never thought of a plane having the wings of an angel until this moment.

Ben had received minimal information from Hank on the two-way radio. They were apprised only that a rescue plane was en route with a doctor and supplies on board, and what approximate day to expect it. The missionary team at the station consisted of three families, a nurse, Ben, and one other translator. Rachel and Rosalie sprinted with Josh to meet the aircraft as it made a reasonably smooth landing on the jagged valley floor.

The door of the plane opened. Roberto jumped to the ground with outstretched arms to greet them, while Josh abruptly froze in his stride, stunned speechless.

"It is good to see you are well and in one piece, my friend," Roberto grinned. "You look surprised that it is I, *sî*?"

"And you look exactly like an angel appearing out of the blue!" Josh flung out his huge arms of welcome to the usually impeccable Italian in his rumpled cotton khaki shirt and trousers. "Just when we thought every possibility had been exhausted, Hank radioed the good word. He said a Lear jet originating in Europe was making the long flight to Wamena to connect with a privately owned Cessna 206 coming from the Marshall Islands, to be flown in here by a missionary pilot. What a horrendous trip!"

The magnitude of orchestration necessary to accomplish such a junket only now registered in Josh's mind. "I should have known only you could pull off such a miracle! And you don't realize what a wonder it is to have permission from the Indonesian government to enter the country with goods!" Josh heartily slapped Roberto on the back, laughing in astonishment.

Roberto accepted the praise with a wide smile. "I only make all the pieces fit," he answered modestly. "The pilots are the skilled ones, first my *magnifico* Emilio, and then Karl Werner here," Roberto introduced the alighting flyer.

"It is my pleasure to bring also Dr. Carlo Rossini, my personal physician from Milan. He is fine doctor. Come, let us get the plane unloaded. I see there are injured people."

Villagers had shyly gathered to stare curiously at their benefactors who came out of the sky. Some had their arms in makeshift slings, others looked pained, wearing only the last shreds of bandages to cover head injuries, while many had ominous-looking open wounds covered with jungle remedies of mud and herbs. The American missionaries were followed by a small assembly of virtually naked tribal men who streamed toward the plane, while Roberto and Karl gave directions for unloading.

Josh hoisted a carton onto his shoulder and escorted Dr. Rossini to the clinic they'd just finished rebuilding, followed by an entourage laden with bulky boxes of medical supplies.

Rachel beamed, "Praise God," at the volume of lifesaving provisions. "This will take care of us for quite a while!"

A tribal man began pounding on an enormous aluminum kettle, never having seen such a large cooking vessel, surmising it must be a drum. Josh paused to laugh at Roberto, who was going through a series of charades in an attempt to demonstrate its practical use.

"Better leave the explanations to Rachel—she's been here the longest, and she speaks their language," Josh laughed again. "*Si,*" Roberto flashed a smile. "Usually my hands help me to communicate. Here we have what you call, *ce tanto differenza* . . . a *wide* culture gap!" he shrugged his shoulders with a grin as perspiration streamed down his handsome face from the heat and humidity.

Near midnight, Josh and Roberto at last found a moment to talk privately by lantern light in a small grass hut to escape the chill of the night air.

"I am happy to be here." Roberto sank to the ground next to his friend, putting his hand on Josh's shoulder. "I admire you always, and now even more, for I see how you have lived, what you have done for God, and at last I too can do something for Him. But where is Ben? I thought by now I would meet David's fine son. . . ."

"I expected Ben to return to the missionary station sooner, and he'd be surprised and excited to find you are our angel of mercy. He's been in one of the villages hard hit by cholera, comforting a grieving family whose four young children all died yesterday. I don't know when he'll be back."

Josh went to the side of the hut to an object wrapped in a blanket. By the light of the lantern, he held it out to Roberto.

"What is this you are handing me?" Roberto stared at him.

"Open it. It's from Ben, who would want to give it to you himself. But who knows when he'll have an opportunity? I think you should have it now."

Roberto peeled back the blanket wrapping of the gift. He gasped, holding the legendary stone axe with the appearance of precious jade as though it were delicate crystal.

"It is *magnifico*! More amazing than I could imagine from what I have heard. When I see these people, with no implements as we have, and recollect this stone is only ordinary before the shaping, the polishing, the time, and patience that make it a beautiful object, my heart—it is touched." Roberto's genteel fingers traced appreciatively over the smoothness of the axe, the product of some village artisan he would never meet, and to whom it had symbolized protection, the sustaining of life, as well as the pride of craftsmanship. "It is a precious gift. I shall hope to thank Ben myself.

"Josh," he said wistfully, "I think my life is never the same after this. I have lived for myself and whatever it pleases me to do. The things I give away are gifts that the excesses of wealth provide. We each begin life as raw material, like this original stone. We become rare and beautiful, like you, and Beth, Kerry, and Bob, the missionaries like Rachel, only by the cutting and polishing of what it costs us, more than money, to give of ourselves."

As they spoke the ground suddenly trembled violently, at once bringing wailing from terrified children remembering the horror of the previous week and the aftershocks since. Josh grabbed the falling lantern, reacting before the hut could ignite in flames. He heard a tree fall, a hut demolished, the anguished screams of a stricken village family, and shuddered. Then the shaking stopped. *What havoc has it wreaked this time?* he wondered.

Roberto took a deep breath with a glance at Josh indicating his readiness for action.

The earth shook again, with a quick, sharp jolt, then another, and more wailing pierced the night in the aftermath of further destruction crashing about them. Roberto quickly but carefully wrapped the stone axe and returned it to the floor of the hut where Josh had kept it.

Josh leapt to his feet from their brief rest, having a total of only six hours of sleep in the past two days. Roberto jumped up to follow as they traced the path of devastation to the missionary house where Dr. Rossini and the two pilots had attempted to catch a few hours' sleep.

The doctor responded to the crisis of a fallen tree that had crashed through the corrugated metal roof and pinned Roy beneath it. He issued orders in Italian, although he spoke English well.

"No, no, no!" he shrieked at a wide-eyed villager who endeavored to help by moving Roy, as Roberto, Karl, and Josh struggled to lift the unwieldy weight from Roy's legs.

They gasped in horror when the dislodged tree released its victim, revealing bones protruding from bruised and bloody flesh slashed by the metal roof. Rossini shouted more orders at Roberto to get his bag of instruments, antiseptics, and morphine for pain, cursing the adverse conditions. He yelled at Karl in Italian, which Roberto translated to Josh.

"He says immediately we must get Roy to a hospital. The breaks are very terrible. Surgery is necessary, which he cannot perform here. Karl, the plane is ready at dawn, *si*? Check it, *per favore*, and tell us how soon it is possible to fly out."

Josh bent over his friend, "Roy, can you hear me? I'm praying for you, old buddy. . . ."

"A blanket," the doctor ordered brusquely at Roberto as he stood ready to assist. "This man is barely conscious and he must not die from shock. I'll take care of him. See about the plane, Josh, and radio to a hospital to be on the alert for us to bring this man in."

"Doctor, can you come?" Rachel called. "This village woman's arm is slashed nearly to the bone."

Another tremor shook the ground. "I cannot," he shouted back. "Apply pressure to slow the bleeding." The sophisticated Rossini, accustomed to equally sophisticated facilities in Milan, was radically unnerved. "We must get this patient ready to be transported," he yelled even louder.

Josh returned breathless. "The villagers are clearing the airstrip by torchlight. Karl's preparing to fly out at dawn," he reported to Roberto. "Pray the plane's not demolished by falling trees and flying rocks before we get off the ground!"

Roy was a large man, almost the stature of Josh. They fashioned a crude stretcher capable of bearing him onto the plane; then propped him up on the rear bench seat in his pain-ridden, semiconscious state, which presented a nearly impossible task. With their sparse gear on board, Karl started the engine with Josh, Roberto, and Dr. Rossini warned to brace themselves for a steep ascent necessitated by the short runway. The first rays of morning silhouetted the perpetually snowy peaks of the towering mountains above Langda.

"Get ready for takeoff in a few minutes and close the door," Karl commanded above the engines.

"Wait! I have to go back!" Josh shouted, calculating in his pilot's mind that he had precisely enough time to run back to the hut.

"What's he doing?" Dr. Rossini complained irritably, peering through the window. Within moments, Josh was dashing back to the plane, victoriously brandishing a blanket-wrapped object in the air as Karl revved the engine.

Josh leaped through the door with a broad grin. "Got it!" he roared, thrusting the protected stone axe at Roberto, his free hand reaching to close the door.

At that precise instant the earth shook as though hell itself were breaking loose. A shower of rocks pelted the fuselage and a jagged rock, the diameter of a large coconut, glanced off the open door of the plane and struck Josh in the forehead. He collapsed into the plane, blood pouring down his face. Roberto pulled Josh up over his own body in the cramped seat while the doctor secured the door. Within seconds they were airborne.

On the ground, Ben watched in horror, sickened by what he had seen and distressed that he had missed the opportunity to meet Roberto and say goodbye to Josh. Oblivious to his own danger, he stood riveted in disbelief. Mixed tears of grief and gratitude flowed down his dirt-smudged cheeks.

Screams of the village men, women, and children fleeing senselessly in all directions jarred him into action. He scooped up a wailing toddler abandoned in the confusion and ran with him toward a clearing amidst the thunder of an avalanche as it demolished the small airstrip.

The thought flashed through Ben's mind that Langda and its ancient tribe, he and the missionaries, were again isolated from the civilized world. Within the week that Josh and Roy had come to their aid and lived among them, followed by Roberto, Karl, and the doctor, they'd become and would remain living legends of mercy among the people.

Ben had listened as the believers in the villages talked of the one Great Living God. This God had first sent strange men with white skin from the sky to their fathers or fathers' fathers many years ago; He had sent the present missionaries and translators, and now these to help them in their time of desperation. . . . And they concluded that this Living God had a great love for them. The isolated tribes of the mountains had proved to be overwhelmingly more receptive to the gospel than those in the lowland swamps, and Ben had grown to love them and their simple faith.

Throughout untold centuries, the primitive culture of these islands continued to bedevil the people, and they sought to placate their pagan gods and demonic spirits with strange rituals. They attributed earthquakes, floods, avalanches, and especially disease to the wrath of these gods. Whatever the catastrophe, a fragment of the population perpetually managed to survive extinction.

Ben pondered. But for Josh, Roberto, and the others mercifully bringing food, medicine, and supplies, might this have been the chapter in history when they would all have perished? And he and the missionaries with them? He shuddered at the thought, certain they'd already endured the worst. While he clutched the screaming, terrified child and searched for the parents, he imagined how the horror stories of the disasters would be embellished and the courage of their rescuers would be woven for generations into their folklore. The frantic mother ran wailing toward him. As he thrust the naked child into her arms, he was struck by the full impact of what had happened only moments ago.

A great sorrow engulfed him and he wept. He had witnessed what surely must have been a mortal blow to Josh's head. The sickening fear haunted him, that this mission of mercy may have cost Josh his life.

The small plane had an impossibly cramped area to minister to Josh's wound.

Rossini strained to reach his bag. In anguish, Roberto tore off his stained shirt to staunch the blood from the terrible wound flowing into Josh's eyes. Josh lay semiconscious across Roberto's lap as when he'd been pulled into the plane.

Barely above a whisper, Josh murmured, "God . . . yes, God." His head dropped as his body went limp in Roberto's arms.

"No! Josh, you cannot die, Josh, you cannot," Roberto pleaded. He knew the precious friend enfolded in his arms was gone, and a terrible sob caught in his throat. "It should be me who dies, not you. I came to save you." He held Josh's head tenderly and sobbed in despair. Grief welled in his chest to the point of bursting.

Throwing his head back, he cried, "I have failed you, *Bella Rosa*! I would gladly give my life for you, Josh, for you, Beth," he spoke as though she were there, "and I have failed," he repeated, weeping.

Roberto tenderly caressed Josh's forehead, gently wiping the blood away, lovingly stroking his thick brown hair. "I loved you, Josh. Your life was good, and pure, you are the best of all men. Would that I could have died in your place, I have failed you. . . ." Dr. Rossini touched Roberto with a compassionate hand, fearing Roberto was near collapse, for they were both overwhelmed with physical, mental, and emotional exhaustion. His elite practice as physician to Milan's aristocracy had not prepared him for the drama he had encountered in the jungles of Irian Jaya.

Under the never-ending demands he faced there, the invincible Rossini saw for the first time that his steely persona was merely a facade. Outside the idealism of his pre-conditioned environment, he had fallen apart. He turned to glance at Roy in his terribly adverse position, the patient on whom he must now concentrate, breathing easier with the shot of morphine to aid him in enduring the rigors of the trip to the hospital in Wamena. But Roberto's pain, which he felt powerless to alleviate, pierced his soul.

"Roberto, my friend, hear me," Rossini pleaded. "We mature ones should have learned the common error of the young, which is to assume if you cannot save all of mankind, you have failed. In medicine, in life, try as we may, we cannot control destiny, or God—whichever one believes in. As a doctor, I must consistently question my performance in adversity. Did I neglect an option, lack perseverance, skill, knowledge? When one does all things right, failure to save a human life is a dreadful thing to bear. Unfortunately, it comes with being a doctor, or a hero.

"Roberto, you are a Christian. You have been earnest in telling me while in my office that you have a God who comforts, who is the Great Physician for hurting hearts. Take His comfort, which I have never learned how to give. Someday, I want you to tell me about your God. I am a man who worships only excellence. There is something in you that is absent in me, which became obvious moments ago. Perhaps I need your God, too."

"*Sí*, good doctor," Roberto's face brightened. He looked lovingly at Josh who lay across his lap in the small plane. "This extraordinary man whose weight I gladly bear is the one who first told me about God. His lips are now silent forever, so I will speak for him. I would be honored to tell to you just like he said to me about Jesus Christ. You shall have a Bible I will bring you. I will introduce you to it, like Josh did to me. And if you have eyes to see and listening ears, you will be blessed. And if you believe, you will never be the same."

Karl radioed Wamena, preparing the field attendants for their requirements—that upon landing they should anticipate one man on board dead and another seriously injured.

They were met by a battered ambulance, whose Javanese drivers dispassionately placed the two men on stretchers side-by-side. While Roberto grappled for a shirt from his satchel, they impatiently motioned for him and the doctor to get in.

At the hospital, Dr. Rossini accompanied Roy through the admitting process, discussing details and vital signs since the time of the injury, never leaving his side until he was wheeled in for surgery.

Roberto furnished information to the authorities for Josh's death certificate. Josh's perpetual smile and his ebullient good nature were indelibly imprinted on Roberto's memory. The very thought of Josh invoked an echo of his jovial laughter. His death left an immeasurable void, and Roberto felt his heart would break. Josh's body was wrapped to be immediately flown to San Francisco. Throughout the interminable labyrinth of government policies, Roberto thought desolately, *It is un-real—this is not happening.*

Hours later, when time had totally lost its relevance, Roberto nervously phoned Rosehaven. It was morning there, and Becky was at the switchboard.

"Do not tell Beth I am calling, *per favore*," he requested. "Not just yet. May I speak with David?"

"Yes, Roberto. I'm relieved to hear from you. How's it going?" David sounded bright, elated over the anticipation of an update of information on "Operation Rescue Langda," as they'd prayed for it.

Roberto had mentally rehearsed the chronological order of events, painstakingly organizing the details to cushion the shock. Instead, he melted at the warm tones of David's voice. Quivering with emotion, he blurted, "Ben is safe. Josh is dead." He sensed David reeling from the impact.

"Oh my Lord, no! What happened, and when?" David gasped, at once thankful Ben was alive, but paralyzed at the thought that the man who flew from the other side of the earth to save his son had lost his life in the process.

Roberto winced, despising how insensitive the words that burst forth sounded even to himself. "*Scusi*—I am as they say . . . shook up to tell you these things. It happened like this. . . ." and he unfolded the account from the hour of their arrival in Langda to the present.

"Beth must be told," Roberto concluded. "I am bringing Josh home. Emilio will fly us to San Francisco. The doctor then takes a commercial flight to Milan. Ben is safe. It is over. . . ." His voice broke while he battled for composure.

"David, I cannot bear to tell Beth this terrible thing by telephone, and it cannot be withheld from her. You will be tender. You will be gentle. Please tell her of the smile on the face of her godly husband before he died. But tell her for me, *per favore* . . . I cannot do it."

David swallowed hard. His heart pulsated as though twice ripped open and left to beat with an exposed raw wound. He mourned Josh whom he loved as a brother, and the sorrowful duty of informing Beth and the family fell solely on him. Words could not get past the lump in his throat.

"David," Roberto's voice choked with further emotion, "*per favore*, you are the only one to tell me . . . how do I live from this point on, with my guilt?"

The question pierced deeply into David the man, as shadows of the same question repeatedly stirred within his breast. . . . Josh died, answering the call to save Ben. David, the psychologist, tried to find a compassionate answer.

"Roberto, I believe godly men, like God Himself, respond to human need because it is their nature to do so. And you mustn't disregard that you also responded to the need without counting the cost, saying simply—'I will do it!' You also could have died."

Roberto interrupted, "David, the stone axe, it was not a need. Ben is a thoughtful man to provide the object of my fascination. But is God demonstrating the futility of *things* to me? If Josh had not gone back to get the stone axe for me, he would not have died! And you are correct. This time I did not count the cost of giving of myself, for long ago, I did that, and paid the price of losing more than I could bear."

"Let me ask you," David proposed, "are you truly convinced Josh intended to risk his life to run back for the axe?"

"I think that is not so," Roberto answered. "He jumped off the plane, it being *impossibile* to know another earthquake was coming. But he did that for me."

"All right. Think about this. A former pilot, such as Josh, immeasurably impressed and grateful for the magnitude of your intrepid rescue, desired with all his heart to show his personal gratitude. The most noble of men have been subject to serious errors in judgment, Roberto. I've often mused that such a man is born a deliverer. At any given moment in life, he is predestined to react by impulse, by throwing himself even into the mouth of death because his basic nature catapults him to respond to a person or a cause beyond himself."

"I still do not know how to live with the guilt. He did it for me!" Roberto cried in anguish.

"I do not have the answer to these things, Roberto, but God does. As we all do, Josh made a choice. To proclaim it as foolishness, to blame him, to make ourselves live in guilt, is perhaps to deny Josh of being who he is. One thing I know—the smile Josh wore during his life reflected the joy of his salvation. Only his body is dead. Josh himself is alive, and his smile will never fade through all eternity.

"Words from Proverbs come to me," David continued. "'Trust in the Lord with all your heart, and lean not on your own understanding.' Many things are not for us to understand, but to trust. He is called 'the Father of mercies and God of all comfort,' and we must allow that comfort to work in us to comfort Beth and all who love Josh."

With heavy hearts, the men concluded the painful call and hung up. David wept after endeavoring to console Roberto by telephone. "God help me," he moaned in prayer. "Give me gentle words for the terrible task of telling Beth and Kerry that Josh is dead."

16

A floral bouquet of April's lilting fragrances floated through the open windows of Beth's study, drawing her from the stack of applicants' files on the desk to pining for Josh and the day of his return.

The pristine morning air sparkled with a heady perfume of narcissus, hyacinth, and jonquils from the gardens below. Beth swiveled her chair to the window. Leaning back into the soft leather, she inhaled deeply of the scents unique to spring.

Her thoughts drifted to the rich promises of their tomorrows, the fulfillment she and Josh found in each other, their family, the challenges of lives being changed at Rosehaven. Her daydreams floated among the swirls of white clouds suspended in a backdrop of clear blue.

She blinked at a circle of light in the heavens, mesmerized as it gradually grew brighter in a brilliant golden sphere with Josh's face shining through it.

His wide smile loomed more radiantly than she had ever experienced it face to face, while irrepressible joy triumphed in his eyes, overwhelming the fullness of his countenance. His smile centered intimately on Beth, penetrating her soul, reaching out to touch her and seeming so near she felt impelled to rise to touch him. Then he vanished into the vapor of a cloud. Was it a vision? Her imagination? No! She saw him. What did it mean?

Peace and a sense of his presence washed warmly over her. She cherished their life together, living each day in one accord, to the fullest, taking nothing for granted between them, no regrets, feeling nothing could ever separate them. She closed her eyes, clinging to the moment, marveling again in its peace.

She heard a soft rap at the door.

Unheeding, she whispered, "Come back, darling," but the jubilant vision had evaporated. She longed to draw it near and press it into her heart.

The tap at her door gently persisted, while the reverie faded away like a mist—as she knew it must. Reluctantly she called, "Come in, please."

Kerry, Bob, and David could not hide their anguished expressions as they entered the study. Her mind flashed to another scene, and as if in slow motion, she saw herself approaching three figures from the past. She felt her lungs expanding as though pedaling a bicycle up a steep grade. The three faces she saw were those of Dr. Hall, Richard, and Tim as they'd waited for her return from cycling by the gates of Charles's castle-like home in Monterey.

Her heart lurched in panic as it had the moment she instinctively knew death had stolen Charles from her, and she would never see him again.

"No!" she screamed. At once, Beth understood her beautiful vision of Josh. She knew then that he had died, that he had left his mortal body. The vision assured her he lived, resplendent in his heavenly body, eternally secure.

"What happened?" she stared with tormented eyes.

Kerry and Bob likewise turned to David, aware only that something catastrophic had occurred. Kerry took her mother's hand on one side, Bob on the other, joining with David's for a circle of support.

David choked with the heartrending task of relating how Josh and Roberto's heroic mission to Langda had saved the missionary station and villages from almost certain annihilation. But it cost Josh his life.

From Roberto's description, David told of Josh's triumphant smile and the upraised arm of victory as he'd bounded onto the plane. And though incoherent from his mortal blow, Josh's dying words affirmed a *yes* to a sovereign God.

David was sensitive to spare Beth the details required for Roberto to return Josh's body to the States and held off approaching the arrangements necessary when the Lear jet landed in San Francisco. But he did relay exactly what Roberto said to him.

"David, tell Beth and Kerry and Bob, it is my honor to take care of anything they wish me to do. I will do it. Tell them that until I come," Roberto urged him.

Kerry sobbed, embracing her mother. Bob and David wept, enfolding the two women, binding them all together in a capsule of shared sorrow. Beth stood rigid with shock, a stream of tears flowing from eyes shut against the pain of her incomprehensible loss. They clung to each other for long, silent moments as in a vacuum of interminable grief.

Beth tore loose from the circle. "Why? Why, God?" she screamed. "What do You want from me?" she shouted angrily toward the ceiling. "Who are You, that You could allow Charles, then Josh, who both served You with their whole hearts, who both loved You with their last breaths, to die this suddenly, to be taken from me, without warning, without reason? Why?" she collapsed in weeping on the deep leather sofa.

Kerry kneeled over her, her own heart shattered with sorrow. Beth looked up at all of them as tears streamed down her cheeks. "What does God want from me?" she asked piteously. "Haven't I given over my whole life, my home, my heart to build up others' faith, to bring them hope and healing, desiring from the depths of my heart that they might fully understand God's love? How could a loving God permit us to suffer this pain and loss *twice*, in so short a time? Why?" She searched Bob's then David's face.

The men exchanged compassionate glances that affirmed she was too full of pain to receive comfort at that moment.

Shelby flew into Bob's study that afternoon, unannounced and without knocking, her eyes red and swollen. Her body shook with rage. "You lied to us. You said God would never leave us or forsake us. If He's my heavenly Father, He's no different from my earthly one—He's cruel, heartless, not to be trusted to keep His word." She stood opposing Bob, glowering. "You also said God is loving, kind—that nothing is impossible with Him! Why then, is Josh dead?" She plunked herself down in the chair opposite the desk, arms folded across her chest.

Bob walked around the desk to the chair next to hers. He took Shelby's hand, holding it gently in his. She began to cry. "I really loved him, Bob," she murmured. "Why Josh? Why do some of these terrible men who seduce and abuse their own daughters continue to live and go on ruining lives, while a godly man like Josh dies so senselessly?"

Bob answered, "The psalmist tells us that the way of the wicked will perish, that justice is God's job. Shelby, if you trusted Josh, trust also that he lived by the Word of God. Josh lives—only his body is gone. He's with God, and God loves *you*. Nothing any of us have ever told you about God is less than the truth."

"I'm confused, Bob," she whimpered. "Twice—no, many times— I've almost raised my hand, or come forward, or cried out to God when I'm alone, that I want to believe He is a loving, caring father, like Josh was to Kerry, like he was to me. I've watched and listened to Josh. Every time he opened his mouth love flowed from it.

"I've struggled, wanting to believe that Jesus is the Savior, the Son God sent to show me what love is about. But then I've hidden in shame, knowing I'm too damaged, not worth Christ's dying for me. I'm disqualified. Many times, I've been within a breath of saying yes to God. Now He lets Josh, this wonderful man, die. So I wonder . . . how can God love me, a nothing in His sight?"

"Everything God created is precious in His sight," Bob assured her. "Do you remember hearing me say God loved the world so much He sent His only Son to die, to cleanse us, free us from sin, bring us into a forever love relationship with Him? If you were the only one on earth, Jesus would still have loved you and died for you."

Shelby buried her face in her hands. "All the more reason I cannot comprehend that these tragedies fall on God's people."

Bob rubbed her hand. "We did not come into this life with God handing us a contract, saying 'You have this many days on earth.' We couldn't handle that information. Death is part of living—life is but a vapor, and then it's gone. Only God has the big picture, Shelby. Nothing He allows is without a purpose, nothing is wasted. We mourn for ourselves and our loss. But Josh is alive and with Jesus."

Tears filled her eyes again at the name of Josh. "I'm not ready for the big picture. But I do know the love I've received at Rosehaven could only begin with a very big God. Tell Beth I love her. . . ."

"You bet I will," Bob smiled tenderly.

In the midst of her own bereavement, Kerry consoled staff, patients, and friends with a strength not her own. She amazed herself—or rather God did. Too many times in her life she'd felt weak when she needed strength, or worse yet, angry. Now, her own encouragement came in comforting others as she centered her vision on the remembrance of Hope's memorial service, the glorious inspiration of faith her adopted mother's "Graduation Day" into eternal life personified.

She called up the memory of sunshine spilling over summer's yellow roses in the little church; the Scripture from the service that gave thanks to God, who gives victory over death through Jesus Christ. "Therefore . . . be steadfast, immovable, always abounding in the work of the Lord, knowing that your labor is not in vain in the Lord."

The words meant more today than they did then, for she saw how naturally they intertwined with the joy of Josh and Hope Sterling's lives. She purposed that every thought and word about Josh's life would glorify God and not be squandered in questioning the Almighty. And above all, Kerry purposed to keep her faith strong enough to lift up Beth's.

Her adopted parents had passed on, her birth parents were absorbed in sorrow, and she marveled at God, how He'd interwoven the provisions He'd made for her life before she was born. She could easily have been a statistic, one of the millions of aborted babies who'd died before they'd been born. But God, in His infinite love, chose a mother whose sacrificial love transcended every thought of self. He'd given her adoptive parents who by application taught her the love of the heavenly Father. Incredibly, He'd transformed her biological father from all former thoughts of self to ultimate abandonment to loving God with his whole heart and soul.

As when holding a prism up to the light, the intricate facets of God's love and provision shimmered with the clarity of finely cut crystal. Did the crystal mourn for that which had been cut away? Or did it embrace the polishing grit of the Master's hand?

Kerry knew this was her appointed moment, her time to hold her mother up to the healing light of Jesus. To focus on the loss would divert her from that which would remain forever.

Beth sequestered herself in her suite, seeing only Kerry, Bob, the children, David, and Golda. She wanted to know the instant Roberto's jet landed in San Francisco, but no details about Josh's body. Bob and Kerry offered to assume the responsibility for his memorial service as well, and she gratefully accepted.

She made valiant attempts to pull her thoughts together, yet they scattered like crisp, dry leaves in a cold wind. From their suite, she'd stare into the heavens in the direction where she'd encountered the reassuring vision of Josh, hoping to see it again. Her body, heart, and soul felt numb, as though nothing existed, nothing was real, not even herself. While waiting for the vision she failed to comprehend even the beauty of the clouds.

In the evening Roberto slipped sadly into her room with Kerry beside him. "*Bella Rosa* . . . I came as quickly as I could. My heart, too, is breaking."

"Roberto," Beth jumped to her feet, releasing a torrent of tears upon his shoulder. "Sit here, and tell me of every moment you were with Josh, what he did and said, everything—up to the smile. I can't bear to know about the last."

The memorial service for Josh overflowed the ballroom with Rose-haven's bounty of garden roses, masses of floral arrangements, and friends who came to honor his life.

"He was dearly loved," Beth sobbed to Kerry as she noted the people. "I know God will help me through this day, somehow. It comforts me to see Shelby, Trent, Rochelle, Howard, Allyson, and all the others who became Christians because of Josh's effect upon their lives."

With misty eyes, Bob told the people, "Our hearts are heavy today as we grieve the loss of our beloved Josh. He had but one desire in life and that was to share God's love, as a husband, father, friend, in the mission field, and with whomever he met. In the likeness of Christ, he lived that others might have newness of life.

"He listened and followed Jesus' Great Commission—to go into the outermost places of the world. He touched those of us who walk on seemingly ordinary paths with the meaning of extraordinary love.

"Josh also listened and followed Jesus' parable of the lost sheep and became the shepherd who left the realms of comfort and security to minister to Ben and one isolated group of humanity in the jungles of Irian Jaya.

"John 15:13 says, 'Greater love has no one than this, than to lay down one's life for his friends.'"

Roberto smothered a sob, and Kerry took and held his hand.

"Dear ones, we grieve for our loss, but not for Josh, who like the apostle Paul would say today, 'For me, to live is Christ, and to die is gain,' for like Paul he would be hard pressed from both directions, 'having a desire to depart and be with Christ, which is far better' or to remain on in the flesh for our sakes.

"Finally, let me assure you Josh is still smiling, and the resurrected Christ has taken away the sting of death. I think back on a conversation we had regarding death one day. He laughed and said, 'If I had my druthers, I'd die with my boots on, somewhere in the mission field.'

"And now may these words of Jesus from the gospel of John chapter 14, bring peace and comfort to your hearts. 'Let not your heart be troubled; you believe in God, believe also in Me. In My Father's house are many mansions; if it were not so, I would have told you. I go to prepare a place for you,' and a few verses on, 'that where I am, there you may be also.'

"Yes, Josh is still laughing, walking, talking with Jesus, the Master of many mansions. Let us pray. . . ."

When her baby died, and her father, and Hope, and even Charles, Beth received the words of God's truth such as she'd heard from Bob, and used them to comfort others. Not now. She couldn't. She didn't understand why. She just couldn't. While tears streamed down her face, she felt incapable of uttering more than, "Thanks for your love . . ." to those who offered condolence.

Shelby approached them with swollen, searching eyes. "Go to her," Beth urged Kerry. "She needs you."

Kerry hesitated, but Beth's eyes insisted. She took Shelby aside.

"I'm—I'm perhaps unforgivingly selfish," Shelby stammered, "but I have to know, because of Josh. Do you think God could work as lovingly and meaningfully in my life as He did in his?"

Kerry threw her arms around Shelby, smiling through her tears. "Yes—yes, of course. He welcomes every willing heart."

"How can I know Christ the way Josh did?"

"You invite Him to come into your life. I'll tell you how to do it, right now. We'll find a quiet place."

"Can we go into the Tea House? Somehow I've always looked for God there. It's tranquil, filled with peace."

"Yes, of course," Kerry took her hand. They went in to pray, and when they'd finished, Shelby's face glowed with a light Kerry had never seen there before.

Standing in the doorway to leave the Tea House, Shelby beamed, "I'm ready to step out and become that new person in Christ, the one Josh promised I could be. I want all the old garbage, the old hate for my father, the old wounds to pass away. I want to experience this 'newness of life,' and to share it with others."

"How about sharing it with me?" Trent smiled, waiting a few feet away. "I watched you two coming over here and know you've always been drawn to the Tea House, Shelby. I kept my distance but followed because I've been praying for you. I knew this time would come someday, and I praise God I was near when it did."

Shelby held out her hand, but Trent opened his arms.

"Many people were praying for me, I think," Shelby smiled, welcoming his embrace. "I'm glad one of them was you. Thanks. I feel like I've just graduated, or done something worth celebrating!"

"You have and we should! Let's sit in the Tea House a while and discuss this 'new life,' and then maybe go to dinner," Trent suggested.

"Yes, let's," Shelby glowed. "Suddenly, the whole world looks brighter, except I'll miss Josh terribly, Kerry. But would you tell Beth for me that Josh and Jesus have turned my life around? I know it! I can already feel it! I am that new creation!"

Kerry put her arms around Shelby and Trent, her eyes smiling through her long, dark lashes. "It will take you a little longer to appreciate what a blessing that will be to Beth. I'll tell her, and God's blessings on you both."

As Bob and Kerry bid the last guests goodbye, Beth said, "You're a great comfort to me, Roberto. Your generosity, in ways too vast to count, consoles me more than you can know."

"I only wish it was different—that I had brought Josh back to you, alive," he said sadly.

"It was not yours, or mine, to control," Beth sighed again. "Maria is very generous in her understanding. Please tell her I appreciate your time away from her to meet the needs of Ben, Josh, me, and the family."

"She is gracious in all ways. I will tell her. But I will stay, until you say to me, 'I do not need you anymore, Roberto.' Only then will I go."

Over the days and weeks, hundreds of letters and telegrams of condolence inundated the mail deliveries to Rosehaven. They poured in from old college classmates, missionary pilots and their families, the congregation from the little church in San Jose, working associates of Hope's from Stanford Med Center, past patients of Rosehaven. They conveyed a common message: Christians said that the joy of knowing Josh was his modeling of Christlikeness along with his lightheartedness. Others said he brought out the best in them by his encouragement—and the same strong cord abounded, steadfast, immovable, throughout his life. San Francisco and local newspapers contacted Rosehaven for the family's preference for memorial bequests. As a result, thousands of dollars in contributions were made to the New Hope Center downtown for counseling the less affluent.

Merribelle called, making superfluous overtones about a major gift to the center, and while the phones were going wild, she somehow cajoled Becky into letting her see Beth.

"She's mah dearest friend in the world," she wailed, "and Ah'm remiss if Ah'm not allowed to console her after this horrible catastrophe," she pleaded in sad, sugary tones.

Within two days following Josh's memorial services, Merribelle crashed into Beth's time of bereavement. They had not seen each other since before the earthquakes, or talked since the telephone conversation when Merribelle rudely hung up at Beth's encouragement to get on with life.

In the midst of Roberto's retelling of the regard the missionary team had for Josh, Merribelle burst in. "Mah heart cries for you, deah. Ah can't believe the sorrow you've been through ovah the years! You have had more than your share."

Roberto arose, standing protectively over Beth though she could not see his dark eyes flashing in indignation at Merribelle's insensitive timing and comments.

"Mah problems have been minute in comparison to your heartaches. Ah've never asked God for anything. Oh, mah husband's never been madly in love with me, the way yours have, but he's still livin' and breathin' and so are mah ungrateful children. Pitiful as we are, we're still a family. I have to ask you, Beth deah—where is your God now?"

Beth paled under the unprovoked attack, appalled that this woman she'd prayed for, cared deeply about, worked diligently with in the name of charity and good will, could so mercilessly descend upon her at this most vulnerable point in time. *Where is your God now?* The question burned in Beth's heart.

"He will never leave me or forsake me," Beth answered weakly.

Roberto's dark eyes flashed at Merribelle. "You have no love in your heart, and so you will never know where God is. You will never find Him, for you ask only out of demand that He come to you while you scoff at Him. That will never be. God have mercy on you."

"Well, Ah nevah! Who does this foreigner think he is, tawkin' to me that way?" Merribelle demanded of Beth.

"One who loves God and hopes you'll listen, as I have done through the years," Beth courageously replied.

"Humph," Merribelle turned to Beth.

Beth gasped in hurt and disbelief at the viciousness of this one who professed loving friendship over several decades.

"Count Cabriollini is a true friend, who has stood by me through the years. Please excuse me." Beth stood to leave the room, determined to retain her composure. She trembled with emotion, stunned by Merribelle's hostile, goading spirit.

"*Scusi, Signora.* It is best you leave. Beth must rest now."

"Well, it's hardly necessary to tell me. It's obvious mah friendship is no longer desired!"

After she'd left, Beth explained, "Merribelle wasn't always so bitter, Roberto."

"I can see, she has spent too many years running from God. She is, as they say, at the end of her rope."

"There was a time when I'd hoped desperately she'd turn around. And now I feel powerless to try to help her," Beth sighed.

Responsibility, commitment, dedication to the task at hand had represented the themes of Beth's life. Any action toward a given direction on her part now seemed as that of a puppet controlled by unseen strings. Yet the strings lay limp, idle, doing nothing.

"I think I've lost my faith in God to sustain me," she confessed to Bob one afternoon in the rose garden. "I'm grasping for any analogy that fits. I feel like a ship without a rudder, adrift, content to let you and the others take the helm and direct the course."

"Think of it as a time to seek shelter in a quiet harbor," Bob suggested, "and let the journey go on without you for a while."

"That's an unfamiliar role for me," she admitted, "but I'll try."

Roberto encountered her sitting above the high knoll at dusk. "You are here, alone with your memories. What are you thinking, *Bella Rosa*?"

"You were right, many years ago, in saying love is too demanding, especially God's. Yet whether it's human or divine, love shakes one loose from following one's chosen path, it gathers one unto itself—for its own purposes. It kneads you until you are pliant, molds you like clay in the likeness of itself if you allow it, and demands all you possess. Roberto, I never imagined I could say, think, or feel such a thing—but I have no more to give. Love of God and love of others have cost more than I have. I am empty. Hollow. Useless," she said dispassionately.

"I cannot accept that. It is not you. In time, it will be different."

Beth stared blankly down the corridor of yew trees, beyond the wedding garden, the Tea House, the pools, over to the guest cottages, the gardens, to the mansion.

"Rosehaven has been part of my very being, as the Villa is for you," she said. "Charles and I breathed life into the raw materials of wood, stone, and glass, every tree and rose bush, not as a monument to ourselves but in thanks to God and to be shared with others. And believing in Charles's vision, that it was created for even higher purposes, Josh and I again breathed new life into providing a sanctuary and place of healing for hurting hearts. Rosehaven has been my home, my life, my joy, the gift of all I am and possess to those who entered in search of hope."

She looked directly into Roberto's compassionate face. "It torments me now to admit that everything I see reminds me not of what is, or what is yet to be, but of my loss. Frankly—this time I don't feel I have the heart to go on."

"Oh, *Bella Rosa*. It is all the love you have given away that makes you a truly beautiful woman. You have given freely, with no expectation, and received much love in return. But sometimes not, and when you were rewarded only with disappointment, you kept on giving. I think you cannot stop being who you are."

He paused, weighing whether to expose his thoughts. "I am different. I have sought only love's peace and love's pleasure. It was a seasonless existence, and *si*, I have laughed, but not all of my laughter like Josh, and cried, but not all of my tears—like you have. I have lived, lavishly, but on the surface. I too have given profusely of my wealth—but seldom of my substance or my heart—except to you—too late. I know what it is to feel hollow inside."

The thought flashed through Beth's mind—*Has he given Maria only his admiration and respect, and withheld his heart?*

He was saying, "Now it is different, since I've given my heart to Christ. Willingly, I know the pain of too much tenderness, for I know Jesus chose the ultimate crown of love at His crucifixion. Whatever God asks of me, I have prayed He will help me do it.

"*Bella Rosa*, I have worried about you, and talked with David. He tells me you are grief-stricken, and this is natural for you to feel this way. It is a process, which you already know.

"But now it is I who remind you," his eyes pleaded sympathetically for her attention, "God will never leave you or forsake you. In your heart you know it is true; in your darkest hour He understands your broken heart. He walks with you—as I do."

Only a muted "thank you" escaped her lips beyond the tightness in her throat. Through a fog of numbness she faintly heard the Voice she'd heard many times before, implying complete adequacy in joy or sorrow: "Be still and know that I am God."

17

I t is time I think of going home," Roberto expressed to Kerry a
week later at breakfast. "I have done all I can here. I've repeated
many times to your mother everything I knew of Josh's last week of life
and the brief period we were together. I do not wish to overstay my
welcome."

"You could never do that, Papa. Those details are a comfort only
you can provide. In David's opinion, this phase of her grief is not unusual.
It seems so to us because she's perpetually been the strong comfort-giver.
I'm drenched in my own sorrow, but to see her depressed is an even greater
heartbreak. It will take time. . . ."

"But surely you've been gone far longer than you anticipated. Did
you say your pilot is staying in San Francisco, waiting for you?"

"That is no matter, and let us say it is a little 'all expense-paid
vacation' for Emilio. I take care of him handsomely—he is not in a hurry.
Beth said something days ago that persists in my mind, and causes me to
seek your advice, *per favore.*"

"What is that?" Kerry asked, touched by the gentleness in his voice.

"She said with much sadness—that which was dear to her at Rosehaven now only serves to remind her of her loss. She cannot bear it, and
that is why I think she stays to herself, living in the past.

"This is what I want to know—would you judge it improper if I
should invite her to come to Lake Como? She will have her own suite of
rooms in the Villa, total privacy and freedom to come and go as she wishes,
my chauffeur to drive her about, but I will be nearby to watch over her. I
believe it would be a good thing. . . ."

Kerry caught her breath, avoiding eye contact, uncertain of what he
would read into her stunned expression, for she didn't know herself.

Her thoughts flashed back to the day of Hope's memorial service. The hurt and anger she felt in learning that Josh was going to the mission field in Thailand so soon after left her devastated. She'd failed to comprehend his valid need to get his life in focus after Hope's years of cancer. Beth had walked hand in hand with Kerry through their shared sorrow, and now only a few years later, their grieving was for Josh. If Beth went to Italy, Kerry would again suffer a double loss.

Tears welled in her eyes, as deep and dark and brown as the ones that searched them for an answer. She kissed her father's cheek, silently thanking God for him. "I agree, and think you should ask her. You have my blessing."

"*Scusi*, I forgot to say, I of course wish you to come also. That would be the proper thing. And, and . . . and the children if you like," he stammered. "I think your mother would not come by herself."

"Oh Papa, you are right! She wouldn't. I didn't think it through." Her mind raced on. "But Rosehaven has been short-staffed without Josh, and everyone's pitched in to cover the administrative responsibilities. Beth is the key figure and I don't know who will take her place, but she can't cope with that now anyway, then if I went . . . hmm, that would take some doing.

"But to invite the children—you are gracious beyond belief! I don't think so. I remember pictures of the Villa, and all that marble wouldn't look too spiffy smudged with little handprints. I'll talk to Bob. We'll pray about it and give you an answer as soon as we can."

"I will say nothing until you tell me," he promised.

Bob walked out to the tennis courts as David and Roberto finished a set. David flicked the perspiration from his forehead. "The Count is a true competitor—he got me again today. I've had to squeeze my schedule to get my exercise and these games in, but Roberto, I'm going to miss you—and not only on the tennis court."

"*Grazie*, David," Roberto patted him on the back. "Bob, you have an answer for me?"

"Yes. Kerry and I gave your invitation top priority today, first confirming with David and Golda that getting away now was right for Beth; second, that we could keep Rosehaven operating smoothly. We'll all have to wear many hats, but it's an excellent idea. Go for it!"

"Kerry, would you have tea with me this afternoon?" Beth phoned her suite. "Only without the children. I've something to discuss with you."

"Of course, I'll see you around four."

They met in Beth's suite. Kerry sat next to her by the window.

"Josh was my solid rock. Now the rock is gone. Everything I see, say, and do mirrors how I'm floundering. I can't get it all together. I've felt like a displaced person. I can't bear to be here, but for once, I can't imagine I'd find peace in Monterey either—I fear that would compound the loss of both Charles *and* Josh. I've thought about visiting Mum, but she'd take on the burden of my pain and sorrow and that's too heavy to put upon her with the heart condition she's developed. I've always found a way to comfort others—now I feel useless, even to myself.

"Maybe running away isn't the answer," Beth continued. "Perhaps I should stay here and grind it out, spend my time counseling with David and force myself to get back in the race. I don't know what to do." Tears stung her eyes. She paused to wipe them away and went on.

"Before I spend another minute considering Roberto's kind invitation, I must know how the rest of you feel. Especially you, and if you would go with me. Otherwise, it is out of the question. I appreciated Roberto's judgment in discussing his suggestion with you before bringing it to me. He knows me well, doesn't he?"

"Mother darling, through my whole life, Dad was my rock too. But only you can decide. I'd be delighted to go with you, and we can work it out. But in joy or in sorrow, God is our solid rock wherever we are. I've heard you counsel others that God will not allow more than one can endure. And you know better than anyone—the stages of overcoming grief cannot be programmed on a time schedule and they *are* real. Don't think of running away *from* life, rather of moving on *with it*. What do *you want* to do?"

"Therein lies the problem. I honestly don't know. I'm afraid I do think of going to Lake Como as 'running away,' and I guess I want someone to tell me it's the right choice. When I talked to Roberto, I was confused—I never thought about how Maria might feel! Surely Roberto would discuss this with her before mentioning it to us. Did you ask him about Maria?"

"Yes—I thought of her right away. He said rather evasively as he has before, 'she is gracious, she will understand, it will not be a problem.' You and Maria are of like temperament and interests. The two of you could have a sweet relationship."

"Surely Roberto must be as confident about that as he is of Maria. I'll talk to David, and yes, my darling, I'll pray about it. I'm grateful you brought my focus back to God—and for the spiritually wise woman I have for a daughter."

"I've had excellent models." Kerry opened her arms and they held one another in a long, close embrace. "I'm going to see what my children are up to. I've never been away from them, and the hardest part would be telling them goodbye."

Teddy and Angela clung to Kerry, not allowing her out of their sight from the moment she and Bob told them she was going away.

"I don't want you and Mommy to leave us, Gammybeth," Teddy sniffled. "I'll miss you," he cried.

"Miss you," Angela echoed, stretching out her arms for Beth to pick her up. The baby planted a big, wet kiss full on Beth's lips while her tiny body comically vibrated in the fervor of hugging her grandmother.

"I'll miss you, too, Papa," Teddy looked up at Roberto.

"Miss you, Pa-pa," Angela bent so far over she fell out of Beth's arms into Roberto's.

"*Addio*, little ones," he embraced the children. "You are precious to my heart."

Roberto waved *arrivederci*, Kerry blew kisses, and Beth stared straight ahead, struggling with her emotions as if in a daze, unable to see through her tear-filled eyes.

Emilio flew the Lear jet to Milan, and from there by Roberto's elegantly appointed Cessna to the Villa's private airstrip, where Renzo awaited them in the black limousine.

"Lake Como is infinitely more spectacular than Mother's description or photographs. It's been like a legend since I was a little girl, and now it's come alive," Kerry commented appreciatively of the lush green landscape.

"Welcome to my home," Roberto made an encompassing gesture as he assisted Beth and Kerry out of the limousine. Kerry gazed in awe down the drive past the cypresses that marched to the lake's edge. "I thought only Hawaii had water this blue, but then I've never been anywhere else. May I go see?" she asked, as Renzo began unloading the luggage.

"But of course, my home is your home, and I plan for you to have a *magnifico* holiday."

Roberto escorted them into the marble entry and through the grandeur of the halls to their suites. Beth expectantly glanced about for Maria, assuming she would appear to welcome them. When she could suppress her concern no longer, she commented, "I'm looking forward to seeing Maria."

"*Un momento, per favore*, you shall have a time to refresh yourselves. Then we shall gather on the terrace with something cool to drink, watch the splendor of the sun blending its enchanted colors over the lake, and we will talk together."

"Sit here," he motioned to Beth and Kerry in the late afternoon. "This is most difficult for me. You have both inquired kindly about Maria numerous times. I regret that the words would not come out of my mouth in January. I could not bring myself to it, and after that an opportune time did not present itself. It seemed inappropriate as these other unfortunate circumstances evolved. The only way to tell you—is to tell you. I have spoken nothing that is not true, and Maria is all that I said—beautiful, gracious, compassionate. She did not wish to marry me. She is not here."

Beth's eyes widened in astonishment. *How hurt he must have been! And to think he'd been carrying his own grief and considered it "inappropriate" to speak of in light of my sorrow,* she thought. It pierced her heart to remember Roberto's proud smile in announcing his engagement to Maria—and this kind, generous man laying his heart and the sharing of a fortune at her feet, only to be rejected. Questions swirled through her head, compelling her to ask, "Why did she change her mind? You two seemed very much in love."

"Do not think badly of her—she was correct in doing so."

Beth shook her head sadly, attempting to discern a chink in his composure and read his expressive eyes, yet they gave no clue to his heart. "I don't understand," she said softly.

"She wished to be loved for herself," he said without looking up.

Beth and Kerry virtually stopped breathing, waiting for him to explain.

"Did you not notice, Beth? Her hair, her eyes, her figure? When we returned from Christmas at Rosehaven, Maria wept. She said she would always think I was looking at her and seeing . . . someone else."

Immediately Kerry thought, *Yes, they resembled twin sisters.*

"I admire her greatly," Roberto said, "and she knew I *wished* to be in love with her but I am, ah—*transparent, si?* It would be a very terrible injustice. She immediately fled to Rome. I became literally ill for weeks that her heart was broken. I could not speak of it.

"We have reconciled our hurts and cherish our unique camaraderie. Maria values her friendships and is here in Lake Como with a family escaping the city for the season. She desires for all of us to be friends and sends her condolences. When you are ready, Beth, she wishes to have dinner with us and see you two again. Someday the right man will come to her, but it is not I."

Roberto's eyes probed theirs for affirmation. "My intent was not to deceive you," he pleaded with open palms. "Every day I thought I would say something while I was with you at Rosehaven, then each day's circumstances seemed worse than the day before. Forgive me, *per favore.*"

Beth's thoughts reverted to the day she learned she was pregnant with Kerry and consumed with the valid reasons why she couldn't tell Roberto or her parents. Then how impossible it became to divulge the circumstances to them, or to Charles, or anyone, and the consequence became years of secrets.

"There's nothing to forgive, Roberto, and haven't I been in a position to understand better than anyone?" Beth said sadly. "I'm sorry. We surely expected you and Maria to find a happy life together." Beth rose wearily from her chair, as though it required all her strength. "Excuse me. I'd like to go to my room for the evening."

Roberto shot a worried glance at Kerry. "*Buona notte, Bella Rosa.* I shall have something brought to your room."

"That won't be necessary, thank you. I'm not hungry."

"Rest well, Mother. Good night."

After Beth left, Kerry said to Roberto, "She's emotionally exhausted, Papa, and I'm sure she'll rest better here than any place in the world."

Roberto and Kerry remained on the terrace, watching the long black shadows of the cypress trees shimmering far out into the inky blue of the lake. They sat in silence for several minutes and still she found no words to acknowledge his relationship with Maria. She now understood his elusiveness at the mention of her name. Somehow, she must give the topic closure.

"I'm glad you and Maria have remained friends."

"It is best this way," he sighed.

Each day as Kerry urged Beth to enjoy the excursions Roberto had planned for them—drives around the lake area in the red Ferrari, picnics on the boat, outings of quiet beauty he thought she'd most enjoy—Beth would say, "You go ahead, perhaps I'll join you tomorrow."

Instead she'd lie alone in the sun by the edge of the lake, or occasionally sketch the rhododendrons as she'd done when she and Josh were there on their honeymoon trip, or sit on the terrace and stare into the clear blue sky. Kerry's greatest encouragement came the day she noticed Beth's Bible by the terrace lounge chair.

On their tenth day, and mostly out of courtesy before the end of their stay, Beth suggested to Roberto, "Whenever you would like to invite Maria to dinner, that would be lovely."

"*Si*, I will do it!"

"It is a good sign, that Beth is ready for company," Roberto later commented to Kerry. "Also I would like to invite Dr. Rossini from Milano, who wished to personally tell Beth of his great admiration for Josh. What do you think?"

"I'd hope she'd rise to the occasion. Meeting new people may help her emerge from her cocoon and gradually become social again."

"*Buono!*" Roberto reported triumphantly. "This will be wonderful evening."

Beth chose a silky dress of a light and flowery print, exhibiting a greater interest in what she wore than since they'd arrived. Amazingly, Maria's dress was similar in color and style, casual yet obviously couture. Roberto blinked in astonishment at their likeness to one another as Maria arrived, and she responded graciously to cover his awkward moment, extending a cordial hand to Beth.

"We are kindred souls, aren't we? I'm delighted to see you again," Maria smiled.

"Let us go into the drawing room," Roberto gestured. "The doctor should arrive *un minuto*. Emilio flew him from Milano and Renzo is bringing him."

Moments later, Roberto stood in the richly carved doorway of the Venetian tapestried walls of the drawing room. "May I present Signoras Beth Sterling and Kerry Daniels, and Signorina Maria Carducci . . . my dear friend, Dr. Carlo Rossini."

Maria's and the doctor's eyes met as though a magnetic force drew and held them together.

"*Buona sera*, it is my pleasure," he greeted the ladies, while his eyes remained riveted on Maria.

Dinner conversation flowed easily. Beth responded warmly to the sincerity of the doctor's respect for Josh and empathized with the loss of his wife and daughter killed in a ski resort accident in Switzerland. She discovered that Maria shared her love for the ballet and had seen Mum perform in Rome. Maria and Carlo drifted into their own dialogue, ascertaining friends they knew in common in Rome and Milano, unable to take their eyes off one another.

Near midnight Beth said, "Kerry and I leave the day after tomorrow at noon. I know she's missing the children, as I am. But Maria, whenever you are in the States, you are welcome to come to Rosehaven, and you as well, Dr. Rossini."

"I've no travel plans at present," Maria smiled, "but thank you. I'd be pleased to accept your kind invitation. I feel I've known you a long time, rather than a few hours here and there."

The next morning Kerry knocked on the door of Beth's room from her adjoining suite and entered at the faint bidding, "Come in, dear."

"I'm nearly packed, so we can drive to Lake Lugano. How are you doing? You don't look like you're ready to go anywhere today. Roberto's plans were designed to get your mind on relaxing with the gorgeous scenery." Kerry's face fell as she saw the tears in Beth's eyes. She dropped to her knees and wrapped her arms around her mother, putting her head on her shoulder.

"I can't get myself together, love. Isn't that stupid?" Beth looked tired. "I haven't even thought about packing," she answered listlessly.

"Then come with us, and I'll do it for you later."

"Um, no. I haven't the energy. Can't put one foot in front of the other."

"You haven't had any exercise, and you're not accustomed to lying around like this. This is the most beautiful place in the world to walk or bicycle. Or you could play tennis with Roberto."

"You and Roberto go to Lake Lugano. This is a precious time for the two of you."

Kerry objected. "We came here for a change from Rosehaven, a healing time for you. That's more important to Papa and me than anything."

"I suppose I just need time. . . ." Beth stared toward the lake.

"Time where—here or there?"

"Anywhere, or nowhere. I don't know. This is terrible to say, honey, but can you believe I dread to go home? I can't face it all yet, the staff and patients who are expecting me to be the paragon of faith and strength."

Kerry thought she hadn't heard correctly until she looked at Beth again and saw she meant it. *Oh, God, please open her ears and her heart to Your comfort, in the same way she's comforted others. We've got to go home, rather I do—to my children.*

"We'll not go to Lugano," Kerry said softly. "I'll be on the lake terrace. Why don't you come down in a little bit, for a swim or a walk?"

"I'll try," Beth sighed noncommittally.

In thirty minutes Beth dutifully appeared in deep pink linen walking shorts and shirt, her black hair tied back with a matching ribbon.

Kerry quickly closed her book and popped up from the lounge. *"Mama mia!"* she laughed. "Which way do you want to walk?"

"Makes no difference."

"Well then, come with me." Kerry led them up a flagstone walk bordered by Italian pines and fir trees, with bright pink azaleas contrasting the restful green landscape.

Kerry thought surely the delicate rose vines artfully twisting up a pine tree would evoke a comment of admiration from Beth. Yet she uttered not a word, walking silently and stoically beside her as the garden sloped dramatically up from the lake to the woods at the top of the hill.

Kerry stopped. "Mother, why don't you stay?"

"Stay where?"

"Here. You actually came alive at dinner last night with new people, generating new thoughts rather than recycling the worn-out ones. Today, contemplating going home, you're back in the doldrums. I'm going to quote your own words—'You must get outside of yourself'—and you did that last night. You're not ready to return to Rosehaven."

"What if Brenda Walker got hold of that!" Beth responded. "Think of the scandal it would create if I stayed here without you."

"Silly, Brenda received her due and you know it! You and Maria have the beginnings of a lovely friendship, and you can see what a comfortable relationship Roberto and she have. What if she stayed, too? Do I have your permission to discuss this with him?"

Beth mulled over the idea a few moments. A wide smile spread across her face. "I've heard there comes a time when parent and child experience a role reversal in care-giving but didn't think I'd come to that this soon. You may!"

"Maria thought it a most wonderful idea, Beth!" Roberto beamed after arranging it with her. "She adores the beauty of the Villa, also your new friendship, and has no problem extending her holiday. *Scusi*, but in two days I go to London and on to Paris. I must get back to business. You two ladies will have a *magnifico* time together.

"And for tonight, I will order chef to prepare his *speciale* veal in wine sauce and we will have a farewell dinner for Kerry and celebrate that you are staying!"

The following week Beth received a thick letter from Kerry.

My darling Mother,

The children still ask everyday when GammyBeth is coming home. They're satisfied, however, when I tell them you are "getting better," as they perceived that you were physically ill and showed greater concern than you realized when you were home.

All are delighted that Maria is a friend with whom you are getting out and having fun, but also one who knows and loves God and that you are finding strength and comfort in His Word together.

I couldn't tell you everything that has transpired at Rosehaven over the phone Sunday night and shall endeavor to limit this letter to less than book-length. I want you to see how the seeds you planted here have taken root and are growing strong. . . .

Shelby is blossoming—a totally different person than the suicidal girl you rescued, loved, nurtured, and brought back to life. She's doing well with her Master's studies, and seeks one of us when confronting a new facet of healing. She's consistently here for Wednesday Bible study. On Sunday mornings she sings robustly off-key with her whole heart and radiates a loveliness from inside her soul. We think she and Trent are falling in love!

Hear this! Shelby and Allyson's support organization for incest victims was featured on the evening news as a "success story." The Examiner followed up with an article in the Sunday magazine section lauding "victims helping victims" and said that their concepts of reaching out were derived from therapy and healing received at Rosehaven. Isn't it exciting (and refreshing) that the media is reporting the positive after the thrashing they gave us all?

Speaking of falling in love . . . Bob and I are more deeply in love than ever! Tragedy had its way of forcing us to focus on the things in our marriage that really matter, of not taking each other for granted, cherishing the little moments of life together, realizing they may be taken at any time.

I'm focusing my Bible study on "God's Plan for Husbands and Wives" and Bob and I have begun a program that we've extended to the community as well as to patients to restore marriage relationships. Bob is also centering on a series in his Sunday services on the restoration of the family as a unit. We've had excellent response and just last week went to holding two services.

Beth put the letter aside, closing tear-filled eyes. "Thank You, God," she whispered.

The next page read:

Mother dear, I know you're vitally interested in life at Rosehaven, and I want to affirm your vision, the heart you have for hurting people that transformed Rosehaven into a place of refuge. This truly is a sanctuary of renewed hope, and in the beauty of the gardens you planted they are discovering the love and grace of a sovereign God, new life in Christ, and healed relationships that seemed irreparably damaged.

So, my darling, I pray daily that as you rebuild your life you will take comfort that all you, and Charles, and Josh began will never die, but live on in an ever-widening circle of love.

I close with this further affirmation of Paul from Philippians 1:6: For I am "confident of this very thing, that He who has begun a good work in you will complete it until the day of Jesus Christ."

Enjoy your holiday. I love you.

Kerry

Beth folded the letter carefully and put it into her Bible. "I needed that. Help me to remember You're still at work within me, God, even when I can't see it," she whispered.

With the letter still in her Bible, Beth slipped into a swimsuit and gauze shirt, heading for the pool on the lake terrace to read it again.

She paused to admire a rose of an unfamiliar variety as one stops to speak to a friend. *The saying is true,* she thought as she held the ruffled face of the rose, *one's heart is nearer to God in the garden than anywhere else on earth.*

The deep greens of the forested hills that rose steeply above the villa reflected turquoise in the smooth waters. In them rippled the images of the Shelbys, Allysons, Trents, and Marys who had come shattered, buffeted, and bruised by the snares of the world and every form of the common ills that twist the mind and soul.

Beth imagined droplets of the sparkling waters on their shining faces rising up through the lake's surface, their bodies emerging cleansed and whole and walking with resolve into a victorious life. A thrill of exhilaration flowed through her, releasing a spurt of energy that lifted her up from the lounge. Arching her lithe body, she dove smoothly into the pool.

With each vigorous lap, she felt her increased heart rate pumping out the toxins of lethargy she'd wallowed in for weeks. Slowing her tempo, she flipped over in back strokes, diving down and coming up over and over, as playful as a dolphin. She cupped the water into her hands, holding them as high as her head, and took delight in watching the drops trickle and splash like liquid crystals.

Energized, Beth stepped out of the pool, her eyes sweeping the wonders of the peaceful village across the lake and her secluded surroundings.

"It is good to be alive," she inhaled, with an emerging awareness that her present grieving for Josh had been further stirred by the deep, dormant pain of the past—first with her baby, then her father, and Hope, and Charles. Perhaps in her courageous resolve to console others in this series of deaths, she'd anesthetized areas that still required healing and had moved on too quickly. *God only knows,* she thought. *Looking back isn't what matters now—moving forward does.* She inhaled deeply once more, lifting her head heavenward, "Thank You, God—I'm beginning to feel progress at last!"

Smoothing on sun-screen, she settled back on the lounge, luxuriating in the warmth of the sun. With closed eyes, all the Shelbys, Allysons, and Trents filed past again, returning to Rosehaven for counsel and encouragement. They'd have new issues or former ones not completely resolved. This was their refueling station, spiritually and emotionally. And rather than being temporarily pumped up by collecting fruitless worldly treasures, they'd go get back in the race—but for imperishable rewards.

With closed eyes she smiled up at the sun warming her to the heart. In that peaceful moment, the Voice returned . . . "Be still and know that I am God."

This time she answered . . . "Yes, God—I'm listening."

18

"Beth, when I was a little girl, I longed for a sister," Maria confided over lunch in the quaint village cafe.

"I imagined her as someone to huddle with on dark and stormy nights when the lightning would flash across my room, who would understand my every fear and feeling. And especially after the murder of my parents, in the convent I would cry at night for someone to hear my heart, like we are hearing each other's now. I must tell you, you are a special person in my life—for many reasons."

"I also felt lonely being an only child," Beth consoled her, "but I could share *everything* with my dearest friend, Hope. I moved to London from San Francisco when I was ten, and we wrote copious letters. Her death a few years ago left a tremendous void in my life. We may call many people friends when they're actually only a step above acquaintances, but a friendship like that is one to cherish.

"Maria, I appreciate your sensitivity. In fact, I consider our friendship incredible! And with both of us loving God, we are sisters in the Lord," Beth smiled.

Maria nodded in agreement, "Like you, I know many people, but my deepest friendships are with three or four individuals whom I most admire. Roberto is one of those, and you are becoming another. And perhaps Carlo. . . ."

The thought flashed through Beth's mind of how Maria could this matter-of-factly speak of Roberto as an "admired friend," rather than the man she came within a day of marrying. Her devotion was obvious, but was she still in love with him? During the past month they'd plumbed one another's spiritual and philosophical depths, yet each woman was covertly reserved that one door to her heart marked Roberto, padlocked and private, distanced and venerated with awe by the other.... But now—what about Carlo?

"Carlo?" Beth echoed with interest. "You both appeared quite enamored that night at dinner," Beth said with a twinkle in her eyes.

"He has invited me to Milano and asked if you would like to accompany me. But first—what do you think of this man?"

Beth suddenly felt the intimacy of two schoolgirls discussing their first date for the prom, which was another experience she'd missed at that age.

"My first thoughts, even before meeting him, were that he is an extraordinary humanitarian to leave the luxuries of his practice in Milan, or Milano as you Italians say, for the primitive jungles of Irian Jaya. I cannot begin to imagine what Roberto paid him, but what amount could be enough? So beyond a caring human being, he must also be an adventurer. Then, he has the reputation of being an excellent physician. We know he is family-oriented and grieving the deaths of his wife and only child, so perhaps he's lonely. He's an excellent conversationalist, is maddeningly attractive, and couldn't take his eyes off of you all through dinner. Will that do for an answer?" Beth laughed.

"*Mama mia!* I did not realize your talents included such an analytical mind. One more thing—I wonder where he stands with God? That is important to me. Do you know?"

"Roberto told me of their spiritual conversation on the plane moments after Josh died. He's a deeply tender man. He's searching. Roberto promised he would tell Carlo of Jesus and bring him a Bible, explaining the holy Word of God as Josh did for him."

Beth amazed herself, realizing she could speak of Josh without tears in her eyes.

"Carlo is Chief of Staff at his hospital and on a heavy schedule that will not permit him to be out of the city for the next two weeks. That is why he invited me—us—to come there. I would like that. Will you join me?"

Beth pondered the question. "Is he asking out of courtesy to me, or to make you comfortable in accepting?"

"Both, I am sure."

"Would you go if I didn't?" Beth asked.

"I would not enjoy leaving you alone. The servants are there, of course, but—"

"Maria," Beth spoke softly, "we're being candid, remember? Would you go to Milano if I did not?"

"Yes. I would. If you think it is proper."

Beth grinned and placed her hand on Maria's across the checkered tablecloth. "I can't imagine you'd allow anything *improper*, for you live by God's standards, which the world's viewpoint unfortunately considers irrelevant. But it's time you experienced a little romance."

"This is true." Maria's eyes sparkled. "I left the convent five years ago and went into shock at the immorality in the world. Through all of our getting acquainted I've told you I enjoy designing the *Maria* line of handbags for Carducci, my family's leather empire, but I do not have to work. Somewhere in God's plan for my life, I hope there is a husband. I am almost forty."

"And I'm pushing fifty, so listen to your *old* friend."

"*Incredibile!* You do not look a minute older than I do. But what will you do while I am gone?"

"Maria, you're a love. Mum's been on my mind. I've longed to be with her, yet my emotions have been too fragile. I'm more stable now and I think her doctor's going to give her a pacemaker. I want to be there when he does."

"Then you go to your mama and I shall go to Milano. Yes?"

"Oh, yes!" Beth laughed, picking up the lunch check. "I'll phone her immediately."

"Cheerio, love! How marvelous to hear your voice," Mum answered when Beth called. "I've scurried to the post every day for even a snippet of a letter, but I'm a dreadful correspondent, too. Kerry's been superb to ring me up and keep me apprised. Are you bearing up better now, darling?"

"Much better. Those first months were a blur. Forgive me, Mum, for neglecting you. Up until early June I felt emotionally like you did physically during your encounter with pneumonia last Christmas—utterly miserable company."

"You know you've had my prayers and deepest sympathy, love. I shall never forget Josh, his kindness, and his smile. Be assured that time will bring healing, and life goes on, but I'll miss your dear father until the day I die."

"And so will I. Now, Mum, about your heart condition—is the doctor going to put in a pacemaker?"

"Mercy! It's already done. I'm feeling fit as a fiddle. Simply marvelous!"

"Mum, that's *wonderful*. I'm greatly relieved. Perhaps you're ready for a visitor? I'm considering coming over."

"That would be . . . lovely." Her mother sounded hesitant.

"Is this not a good time?" Beth quickly responded, not wanting to impose on her mother's plans.

"It's a fine time, except—I've made some plans." Silence followed. "Darling," her voice brightened. "You could join me!"

"Where, Mum?" Beth delighted in her mother's spirit.

"I've been fascinated by a marvelous travel article. There's a superb *auberge*, a small hotel, in the south of France in Provence, not far from Marseilles. From there we shall run the gamut of that fascinating area, as I abhor tours and rummaging about in one's valise for weeks. It sounds naughty, but they tout it as 'the landscape that seduced the Impressionists.' Hold on, love, I have the article right here. Listen to this. 'Roses climb upon ancient stone walls green with the patina of years. Where summer fields are filled with a riot of colors; purple irises on slender stalks—sunflowers bending in the wind.' It rambles on about herbs sprouting in parks along country paths while lavender carpets the valley like spilled wine. It's the landscape that immortalized painters such as Cezanne, Matisse, Van Gogh, and Chagall. Doesn't it sound luscious? What a pity you can't see the glorious photos. Picture it in the vicinity of Arles and Avignon. Bring your paintbox, love."

"When are you going? Have you already made the reservations?"

"Next week, from July 1st through 15th. And the old gentleman who has owned the *auberge* forever, and took my reservation himself, will be ecstatic to learn I'm bringing an *artiste*. I'll have Edward fax the article and information to the Villa, and we'll be romping in Provence on the first. Cheerio, love."

"Mum, wait, don't hang up! I need to know how you're getting there, where you make connections, etc." Beth's head swam with questions about her aging mother traveling alone.

"Not a problem, love. Air travel from London to the south of France is but a hop, skip, and a jump. The *auberge* will send a motor car for us. I've trooped all over Europe in my day, so not to worry. *Au revoir, mä cherie!* I'll meet you in Marseilles."

As Beth advanced toward the British Airways Passenger Arrival area she heard, "Over here, love!" She ran toward Mum, who was by far the most stylish and sprightly eighty-ish woman in sight.

"You look smashing, Mum. Oh, it's been too long since I've had a hug!" She held her close, then at arm's length to admire her again. "You are simply wonderful to arrange this adventure for us!"

"Well, my heart is good, my knees are holding up, and my head still works, so we shall have a lovely time. And you look like my Beth again. My heart ached for you, dear. But we shall put heartaches behind us and get on with our jolly holiday. Righto?"

"Righto," Beth hugged her again and picked up her tote. "The information you had faxed was perfect. My luggage is already in your driver's van and he's fetching yours from the baggage claim. We'll meet him at the loading zone."

As they drove, a crumbled marquis's chateau came into view a few miles from thriving villages, and a medieval castle sheltered a burgeoning artist's colony.

Walls of pale butterscotch-yellow, worn from generations of polishing with wax and turpentine, greeted them inside the eighteenth-century *auberge* with a soft, peaceful glow.

In their rooms were gondola-shaped beds, 300-year-old wardrobes, Oriental rugs, and teardrop chandeliers. Thick, snowy white towels hung in the pink and green marble bathrooms.

When the grand-nephew of the elderly owner had brought in their bags and left grinning with the gratuity Beth pressed into his hand, Mum gazed about the room that was polished, elegant, and homey all at once. Her eyes twinkled. She looked enormously pleased with herself.

"It exceeds my imagination, Mum," Beth commented, contemplating the inn's azure pools set against a background of odd rock formations and ancient caverns.

"The vaulted dining room is said to be the heart of the inn and the cuisine exquisite, with vegetables grown on their own farm."

"Everything is exquisite, but especially sharing it with you, Mum. This is what dreams and memories are made of. I see the price is exquisite, too. You made the arrangements—allow me to take care of the bill."

"You'll do nothing of the kind! You won't take this pleasure from me, so I jolly well shan't have another word on the subject."

"Yes, Mum," Beth bit her tongue like a small child being chastised, hiding her amusement.

"But thank you, love," Mum patted her hand.

Over tea on a relaxed afternoon after days of touring the sights of the sun-drenched countryside, Beth finally had an opportunity to ask, "Tell me about Hampstead and your friends at the Spaniard's Inn. Do you still 'hang out' at the pub about this time of day?"

"That is one of the glories of English tradition, while concurrently a bore at times. I do believe it's a petulant paragon of old age to enjoy one's past with essentially greater relish than the present. It's quite an odious sign to flit away one's time in the pub day after day and rehash the same old yarns. The young neighbor family that comes to take tea with me from across the heath is always popping over with something riveting to share with me. But one pastime I refuse to indulge in if I feel blue is the pity party. I posted a note on my refrigerator that says 'Old age is not for sissies.' Believe me, my dear, it takes courage."

"Planning this trip by yourself took courage. You didn't have any friends you intended to ask?"

"Goodness, no. They were petrified they'd take a spill or have their valises ripped off. I said, 'Let's live a little,' and they kept on rocking and said, 'Go right ahead, my deah,'" Mum giggled. "But see, love, it turned out precisely the way the good Lord intended and we had our 'stolen moments' together after all."

"Next time you come across an irresistible travel article, count on me," Beth commented with an appreciative glance about the rooms the morning they checked out of the *auberge*.

Mum took Beth's hands as they parted at the airport in Marseilles. "Are you quite certain you won't come home to London with me?"

"Maria's waiting for me in Milan. I talked with her this morning. She's dying to have me meet her Carlo again—I think she hears bells ringing. She wants to show me the shops, too. I only brought clothes for a two-week stay. Why don't you come to Milan and on to Lake Como?"

"But love, my luggage is heading for London—I'd best go with it."

"Of course. Thanks for the fun—and the memories. Love you, Mum," Beth waved. "I'll see you soon in London."

"Buona sera," Roberto surprised Beth and Maria with outspread arms on the driveway. As Renzo opened the trunk to unload the boxes from Milano's boutiques he explained, "It is *magnifico* to know I have my friends here when I return to Como—so I accomplished my business in half the time," he grinned.

"I'm embarrassed to admit, I didn't even inquire about the nature of your trip. *Scuzi*," Beth apologized and Roberto smiled at her use of Italian. "Tell us about it. And how sweet of you to come out to greet us."

"I arrived two hours ago and am most gratified," he flashed a smile. "The Cabriollini Collection, the most complete in the world of eighteenth-century Italian art, will go on world tour in the fall. The works are catalogued and the schedule of art museums is finished. Never has it been done so expediently, but never have I been as motivated," he beamed. "And you have a letter from Kerry waiting for you, *Bella Rosa*."

"Wonderful! I'd hoped there would be. Congratulations on the arrangements for the tour. But I've never seen this Collection—is it here in the Villa now?"

"*Si*," he smiled simply.

"And would you show it to me?"

"But of course. I am anxious to do so," he grinned honestly. "Oh and here is the letter."

Beth quickly began reading.

My dear Mother,

> *When we call on Sunday evening you can tell us about your trip with Mum to Marseilles and Milan.*
> *We have exciting news that merits a letter. . . .*
> *The success rate at Rosehaven is becoming a model for other resident counseling centers that are rising up across the country. Suddenly, we're the experts!*

As a facet of her Master's studies and especially for the patients' encouragement, Shelby has spoken to the group therapy sessions. Her theme for healing is "getting outside of yourself."

And guess what? They are! You would be thrilled with the sense of community that is being perpetuated at Rosehaven, rather than the "each person surviving for him- or herself" mentality. Our patients were inspired by the large sum of the gifts received in honor of Josh to assist in the support of the New Hope Center in the city.

They were further motivated by the excellence of Rosehaven's program and their individual results. Two of our "Type A" corporate presidents developed a perpetual fund for patients who wish to participate in expanding the level of services available to the moderate- to lower-income groups through the New Hope Center.

Trent is here frequently, not for therapy but to come alongside Shelby (where he wants to be anyway!) in giving testimony in forgiveness. He coined the name for the "people helping people" project: The Rosehaven Guild for the Support of the New Hope Center.

They drafted a letter that Becky will send to all former patients inviting them to join the Guild. Some who demonstrate the proper skills have asked to be trained in lay counseling and volunteered to serve at New Hope! Isn't that amazing?

Our patients' backgrounds have typically been from the elite—obviously soaring above the average to have attained their present status in the world. David tells them the ability to live "outside of themselves" will be their highest accomplishment in arriving at wholeness and happiness.

Mother—Bob, David, Golda, the entire staff, and I want you to know this is the most rewarding purpose for our lives we could ever hope or dream of! Once again, we want you to remember . . . it all began with God at work in you, and we exult in the glory of God. . . . Listen to how appropriate Romans 5:3–5 is:

"We also glory in tribulations, knowing that tribulation produces perseverance; and perseverance, character; and character,

hope. Now hope does not disappoint, because the love of God has been poured out in our hearts by the Holy Spirit who was given to us."

Precious Mother—may you bask in your well-deserved time of rest and healing, daily abounding in God's love poured out within your heart through the Holy Spirit.

I love you,
Kerry

Overwhelmed, Beth closed her eyes and felt humble tears of joy spilling down her face. She remembered how in the past her formerly free spirit would have danced triumphantly in fulfillment of her heart's desire for Rosehaven. At the moment, though, she sought only to retreat into a quiet haven of intimacy with God.

"Excuse me," she murmured in a quivering voice to Roberto and Maria, confident of their unspoken gift of the freedom of privacy. She kissed each of them on the cheek, exiting with her letter toward the vine-covered arches on the terrace.

Beth reached for her Bible beside the lounge. As she'd read Kerry's letter, a passage from 1 Corinthians 3:7–8 came to mind. "So then neither he who plants is anything, nor he who waters, but God who gives the increase. Now he who plants and he who waters are one, and each one will receive his own reward according to his own labor."

Beth meditated momentarily and read on. "For we are God's fellow workers; you are God's field, you are God's building. According to the grace of God which was given to me, as a wise master builder I have laid the foundation, and another builds on it. But let each one take heed how he builds on it. For no other foundation can anyone lay than that which is laid, which is Jesus Christ."

She gazed across the lake and into the pristine sky. "Charles," she whispered into the heavens, "you were a wise master-builder who laid a foundation, giving me the unspeakable joy of being your helpmate. Then Kerry, Bob, then Josh, labored beside me, building upon it. God brought further workers from His vast resources, and now others continue to build upon it. Charles, Josh, because you live—share this moment with me . . . for the foundation was, and is, Jesus Christ."

Suddenly, through her tears Beth saw the shining triumph of both Charles and Josh. She felt the reassurance that their good work had expanded on earth and she would also share in their rewards in heaven. By the promise of His Word, God had released her pain.

"Thank You, Jesus," she whispered, "for what You have done and are doing."

Uplifted to the sensation of floating through the marble halls, Beth sought her friends who would welcome receiving these scriptural gems. Through the words, new dimensions had been added to the victories of Rosehaven and must be poured out, like a praise offering for their love and support.

Roberto rose to his feet with a smile. "*Bella Rosa,* you appear so happy," he stretched out his hand. "Come, share it with us!"

Beth repeated the highlights of the letter, then related her meditations on the Scriptures.

Pensively, Roberto responded, "There was much that I could not comprehend when first I encountered what you were doing at Rosehaven. From the worldly viewpoint, which was all I knew, it seemed a strange and foolish thing to do with wealth and possessions. *Si,* I did not even perceive what the New Hope Center hoped to accomplish. You and yours planted and watered me," he grinned, "and God has caused me to grow. I pray that is one of your rewards, *Bella Rosa.*"

"Oh, it is!" Beth instinctively threw her arms around Roberto, then as quickly withdrew. She'd inadvertently struck the chord of a haunting melody that had long been silenced. The strings of her heart could not endure playing its music again.

A page of the letter fell to the floor. She and Maria simultaneously bent to recover it, and at that moment Beth caught an intuitive flash of perception in Maria's eyes. As if denying its existence, Beth drew her attention back to the letter.

"Here's a P.S.—I missed a page," she said in surprise.

P.S. There's more good news. Kathleen Sherman has joined our staff. You'll remember her and her husband, Jeff. They came for help in recovering from the death of their daughter and later formed a support group for parents of children with cancer. She calls regularly. She was formerly Personnel Director at Stanford Med Center and volunteered her services. While the Board of Directors continues to interview for an administrator, she's capably filling in for a few of those responsibilities and demonstrates great potential in interviewing and assessing new applicants until you return.

Bye again, K.

"*Magnifico!*" Maria smiled. "Then there is no need for you to feel pressed to go home."

"*Si*, my home is your home," Roberto said tenderly. "You may stay . . . forever," he turned up his palms and smiled.

Allesandro, Roberto's dignified houseman, appeared. "*Mi scusi, signora*," he bowed to Beth. "You have a telephone call. If you wish you may take it here," he offered the cordless instrument.

"That's fine. Thank you. Hello? Yes, Kerry. I've just finished reading your letter. I'm delighted about all the exciting news. Is there more?"

"Mother, your old friend Catherine Chandler phoned. She was unaware you were out of the country. I took the call. She didn't know if you'd heard that Merribelle had a stroke. I went to visit her in the hospital on your behalf. Her mouth droops badly on the left, and she's lost the use of that side as well as her speech, but she is able to write with her right hand. Terror and loneliness filled her eyes, and she cried when I told her you were visiting a friend in Italy."

"Oh dear. I wish I could be with her. You were sweet to go see her. How long will she be in the hospital?"

"I made inquiries at the nurses' station. They're about to release her to a convalescent hospital. She could have a nurse and therapist at home but the head nurse says she gets angry every time she sees her husband and they're afraid she'll have another stroke. She seldom has visitors.

"I couldn't believe it. While I was simply chatting she wrote on the slate, 'This is Henry's fault.' I told her 'God loves you and so do I, and so does Beth.' She wrote, 'Beth is the only one who has ever loved me. There is no God.' I told her, 'Yes, there is. I'll pray for you.' She wrote, 'Don't bother.'

"Mother, I thought you and Papa and Maria would want to know immediately so you could pray for her. I've never witnessed despair that deep and bitter before, even among our most disillusioned Rosehaven patients, and I know she considers you her best friend."

The indifference followed by the contempt Merribelle revealed toward God sent a shiver through the core of Beth's being. Rejection remained the one sin God would not forgive. Considering being separated from Him in eternal damnation as one who'd spurned the love of His redemptive grace was terrible beyond her imagining. Beth shuddered.

"I appreciate your thoughtfulness, Kerry. I'll write to Merribelle and we'll pray her heart will be open."

Roberto flinched as Beth related Merribelle's plight. He knew he could never erase the remembrance of her caustic lack of sensitivity as she heartlessly burst upon Beth's moment of deepest grief to satisfy her own vindictiveness toward God.

"Have mercy upon her, Father," he prayed, and Maria added, "Open her ears, Lord."

"Considering our sadness for Merribelle, think how God's heart feels." Beth then exchanged a sigh for a look of elation, "Each day I'm encountering God's blessings as opposed to the anguish of defiantly shaking my fist or turning my back upon Him. And in His grace, He understood that, too, for when I couldn't see Him, He was holding me up. He shows me the depth of His love through His Word, through the two of you, in the beauty of all His creation which He lavishes upon me. And He's revealed something else to me as I've journaled my emotions over the past months."

"What is that, *Bella Rosa*?" Roberto asked.

"It came to me on a day when Mum chose to stay at the *auberge* and chat with a couple from Bath and I went to Avignon to sketch. I attempted to capture the clouds as they hurried across the sky as if to keep an appointment. I lost them, they scattered, and so I drew in facsimiles of my feelings at a leisurely pace. I returned as a walker coming home with a medley of souvenirs."

"And what was in your pocket?" Roberto asked wistfully.

"Bits and pieces of myself responding to the Word of God, a collection of my journal writings, the balms that soothe my soul. As I've laid them out before me, I see I've come along a steep and winding path, and am yet climbing to rise above the sufferings of loss. Through the pages of a book, I want to write and illustrate for others the ways in which God takes us by the hand. He walks beside us out the other side of the valley of the shadow of death of our loved ones."

"That's beautiful," Maria whispered with misty eyes.

"Does your book have a name?"

"*The Garden of Grace.*"

"*Si,* you will write and paint beautiful word pictures with such a theme," Roberto nodded in agreement.

Throughout the remaining days of July, there were periods when Beth saw nothing of Roberto, yet felt the security of his watchful presence as he worked in the library wing of the Villa with his male secretary, Georgio. Maria spent increasingly more time in Milan staying with friends, and when Carlo's schedule permitted, they came for weekends in Como.

Beth luxuriated in allowing her spirit to soar free of the constraints of the disciplines of art forms, of business, social, and family responsibilities for the first time since the age of three when her rigorous ballet training had begun. Her days were filled with walking through the lake and forest paths, bicycling along the narrow road that edged the blue waters, swimming and bronzing in the sun. She read—everything from the Psalms, Isaiah, the letters of the apostle Paul, to John Donne and Shakespeare. Among Walden's ancient oaks, Thoreau had written, "Nature is our widest home," which unfurled fresh images, releasing a prolific flow of her pen.

Roberto possessed an affinity for knowing when they both needed a diversion from their work.

"I wish to relax, take the boat across the lake, and paint the gardens. Will you paint with me?" he'd ask.

She always said yes. His companionship and unobtrusive compassion granted her time and space for regeneration. Yet when he set up their easels and they'd begin to paint, a mute form of communication passed between them. With maturity, he'd developed even greater competence in his bold style and use of color, yet a finer quality had emerged, shaded by benevolence toward the mysteries of life.

"I shall fondly remember the beauty of these days at Lake Como, Roberto, and the epoch when I learned that joy and sorrow are as inseparable as life and death."

"*Si.* We are suspended like scales between joy and sorrow. We must willingly go through one to experience the other. But I shall be sad indeed for you to speak as though this time is coming to an end, *Bella Rosa.*"

"Not yet. I am totally content. *Grazie,*" she sighed.

By midsummer a series of stunning events commanded the attention of the world and intruded upon the tranquil life at the Villa. . . .

On August 2, 1990, the tank-led troops of Iraq's Saddam Hussein invaded the small nation of Kuwait in an unprovoked pre-dawn attack, arrogantly boasting the overthrow of the Kuwaiti government in lightning fashion.

News from the Soviet Union highlighted its political transition, as the first freedom of the press law broadened journalists' and mass media rights, forbidding censorship by the Communist party. Also, signals came loud and clear that a break in the political stalemate of its leaders would produce massive economic change for the Soviet Union.

Into September, U.S. newspapers warned that shaky banks could create a second economic nightmare.

A historic treaty was signed, which cleared the way for a unified Germany after forty-five years of occupation. Roberto commented, "Perhaps more clearly than any other event, the treaty demonstrates the retreat of communism from Europe."

The U.N. Security Council adopted another resolution condemning the aggressive insanity of Saddam. U.S. President George Bush, appearing on Iraqi television, warned the nation it was on the brink of war. "No one wants war. But there are times when all nations must stand against aggression."

Threats by Saddam to attack the oil fields of Saudi Arabia and other acts of terrorism continued to dominate the news.

"Look at this headline from Rome!" Maria exclaimed on December 1, " 'Soviets Soften Stance on God.

"'On the eve of an historic encounter with Pope John Paul II, President Mikhail S. Gorbachev said that the Soviet Union had erred in long rejecting religion and now needed its moral force to help make his plans for a restructured society work.'

"*Mama Mia!*" Maria exclaimed. "It is wonderful! And listen to this: 'We also say that the moral values which religion generated and embodied for centuries can help in the work of renewal in our country, too.'"

"I know Josh is smiling over that good news, and surely the Bibles he helped get behind the Iron Curtain paved the way for it," Beth agreed.

"Here's another article from the same meeting," Roberto added. "Gorbachev says there is 'No return to the past. In the vision of a new Europe, the world is on the threshold of an entirely new era.' That is good news! We must pray it is true. It impacts the whole world.

"But I am ready not to think of the whole world and the succession of events coming to us every moment which I cannot do anything about. I wish to think of a time to celebrate the blessings God has given us, right here. I have a *magnifico* idea."

"Tell us, *per favore*," Beth's eyes sparkled.

"We must act quickly if it is to be. . . . I have never had a family of my own, so I have never known the joys of a family Christmas in my home. I wish to celebrate the birthday of our Savior Italiano-style and send tickets for Bob and Kerry and the children and Mum, and whomever else you wish."

"And to Carlo?" Maria asked hopefully.

"But of course to Carlo," Roberto grinned. "And you ladies will plan with Guido our chef, for *Italiano* and *Americano* favorite holiday dishes. Beth, I will tell you of the florist and you shall make the Villa as cozy as you always have Rosehaven if you wish, wielding your magic with flowers and fresh greens. It will be *magnifico!*"

"Oh, Roberto, *you* are *magnifico*," Beth clapped her hands. "I'm certain they'd all be delighted to come!"

Having been away from Rosehaven for almost nine months, how could she bear to go back to Christmas without Josh? But then, how could she choose not to be with her precious family? The questions had plagued her for weeks, and now Roberto's thoughtfulness had again resolved her anxiety.

Beth impulsively kissed his cheek in gratitude. *Was it merely my imagination?* she wondered, *or did Maria just send me a cautioning glance? And if so—what did it mean?*

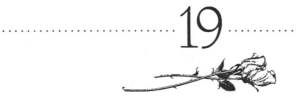

19

Here, my Angela, Papa found this ornament especially for you. It is an angel, too, and you may put it on the tree. Teddy, you must have a Teddy bear ornament. Look at the designs GammyBeth and I bought in the village for you. I have never decorated a Christmas tree before," Roberto laughed, holding Angela up to reach a branch.

"Not even when you were a little boy?" Kerry asked incredulously.

"Strange, but I do not remember being a little boy. I remember my father impressing upon me, 'You are a Count.'" Roberto puffed himself up to his full stature, mocking a heavy frown and tucking in his chin. He towered ominously like a rocking robot over the children, glowering sternly until they giggled. "'And furthermore,'" he continued in a stern, deep voice, "'one day the Cabriollini estate, the Villa, and all its treasures, and one of Italy's great twentieth-century fortunes will be yours. You must learn to be *responsibile*. You do not have time to be a little boy.'"

"Did he really say that—the last part, I mean?" Kerry looked shocked.

"Not in words, but the message could not be mistaken. But it is true—this is my very first Christmas tree to make beautiful, so Teddy—where shall we put this little drum, hmm?"

When they had finished, Roberto stood back to admire their handiwork. With the eye of a connoisseur he assessed the highly prized features of the drawing room—the patina of the richly carved Venetian panels, the rouge marble fireplace, the bronze and crystal chandelier. His appraisal shifted to the tree and the luxuriant fresh green garlands with ruby velvet bows Beth had festooned about the room.

"These simple touches give it the splendor of a home. Even the rooms in which I live feel like a museum."

"I thought that at first," Beth commented, "because the furnishings are formal and classic in design, but I grew up appreciating rare antiques. Your rooms have richness, yet also *soul*, and a welcoming ambience, Roberto. All rooms become endearing when we embellish them with the traditions of Christmas."

"I have a tradition in which I would like you to join me early on this Christmas Eve. Carlo and Maria will not arrive until later tonight."

"What is it, Papa?" Teddy asked with shining eyes.

"Being with some special children who are my friends. You're all invited. Mum, will you come also?"

"Where are we going?"

"You will know when we get there," his dark eyes danced.

"You've presented the invitation with such intrigue, I jolly well must," Mum chuckled.

"Come, I will drive you myself so we may all ride together. Renzo will follow in the truck."

Within twenty minutes they were passing through old iron gates into a heavily wooded area. Roberto drove on to an ancient vine-covered building resembling a church, to which several large new buildings had been annexed. Over the freshly painted doorway a sign read *Casa da Bambino*.

"We are here," he announced joyfully, opening the limousine doors. "Renzo," he called, motioning for him to proceed with their plan.

While Bob, Kerry, Mum, and Beth complied with bewilderment, Renzo loaded each person with as many Christmas packages as their arms would hold. "Follow me," Roberto grinned, while Renzo finished the unloading.

Upon entering the hall, the clamor of children's voices came from all directions. Suddenly children scampered everywhere.

"Papa! Papa Cabriollini . . . *Buon Natale*," they danced about him in a procession to the dining hall.

"*Buon Natale*, Merry Christmas, *bambolinis*." Beth caught the word *famiglia* and understood he was introducing them as his family who came to wish them a merry Christmas. The children clapped their hands and turned in welcoming smiles.

The nuns came over to greet them, "Welcome to the Home of the Children. I am Sister Maria Teresa. The Count is the dearest friend and our own patron saint of the orphans. We are happy to meet you."

One of the sisters began to play her concertina. The children sang, played games, and enacted a play of the Holy family and the birth of the Christ child. Renzo had brought in endless trays laden with fruits, cookies, and sweets. They devoured them all.

"Come, Teddy and Angela, you may help me, *per favore*, we have gifts for each of the children," and he called every one of them by name as Teddy and Angela awarded their presents. The party that proceeded for hours seemed over in minutes when Roberto hugged them and said goodbye.

Sister Maria Teresa encountered the family. "Aren't the new wings the Count has added to this old building miraculous? And how excited he is with his approval to build a hospital on our property for all children! We're delighted he has brought his family to see the vast improvements. Surely you are very proud," she addressed Mum, assuming her to be the matriarch.

Mum blinked in surprise. "Marvelous. It is the work of God's hand," she quickly responded, with a wink at Bob.

Bob smiled as the nun glided away in her black habit saying, "Enjoy your holidays, and God bless you."

"It is the hand of God indeed," Bob turned with a huge smile to the others. "When God touches Roberto's heart and says 'do it,' expect mighty results!"

As Roberto helped Mum back into the limousine, she patted his cheek. "You are a man of splendid surprises, and a love to invite us to share in your merriment. What a delight to see the joy of the children. You've done a commendable thing, Roberto."

"*Grazie*." As they drove toward the Villa, Roberto turned to Beth. "You are very quiet, *Bella Rosa*," he observed. "Did you not enjoy?"

Beth whisked a tear from her eye. "I'm overwhelmed. I didn't know of your love for the children of the orphanage."

"*Si*. Since the Villa became mine, I have given gifts at Christmas, with an endowment for the sisters to buy each child a birthday present. It is only after I became a Christian that I brought the gifts myself and included my heart. Then God opened my eyes and showed me their needs. Bob, did not Jesus say to Peter, 'If you love Me, feed My sheep'?"

"Absolutely, Roberto, and that's the perfect illustration of what He meant."

"It is nothing more than one with an inheritance from the heavenly Father is called to do. That is my richest inheritance. The children are my greatest joy, second only to my own daughter and her family," he touched Kerry's hand next to his.

At the Villa, Allesandro informed him, "Your guests arrived a few moments ago."

"Carlo, Maria—welcome, my friends," Roberto extended his hands. "You are earlier than I expected. *Magnifico!* Carlo, there are dear ones you must meet," he graciously proceeded with the introductions.

"Do they know?" Beth heard Carlo whisper to Maria on the way to the drawing room.

"No—and this is not the time to tell them," she whispered.

"I cannot wait any longer."

"Please, another time."

"You will see," he insisted.

The festive dinner table glowed with candlelight flickering in the prisms of the crystal goblets. Carlo waited until his host had asked the blessing.

"I propose a toast." Carlo raised his glass of sparkling wine. "This Christmas has greater meaning than any other in my life, for Roberto and Maria have introduced me to a new friend. . . . He is my Savior, Jesus Christ our Lord, whose birthday we celebrate. *Buon Natale*—Merry Christmas."

Maria raised her glass. "Wait, darling," Carlo warned. "There is something in the bottom of your glass. Do not drink yet. . . ."

Maria peered into the deeply cut crystal. She dipped in her spoon, lifting out an exquisitely cut diamond ring. Carlo gently grasped it between his fingers, placing it on the third finger of her left hand. He slipped his arm tenderly around her shoulders, "Maria has brought love back into my life, which I feared I would never find again, and she has made me a happy man by consenting to be my wife." Smiles and applause greeted his announcement.

Stunned by Carlo's timing of the announcement, Maria winced. After all, he could not have known that on a previous Christmas Eve, Roberto had announced her engagement to him. But her expression turned quickly to joy as she felt the delight of her friends. She beamed at her future husband. "Carlo, the ring is exquisite," she smiled.

"I am glad for you—*congratulazioni!*" Roberto raised his glass as the others joined in the toast.

Yet Kerry caught the sadness in his dark eyes and glanced at Beth, whose only thoughts seemed to share the felicity of Maria and Carlo.

Later, over espresso in the drawing room, Beth overheard the compassion in Carlo's voice as he whispered to Maria, "The grief I sense breaks my heart, isn't it obvious?" and Beth wondered what he meant.

The sadness of her first Christmas without Josh was undeniable. Yet the children's party at the orphanage and having her family together in this legendary setting, without the reminders of the past at Rosehaven, had lightened her heart. Was she spoiling the party and being more transparent than she realized?

The conversation returned to wedding plans. "When will this happy event take place?" Beth asked with a concerted effort to convey her pleasure, "and where?"

"In June, in Milano," Maria answered, glowing. "And we would be honored if you and Roberto would be our attendants. Beth, you must come to Milano and assist me in choosing the perfect dress for the bride of my handsome husband. I know nothing of flowers and planning a wedding. Will you do it?"

"I'd be honored," Beth smiled.

"One of her gifts is making everything beautiful," Bob assured Maria.

"*Scuzi,*" Roberto slipped out of the room, his eyes clouded with emotion.

Maria quickly launched into a rapid description of wedding plans to cover the concerned glances that followed him. Again Beth felt bewildered. Her heart ached for Roberto, yet she didn't know why. *Could he still be in love with Maria?*

The day after Christmas, Mum urged Beth, "Come home to London with me, love. It's cold and damp, but we shall have lovely days before the fire, and you may write and sketch to your heart's content."

Before she could reply, Maria said, "And after that I shall need her in Milano to help me with our wedding plans."

Kerry had an urge to ask when she planned to return home to Rosehaven but thought better of it. Only Beth could make that decision, which seemed farther away each day.

Beth silently searched Roberto's face for a response to her invitations, certain she'd seen a flash of sadness beneath emotions she'd never known him to mask before. She had no wish to overstay her welcome, yet knew Roberto's gracious open invitation truly was sincere.

Reading her eyes, Roberto responded, "I would miss you, for I have grown accustomed to having houseguests. I may decide to make a personal appearance in Rome with the art exhibition. But with each day I am more concerned for all of you to fly, to the United States more than to London. This madman Saddam's atrocities and his defiance of the U.N. appear as though it may come to war in a few weeks. He is insane, unpredictable. Who knows what terrorism he will cause in the world?"

Saddam failed to pull out of Kuwait by the January 15th deadline, and within two days the twenty-eight-nation allied forces had 690,000 troops in the region. Television audiences around the world vicariously fought the war as Baghdad was pounded with cruise missiles and bombs. TV screens were aflame with Iraq's Scud missiles being exploded by the Patriot radar-guided antimissile missiles. Cameramen were shown next to soldiers in the ground war that began a week later.

Saddam's acts of "environmental terrorism," the oil flowing into the Persian Gulf, hundreds of Kuwaiti oil installations set aflame with the ominous black smoke extending to neighboring countries, outraged the world.

Biblical scholars and those merely hazarding unqualified guesses were predicting the "end times." The uncertainties were reflected by people everywhere being indecisive regarding even the most mundane choices. Finally, on February 27, President Bush declared, "Kuwait is liberated." On February 28, Iraq announced a ceasefire.

Hearing the news in Milano, Beth sighed to Maria, "Thank God, it's over." After a few moments she added, "Looking back on my life, with each cataclysmic event chasing on the heels of another, and whatever the outcome—one thing is certain."

"What is that?" Maria asked.

"We must cling to the truth that God is in control of everything. Our security will never be in the things of this world. Romans 8:38 and 39 say it best." She opened her Bible. "Listen to this: 'For I am persuaded that neither death nor life, nor angels nor principalities nor powers, nor things present nor things to come, nor height nor depth, nor any other created thing, shall be able to separate us from the love of God which is in Christ Jesus our Lord.'

"That says it all, doesn't it?" Beth put her Bible down.

"Whether it's a common disaster or my private tragedy, God's Word reminds me—He alone is our rock."

In March, in Milan's couturier bridal salon, Maria took a deep breath and sighed as the designer fitted her voluminous white lace gown. "Oh, Beth—I'm delighted we decided upon this one. It is exquisite!"

"Perfect. . . . You are beautiful, Maria!"

Over lunch Beth told her, "Helping you plan your wedding has been a joy for me. It will be gorgeous. But I'm beginning to feel like an international vagabond," Beth laughed.

"Of course you will always sense the loss of your Josh, but you are a different person from the grief-tormented woman who came to Lake Como last year."

Beth thought for a moment. "At first I felt powerless to do anything to help myself, as one without hope or faith. That further depressed me. It was out of character. You, among others, are largely responsible for my recovery, Maria.

"And it's as though our great God put pen and paper in my hand and led me to write my way through the grief. I pray *The Garden of Grace* will guide others who hurt. I've had comfort in the Psalms and the support of my family. All of this and the assurance that Rosehaven was running smoothly took me through the most painful, and perhaps one of the most precious, times of my life—precious in terms of seeing the sovereignty of a loving God face to face. And there's been Roberto and his support throughout these months. Isn't he a dear?"

"He is, as you Americans say, 'one in a million.'"

"I must go home sometime, but I'm thinking I'd like to be with Roberto again before I do, for Easter, which is the anniversary of the day Josh died. He and Carlo were the last to see him alive. But why am I saying that? You've heard it over and over. . . . But what do you think?"

"I think you should waste no time in getting to Como. Roberto is an extraordinary man with a deep love for God and care for others' needs. And he is also 'maddeningly attractive' in addition to his unlimited talents and generosity. He is a man of great honor and integrity. And it's time you noticed he can't take his eyes off you—ever."

Beth's eyes widened as she listened.

"You have been in a period of mourning, Beth, but you surely cannot continue to disregard the love he has for you. It is obvious to everyone. I do not know how a man could love a woman as he loves you and keep silent this long. Do you not see it?

"*Mama mia,*" she sighed, "I have done it—it had to come out. Forgive me if I am too blunt, but you asked what I think, and it is this: Hurry back to Como—to the love and the life waiting for you!"

Beth reeled at Maria's forthright advice as the truth began to penetrate.

"Maria, are you aware that we didn't know you had decided not to marry Roberto until over a year had passed—until Kerry and I first came last April? It was difficult for him to tell us. At that time my heart was heavy with its own pain. All I comprehended was your rejection, that you thought he didn't love you for yourself, but for someone he wanted you to be."

"Beth—I can't believe you still do not understand! I loved Roberto with all my heart—but he could never love me completely because his heart has always belonged to you. I imagined him making love to me—and wishing it was you. . . ." Maria's voice cracked, and Beth leaned forward to embrace her.

"It's a wonder you don't hate me, Maria, and you are a remarkable woman to be capable of going from romantic love to the deep friendship and admiration you have for Roberto. It's beyond my comprehension."

"And I knew you had to be extraordinary for a man of Roberto's quality to love you as he does. Since I looked like you, I also wanted to learn how to become like you. I prayed there was another man I could love, who would love me in return. And God gave Carlo to me. Now, Beth—go to Roberto, for I believe in my heart you love him beyond a friend. Go—find out for yourself. . . ."

"Bella Rosa! Si, I am here," Roberto answered excitedly when Beth telephoned. "But of course I would be delighted to have you come back to Como. It is like the sunshine left, and it is a museum again. Allow me to send Emilio for you, for then I will see you sooner."

The elation in his voice and the enthusiasm of his response after her three-month absence caused Beth to meticulously mull over Maria's comments. She recalled Maria's cautioning glances and those exchanged with Carlo. The meaning of Carlo's whisper to Maria, "The grief I see breaks my heart," referred not to her loss but to Roberto's ache of unrequited love. And what of the times Roberto could not cover his pained emotions or the guard he'd raised to mask them from her? It all made sense now.

Roberto had loved her far beyond the passion of his youth. He'd never stopped loving her after he'd asked her to be his wife the year after Charles died, or after her marriage to Josh. Roberto had loved her with a love that would not let her go—even to risking his own life to save Josh, for her sake. He'd loved her with a love that honored Josh and her mourning, and he had hidden it until he could bear it no longer.

As she packed, Beth reached further realizations. Her lost sense of God's love and mercy had been breathed back into her soul by Roberto's own tender compassion. He'd shielded her with boundless space to clear the way for God to regenerate her spirit. She now clearly saw Roberto's love, which had endured through every heartache.

"You've opened my eyes, Maria," Beth glowed as they embraced at the airport annex for private planes. "Grazie. I will call you soon."

"Look and listen with your heart," Maria smiled, waving as Beth walked briskly to the field where Emilio waited.

The distance from Milano to Como was slight, yet it had never before seemed this long. As the plane landed and Emilio taxied down the runway, she scanned the airstrip for Renzo and the limousine. Not Renzo but Roberto stood with a wide smile. A rush of air from the landing conformed his ivory silk shirt and slacks against his lean body as he waved.

"*Bella Rosa!*" He ran to her as she fled down the plane's steps into his open arms.

They laughed joyously, playfully, releasing the past and capturing the moment. Clinging together, they twirled in a circle as the breeze caught Beth's hair, their hearts beating with the same rhythm.

"*Cara mia,*" Roberto tilted her face up to his with tears in his velvet brown eyes. "You have come back to me."

In his eyes she found the reply to Maria's urging . . . *Go find out for yourself.* "With you is where I want to be," she smiled up at him.

At once, they exchanged the tingling realization that they'd embraced a new season of their lives, still beyond utterance.

Emilio took her luggage from the plane and loaded it into the Ferrari. As Roberto drove to the Villa he found it difficult to keep his eyes on the road instead of Beth.

"Maria's wedding is finally planned, *si* ? Tell me about it," he asked.

"I will, but first I would rather hear about you. Have you been away, or are you planning a trip?"

"Now that you are in Como, I have no need or desire to leave. The Villa was lonely after you went away. My secretary is a competent man, things were in order, so I went skiing in Switzerland, then to Paris. I visited the *École des Beaux Arts,* for old times' sake. Perhaps I should not have done it. It stirred many memories of my foolishness, as in a dark mirror I did not wish to see."

"The man in your mirror now is far more beautiful. . . ."

"He is getting a little gray," he sighed.

"I always thought of you as beautiful, not merely handsome, Roberto. And through the years your inner spirit has reflected God's love—I see Him in all you say and do."

"Is that really so? That is my prayer."

"Oh yes, Roberto, and that is why I . . . I mean that is one of the things I love . . . about you." Beth bit back her words, sensitive and appreciative of the time period he'd struggled to honor. An inner admonition cried— "Wait. Wait for God's timing. . . ."

On Easter morning, the chapel of *Casa da Bambino* abounded with lilies, filling it with their sweet fragrance. As Roberto and Beth, followed by the families of Renzo, Emilio, Allesandro, Guido, and the household staff of the Villa, entered for the mass, Sister Maria Teresa approached Roberto.

"Your heart will be glad at the voices of the children this morning," she spoke in English for Beth's benefit. "We are pleased to have the household of your Villa attend the mass. The children especially wished me to tell you how they love the flowers. They said they 'saw the love of Jesus in your gifts today.' *Grazi*. And now *scusi*, I must be about the business of the morning."

Beth listened carefully to the Mass spoken in Italian, but did not need to understand every word to experience the reverence of Easter. She felt filled by the presence of the Holy Spirit, lifting her heart in worship and praise to the living God. English or Italian was of no consequence. God alone mattered.

"Lord Jesus," she silently prayed, "I praise You for the gift of eternal life, that Josh lives and is with You now, that again Your love has lifted me through my darkest hours. With all my heart I seek Thee—do not let me wander from the way You would have me go. I ask that the peace of God lead my heart. Thank You, Father, for Roberto here beside me and for his love for You. Please bless my family this Easter day, and may Your blessings continue to flow upon Rosehaven. I ask these things in the precious name of Jesus. Amen."

As Beth and Roberto left the orphanage chapel in the Ferrari, he explained, "Only on Christmas and Easter do I attend the services here. At those times I wish to see the children. In the village is a small Christian church. The congregation is international, attended by Americans, Swiss, English, and even a few Italians," he flashed a winsome smile. "I have many friends there. The service is in English and the pastor preaches from God's Word—in fact he reminds me of Bob. I would like to take you there next Sunday."

"I'll look forward to it," Beth nodded.

"But let us think only of the beautiful Easter Sunday God has given us to be together. I reserved a table at a small, quiet *ristorante* by the lake."

They talked of many things . . . Maria and Carlo's wedding, their latest communications with Kerry and the events at Rosehaven, places to go and things to do. Roberto spoke only of one day at a time and she found herself longing for the desire of her heart—to share the rest of their lives together.

At the end of the week she'd written her deepest yearnings into her prayer journal with the verse from Psalms, "Delight yourself also in the Lord, and He shall give you the desires of your heart. Commit your way to the Lord, trust also in Him, and He shall bring it to pass."

The friendliness of the little church in the village pleased Beth, along with the quality of worship and Pastor Martino's biblical teaching.

"It feels like home," she offered as they left the Sunday service.

That evening, Beth's heart skipped at the moment she saw the intimate dinner table overlooking the terrace of the Villa. Tucked among a bouquet of white roses peeked a small box covered in gold foil, while the reflection of twinkling lights from across the lake danced among the glow of candlelight and crystal.

"Roberto, the setting is *magnifico*."

"You are the most beautiful being in my life," Roberto smiled as he nervously held her chair. "I must tell you, I cannot endure it *una minuto*—my love for you! My heart is in this gift." He placed a foil-wrapped box before her.

With trembling hands, Beth loosed the ribbon. Delicately she removed the foil, catching her breath at the sight of an aged black velvet box.

"Remember, *Cara mia*?" he asked softly as she opened it.

She beheld the brooch—more exquisite than she'd remembered—a tracery of gold filigree set with amethysts, pearls, and diamonds.

"The brooch is a treasure my father handed to me before he died—worn by my mother, to be given only to the woman who becomes my wife. Many years ago, when I offered it to you, I said you are the only woman I could ever be in love with—that is still true. I *wanted* to love Maria, but my heart belonged to you. I am grateful she became my dear friend, but Beth, it is only you I want to marry. I have prayed you would accept the brooch, and me."

"Yes, oh yes, Roberto." Beth's eyes sparkled with tears. "Yes," she repeated, laying her hand upon his. "And I've prayed you would ask. I love you with my whole heart. I'm in awe that you've loved me all these years and how our love has come full circle. Life has reshaped us since our student days in Paris and that one night of passion when Kerry was conceived. And ever since, when you've known of my joys and sorrows— you've always been there. And through it all I realize now how God's hand continually brought us together."

Beth reverently caressed the brooch and rose from the table. Roberto took the brooch and pinned it over her heart as they melted into each other's arms in a long embrace. She trembled with the ecstasy of his kisses and the desire to be his wife.

"*Cara mia*, I wish for Pastor Martino to marry us in my family chapel, here at the Villa, as soon as *possibile*."

"*Si*," she lifted her lips to his. "And may we ask Maria and Carlo to come stand with us?"

"I have asked God to lead all the way," he kissed her again, "and they have been praying for us since you came. They were already prepared if you should say yes," he grinned. "*Scuzi*, I am being impetuous once more, but each minute is precious and not to be wasted."

"Then I'll ask Maria to bring a dress from the wedding boutique in Milan, and save me the trip," Beth said excitedly.

"First, come, let me see if you like." He took her by the hand into a pristine bedroom chamber smelling of walls freshly covered in silk damask and new carpet, elegantly appointed with baroque gold. A wedding suit of cream-colored lace hung upon a satin hanger.

"I had a couturier in Rome design this especially for you, but I do not mind if you prefer something else," he smiled.

"Roberto, it's gorgeous—and you are completely irresistible," Beth laughed, falling into his arms again.

"You like?" he smiled, pleased, with tears in his eyes.

"I like," she kissed the question from his lips. "Does a marriage license take time?" she asked.

"I will see to that while you select the flowers. And after the ceremony, I wish to have others come, to celebrate with us on the happiest day of my life! Ah—and let us immediately telephone Bob and Kerry and the children with our wonderful news."

"Do you think they will come on such short notice?"

"*Scuzi, Cara mia*—it takes only a bride and groom to make a wedding. They come here, we go there as soon as you are inclined, but if we could marry this very moment it would not be too soon!"

"Dearly beloved," Pastor Martino began the wedding ceremony. A bower of lacy ferns and myriad shades of pink roses surrounded the altar of the intimate little chapel. Maria and Carlo smiled beside the radiant bride and groom. Roberto gazed up at the ancient stained glass window of Christ above them. The words he had once spoken to Josh—*I do not understand this man whose figure is on the cross*—came back to him. His heart silently sang—*Dio! Lord God . . . grazie. You have given life and love to me.*

"We are gathered to unite this man and this woman in holy matrimony," the pastor continued while Roberto beheld his bride. Beth's silky black hair fell softly to the shoulders of the cream-colored lace suit, which fit her slim figure to perfection. In her hair she wore a crown of tulle and roses. Their misty eyes beheld only each other. In hers, Roberto met the deep reflection of his love. They vowed, "Like the ring, our love is a never-ending circle that endures until the end of time."

Beth trembled as Roberto took her into his arms. Their lips met, sealing their vows with the sweet, tender ardor of their kiss.

"*Congratulazioni*," Carlo kissed the bride and heartily embraced Roberto.

"What a sweet ceremony," Maria glowed. "It makes us anxious for our own wedding."

An intimate gathering of international friends from the village church shared in the celebration as the romantic refrains of a string quartet drifted among the dinner tables.

"Do you remember, in Paris?" Roberto asked, as he glided Beth gracefully to the dance floor. "You remember the music of 'Love Makes the World Go 'Round'?"

"I especially remembered you holding me close, and that the nearness of you made my heart beat faster than the music, like it's beating now," Beth whispered.

"*Cara mia*, only your love makes my world go around. I requested the musicians to play this old song, but we shall compose new lyrics sweeter still. Let us begin tonight. . . ."

Their silken white suite glowed in the soft shadows of candlelight. Roberto first embraced her with his magnificent brown eyes and her heart skipped a beat, as it had the first time he'd looked at her.

His eyes shimmered with tenderness. "*Bella Rosa*, I have longed for this moment. For you to be my wife, to love and cherish you, never to let you go."

Roberto took her in his arms, no longer the impulsive, demanding lover. Their love was genuine, their shared passion sweet, as God intended it.

Beth was enraptured by his heartbeat against hers, and felt her own might burst with joy.

Then, as she lay contented in Roberto's arms, his soft kisses against her hair, she felt peace and the shared joy of her first love. She had been as overwhelmed by his lovemaking as on that fateful night in her youth, yet this union had been restored to them by God.

"*Bella Rosa, Bella Rosa mia*," he whispered, kissing her tenderly, "a lifetime was not too long to wait for a love like ours."

20

The roses were in full bloom when Beth and Roberto returned to Rosehaven.

"Welcome home and congratulations!" The entourage swarmed to meet them as Max drove them through the iron gates. Kerry and Bob, Teddy and Angela, Tillie, Cookie, Jimmy, Max, David, Golda, Becky, and the Rosehaven staff engulfed them with their greetings amidst tears of joy.

The quintessence of all Rosehaven had ever been to Beth now received her with open arms. The mullioned windows of the mansion winked their welcome in the afternoon sun, and every rose seemed to smile at the one whose secrets they had shared over the years.

Kerry tenderly embraced Beth in the privacy of their rooms. "Mother, joy is written all over you! God amazes me in the caring way He directs the ones who love Him. I begin each day praising Him and you for the rewards of sharing what you have sown and watered and reaped in your 'garden of grace.' Not only the one you've written about, but the living one right here.

"Before distractions overwhelm us, I must tell you, the love and respect I witnessed between you and Charles, and you and Dad, laid the foundation for the relationship God meant Bob and me to have. God gave me the perfect husband in Bob. We've had our differences. But even because of them, we're able to reach out to others, and it's been by following God's plan as well as your modeling. I simply had to say that before we were deluged with people wanting to welcome and congratulate you and Papa. I'm more in love with Bob every day—and you'll be pleased with the sermon he's planned for Sunday."

The entire community turned out to share the morning services and welcoming reception for Beth as Rosehaven's visiting founder. Bob had a few early wisps of gray at his temples, but it was his increased spiritual maturity and growth that impressed Beth.

"It continually amazes me," Bob began his sermon, "the timeliness of God's Word. It occurred to me that perhaps I should choose a different text than the one we've been studying in the gospel of John to honor our beloved Beth—the visionary who transformed her home into this sanctuary we know as Rosehaven. But listen to this. . . .

"John 15:5 reads 'I am the vine, you are the branches. He who abides in Me, and I in him, bears much fruit; for without Me you can do nothing.'

"It is our *connectedness* to the source of growth and power in Jesus Christ, and the resulting fruit of it, which we have seen in Beth that I want us to consider this morning."

Beth felt humbled to tears. No, she thought—*the glory is God's.*

At the conclusion of his sermon, Bob welcomed sharing from the congregation. Nearly an hour passed, and he was unable to slow the flow of testimonies of changed lives. Finally Bob proclaimed an "amen" as the people applauded Beth.

Bob dismissed the congregation. "Go in the peace of the Lord—and remember, He blesses those who get outside themselves."

"How true," Beth whispered. Charles had set the course for Rosehaven. She and Josh, Kerry and Bob pursued a vision. David and Golda, the medical and psychological staff, Tillie, Max, and Jimmy poured their hearts and lives into it. She thought, *How faithful they've been*, and prayed, *Thank You, God, for the ways in which You've blessed us all.*

That evening, after a day filled with activity, Beth sat alone before the family gathered in the cozy elegance of the living room. Her gaze caressed its polished woods, the colors that had become richer with the passing of time. She smiled at the rose of her own design in the stained glass window. Its glittering prisms caught the soft lights, returning her smile. She'd thought of Rosehaven and its furnishings not as material possessions, but rather as extensions of Charles and herself, and then Josh. She'd called it 'a sanctuary from a wearisome world,' even before it became a retreat center. And now willingly, joyfully, purposefully, her desire was to yield Rosehaven to those who would receive and nurture that which was part of her.

"You've given me a day I'll always treasure," Beth smiled after they'd all filtered in and sat down. Teddy and Angela snuggled like little chicks under her wings with Roberto beside them.

David's warm brown eyes smiled at Beth. "Our rewards in being a part of Rosehaven have exceeded all our expectations. Your vision became the reality of the dream Golda and I had. Lives truly have been changed for eternity in these mere five years. And it's only the beginning."

Bob added, "I've experienced what Jesus meant when He called me to daily take up my cross and follow Him. He was talking about sacrificial love, but I doubt any of us understood the cost. If we had, would we have been willing to pay the price? Kerry and I think we would. And I think each of us has to agree with David: The rewards have been greater than we could anticipate. What further amazes me is what Jesus does with willing hearts—what He's done with mine."

"And mine," Beth smiled. She drew the children closer to her. "Long ago I heard a phrase: 'The rose will fade, and the mighty oak fall, and the mountains shall crumble into dust. Love alone never dies.'"

"*Si, Bella Rosa mia,*" Roberto's eyes glowed in adoration. "From you, and yours, and God, I have learned about love. How foolish I was to have made the statement 'love ruins everything.' Love, true love that honors God, does not ruin everything. Love is the reason for living."

Notes

1. *Rubaiyat of Omar Khayyam*, trans. by Edward Fitzgerald (New York: Garden City Books, 1953), public domain.

2. Rick Hampton, "In New Book Americans Tell Truth About Themselves," *San Bernardino Sun*, April 1991; statistics from book *The Day America Told the Truth* by James Patterson with Peter Kim (New York: Prentice Hall, 1991).

About the Author

Lila Peiffer is a native Southern Californian. She and her husband Rick own and operate Bluebelle House Bed & Breakfast in the resort community of Lake Arrowhead. They retired from corporate life in 1983, where she wrote a publication for the firm for over twelve years. She has served in church leadership throughout her life, leads a weekly women's Bible study, and is also a public speaker. Her love for travel and her background in interior design adds richness to her writing, as does her love for family. Lila and Rick have four married children and eight grandchildren. *Rosehaven* is the sequel to her first novel, *The Secrets of the Roses*.

The Secrets of the Roses

A NOVEL

In the tradition of Rosamunde Pilcher's *The Shell Seekers* comes a moving novel of one woman's journey of faith. Beautiful Elizabeth Sheridan pursues an education in art in Paris only to see it swept away by a crisis in the family antiques business. But Beth brings more than her paintings home to England and then to San Francisco, where a new love awaits her in the city by the bay.

Charles Townsend, brilliant and wealthy architect, creates Rosehaven, a beautiful mansion, for Beth. But can his adoration eclipse the passion her first love, Roberto, awoke in her? She heard the promise of God's love and care as a child. But can the beautiful and wealthy Beth Townsend count on that promise as an adult? And will Beth be able to protect the child she aches to call her own? Only God and the roses in the garden hear her whispered prayers and hopes. . . .

A sample from *The Secrets of the Roses* . . .

A chill spring rain sent its tears weeping slender streams down the windowpane. Beth's shroud of misery hovered over her like the morning mists that smothered the Seine. She could not bear the thought of venturing out of the safe cocoon of her apartment, of the bruising cruelty of mocking eyes awaiting her.

The refrain of the love song, "April in Paris," that she and Roberto had once danced to, played over and over in her mind. Beth covered her ears and burrowed deep in her quilts, as if to shut out the romantic melody that had gone sour.

"Blithering idiot," she cursed herself. "You played a game without knowing the rules. It's your own fault you got hurt. You'll never be able to look at Roberto again—you've made such a fool of yourself."

A persistent rap at the door demanded an answer. A young French delivery boy grinned, "For you, *Mademoiselle.*" He placed a bountiful bouquet of pink roses in her arms. She was too dazed to say anything or think to tip him.

The card read, "Please forgive me, *Bella Rosa Mia.* I am so sorry. . . . Roberto."

Beth broke down in tears again. Roberto's dark eyes and handsome face loomed before her. "I can't blame you too much, Roberto," she whispered. Her heart twisted, and her mind churned in confusion. "I thought it was love—we have so much in common, yet we're worlds apart." The momentary ecstasy after she had stopped struggling and surrendered in his arms was overshadowed by a sense of shame and stupidity. The very thing she had determined not to do was done.

The ring of the telephone jarred her. "Beth, are you ill? It's Ruth. I've never known you to miss a class."

Beth choked out the words. "Thanks for calling. . . . I'm, I'm all right. Talk to you later. I need to be alone right now."

"Is there bad news? Is it your family?"

Beth didn't want to talk to anyone, not even Ruth.

"No . . . they're all right, thanks." She hung up the phone.

Beth mourned the innocence she had wanted to keep for a husband, but also for Roberto's love that could only bring heartache. She had never felt so depressed, nor known that love could be so painful.

The fragrance of the exquisite roses permeated the small apartment. They endured Beth's salty tears upon their velvet petals and caressed her burning cheeks as she buried her face in their cool perfume. Her eyes fell again on the card: *"I am so sorry. . . Roberto."*

"I'm sorry too," she said aloud. "Come along, girl, get yourself together," she told herself. "Life goes on. Private little tragedies happen every day, and no one else will ever know or care. The French girls with their sneers can just . . . well, I don't care."

Beth splashed cold water on her face and dressed hurriedly. A quick whisk of the hairbrush and a dab of lipstick brightened her spirits. She slipped into her trench coat for a walk in the rain.

She saw herself and Roberto passing the painting stalls of eager artists along the Left Bank, closed now because of the rain. Never again would they stroll together across the Pont Neuf with its golden statues, or wander through the Tuilleries gardens. The Champs Elysees bustled with its usual parade of power and sophistication. Parisians and tourists crowded the avant-garde boutiques and cafes. It looked exactly like a Utrillo painting.

She walked for hours, turning her head aside from every set of oncoming eyes that seemed to question the tears swimming in hers.

At last, she found herself in the Notre Dame Cathedral. Here in the parish of the history of France, she gazed in awe of its ancient architecture, the glowing radiance of the thirty-foot expanse of the Rose Windows.

A few reverent worshipers were sequestered in the only quiet section of the vast cathedral. Beth slid into a seat. A tour group passed, talking loudly. Slowly, she came to understand. A search for the presence of God had drawn her here. Somewhere among the shadowy mysteries of the ages, hidden among the crowds and the noise, perhaps she could find Him. She had to. The guilt, the turmoil, the explosion inside her soul demanded release.

"I don't know much about You, God," she whispered, "but I do know one of Your commandments says You don't approve of what happened between Roberto and me last night. It's commonplace for others, but You and I know it's not right. Please forgive me. Help me to forget about Roberto. . . ."

A lecturer gathered her tour group a few feet away and began an explanation of the magnificent Gothic architecture and the flying buttresses supporting the walls. Moving on, Beth paused before an awesome golden statue of Christ on the cross. She looked up in silent prayer. "Jesus, I know You died for people like me. You're real to my friend Hope and her family. Would You please, somehow, become real to me? I need You so very much. . . ."

The tense anguish over her lost chastity slowly released its iron knot. With closed eyes she saw the awful mass of confusion, the delusion she'd substituted for the real thing, spiral round and round, like the water in the streets being flushed down a drain. A calm she didn't understand warmed and relaxed her stiffened shoulders as she stepped outside.

Beth often felt refreshed by a walk in the rain. But she didn't know God could wash away the chains of guilt and revive her spirit, just by her asking Him. Healing the heartache would take some time, but at twenty-one she had her whole life before her. She felt calmer, definitely older and hopefully wiser. Whatever had happened in the cathedral was a mystery—a wonderful mystery, for which she would be forever grateful.

One thought about Roberto consoled her. She believed that in his own way, he loved her as much as he could any woman.

She dodged another wave of tourists crossing the bridge to the Left Bank. Through the drizzle the Seine rippled in unperturbed grey-green silence. Beth quickened her step to get back for her last class.